P9-CAO-440

The Curse of *Sight* . . .

Aeron woke with a cry of horror, a cry that had Gwydion reaching for his sword though he could see no threat in the room.

"Aeron, what is it?"

"A dream—all was blood and fire, the castle fallen, warships in the Bawn, swords on the plain—"

"What counsel did the dream give you?"

"I do not know," Aeron said bleakly. "But there is great evil coming. From friend or foe, I cannot tell; but we are warned!"

As Aeron spoke, a shudder went through her Lord Protector. For that this was a true seeing he had no doubt, and the coming of war could no longer be denied. . . .

THE
COPPER
CROWN

"A rich treasure-trove of high Celtic adventure . . . a long-denied empire—among the stars.
—Morgan Llywelyn, author of *The Horse Goddess*

The COPPER CROWN

A NOVEL OF THE KELTIAD

by
Patricia Kennealy

A ROC BOOK

ROC
Published by the Penguin Group
Penguin Books USA Inc., 375 Hudson Street,
New York, New York 10014, U.S.A.
Penguin Books Ltd, 27 Wrights Lane,
London W8 5TZ, England
Penguin Books Australia Ltd, Ringwood,
Victoria, Australia
Penguin Books Canada Ltd, 10 Alcorn Avenue,
Toronto, Ontario, Canada M4V 3B2
Penguin Books (N.Z.) Ltd, 182–190 Wairau Road,
Auckland 10, New Zealand

Penguin Books Ltd, Registered Offices:
Harmondsworth, Middlesex, England

Published by Roc, an imprint of New American Library,
a division of Penguin Books USA Inc.

This is an authorized reprint of a hardcover book published by Bluejay Books Inc.

First Printing, July 1986
14 13 12 11 10 9 8 7 6

Acknowledgments

My thanks to many, and not diminished for the sharing: to the unnamed and unremembered bards and poets and makers who set down their long knowledge in the old tales; to my parents, Joseph and Genevieve, who read me all those stories; to my grandmother Agnes McDonald, who sent me all those cards; to my sister, Regina, whose advice was worthy of a Keltic High Councillor; to David Walley (Mishkin, scribe and prince!), who never stopped listening; to Janice Scott, who helped launch the original "Kelts in Space" on a Cornish road between Treen and Penzance; and most of all to the true Gwydion ap Dôn, lord of bards and god of writers, who gave me wit and words enough to make this tale.

Notes on Pronunciation

The spellings and pronunciations of the names in *The Copper Crown* are probably unfamiliar to most readers unless one happens to be thoroughly steeped in things like the *Mabinogion* or the Cuchulainn cycle. The Celtic languages (Irish, Scots Gaelic, Welsh, Cornish, Manx and Breton) upon which I have drawn for my nomenclature are not related to any tongue that might provide a clue as to their derivation or spoken sound. Outside of a few loan-words, they have no Latin root as do the Romance tongues, and they are in fact derived from a totally different branch of the Indo-European linguistic tree.

Therefore I have taken certain, not always consistent, liberties with orthography in the interests of reader convenience, though of course one may deal with the names any way one pleases. But for those who might like to humor the author, I have made this list of some of the more difficult names, words, and phonetic combinations.

—pk

Vowels

Generally the usual, though *a* is mostly pronounced "ah" and *i* never takes the sound of "eye," but always an "ee" or "ih" sound. Thus: "Ard-ree" for *Ard-rígh*, not "ard-rye." Final *e* is always sounded; thus: "Slay-nee" for *Slaine*, not "Slain."

Vowel Combinations

aoi: "ee" as in "heel"

ao: "ay" as in "pay"

au: "ow" as in "cow", never "aw" as in "saw"; thus *Jaun* rhymes with "crown," not with "fawn."

ae, ai: "I" as in "high." Exceptions: the proper names *Aeron* and *Slaine*, where the sound is "ay" as in "day."

á: The accent gives it length. Thus, *dán* is pronounced "dawn."

io: "ih" if unaccented. If accented (*ío*), then it becomes "ee."

Consonants

c: always a "k" sound. (To avoid the obvious problem here, the more usual *Celt, Celtic, Celtia* have been spelled *Kelt, Keltic, Keltia,* throughout.)

ch, kh: gutturals as in the German "ach," never "ch" as in "choose"

g: always hard, as in "get" or "give"

bh: pronounced as "v"

dd: pronounced as "th"

Some of the more difficult names:

Aeron: AIR-on
Aoibhell: ee-VELL
Gwydion: GWID-eeon
Ríoghnach: REE-oh-nakh (guttural "ch")
Fionnbarr: FINN-bar
Slaine: SLAY-nee
Caerdroia: car-DROY-uh
Tuatha De Danaan: TOO-uh-huh Day DAH-nahn
Gwynedd: GWIN-ith
Melangell: mel-ANN-gel (hard "g")
Criosanna: criss-anna
Kymry: KIM-ree
Ard-rían: ard-REE-uhn
Ard-rígh: ard-REE
Taoiseach: TEE-shokh (guttural "ch")
Turusachan: too-roo-SAKH'N (guttural "ch")
Rath na Ríogh: rath-na-ree
Ban-draoi: ban-dree
Fáinne: fawn-ya
Fianna: FEE-unna
Aoife: EE-fa
Sidhe: shee
Annwn: annoon

Characters

Aboard the Sword:

Theo Haruko, Captain, FSN
Sarah O'Reilly, Lieutenant, communications officer
Hugh Tindal, Lieutenant, science officer
Warren Hathaway, Lieutenant, astrogator
Athenée Mikhailova, Ensign, technical officer
Tarquin Gro, Ensign, engineering and weapons officer (died in coldsleep)

Aboard the Firedrake:

Elharn Aoibhell, Master of Sail, High Admiral
Gwennan Chynoweth, Captain
Anluan mac Rossa, First Officer

In Keltia:

Aeron Aoibhell, High Queen of Keltia
Rohan, Prince of Thomond, her brother
Gwydion ap Arawn, Prince of Gwynedd, First Lord of War
Morwen Douglas, Duchess of Lochcarron, Taoiseach of Keltia
Gavin, Earl of Straloch, Lord Extern
Idris ap Caswyn, Chief Bard
Lady Douglass Graham, Earl-Marischal
Ffaleira nighean Enfail, Magistra of the Ban-draoi
Auster, Lord Chief Brehon
Teilo ap Bearach, Archdruid
Ríoghnach, Princess of the Name, sister to Aeron
Niall O Kerevan, Duke of Tir-connell, her husband
Sabia ní Dalaigh, friend to Aeron
Morgan Cairbre, master-bard and spy
Melangell, cousin to Aeron
Arianeira, Princess of Gwynedd, Gwydion's twin sister
Kynon, her retainer
Fergus, Lord of the Isles, husband to Morwen
Kieran, brother to Aeron
Eiluned of Garioch, his wife
Declan, brother to Aeron, Kieran's twin
Gwyneira, Dowager Queen of Keltia, grandmother to Aeron
Desmond, son to Elharn, cousin to Aeron
Slaine, his twin sister
Macsen, their younger brother
Fionnbarr, late High King of Keltia
Emer, his late wife and Queen
Roderick, Prince of Scots, Aeron's late consort
Fionnuala, sister to Aeron
Struan Cameron, Master of Horse
Denzil Cameron, his brother, cavalry commander
Fedelma ní Garra, Fian general
Tanwen of Marsco, infantry commander
Donal mac Avera, Captain-General of the Fianna
Grelun, an officer in Gwydion's service

Indec, an Abbess-mother of the Ban-draoi
Ithell, a woman who lives in Upper Darkdale
Brioc, her husband
Allyn, son of Midna, a lord of the Sidhe
Gwyn ap Neith, King of the Sidhe

On Alphor:

Strephon, the Cabiri Emperor, political head of the Imperium
Jaun Akhera, Prince of Alphor, his grandson and heir
Tinao, Jaun Akhera's mistress
Sanchoniathon, brother to Jaun Akhera
Hanno, Captain-General of the Imperial armies
Garallaz, an Imperial envoy

On Fomor:

Bres, King of Fomor and Archon of the Phalanx
Elathan, Crown Prince, his son and heir
Talorcan, Bres's son by his legal concubine Thona
Basilea, Bres's wife and Queen, mother to Elathan
Camissa, Elathan's betrothed
Borvos, a Fomori captain

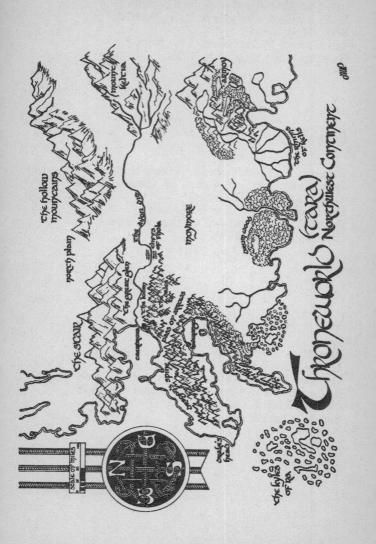

To James Douglas Morrison.
Without whom.
Bydd i ti ddychwelyd.

PARTIAL DESCENT
of the Ard-Rían Keiron
from the royal and noble Keltic houses

(not every generation shown)

House of Dân   House of Arvon

Gwynek = Arthur Morgan

Gwenhwyfach = Arawn Arawnfab Mabac

    House of Dâra
    (Royal line of Doirbell)

Arawnwen = Macsen Lloyd   Malen = Brendan Ivor Doirbell

Gawyr (2) = Marawnwen (1) Sempre   Keiron XVI   Erithys = Taighlann Van Cathal

Brennya = Keirios   Margal = Corymc   Declan VIII   Raynall III   Anghapas X   Tiegernach = Soretja

Princes of Gwynedd   (not every generation shown)   Kerrodec of Gwalaryc Tergonkfra IV

    Telern = Rhybian   Bryfon or Bretyn = Lessarina V

Guydion   Ridd of Powys   Brendan XXVIII = Eloween

     Lords of the Isles   Sioba = Declan IX

     Glesyn = Sompayle   Kaoan = Rohan

       Sultoun = Fionnbarr XIII

       Grefan = Aoife VI   Conn Iungo

       Guynena = Lessarian III   Reklin Dartjac Elfagn

Lords of   Princes of
Brecordea   Lennscér

Brydan = Malwyn   Copraine = Fiora

Gwenran Athes = Farrell Cophall   Coplsyn   Guynena Eocyn Keira Emer = Fionnbarr XIV   Orlairch Deian

Morlaus Taithya Eocyn Keira Emer   Aeron Rohan Ríoghnach Keiren Declan Fionnuala ... mm?

(In early generations, not all issue shown)

'Sé deireadh gach cogadh síth.
("The end of each strife is peace.")

Kish-Somhpa: The Royal Family of Doishell and Collateral Kinships

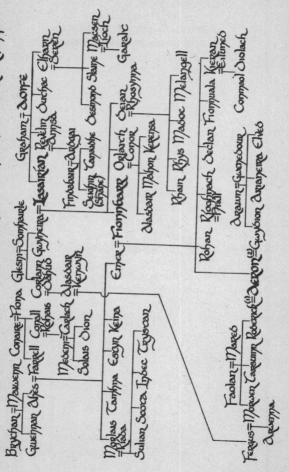

Prologue

Extract from Federacy Space Navy Records, Terran Admiralty:

SHIP REGISTER: Code AA–360–9–B14D.
Clearance: Level 5, Military.

FSS *SWORD*. Registry number: 7568-DGW.

Vessel Class:	Long-range cutter. General assignment: Sector R12–24670.
Duty rotation:	Five years Earthstandard.
Standing orders:	Alien contact. Investigation of inhabited or inhabitable planetary bodies; diplomatic prime contact.
Modifications:	Refit of emergency and cruise capability hyperdrive; hypospatial radio link; two escape pods, engineless; two powered escape boats; coldsleep berths; shuttle.
Armament class:	Light.
Attack capability:	Contraindicated. Specifications: forward and rear gunnery consoles; inboard and outboard shields; double-strength hull plating.
Droid complement:	Various all-purpose units.
Crew complement:	Captain, five crew.

* * *

Current status: active patrol, Orion Sector.
Time elapsed since last logged communication:
   two months, Earthstandard.
Nature of last logged communication:
   automatic, droidoriginated.
Last reported position: Orion Arm, outward bound.

The Federacy Space Ship *Sword* was almost ready for turn-around when the incident occurred, and after that nothing was ever the same again.

The *Sword* was a deep-space interstellar probe ship, light and sleek, designed for long, boring journeys of incalculable length over inconceivable distances, with one purpose only: to find life on unmapped planets, preferably humanoid and preferably friendly.

She was small but trim; as sea-sailors used to say, a "lady" of her kind. Ever since the Federacy had rediscovered a cheap, easy and almost ridiculously simple method of propulsion for its faster-than-light ships, voyages like this of the *Sword* were becoming routine.

The principle behind them was minimal: At regular intervals, the Admiralty would send a wave of light, fast cutters, each ship programmed for a different distant area of unexplored space. The craft would fly themselves at first, on automatic hyperdrive with their crews in coldsleep suspension, for varying periods, also predetermined; some went for one lightyear, others five or ten or fifty.

Then, after that first big jump, the ship would take itself down into space-normal and proceed automatically on course at just below lightspeed. This was where the mission really began. Once out of lightspeed, the ship was in its assigned search target area, and its scanners would then begin to sweep the passing star systems for signs of life. At the same time, the ship would send out signals of its own; with luck, any spacefaring civilization in the neighborhood would pick up those signals and make contact. If contact should be established, one way or another, the droid crew would then awaken the human crew. If not, well . . . five years in hypersleep suspension had one big advantage: It didn't age you.

Captain of the *Sword* was Theo Haruko. He was career Navy, Japanasian by birth, of middle height, middle age, and above-average intelligence. This present voyage would be his last diplomatic exploratory in the *Sword*. Perhaps his last ever, though that was yet to be decided.

And, befitting his final tour as master, his crew this time out was an exceptional one: Warren Hathaway, astrogator; Sarah O'Reilly, communications officer; Athenée Mikhailova, technical officer; and Hugh Tindal, science officer. Since the accidental death in coldsleep of Ensign Gro, these last two had taken on his duties of weapons officer and engineering officer, respectively.

In the bright crowded endless "now" of hibernation, Haruko dreamed—of food, of women, of his family, of promotion into a destroyer, or a dreadnought, maybe even . . . ship of the line. Or perhaps this time he would finally take that long-postponed retirement, go into the merchant spacefleet and make himself a packet. With his Navy experience and seniority, he could quickly get to be skipper of something really classy, one of the big plush luxury liners like the *Empress Elisabeth* or the *Aefensteorra*. Next to ships like those, the *Sword* was little more than a dinghy . . .

He never knew what the others dreamed of.

When the automatic alarm pinged gently, insistently, on the bone behind his ear, Haruko, though he would not know it for several minutes yet, began to wake up out of coldsleep. By the time he was fully conscious, the medidroid was already standing at his elbow administering a sprayshot. By force of long habit, Haruko's first focused glance was upward, at the small monitor screens set into the ceiling of the coldsleep cell, and he gasped at what he saw.

"Oh my God." He sequenced the droid to wake the others, scrambled into his flightsuit, and soon he was standing in the control cabin, the rest of his crew crowded in behind him, all of them staring rapt at the screens.

The screens all showed the same picture: a black and silver ship, of no known configuration or affiliation, bearing no markings of any kind. It was coming straight at them, and it was coming fast.

Mikhailova broke the silence. "There's not supposed to be anyone around here for parsecs. Who could they be, do you think?"

"How the hell would *I* know?" muttered Tindal, who did not much care for the technical officer. "O'Reilly, say hello to them."

But her fingers were already busy tapping out greetings on the light-coder, in Englic, Russic, Chinese, French, Germanic, Arabic, Hebraic, Swahili, Japannic and the twenty-three other spacegoing tongues, human and alien, that were currently known to the Federacy.

The reply, when it came, was in no language any of them had ever heard.

Then . . .

"LATIN!" screamed O'Reilly. "They speak *Latin*! Oh my God—"

Well, she was the linguist. . . . Again quick tanned fingers flickered over the light-coder keyboard, and this time without even a pause more of the weird language came flooding back.

From his chair on the port side, Tindal called out, "They're coming on visual."

Human. Well, human*oid*. Very big, very hairy, and very oddly accoutered . . .

"What's that?" snapped Haruko, and instantly bit the inside of his cheeks, hoping the others had not noticed how nervous he had sounded. He was swamped with shame at his reaction; he had done this very thing dozens of times before—why now, on his last go-round, should he be so suddenly and unaccountably edgy? But there it was: a vivid and dread-imbued feeling of something cataclysmic impending, some monstrous and colossal and totally unavoidable doom. Karma.

Well, whatever it might be, there was nothing he could do about it now. But the strangers had spoken again, and it was that which had startled him: not the Latin this time, but something that sounded like an unbroken string of consonants; all of them hard and most of them guttural, but an oddly musical tongue nonetheless.

O'Reilly, who had by now realized that for once she was out of her depth, had cut in the computer, and she was looking stunned at what it was apparently telling her.

"Lieutenant O'Reilly?" Haruko's voice, though unraised and unaccentuated, had nevertheless sharpened sufficiently to pierce the communications officer's sudden bemusement.

"Yes, sir. Sorry, sir. Gaelic. I mean, that's what they're speaking. Gaelic. It's not possible, but there it is."

"*Gaelic*? You mean these people are IRISH? The Irish came from outer space?"

O'Reilly riffled off some more Latin, got a great slab of it back. The first smiles, then, on both sides. "No . . . no, they're from Earth. Earth! Well, originally from Earth. I mean, not this lot, but—" She appeared to be caught in the grip of some intense emotion.

"Pull yourself together," said Haruko automatically.

"Sir." She composed herself with visible effort. "They *said* they are from an interstellar monarchy known as Keltia, and they, or their ancestors, I should say, have been out here since Earth year 453 A.D."

"Ri-i-i-ght." Jade Emperor of Heaven! It had been bad enough when one of the other probes had come across the Lost Tribe of Israel on Procyon VII, but *this*— "Do they speak Englic?" asked Haruko hopefully. Englic, the Federacy's official language, had become a sort of unofficial galactic common tongue, almost all aliens could speak a little . . .

"Not these two," O'Reilly informed him after inquiring. "They're just scouts, on patrol from a destroyer in the area, and their sloop has no language computer. But they've sent a message to their ship; there are people on board her who do speak Englic, and down on their worlds plenty of people speak it, too, so they don't think we'll have too much trouble. Latin is their own diplomatic language, though, and they suggest we all sleep-study it intensively, and maybe a little of the Gaeloch, as they call it, too, before . . ." Her voice trailed off.

"Before what?" asked Hathaway, speaking for the first time since the stranger ship had appeared on the screens.

O'Reilly gestured helplessly. "Before whatever."

Chapter One

As worlds change, and time comes to all nations that they must stand open at last to the strong cold sweeping tides of the Alterator, still it is people who must abide these changes, and do the same simple things they have always done, no matter the gale that howls at their backs.

It was cold that night on the heights of Caerdroia. The stars of autumn blazed diamond-hard overhead, the great stars that lay in no configuration Earth had ever seen. The Plumed Dancer, the Spearhead, the Warrior: All their cold gleam fell upon the frost that lay in the cracks of the street cobbles and glazed the roofs of the towers and rimed the high fields up in the inland valleys of the mountain range called the Loom.

Few were abroad, for the northwest wind the Kelts named An-Lasca, The Whip, blew straight and strong off the early sea-ice in the bay, and its sharp glassy bite was edged with salt. A knot of homebound souls here, hurrying down along the curving streets of the Stonerows from a late lively party; a lone walker, there, or there, moving with steady stride, untroubled by the wind, who could not stay indoors on even so bitter a night as this. Whatever their errand, all were cloaked and hooded and muffled well against the weather.

Late though it was, there were still cheerful yellow rectangles of light visible all through the ten-mile stretch of the walled city, where talk or merriment or duty kept some awake, or where some others courted sleep in vain. Many of those lights shone far up in the sheer basalt walls that climbed the shoulder of Mount Eagle, culminating in Turusachan, Place of Gathering, the immense fortress-palace-citadel that crowned Caerdroia. There, a ball was still faintly in progress in one of the splendid festal halls; up in a small tower a cool blue light spoke of computer-rooms still active; in a wind-swept courtyard a cloaked Fenian guard stood unmoving at his post. For this was the heart of Keltia, and it beat though all else slept.

On the extreme western edge of the city, black granite cliffs plunged their bastions two thousand feet straight down into the sea. The battlemented walls that encircled Caerdroia were here cut from the living rock of the mountain, and hanging above the sea, not the tallest nor yet the largest, was one round tower.

Its topmost story was pierced with twelve narrow windows, their stained glass worked in patterns both heraldic and magi-cal; at night their glow could be seen well out to sea. Just below, slightly to one side and facing square on to the sunset, a wide mullioned window opened upon a turret walk, and here a light still showed.

This was Aeron's chamber, Aeron's tower, and it was warm and cheerful this night despite the blast that buffeted it from the northwest. Her private chambers were very different from the picture most of her people probably had of them. The solar, the main room, where everything usually happened and where she now worked so late, was a big round chamber, high-ceilinged and generously proportioned, with walls of plain white stone that reflected the light-wash off the sea in the afternoons. It was furnished in a curious and highly personal blend of the severely functional and the traditionally ancient, with things the room's owner needed to have there and things she simply liked. Computers and viewscreens and monitors and control panels stood along the walls, alternating impartially with ceiling-high bookshelves and huge tapestries and weapons both ancient and modern. Anachronistic fires blazed in marble hearths, candles flickered on the carved iron-oak tables black with age—all for atmosphere: The real light and heat and energy came from solar insets and that universal Keltic power source, the crystal. Two huge shaggy wolfhounds dozed peacefully in front of the fire.

Aeron herself was wide awake, sitting cross-legged in the middle of her enormous tapestry-hung bed. She was clad in an old ragged gúna of thick nubby brown wool, its hood thrown back on her shoulders. Her hair, only a thought darker than the flames on the hearth, was pinned up anyhow in a half-braided knot at the back of her head, and so long was it that still it cascaded down onto the fur coverlet. In front of her on the bed was a computer pad, and she was leaning over it, chin in hand and elbow on knee, scribbling intently with a lightpen. Her face, of a calm beauty, pale, fine-featured and delicate, showed only the singleminded absorption of a child or a scholar.

Aeron Lassarina Angharad Aoife Aoibhell was thirty-seven years old, barely of full legal age by Keltic standards, which postulated an average lifespan of a hundred and sixty. She had been Ard-rían, High Queen of Keltia, for just under three years. She was the seventeenth monarch of her House to rule the Six Nations, and tonight she faced a problem that had been three thousand years in the making.

After a while, she paused, putting down the lightpen, and stretched like a palug to ease the ache that cramped her shoulders. She reviewed her work on the computer screen, coded it for automatic storage in the big wall computers, then fell back onto the piled pillows and ran her hands through her hair. The dogs, as dogs will, sensed her break in concentration and came bounding delightedly onto the bed. She smiled absently and ruffled their ears, but her thoughts were plainly elsewhere.

Her wandering gaze was caught and held by the portrait of her mother over the marble chimney-breast. The ethereal face of Emer ní Kerrigan looked back at her with an enigmatic smile. Emer, youngest daughter of the Prince of Leinster, who had run away from home to marry the Crown Prince of Keltia at the unheard-of age of twenty—the scandal had been appalling—and who with her husband Fionnbarr had ascended the throne only twenty-four years later. She really had been lovely: cornflower eyes, amber hair, a small sweet heart-shaped face—Aeron laughed suddenly, in half-grudging, half-amused admiration of the brazen fraud her mother had perpetrated upon an entire kingdom.

Queen Emer had been a woman of flinty resolution and surpassing deviousness; behind that pale frail loveliness had lain a will of findruinna and an unforgiving heart. She and her explosive eldest child had had more than one earthshaking passage-at-arms; even King Fionnbarr himself had not dared intervene, when his wife and his heir were in posture of war and all Turusachan became an armed camp and everybody in the line of fire went swiftly to ground.

Always it went the hardest on the eldest, thought Aeron, with a sudden sharp flare of unreasonable annoyance. And it mattered no whit whether one was heir to a throne or a croft or a merchancy . . . Still, she *was* firstborn, and the knowledge that she would one day be Queen of Kelts had been part of her first awareness. If those whose duty it had been to train her for the role had emphasized the burden far more than the glory, that too was as it should have been. All was lesson: Even family warfare had taught her much. Sibling battles were primary learning experiences for a young princess, and the shifting alliances among the Aoibhell brothers and sisters and cousins and fosterans were early training for one who would someday have to deal in galactic alliances.

Queen Emer had died with her husband three years ago, their son-in-law of five weeks, Roderick, only moments before, in the savage space ambush that had made Aeron Queen, orphan and widow all in one burst of Fomori lasers. She ignored the usual stab of sorrow at the thought, setting both grief and thought gently aside with discipline of three years' practice. For now, there were bigger things to consider, and the flood of change this night beat upon high far shores. Aeron gave the portrait one last long thoughtful look, then leaned across the pillows to punch up her brother Rohan on the transcom.

"Did I wake you?" she asked, when the cheerful countenance of her heir appeared on the multiscreen beside the bed. Telepathy was as common as speech among the Keltic peoples, though it involved considerably more effort, but there was something somehow reassuring about mechanical methods of communication, and Aeron was not alone in preferring to employ them whenever she could.

Rohan shook his head, raking his fingers through rumpled red-brown hair.

"You did not. I was playing fidchell with the computer. Everyone else is asleep long since, I think. What is it?"

"A moment." She cut in two more channels. "Morwen, Gwydion?"

"Ah, Aeron, can you not leave it till the morning?" The voice was sleepy and exasperated; the face did not appear on the screen, but Aeron knew it well: the gold hair, the startlingly blue eyes, the creamy complexion, all of which made Morwen Douglas, Duchess of Lochcarron and, more importantly, First Minister of Keltia, look even younger than her years.

"I fear not, Taoiseach. Gwydion?"

"I am here, Ard-rían." The deep bard's voice of the Prince of Gwynedd came untroubled, though he too chose not to be seen.

"Then come up, all of you. There is something you must hear."

The transcom went silent. Aeron re-settled herself on the bed to await the arrival of the three who, together with herself, really ruled Keltia. It was not only politics that united them; there were also other, more complex bonds. There was fosterage, as binding in love and law as blood-kinship to the Keltic mind: and Aeron, Morwen, and Gwydion's twin sister Arianeira were all foster-sisters, having been brought up together from infancy. There was marriage: Morwen's husband was Aeron's second cousin Fergus, and Aeron's dead lord Roderick had been Morwen's adored elder brother, the Prince of Scots; and palace gossip had it that when Aeron chose to wed again her choice would fall upon Gwydion Prince of Dôn. And there was fealty, a bond of loyalty made easy by a strong and popular Crown. But above all else there was deep wordless affectionate warmth: These four were true friends.

The wind, which had fallen off a little, suddenly slammed into the leaded windows with all the force of a fist. The dogs looked up, startled, and Aeron padded barefoot over to the casements, flinging them open to the wild night and leaning out into the wind. From here, high on a spur of Eryri, it was nearly three thousand feet straight down to where the giant waves crashed in fury on the slick slabs of rock, leaving their streaming foam-lattices halfway up the cliff. A few miles to the north, where the Avon Dia ran down to the sea, there was a fine sandy strand, wide and white, where Aeron often rode alone. But here was only the eternal clash of stone and water, bone and blood of the planet itself, neither one to outlast, or defeat, the other.

Aeron looked up, to where the Criosanna glittered in the light of the two small moons, both now fully risen, though Argialla was still only a slim crescent curve of silver-blue. The Criosanna, the Woven Belts, were the glory of Tara, flat shining rings that girdled the planet at the equator. Scientists disagreed on their nature: Some said they were the remains of former satellites, late moons, while others contended they were rather moons in the making. Any road, they were beautiful, and unique in the seven Keltic systems: they had been the first spacemark of the original Danaan starfarers, their first assurance of journey's end safely reached, when they made planetfall three thousand years ago after the great emigration from an Earth that was no longer home.

The Criosanna seemed to put everything into perfect perspective. Aeron smiled, and turned as the door opened behind her. Her smile widened and warmed as she saw her brother.

Rohan was as a rule the first to arrive for anything, and tonight he had been not only awake and dressed, but the closest at hand of the three she had summoned. The many towers and brughs and courts that constituted Turusachan were not merely governmental; they served as official residences for the chief Keltic nobles and officers of state, as well as home to the rather extensive royal family. As Tanist, heir-presumptive to the Throne of Scone, Rohan Revelin Aoibhell, Prince of Thomond and Duke of Ythan, occupied a tower not far from his elder sister's, with his own household and guards and dependents and duties.

He came in now, dressed in the bardic dark-blue he favored. The wolfhounds leaped joyfully upon him, standing on their hind legs to lick his face. Those immense beasts were but little loftier than he: Tallness of stature ran in the Keltic race, and in the Aoibhell family; Rohan and his brothers Kieran and Declan all towered seven feet high or more. Even their sisters, save for Ríoghnach, stood well on the far side of six feet.

Laughing, Rohan pushed the dogs away and went to a sideboard.

"Wine?" At Aeron's nod, he poured out four cups and passed one to her. "Morwen is on Lochcarron time as ever, I suppose."

His sister laughed. Morwen's unpunctuality, a family jest for years, was deplorable in one who was after all the second most important person in the realm; but it was also as unchangeable as the stars.

"Gwynedd at least is not laggard," said Gwydion lightly, coming in through the library doors.

"Nor has ever been," said Aeron, and he bowed in acknowledgment of the compliment. But that was only simple truth: Those who belonged to the House of Dôn, over which House the Princes of Gwynedd were Chief, had always been in Keltia's vanguard was it peace or was it war. They were rivaled in their antiquity, rank, honor and divine ancestry only by the House of Dâna—whose Chief was the head of the line of Aoibhell.

Indeed, Aeron reflected idly, watching the two men talk bard-lore over their wine, at one time the Crown itself had been seated in the House of Dôn; from there it had passed peacefully into the keeping of the Douglases, Morwen's clann; and, eight hundred years ago, equally peacefully, to the Aoibhells, who had held it ever since—making the rulership of Keltia more than ever a family matter.

Gwydion had taken his cup of wine and stretched out on the fur rugs by the fireside; one of the wolfhounds laid its head upon his knee and gazed up at him soulfully. He was tall even among a tall people, the Prince of Dôn, with a build at once lean, graceful, and powerful. His dark hair and beard were flecked with gray, and his eyes were sea-gray in a stern handsome face. He was a master-bard, and a brilliant general, and a towering magician, and there were few finer swordsmen in all Keltia.

Also he was First Lord of War on the Keltic High Council, and for that alone he would have been summoned by Aeron to this owl-time parley. The gray eyes looked up consideringly to meet Aeron's green ones, and after a moment she smiled.

Again the oak door swung, and Morwen entered at last, unhurried, casual, looking faintly aggrieved and supremely unconcerned for her tardiness.

Aeron raised her fine brows. "Have some wine," she said politely.

Her sister-in-law cast her a dark look. "Gods help you, Aeron, if this is aught less than war or treason or galactic pestilence. Fergus leaves tomorrow for Duneidyn, and a royal chat was not part of my plans for tonight. It had better be important, Ard-rían, or I shall rip your throat out, truly." She took the cup of wine Rohan offered her and drank it off.

"Your Grace of Lochcarron will doubtless decide for yourself. As for Fergus, I suggest he change his plans for departure and remain at Turusachan." Aeron had returned to the middle of the bed, and now she drew up her bare feet beneath her and fixed her company with a level green gaze. It had been Aeron in her threadbare old robe who had sat crosslegged on the bed; it was the High Queen of Keltia who now spoke.

"Well then, my children, an hour ago I received a first-urgency communication out of Falias sector, from the commander of the *Glaistig,* a destroyer on routine patrol just outside the Curtain Wall. One of her scout sloops has made contact with a stranger ship."

Rohan groaned. "Galláin?" he asked, using the Gaeloch word that served as a blanket term for all alien humanoid races. "Is that what you dragged us up here for? Where is the urgency there? We have made contact with strangers often enough before. All we ever do is quarantine them for a time, receive their ambassadors here at Caerdroia, and give them audience with you. What is so different now?"

For answer, Aeron activated the big wallscreen at the far end of the room. Against a sharp-edged background of starfield, a small, rather old-fashioned ship hung motionless in hologram. She increased the magnification, and as one her companions sat up startled.

"A deep-space interstellar probe ship, with its crew in

coldsleep,'' commented Aeron, in a dry lecturer's voice that fooled nobody. She added almost casually, "From Earth."

Now she had their undivided attention, and she waited quietly while they stared at the image, studying it, gathering their own thoughts and questions. She had done the same herself scarcely an hour since; their thoughts and questions would be much the same as her own . . .

"Terrans," breathed Morwen at last. "Have they spoken to you?"

"What are you going to do about them?" asked Rohan at the same moment.

Gwydion remained silent, though he glanced up sideways at Aeron for her response. This event had been long expected; ever since, three millennia ago, the Kelts had first settled in their new home, the eventual, or inevitable, reunion with Earth had been anticipated—with varying attitudes.

Some monarchs over the centuries had counseled extending the hand of friendship and alliance and common kinship to Earth, should that day ever come when Terra and Keltia must meet again at last. Others had set their faces against it, and had called for hostility, or at best a policy of severely neutral disregard. As First Lord of War, Gwydion had his own ideas; as Pendragon of Lirias, leader of the awesome magical-military order known as the Dragon Kinship, he had others. But he kept his own counsel for the moment, and waited to hear his Queen's thought.

"They have not yet spoken to any Kelt, save the two pilots aboard the scout vessel and the commander of the *Glaistig*," Aeron was saying. "And as for what I shall do—well, first of all I shall do as we always do when strangers are in the gate: show them sacred Keltic hospitality." She slid off the bed as she spoke, crossed the room to a wardrobe and began pulling out clothing. "Have the *Firedrake* and an escort brought in and stand ready in orbit. I am going to greet our guests."

An instant rigidity seized the room.

"Is that wise?" murmured Gwydion. He did not look at her.

"They will not know who I am," she said reasonably, "if nobody is fool enough to tell them . . . I know what you are thinking, Gwydion, but I shall worry about that later. Tonight, I need very desperately to know what like are these Terrans. I need to know how came they here, what they do seek, what more they may know of us, and who it was told them. And I need to know all this before I take the news to the Council.'' She sensed the disapproval in the silence, turned to face them. ''It is but a probe drone, after all, not an armada.''

''Then why go out on *Firedrake*?'' asked Morwen immediately. ''The Starfleet flagship, with a destroyer escort, going to meet a probe—does that not seem something strange?''

''Not to my mind! These Terrans already know some little about us, from the scout ship if from nowhere else. By now, they undoubtedly are aware we are originally of Earth, and if I were one of them, I would certainly think it peculiar if some dramatic first gesture were *not* made. I might even begin to wonder what was being hidden . . . If my going chafes you so, Elharn shall come; he shall be my official representative, and I only an anonymous observer. But I *will* go.'' The green eyes glinted, and there was sudden steel beneath the light tone of her voice.

Morwen sighed, resigned. ''And what to us?''

''I wish you, Taoiseach, to inform my High Councillors, or as many of them as you can locate at this time of night. Call an immediate session for all those in Caerdroia, and summon the others who are not in the City or who may be off-planet. Tell them what has happened, so far as you know, and decide how best to announce the news to the people. Rohan, you will of course take my chair in my absence. Then, call another meeting to be held when I return: a joint session of High Council, Privy Council, and the leaders of Senate, Assembly and House of Peers. By then I shall have a better idea of the Terrans upon which to act.'' Aeron flashed them a smile. ''And perhaps the Rechtair of Tara should begin planning of a suitable ceremonial welcome. Earth seems to have found us at last.''

After they had gone, Aeron stood motionless in the middle of the room. She seemed to come back to herself, abruptly, shaking her head as if to clear it, then took a cloak from its peg and wrapped herself in its voluminous folds. Pulling the hood up about her face, she let herself out onto the turret walk through a door set in the thickness of the tower wall.

Out on the battlements, the full force of An-Lasca came at her, flattening her against the wall and whipping her cloak out behind her. It was hard to catch her breath in that fierce unslackening rush of air, and after a few yards she turned aside to shelter in a small recess cut into the stone.

The ramparts shone wet and black in the light from her windows; the mist that lay as frost farther inland was here still sea-mist only. Below, the waves sounded, their sullen boom amplified by the niche in which Aeron huddled on her bench. Overhead, the Criosanna still arched luminous milky veils over Tara.

That at least was unchanged, no whit altered by this vast new thing that had come to change all else. But beyond those circling bright ribbons, out there—her eye quickly oriented the direction—out beyond the Spearhead, a ship from Earth lay hove-to in deep space outside the Curtain Wall, and a Keltic scout ship had hailed it, and a Keltic warship kept watch on it, and a Keltic fleet would soon be racing out to meet it, and she with that fleet.

Why had she been so insistent upon her own going? Was it, as Morwen and Rohan and Gwydion clearly thought, just mischief? In the past, when contact had been made, she had always waited regally for aliens to come to *her*; sovereigns of mighty nations did not dash off to meet any little curragh that ventured into their territory.

Oh, but this was so different, she thought, and a thrill of anticipation shook her from head to foot. Surely the others had seen that? A ship from *Earth*, the ship Keltia had been awaiting for the past three millennia! And now it was here, in her time, in her reign; the gods having for their own reasons so ordered it that Aeron Aoibhell and no other must be the one to face this moment.

What would her people think? Would they see it as it appeared in her eyes, as a high moment of destiny for Keltia, for all the galaxy, even? Would they remember in their bones, in that inner certainty of race-memory, in that cell-coded dim place within them that spoke to all Kelts alike, the beautiful blue-white planet that had been their home? Or, remembering, would they wish to affirm that kinship of old with the Terran world-family? They could never go back, of course; Keltia was a power in the galaxy now, for good or for ill, very possibly mightier than Earth herself, though that remained to be proven. Alliance, then? Was it possible . . . or even desirable?

And the Terrans, what would *they* think? What would they be *like?* After three thousand years . . . Aeron felt herself shiver, pulled her cloak closer around her. For the Kelts had not left Earth in happy time, nor even for high adventure's sake. They had gone as refugees, fleeing persecutions, desperate, hoping to find the home they had been promised out among the stars, but never knowing if they would live to see it. Who aboard that first emigration, that first staggering leap into the dark, could have foreseen the Keltia to come; having foreseen, who would have believed?

Except, of course, Brendan . . . Her thought spun back to contemplation of her great ancestor, founder of her House. St. Brendan the Astrogator. *He* was the one who had gotten her into this. *He* was the First Cause of this present moment. It was all his fault. When everybody else in fifth-century Ireland had been busy with leather boats and the New World across the western seas, Brendan had been busy plotting mass exodus. No leather boats for *him*; no, Brendan had had to get involved with the Danaans, the last of Atlantis, and end up with starships and magic. So that when the monk Patrick came, with his preachings and his prohibitions against magic and all the high lore preserved so long at such cost, Brendan had seen the way of it, and had revolted. Supported by his mother Nia, guided by the old man Barinthus's half-mad memories of a long-ago voyage, Brendan had built ships to sail the stars again, as the Atlanteans had done, and in those ships he had taken the last of the Danaans back out to the heavens.

With them went many others, Milesians and Kymry and Scotans, Picts and Prytani, Kernish and Vanx, who would no longer stay if magic died, and so Keltia began—here, in this very place from which Aeron now stared at the stars that had led her people home. And those same star-roads now had led

Earth to meet them again; Time had spun round, flung free of the Wheel, and worlds stood waiting for her to raise her hand.

Out of the corner of her eye, she caught the flash and smear of starlight that signalled the emergence of a ship from hyperspace, and then six golden objects, the central one far larger than the others, were moving steadily in a graceful arc out beyond the Criosanna. The fleet had arrived; she must now finish dressing, then go by aircar to Mardale Port, twelve miles away, for the shuttle out to the orbiting flagship.

In any case, the time for reflection was past. Brendan, no doubt, would have understood. She brushed the sea-damp from her face and went in.

Chapter Two

As the bright needles of light that were the approaching Keltic fleet drew steadily nearer, so too did the crew of the *Sword* draw together to huddle companionably close around the screens, shoulders touching as they watched. No one admitted, even to himself, that reassurance was the reason for this unaccustomed nearness, but that was it all the same. Instinctive. Atavistic, even. But singularly comforting.

For the rest, they watched in silence.

Which was broken first by Hathaway. "Mother of poodles!"

Haruko had to agree. There were six ships out there now, fully visible to the scanners, and one of them was the biggest thing he had ever seen in his life. Even the five smaller vessels were imposing enough. Escort attack craft, undoubtedly: light cruisers, or destroyers. Sleek, deadly, and, judging from their gunports, carrying enough weaponry to take out ships several times their size.

But the central ship, the one they escorted—that was something else entirely. It looked like a golden dragon. An enormous sculptured head with open jaws, outstretched claws on stylized forelegs, swept-back wings and a curved forked tail; and it had to be ten miles long at the very least . . . It was a statement of arrogant and ostentatious power, on a scale that Haruko could not quite grasp just yet. *A military vessel like a work of art*, he thought numbly. A warship deliberately designed to flout astrodynamic conventions, as if the race who had launched her could afford aesthetics even in battle, were so mighty as to be able to ignore the demands of interstellar physics that bound ordinary mortals. And God was it big—

"I make her more than twelve times bigger than the *Empress Elisabeth*," said Mikhailova, looking stunned. "*Four times* the size of *Leviathan*! I don't even want to *guess* at her armaments."

Haruko nodded in abstracted wonder. Comparing the foreign flagship—for she could be nothing else—to the largest civilian and military craft that the Federacy could boast was a fairly pointless exercise. For one thing, such comparisons conveyed nothing of the beauty and sheer impact of the alien ship, and as she began to slow for the rendezvous with the invincible stateliness of an avalanche or a tidal wave, Haruko gave himself up to dazzlement and envy. She seemed hulled in seamless sheet gold that glittered in the wash of starlight across her, and for all her tremendous size and bulk, she was fast, graceful and impressive as hell.

Sudden cold panic clamped itself around his middle. This, he knew now, beyond any faintest doubt, was what he had been afraid of for the past few hours, ever since they had met the scout ship. This dragon sailing toward him from unknown stars was the embodiment of that prescient numbing dread. That ship held his doom. Whoever commanded her knew the value of psychological warfare. Whoever ruled the race that had launched her . . . His mind faltered into silence before the possibilities. For the first time in his career, Captain Theo Haruko, FSN, feared contact.

Aeron stood on the vast main bridge of the *Firedrake*, arms folded across her chest. She was in her usual shipboard position—leaning casually against the huge viewport that formed one facet of the right eye of the dragon—and she was dressed in her usual shipboard attire, the same dark-green flightsuit worn by every kern and officer in the Keltic starfleet, the same knee-high black boots. Her uniform bore no decorations, no mark of rank, no insignia of any kind save the royal device of the winged unicorn upon her left sleeve. Her hair was loose, and rippled down to her knees.

She was staring out at the blazing starfields forward as if she could somehow detect in all that velvet immensity the one significant speck that was the Terran ship. All around her, the bridge crew worked smoothly, unconstrained by her presence.

Still, that presence was very much in the forefront of their awareness. It was always an occasion when the great flagship had the Ard-rían on board; but the crew was well used to it, and Aeron had nothing to do but be a passenger, even though she was qualified to sail this ship herself. The *Firedrake*, as always, was under the command of Mistress and Captain Gwennan Chynoweth, a full century Aeron's senior and latest of a long line of spacegoing Chynoweths.

Even that, though, was not enough; and Aeron's presence in any capacity whatever would not have been accepted by her counselors—they had accepted it reluctantly enough even as it was—were it not for the presence of the Master of Sail himself. Elharn Aoibhell, called Ironbrow, High Admiral of the Keltic Starfleet since before his grandniece Aeron's birth, stood beside Chynoweth on the cithóg side of the command deck.

Under the terms of Aeron's promise, Elharn was her official royal representative to this exceptionally unorthodox diplomatic meeting. It would be he, with Gwennan Chynoweth, who would formally greet the Terrans in the name of Keltia and the Queen of Kelts; not Aeron, who was bound by that same promise to the role of unidentified onlooker, nameless and rankless.

Aeron was irritated all over again when she remembered that. To hide her ill temper, she turned her gaze out again at the stars, feeling the *Firedrake* begin to slow around her. They must be very near now.

Confirming her guess, Elharn approached. He saluted gravely, fist to shoulder in the Keltic fashion, and, at her nod, spoke.

"We have arrived at the coordinates, Ard-rían."

All her annoyance vanished, and her face lighted with a burst of unqueenly eagerness.

"Let us see what they look like close to, then." She uncoiled from her position against the bulkhead and went to the railing that overlooked the huge control bay twenty feet below. Elharn, a step behind her, signalled unobtrusively to a tech.

Immediately the big main screen blurred and cleared to reveal the *Sword*, looking much as it had done on the screen in Aeron's chamber. Off to one side of the picture, the scout sloop was visible a short way away; and, even more discreetly distant, the outlines of the destroyer *Glaistig* blocked the farther stars. The *Glaistig* had been there ever since first summoned by her scout vessel, taking up a watchful position at a safe distance, lest there should be some trap sprung before the fleet, and the *Firedrake* which was a fleet unto herself, should arrive.

Taking almost automatic note of these military dispositions, of which she thoroughly approved, Aeron leaned against the railing and allowed herself to be entranced, much as was Haruko at that same moment aboard the *Sword*. Out here in deep interstellar space, that strange hollow sunless country of cold stars and galaxies adrift, the metal artifact of man's devising that was the *Sword* took on overtones of glamourie. *It was almost a fith-fath*, thought Aeron, bemused; a shapeshifting spell. First it looked totally natural, then it most unsettlingly did not, and then again, after she had stared at it a while longer, it did. She could not make up her mind about it. Whatever, this was what had come all that way from Earth after all those years.

"She is very small, my lord," remarked Aeron at last to Elharn, who stood patiently at her shoulder. "How many are aboard her?"

"Five, Ard-rían. All were in coldsleep, of course."

"Of course." Aeron stared a while longer, then with visible reluctance stepped back from the rail, and Elharn quickly schooled the smile from his features. "Well, Master of Sail, I give place to you—as promised. Send appropriate greetings, and invite the Earth captain here. After simple decontamination, of course."

Gwennan Chynoweth, who had joined them in time to hear this last, shook her head.

"Forgive me, Ard-rían," she said, a careful delicacy to her tone. "But they cannot come aboard a foreign vessel without, ah, *sureties*. A certain faith on their part would—"

"They are undoubtedly civilized people, gentry and officers, well used to interstellar diplomacy," said Aeron icily, her resentment getting the better of her. "Else they would never have been sent on so delicate a mission. But what do you suggest, Captain?"

Gwennan smiled, unruffled, for she well understood her ruler's wish to be more actively a part of this breathtakingly exciting moment.

"He'll come here, I'll go there. Fair exchange. And my lord Elharn will be here to greet him officially. With your permission, Ard-rían."

Both Elharn and Chynoweth saw the idea leap, full-blown and shining, into Aeron's face. Elharn spoke first to scotch it.

"Nay, Aeron, you will *not* go yourself."

"Uncle, it is perfect! They can have no idea who I might be—"

"And that is how it must remain. It is out of the question, Aeron, and *I* am in command of this embassy," he reminded her. "At Your Majesty's order—Besides, you are here as a plain spacer, a kern of no rank."

"I am a Fian commander," replied Aeron a little stiffly. "And a qualified starship captain."

"All very true. But the Terrans do not know that—as they must not; and your uniform says otherwise—as it must. It would provoke an interstellar incident were we to offer to swap one Keltic kern for their captain."

"And when they later discovered—which they would, and sooner rather than later—that their hostage had been our Queen?" Chynoweth pointed out, with the bland guile that so often was required in dealing with Aeron. "The consequences of that could well be—unfortunate."

Aeron, who had been scowling, was brought up short by that. It made sense, she was forced to admit, but no one said she had to be gracious about it . . . "Very well. You may go, Captain. If, of course, the Terrans even agree to such terms."

The tall blonde Kernishwoman grinned. "Thank you, Ard-rían. And you?"

"I? I shall stay here on the bridge, of course, and watch from a distance. A safe, silent distance. Unless you two jurisconsults think even that too much?"

But, as it turned out, they did not. Saluting them both, Gwennan left for the shuttle deck, and Aeron turned disconsolately back to watch the proceedings in the control bay. Elharn maintained discreet silence for a few minutes, then laid a gentle hand on her shoulder.

"Aeron, you do understand why we cannot risk your going, cannot risk even your speaking to the Terrans at this time? Gwydion would cut me to pieces if anything happened to you. And you did promise."

Mutinous green eyes met his, then fell, and Aeron briefly inclined her cheek to touch his hand.

"Ah, uncle, of course I know; who knows better than I, by now? All the same—" She broke off, then continued in a lower voice, turning away so that the crew should not see her face. "How very much I should like to *not* be Queen for a while . . . This is the greatest thing that has happened to us since the time of Arthur, perhaps since the time of Brendan himself. I wanted so much to see it as Aeron only, before I was obliged to see it as the Ard-rían Aeron." She glanced up at him. "Does that sound so very terrible?"

He shook his head, smiling. "Not to me does it sound so, alanna. And so you bullied Gwydion and Morwen and Rohan, the poor bodachs, into letting you come. Nay, I understand that well, and your father would have done the very same, if it were he who sat today upon the Throne of Scone."

Her quick ear had caught the subtle shadings of what he had really said. "You miss him very much."

Elharn's eyes were distant with old, gentle memories. "He was only ten years my junior, though he was my brother's son—we were more like cousins than uncle and nephew. And you are very like him in many ways, you know. But even more are you like your grandfather."

She looked startled. "Lasairían? He was not like—"

But Elharn shook his head. "Your other grandfather. Farrell. And that worries me sometimes."

In truth, it worried more people than just the High Admiral: Aeron's maternal grandfather, Farrell Prince of Leinster, had rejoiced in the possession of a wild strain of impulsiveness, a tendency to leap into action first and think later, if at all, that he had passed on to his daughter Emer, and she to hers. Courage and single-mindedness went with it, but Farrell's unpredictability made for a certain recklessness not entirely appropriate in a High Queen. After all, look where it had led her tonight . . .

Aeron, catching much of this telepathically, smiled, for she well understood her great-uncle's concern, and now she was the one who laid a comforting hand on the other's arm.

"Never mind, Master of Sail. As of this moment, it goes from our hands to the laps of the gods." She pointed. "Look there."

On the deosil screen, Gwennan Chynoweth's gold and black shuttle now hovered alongside the Terran ship, and another, smaller, shuttle was on the main screen, gliding into the hangar bay of the *Firedrake* like a falcon alighting. The Earth captain had arrived.

Chapter Three

As his shuttle moved smoothly through deep space toward its rendezvous with the dragon ship, Haruko had leisure to speculate upon the probable nature of his imminent hosts, and perhaps also to regret his haste to meet them. Maybe Tindal and Hathaway had been right to urge caution. Maybe he *had* been too precipitate, too eager, in his instant acceptance of the Keltic offer. True, his presence on their flagship was counterbalanced by their captain's presence on the *Sword*, but treachery was everywhere in the universe and what guarantees did he have, really? All they knew about the Kelts up to this moment came from some antiquated anthropological tapes on the Kelts of Earth that Mikhailova had dug up, and from what little the scouts had told O'Reilly. And all of it could be a pack of lies, and in any case it had all been in one or the other of those incomprehensible languages.

Haruko gnawed thoughtfully on his knuckles, as he always did when he was really upset and thinking hard. In the end, it had been O'Reilly who had given him the push he'd needed—and he shouldn't have needed it—to climb into the shuttle. She had talked, long and eloquently and insistently, and her arguments had been impossible to refute.

"To begin with," she had said, with some asperity, "what they propose is traditional and honorable diplomatic practice, and what are we if not diplomats? Why the hell else are we even here? Anyway, it's not as if you hadn't done this sort of thing before." Well, she had him there; and since her duties

42

as communications officer also included protocol, Haruko had not felt qualified to gainsay her.

But her other reasons had been rather more intangible. What it all seemed to come down to was the contention that the Kelts would be irretrievably insulted if their offer was refused. Again according to O'Reilly, who was after all herself of Irish descent, the Kelts' sense of face, their personal valuation of honor and dishonor, was as great and as lunatic (though she didn't use that word) as any Japanasian's, and Haruko of all people should be able to understand *that*?

And he *did*, he *did* understand it, that wasn't the problem. No, what was troubling him was much more basic than that, and much less noble: Haruko was terrified. He would go aboard the Keltic ship because he had to and he knew it, but all the reason and logic O'Reilly could marshal up were utterly powerless against the almost superstitious panic he was feeling. As soon as he had seen that gold ship coming at him, he had been swamped by a sense of cosmic doom that had nothing to do with the obvious technological superiority of the strangers, or even merely their stranger status of itself. He had met aliens before, on other voyages, plenty of times; sometimes they had been more advanced than the Terrans and sometimes they had not. But never once on those trips had he felt so much a pawn of the unknown. This time it was different; and as the golden ship loomed up before him, its glowing bulk shutting out the stars and filling his screens, a vast black bay suddenly yawned in her side where no opening had been a moment before, and the shuttle was swallowed up into it.

Haruko realized with a blink of surprise that his control of his own craft had been usurped; some unknown hand was landing the shuttle automatically. He sat back to compose himself in these last few seconds, and then jumped uncontrollably as his ship-to-ship communicator came to life. A pleasant male voice, welcoming him to the *Firedrake*—the *Firedrake!* that was perfect!—in excellent Englic, though accented a little strangely, and requesting his compliance with some minimal decontamination procedures; would Haruko be so kind as to oblige patiently?

The voice evidently took his startled silence for assent.

There was a flash of warm rose-colored light, a low hum, then another flash of light, white this time. Then the voice again, now politely asking him to step out of the shuttle.

Jade Emperor of Heaven, raced Haruko's last panic-stricken prayer, *just get me through this one* . . . He took a deep breath to steady his *hara*, according to the teachings he followed, then pressed the door control.

He emerged into a cool, breathable atmosphere almost indistinguishable from that of the *Sword*, and an artificial gravity only fractionally less than Earth's. Surprised, and subtly reassured, Haruko followed the loudspeaker's instructions and stepped into a lighted alcove in the wall of the landing bay. Again the pulsing rosy light, the flood of white light; then a klaxon brayed and doors seemed to whoosh open all over the hangar and people seemed to pour through all those doors.

His first reaction was alarm. Haruko blinked, a little nonplussed, but saw that it was no army but only about ten or fifteen poeple, most of them techs to service his shuttle. *But they were all Kelts* . . . He knew he was staring, but they were regarding him just as frankly. It came to him with something of a shock—and with chagrin that it *should* shock him, and that he had not thought of it sooner—that he, Theo Haruko, was probably the first man of his race these people had ever seen, the first Terran of *any* stripe for more than three millennia. The thought rocked him.

But they were fascinating too. The first thing that struck him was all the hair they seemed to have: hip-length, shoulder-length, mustaches, beards— Three women and four men, who were most definitely *not* techs, had drawn themselves up in front of him and were now waiting politely for him to speak. Still he stared. They were all clad in the same dark-brown uniform—the uniform of the Fianna, as he would later learn—and all of them were quite amazingly tall. There were no weapons in sight.

Haruko got a grip on himself. "Permission to come aboard," he said, and saluted smartly.

At that the formality thawed. The man who seemed to be in charge of the detachment returned his salute, with a smile.

"Permission granted. You are very welcome to Keltia,

Captain Haruko. I am Lieutenant O Fiura, and we are here to escort you to the bridge.''

He fell cordially into step beside Haruko, though he towered over the Terran by more than a foot, and they left the landing bay and headed for what was unmistakably a turbolift. Not many moments later, the lift deposited them on what could only be the command bridge of the giant ship. Haruko had time for only the briefest glance round before his attention was claimed by the two men who came forward to meet him.

O Fiura saluted. "My lord Admiral, my lord mac Rossa— may I present Captain Theo Haruko of the FSS *Sword*." He withdrew, and the escort followed suit. Haruko stood alone on the bridge with the two officers, all his diplomatic instincts on red alert.

The gray-haired man with the piercing dark eyes spoke first.

"The greeting of the gods and man to you, Captain. I am Elharn Aoibhell, Master of Sail, High Admiral of the Keltic Starfleet, and I have been commanded by Her Majesty Aeron the High Queen to welcome you in her name."

Haruko had guessed the man to be a ranking spacer, and he returned the civilities.

"I thank you, Admiral. In the name of the Terran Federacy, I extend to Her Majesty and to all Keltia the salutations of Earth."

Smiles all round. "Another Navy man," said Elharn pleasantly. "Well met indeed. I am sure you will enjoy your visit to the *Firedrake*. We will talk later, you and I; not often do I have the chance to trade stories with a new listener. But may I present the *Firedrake*'s first officer, Anluan mac Rossa. Captain Chynoweth is, of course, at the moment on board your own ship."

The tall brown-haired man called mac Rossa bowed, and Haruko did likewise, but with a certain distraction. In all the excitement he had managed to forget completely about the *Sword* and what must be going on back there. But there was nothing he could do.

Elharn gestured, and the three men moved to the railing of the command deck, looking down on the activity below.

"This meeting must be fairly brief, Captain, for a number of reasons," he said, with just the right note of regret. "But I have been instructed by the Queen to convey her formal invitation to you and your crew to accompany us back to our capital of Caerdroia, and to be our guests there, until our diplomatic dealings are concluded, or until it is your pleasure—or your duty—to depart." He glanced to his right, past mac Rossa's shoulder, a glance so swift as to be almost imperceptible.

But Haruko's hyperawareness caught it. He followed the flick of eyes, saw only a woman standing motionless some fifteen yards away in the bubble curve of the enormous viewport. Silhouetted against stars, she was tall, slender, dressed in the green Keltic uniform. Her face was in deep shadow, but Haruko's notice was caught by her hair: bone-straight, silk-smooth, the color of polished copper. *A guard?* he wondered. No, she was unarmed. But then, no one he had yet seen had borne any weapon . . .

"We would be pleased and honored to accept Her Majesty's invitation," he replied aloud, looking again at Elharn. "I will confirm this acceptance when I am back aboard my own ship, and we will then receive your sailing orders." He paused before he spoke again. "As your scouts no doubt have informed you, Admiral, we are a long-range probe sent out to contact civilization outside—usually *far* outside—our own immediate sphere of influence. Which is, if I may say so, considerable. Although this is the farthest we have yet ventured in this direction, I still wonder that we have not met you before in our travels—or at least had word of your existence."

"We keep ourselves rather *to* ourselves, Captain," said mac Rossa with a smile. "As you will come to see. For our part, I think we were just as shocked to encounter you."

"Yes, it was quite a surprise all round," agreed Haruko. *And the biggest surprise of all was your Queen's sending her flagship to meet us when a simple, unostentatious destroyer would have done just as well. Unless she really wanted to impress us—or intimidate us . . .*

It seemed Elharn had read the thought. "The Ard-rían is very eager to meet you," he remarked. "And in light of that, and also in view of our mutual kinship from afar, it seemed good to her to send the *Firedrake*, and myself, as earnests of her friendship and honor.''

Haruko was taken aback, less at the answer, which however flattering was still only partly true, than at the fact that Elharn had apparently responded to an unspoken question. *Are they all telepaths, then?* he wondered, very privately indeed, all his mental shields having slammed up at once. If so, he must order the others to guard their thoughts as well as their tongues; and do so himself, of course. All at once he felt extremely uncomfortable, and glancing over his shoulder, he saw the red-haired woman watching him, a faint smile on her face. She had emerged from the shadows by the viewport and now stood in the light, close enough for him to see her face: fine-featured, and very lovely. Catching his eye, she nodded politely, setting fist to shoulder in the Keltic greeting he had already received several times; and before he could stop himself, he was bowing back. Obscurely unsettled, he turned his attention again to Elharn and mac Rossa.

To his utter astonishment, both Kelts had the same expression of rigid control on their faces, and for a moment he stared at them in confusion. What could possibly cause those two officers to look so appalled? Again he glanced around, but, except for the woman, who had withdrawn to her original position near the port, he saw nothing to justify any panic.

After a moment, Elharn spoke, and his tone was carefully neutral. ''In the time remaining, Captain Haruko, perhaps you would care to hear something of our history?''

''I'd be delighted, sir,'' said Haruko sincerely. *A few answers might well be in order here . . .*

''You have heard, I think, that we came originally from Earth.''

''That could have been inferred,'' said the Terran, smiling. ''Your scouts did tell us a little. But hardly what you'd call a detailed history.''

''No, well, that does not surprise me. It takes somewhat longer than that. But I can certainly tell you enough now for your satisfaction, and later you shall hear all our story.'' They had crossed the command deck to stand by the deosil viewport. From here, Haruko could just discern the sliver of silver that was the *Sword*.

"Where to begin," said Elharn. "Well, we left Earth for galactic space in the year 453, by your old-style reckoning, and we came to Keltia two years later."

453! The scouts had not been lying, then; but it was still almost unbelievable . . .

"If you'll forgive me," said Haruko, shaking his head in wonder, "I find that astounding. I know I am not mistaken in thinking that a good many centuries pre-space."

"Fifteen centuries pre-space, in fact," said mac Rossa. "We knew you'd be surprised. But we were lucky—we, meaning the Kelts of old. We were able to rediscover faster-than-light travel and get out."

"*Re*discover?" repeated Haruko.

"I warned you there was much to explain." Elharn's voice was amused. "Our ancestors on Earth were the Danaans, the original Kelts, who settled in Ireland and the other Keltic countries. But before they lived there, they had lived in Atlantis—that is right, the place you Terrans always thought such a myth. I promise you, it was very real indeed, and the Danaans were not the only race to live there. But before they lived in Atlantis, they came to Earth from a distant star."

"You are saying the original Kelts—these Danaans—were actually extraterrestrials?" Haruko had been listening intently, desperate to learn, but this he thought he must have misheard. Or hoped he had.

But both Kelts were nodding. "Yes, exactly," said mac Rossa. "There is no record now of their planetary origins, though we have plenty of other documents. Any road, they came to Earth, they settled in Atlantis—Atland, as we call it—and after a time they had to flee again when Atland was destroyed. But at the moment, Captain, I'm afraid we can't possibly go into the story of the Atlandic Wars. Suffice it to say that when Atlantis sank, the Danaans fled to Ireland and became the Kelts."

It was fantastic. "And then what happened?" asked Haruko.

"After a few thousand years, a few wars, a few invasions, Ireland had grown sufficiently unpleasant so that most of the Danaans felt the need to depart." Elharn's voice was even, unstressed. "Christianity had come in, all magic was condemned, there were persecutions . . . And that was when St.

Brendan the Astrogator built ships according to the old patterns, organized the immrama, what we call the Great Migrations, and got us out. He led the first exodus himself, and brought us here. And here we still are.''

They had been out here all this time, thought Haruko. All this time, while Earth reeled through the Dark Ages and the Renaissance and the Industrial Revolution and the Space Age and the Age of Exploration and the Colonization and the Wars of Empire and the Peace of Dzyan and the formation of the Federacy . . .

''You still haven't told me how it is we haven't met you before,'' he said presently.

''Ah, that.'' For the first time, Elharn seemed a little uncertain of his ground. ''Well, partly, I would say, because such off-world trade as we have is outward from Earth, and our paths would not have crossed in that way for a while yet. But chiefly I think it is because we have not wished you to find us. Doubtless Her Majesty will tell you in a more satisfactory fashion, when you do meet her.''

''*Will* we meet her?''

''Oh, aye—'' Mac Rossa flushed unaccountably.

Elharn retained his poise. ''As I said earlier, Queen Aeron is most eager to meet with you. Whatever monarchies you may happen to be familiar with, I think I can safely say that ours is quite different. But this is a very important event in our history, Captain! Our first contact with Earth in three thousand years, and you the first Terrans we meet . . . You have already become historical figures.''

Haruko passed over the compliment, intent on his point. ''If you have lived isolate all these years,'' he said, choosing his words with care, ''I wonder that you elect now, at this particular moment, to initiate contact between our worlds.''

Again Elharn gently refused the gambit. ''As to that, I am no politician, but only an old sailor. You must ask that of the Queen, so that you may later convey the information back to your superiors.''

''A subspace communication has already been sent out to my Admiralty,'' said Haruko bluntly.

''Yes, we know. It's of no matter,'' replied Elharn with

equal candor. Changing the subject, "Would you care to see something of the *Firedrake*, while we discuss further plans?"

Haruko accepted gratefully, hiding the frustration and bafflement he felt, and followed Elharn into the turbolift. Haruko's original Fian escort now rejoined him, though mac Rossa remained on the bridge; the party also included two towering kilted warriors and the silent red-haired girl who had stood by the viewport.

They emerged on a lower deck and headed down a brightly illuminated companionway. On such a brief tour of inspection, only the barest of ideas could be obtained as to the true nature of a vessel the size and complexity of the *Firedrake*, and Haruko was well aware that no secrets would be given away. Nonetheless, he found the tour fascinating, and he wondered idly if his Keltic counterpart was finding the tiny *Sword* equally interesting. Very likely she was; strange vessels were always enthralling, no matter their size. But there was certainly a lot more to see aboard this beauty, and a lot to think about as well . . . and all of it totally foreign to the Terran's experience.

Haruko gave himself happily up to the wonders of the *Firedrake*. The interior of the great ship was as unusual as her outer design. Though all appeared frighteningly functional, everything was also invested with a very definite artistic value that he had never thought possible aboard a ship of war. And everyone he met was so *courteous*, saluting their Admiral and bowing to their alien visitor without the slightest hint of surprise or ill-bred gaping curiosity. Most interesting! In fact, almost Japanasian. Haruko began to relax again.

As she paced down the corridors of the *Firedrake*, a few steps behind Elharn and the Terran captain, Aeron kept her face as blank as she could, though her mind was whirling with excitement. They passed many members of the crew, all of whom smilingly acknowledged their Admiral and the guest from Earth—and all of whom were under strictest orders to ignore completely the presence of their Queen. So far, everyone had obeyed, though it was probably very hard on them.

At that thought, Aeron did smile, and the tall Dragon who strode beside her looked down sidelong at her with shy curiosity. He had never before been at such close quarters with royalty of any degree, let alone the Ard-rían herself—though of course he had seen her often enough on the farviewers. She was much prettier in person, he decided; warmer, and merrier. And so young: Three years as High Queen had not been enough to perfect the royal mask that all monarchs must learn to don, and Aeron still wore much of her thought in her face.

She felt his glance, though she did not look at him. She was well aware of the curiosity that was consuming everyone aboard the *Firedrake*: Why was Aeron here, and why was it such a secret? She cared not at all for that; it was worth all the trouble, every bit, just to have been here, to have seen the Terran ship and stood on the bridge with the Terran captain. It would even be worth the harrowing that was awaiting her at the hands of her Council when she returned to Caerdroia. She spared a brief thought, and pang of sympathy, for Gwydion and Rohan and Morwen, who even now were most likely trying to explain away an action they themselves neither fully understood nor entirely approved. But she would mend all later.

"A word to you, my friend," she murmured to the guard beside her. "Nay, do not speak—but watch the Terran closely. What you see or sense may be of use to me later."

He nodded, his eyes straight ahead, and after a while Aeron began to smile quietly to herself.

The perambulation of the *Firedrake*, limited as it was, still lasted more than an hour. Haruko, exerting all his powers of diplomacy, charmed and was charmed by his hosts. By the time the tour came to an end, back in the landing-bay in front of his shuttle, arrangements had been concluded for the *Sword* to follow the destroyer *Glaistig* to a quarantine planetoid known as Inishgall.

Inishgall was not within the boundaries of Keltic space, but was rather a sort of anteroom planet, used only for the brief quarantine period required of those who would be guests in Keltia. There was some slight mystery about what in fact did constitute Keltic space, and there had been mention of something called the Curtain Wall, but no explanation had been given. Finally Haruko permitted himself to forget his manners so far as to ask, point-blank.

Elharn was equally straightforward. "You'd not believe it if I told you, Captain, so I will leave it for the moment. It will be explained to you and your crew in good time, I promise you. Any road, you will be seeing for yourself soon enough." And Haruko had had to content himself with that.

But in all other particulars he thought the Keltic proposal an excellent one. He and the crew would remain on the planetoid in semi-isolation for three days' quarantine, local time. A retinue of Kelts would be dispatched to keep them company and to teach them everything they might want, or need, to know. It all sounded perfectly acceptable.

So he took his farewells of Elharn, casting a final covert glance at the mysterious red-haired girl who still stood impassively a few feet behind the Admiral, and entered his shuttle. The doors slid closed behind him, and almost immediately the craft lifted smoothly out into space.

Behind the thick protective glass that shielded the gallery from the vacuum of launch, Elharn dismissed the escort and turned on Aeron.

"Well?"

She shrugged happily, still staring after the vanished shuttle. "Let us wait here for Gwennan. The board shows her shuttle but two minutes out."

"As you wish, Ard-rían."

"Oh, don't be cross with me," she said. "Not you, uncle."

He shook his head. "You're a hard lass to be angry with, Aeron, but I have the feeling your Council will find it no task at all."

"And therefore do I not need it from you." She slipped her arm through his. "But what did you *think*! Oh, I am glad I was here. But I know we were not what he expected."

"Like as not," said Elharn dryly. "And do you think you learned enough from him to justify the risk you took? Not to mention all the explanations you will have to furnish?"

Aeron dismissed this magnificently. "That pack of camurs will be no great trouble."

"They'd not thank you to call them camurs, and they may

well be more trouble than you think. For one thing, they have the power to vote you a censure."

"They dare not," she said confidently. "They have not the votes, and even if they did— But look, here is Gwen."

"She went *where*?" Gavin Earl of Straloch, Lord Extern on the High Council, went first white, then purple, in his rage.

"The Ard-rían," repeated Morwen, pointedly stressing Aeron's title, "has gone to observe the Terrans from aboard the *Firedrake*." This was going to be far worse than they had feared; she threw a quick look at Rohan, who sat at her left in Aeron's big carved chair at the head of the Council table.

Rohan raised his eyebrows noncommittally. As far as he could tell, the Ard-eis, the High Council of Keltia, felt themselves fully justified in their indignation, though not all of them apparently felt it quite so keenly as Straloch. He could understand their vexation: They had been summoned from their sleep in the middle of the night—at least, the six of them who had been in residence in Turusachan; the others were even now en route to the Throneworld for the later, larger meeting—dragged into emergency session, and with no warning whatsoever been blithely informed not only of the arrival of the Terran probe ship, an event of the gravest importance in any case, but also of the fact that their Queen had dashed out to meet it without even the courtesy of informing them. Small wonder that Straloch fumed: He was, after all, Lord Extern, in charge of all out-Wall affairs, and he should certainly have been consulted on this.

"She has hardly gone alone," added Morwen with pardonable sharpness, though inwardly furious with Aeron herself. "She is with Elharn, aboard the flagship with a five-cursal escort. I *think* she will be quite safe."

"Too impulsive!" shouted Straloch. "That girl never thinks!"

The Chief Bard, Idris ap Caswyn, interposed quickly. "That is not entirely accurate, Gavin, and most entirely unfair—at the very least give Aeron the chance to speak for herself. In the meantime . . . Rohan, why did Aeron say she must go?"

From the way the Council hushed to hear his answer,

Rohan was at once made uncomfortably aware how much depended on how well he explained his sister's actions. And he barely understood them himself . . .

"I think she simply felt a need to be there in her own person," he said at last. "She thought she might perhaps learn more, in the end, by kenning the Terrans herself at the beginning—before any barriers went up, before they knew who she was and so could relate to her only as Ard-rían."

Not good enough, he saw, and Morwen's frown confirmed it. Well, gods, he was annoyed with her himself, Straloch wasn't the only one who thought the Queen had behaved irresponsibly. But Aeron had charged her three closest advisors with the duty of explaining her actions, and they would simply have to do the best they could.

"Kenning, eh? Well, that's something, at least," growled Straloch, slightly mollified. "Don't know what good it'll do, but it's something." Magic was a reason he could understand, though he did not go in for it himself. The telepathic technique known as kenning was one Aeron was known to be skilled in; even a non-sorcerer could buy that, and the suggestion, however flimsy, that Aeron was out there exercising her powers was an excuse that all could accept with reasonable grace.

Across the table, Gwydion shifted in his seat, and instantly the undercurrent of comment ceased.

"Whatever reasons Aeron may have," he said, "—and I for one think them good reasons—the thing we must consider, here and now, is not what has Aeron done about the Terrans, but what we here are to do about the Terrans. Like it or not, Earth has found us; or, more accurately, we have announced ourselves to them. I know a matter of such weight cannot be, and must not be, decided in haste; but we have very little time in which to debate at leisure. The people must be told. And the very first thing they will ask us is what is being done. So, my friends, what are we to tell them?"

The ironic half-smile on Gwydion's bearded face was lost on none of them, and no one spoke.

"No suggestions?" he asked, after a long silent moment. "Well, I have had a little longer than most of you to think about it, and perhaps that is an unfair asking just yet . . .

However, as First Lord of War, my first duty is the battle-readiness of this kingdom, and my last duty is that also. And I will say now there is more here than any could have foreseen. Even Aeron, and she sees twice as far as the rest of us."

"You are speaking of the Imperium, Gwydion." The soft Scotic accents belonged to Lady Douglass Graham. Douglass's sweet voice had led many to overlook the flint in her eyes—to their detriment. As Earl-Marischal, commander of Keltia's attack forces, she and Illoc mac Nectan, the Earl-Guardian who commanded the defense forces, were responsible directly to the First Lord of War, and so shared with Gwydion much military knowledge of which the other Councillors preferred to remain ignorant.

And clearly they would prefer to stay so now, if only they could, observed Rohan with some scorn. Straloch certainly; and Auster, the Chief Brehon; and Lodenek of Gorlas, the Sea Lord. Thank gods that Douglass was on Aeron's side, and Idris's attitude seemed to convey that he very much wanted to be persuaded onto Aeron's side. Pity it was that there even *were* sides in this matter . . . But no one could afford to remain ignorant any longer, and all in the room knew it.

"Not the Imperium alone, though the problem there has been, I admit, graver than usual of late." Gwydion sat silent a moment, and no one cared, or dared, to press him. "I am thinking of what will happen—inevitably—when the Empire and the Phalanx learn we have met the Terrans. When it dawns on them both, as it surely will, that Keltia alone is one thing, and Terra alone another, but that Keltia allied with the Terran Federacy—two realms with common ancestry and loyalties—is something else again. And I am thinking of what their probable responses to such an alliance are like to be."

"Well, we're not allied with the Earthers just yet," grated Straloch. "May never be. Aeron is so damned flighty—"

"The Ard-rían is not so flighty as you seem to think, my lord," said Rohan sharply. When would the older members of the Council stop thinking of his sister as an ungovernable, if brilliant, child— "But Gwydion is right. We have little sword-room here. We are not in posture of war at the moment, but we all know that moment could turn upon a hair. You are all well aware just how delicate is the 'peace' that now exists. Our enemies will use any excuse, however tenuous, to turn that balance. An alliance with Earth, perhaps even the mere rumor of such an alliance, might easily tip the scales to war. In such time, can we stand alone? Gwydion?"

Gwydion's gray eyes were veiled, and he did not answer at once.

"We cannot," he said presently. He rose from his chair, stretched, and went to the windows, where now the sky was lightening to the dawn. All Caerdroia lay beneath him in the growing brightness. "We cannot," he said again, almost casually. "One or the other we could stand against, and probably defeat. But we cannot stand at the same time against them both, whether they come at us one and one, or two united. Not alone."

"Therefore you want the Terrans as allies!" gasped Ffaleira, the Ban-draoi Magistra, speaking for the first time. "You and Aeron—Gwydion, we have only just met them! We do not know what they may be like, or if they even *wish* for alliance, or what strength they might have to lend us—"

Gwydion swung round from the windows, and his smile was that of a swordsman who has just backed his opponent into a corner.

"And what else, Magistra, did you think Aeron went out there to try to begin to learn?"

Idris laughed. "Oh, beautiful! And so Aeron goes to ken the Terrans before they even know they are being tested." His smile turned malicious. "Not much flightiness about *that* move, Gavin . . . Nay, Aeron has played this bout well. She must know and they must not, and she must know first. That's the way queens are supposed to think. Gods, I had given anything to have seen it."

Rohan smiled, but his expression was distracted. "Well," he said at last, "it appears there will be no agreement here, and any road, decisions of policy must wait for Aeron's return. But we cannot keep back the news any longer. Morwen, you must announce it at once to the people." He silenced their protests with a glance of warning. "At the Ard-rían's command, I decide here in her absence, and this is what I decide. Taoiseach, see to it."

"At once, lord."

Straloch rallied for one last throw. "Very well, tell the people if you will, but how do we know the Terrans are not already in league with another, and all this but a trap?"

Idris snorted. "Treachery? The encounter was far too chancy for that; any trap of such importance would have been far better laid."

"We know they are not for Imperium or Phalanx," remarked Morwen with an air of exasperated finality, "because if they were, they would not now be sending probe ships into unknown territory hoping to find possible friends. And—all the moithering possibilities of bluff and double-bluff aside—if they were indeed seeking to carve themselves an empire of their own, they would have dispatched an armada to conquer, not a weaponless drone on an embassy mission. I think they may need us as much as we may need them."

Douglass looked up, her dark eyes thoughtful. "But, Taoiseach, you are not certain."

"Nay, I am not certain." Morwen smiled grimly. "But I'll wager Aeron is."

Chapter Four

On the world called Alphor, a young man hurried down a palace corridor to talk to his grandfather. Guards snapped to crisp attention as he passed them, and when he had gone by they peered after him with a fearing curiosity.

The young man came to a set of double doors, upon either side of which stood sentries with weapons at the ready. The doors were blazoned in gold with the Imperial eagles, and the sentries leaped to pull back those doors for him to enter. He was called Jaun Akhera, and the grandfather he hastened to address was the Emperor Strephon, ruler of the Cabiri Empire—the Imperium.

"Grandson!" The voice, old yet strong, and pleased-sounding, came from over by the tall windows on the opposite side of the room.

Jaun Akhera dropped briefly to one knee, then rose and crossed the sun-filled stoa to the golden longchair where his grandfather reclined upon silk pillows.

The Emperor of the galaxy, for so he liked to think of himself, was playing senet, a game that had been ancient when Akhenaton and Nefretiti had played it on a board brought from Atlantis. Jaun Akhera watched for a while, then pointed out a move with a flick of his fingers, and his grandfather brightened.

"That's won it for me," he said, delighted, and looked up at his daughter's son. "You are well today, young Akhi?"

"I am very well, and so will you be, lord, when you have

heard." Without waiting for an invitation, Jaun Akhera curled up gracefully in a chair and regarded his grandfather. "I have just received a communication from one of my contacts—the one in Keltia."

The Emperor looked interested. "I didn't know you had a spy in Keltia."

But his grandson was not discomfited. "Be that as it may, sire, the news I have is certain and it is good. The Terrans have made contact with the Kelts at last. An Admiralty drone probe out of Earth was intercepted outside the Curtain Wall by a Keltic destroyer, and it is even now on its way to Caerdroia."

"In Seti's name, what is the good news there?" The old, lined face grew petulant. "Are you really so stupid after all? We have been fearing *that* alliance since before you were born, yes, and longer."

Jaun Akhera's face, which had darkened momentarily, cleared again, and his voice was velvety.

"I say it is good news, lord, because it sets up our chance to move against the Kelts at last. And have we not waited even longer for that?"

"Mmm . . . yes, well, perhaps it is as you say." Strephon peered keenly at his eldest daughter's eldest child. Certainly it was as the boy had said; and in fact they had waited nearly fifteen centuries for a chance as good. But best not to be too eager, too approving too quickly, at least not for the boy to see. Obviously he had come here with a plan; but that was to be expected. He was brilliant, this one; he had inherited all his mother's deviousness and had combined it with the cold, calculating intellect of his father's family. His *late* father, Strephon corrected himself. Not that Phano hadn't deserved execution, to be sure . . . But all that unpleasantness was past now. The son of Phano and Helior was unquestioningly loyal; that was, after all, one of the reasons why Strephon had felt safe in formally naming him Imperial Heir. And if Jaun Akhera claimed advantage here for the Imperium, for the Coranian people, and most importantly for the family Plexari, it was surely so.

"Well, tell me, then."

Jaun Akhera leaned forward, his tanned face animated. "I

think the Kelts will not refuse this encounter. I think they will ally themselves with Terra. I propose to come between them before that alliance can be consummated, and in so doing, I shall be able to crush them both.

"As you know, Sire, Terra and Keltia both are easily strong enough to stand against us alone should it come to war, though not, perhaps, with any real certainty of victory. Allied, however, they could threaten us, could inflict great damage on us, could—conceivably—defeat us. But the one thing neither Keltia nor Terra could expect is an alliance on *our* side. If we threw in with the Phalanx worlds, or even just with the kingdom of Fomor alone—and we know well how the Fomori feel about the Kelts—" He paused to let the image sink into his grandfather's mind. "The time for us to strike is soon," he continued. "Before any such Keltic-Terran alliance is concluded. Before there is either commitment or plan for either to come to the aid of the other. If we move at such a time, in common cause with Fomor, Keltia should fall; and, if we play our hand aright, Terra with her."

Strephon drummed his fingers on the senet board. The plan held great possibilities, that was easy to see, as well as great risks. If what Jaun Akhera had heard was even a tenth part correct, Keltia must now be in a state of political uncertainty. And when had there ever been a better time to begin hostilities?

"I like it well," said Strephon. "How do you plan to start?"

"I shall summon certain individuals here for a meeting," said Jaun Akhera. "And then I have a pawn in mind to make my opening move in Keltia." He fingered one of the senet pieces, smiling to himself. "Yes, a pawn to take a Queen . . . May I have Your Imperial Majesty's sanction to begin?"

How very simple it was to start a war . . . Strephon was taken aback for the second time that afternoon. He really must keep closer watch on this very, ah, *energetic* heir of his.

"You have been thinking about this for some time, then, if you went to the trouble of planting a spy in Keltia."

"Two years or three . . . but surely it was inevitable that we move against the Kelts?"

Surely it was . . . Only a matter of time, mused Strephon, before the state of polite hatred that existed between Keltia and the Imperium would have flamed anew into outright conflict, as it had done so many times before. And Keltia's relations with Fomor, the ruling kingdom of the Phalanx worlds, were even less cordial than that; there had already been acts of war between those two powers. It was only surprising that it had taken so long to come to this, especially with that new queen the Kelts now had; they had been strangely quiet since the upheaval that had attended her accession to the throne; what was her name again . . .

"Aeron Aoibhell," he said. "What do you hear of her, then, since she will be your chiefest enemy?"

Jaun Akhera had been anticipating this question, and now he went to a sliding ornamental panel set in the wall, and opened it to reveal a computer screen.

"A great deal," he said. "And all of it bad. At least from our point of view; no doubt she makes the Kelts an excellent monarch."

He punched out a sequence on the computer, and the data he had prepared for this moment began to flow onto the screen as they watched. First a hologram portrait appeared, a young woman's portrait; judging by the smoothness of the pale complexion and the vibrancy of the flaming hair, she seemed far too young for the crushing burden of interstellar sovereignty. But the green eyes that looked out at them so disconcertingly gave that the lie: Those eyes would miss little and had seen much, and they looked as hard and as piercing as an emerald laser.

"She has been High Queen of Keltia for not quite three years," said Jaun Akhera, though his grandfather could read the information on the screen for himself. "And she is a very young monarch, as her people reckon such things."

Strephon appeared fascinated by the portrait. "Has she heirs? Or a consort?"

"Her heir is her brother Prince Rohan. Her consort perished in that, ah, regrettable Fomori raid, the one that killed her parents—you will doubtless recall it."

Strephon remembered it only too well. What a misbegotten idea that ambush had been, though no idea of his. In fact, the Imperium had had no inkling of it until it had happened—that unbelievably stupid Bres of Fomor, it had been his doing from the start—

"And you will also recall," added Jaun Akhera, "the aftermath of Bres's ambush."

That too he remembered. Most of the civilized galaxy remembered it. Aeron Aoibhell's first act as Queen—or her last as a private citizen, depending on how one chose to perceive it—had been to avenge the slaughter of her parents and her lord and their party. And how fearsomely she had done that . . .

"She seems to be a chancy person to risk running afoul of," observed Strephon.

"I agree. And that is why treachery must be the initial weapon to use against her; and why the instrument of that treachery shall be one of her own people." Jaun Akhera had been saving that surprise, and his grandfather's reaction was all that could have been hoped for.

"A *Kelt*? That's not possible! They do *not* betray their own!"

"I promise you, grandsir, this Kelt is distinctly possible." Again Jaun Akhera seemed secretly amused. "Trust me, lord." He glanced once more at the hologram. "Still," he said, his voice oddly tinged with regret, "it seems a great waste of beauty and power."

Strephon hid a smile. "Perhaps she need not be destroyed," he said. "My heir will one day need an empress to sit beside him on the Throne of the Cabiri, a woman well fitted to be his consort. Who better prepared to be an empress than a queen, and what queen better than this one? She is intelligent, is she not; why should she choose to waste herself and her people in war, when she could rule our realm with you in peace?"

Jaun Akhera laughed. "A tempting idea," he admitted, still smiling. "But I doubt Aeron Aoibhell would see it quite as you do. Do you know what they call her on the Fomori worlds? The She-wolf of Keltia. Until three years ago, all thought that merely empty compliment based on travellers' tales. Since then, she has earned that name many times over. And a she-wolf upon the throne—*your* throne—could be dangerous. Who knows where those fangs might snap next? I would fear them at my own throat before an hour had passed since the wedding . . . No, with your leave, grandsir. I think I shall seek elsewhere for my Empress.''

"A pity.'' Strephon touched a stud, and the screen darkened and slid behind its ornamental panel. He reclined once more upon his longchair, studying the big opal on his forefinger. "A great pity,'' he repeated. Then, in a brisker tone, "Go then, and work your plan. —No, do not thank me. If you succeed, it will be for me to thank you.''

Jaun Akhera bowed deeply. "Can you doubt it?''

The Emperor gave his grandson a twisted smile, and his old pale eyes grew suddenly piercing.

"I *can* doubt anything, son of my daughter,'' he said softly. "And I do doubt everything, until it has come to pass. Go, and do as you will. I shall give orders that you have anything you need.''

Again Jaun Akhera bowed, and then he left. Alone in the slanting afternoon light, Strephon contemplated the senet board again, but his thoughts were on the scene just past. After a time, an old philosophical problem came to his mind, and he smiled to himself at the idea: the Irresistible Force and the Immovable Object. Perhaps he was about to receive an effective demonstration of a solution. Only, he wondered suddenly, which element would be Jaun Akhera, and which Aeron Aoibhell?

Even before the airlock of the *Sword* had fully opened, Haruko was surrounded by his crew. Their faces shone with excitement, and they all spoke at once.

"What was it like? Did you meet their Queen? Are we going there? What did they say?''

"Back off,'' warned Haruko sincerely, still flustered from the events of the past few hours. He went into the lounge, fell into a contour couch, and took without even looking at it the drink Mikhailova thrust into his hands.

"Well,'' he said, after emptying his glass in one long swallow, "we have been invited to Keltia. We'll be starting up in a little while, and then we'll be getting instructions on following the destroyer down.''

Tindal laughed. "Why don't they just stuff us into a hangar

bay aboard the flagship? That baby could swallow us about an thousand times over.''

Haruko glared at him. ''Hardly good diplomatic procedure. These people seem to think a lot of good manners, and by God we're going to show them some. *All* of you,'' he emphasized, looking at each of them in turn, but his glance lingering longest on Tindal. ''At any rate, we'll be following them to a quarantine planetoid not too far away. We'll leave the *Sword* in orbit and go down to the surface in the shuttle.''

''And what happens after the quarantine?'' asked Hathaway.

''Good question. I'm tired, and we'll discuss it later, it's rather complicated. But we will be arriving—ultimately—at their capital.'' Suddenly he remembered, and startled them all as he shot upright, his fatigue forgotten. ''But what about the one who was here, the captain of that ship—''

''Mistress and Captain Gwennan Chynoweth,'' said O'Reilly primly.

''She was very friendly, very courteous, very impressive, and gave away absolutely nothing,'' remarked Mikhailova. ''We tried our best, too.''

''Yes, yes, but did you record it?'' Haruko tried, unsuccessfully, to control his impatience.

''Certainly we recorded it.'' Hathaway punched up the monitor, and they watched in silence as the tape unspooled.

When it ended, Haruko sighed. ''Well, that's about how it was with me. They were charming, but not exactly overinformative.''

''So?'' O'Reilly was leaning forward, trying to see as much of the Keltic flagship as she could, through the small port of the lounge.

''So . . . we accept with pleasure their kind invitation. What else? Oh, and extend our compliments to their Queen. You do it, O'Reilly; you know how to say all that formal stuff.'' Haruko paused in the hatchway leading to the crew's quarters. ''I'm going to take a nap. Don't wake me until we're ready to move.''

She who had been so lately characterized in an Imperial sitting-room as the She-wolf of Keltia jumped down from the door of the aircar onto the stone pavement of the landing-yard. Several people who had been sheltering in the door of a nearby tower now came forward, their heads hooded against the weather.

It had turned sharply colder in the hours Aeron had been gone from Caerdroia, and a freak early snowfall had dusted the entire length of the Great Glen. Ribbons of dry snow snaked along the ground, and the trees, still full-leaved in their autumn splendor, raised blazing heads through the thin sprinkling of white.

Aeron glanced guiltily at those who drew near, but when she saw it was only Morwen, Rohan and Gwydion, her apprehension turned at once to cheerful greeting.

They returned her salute with somewhat subdued civility, which Aeron chose to ignore.

"Will you join me for breakfast? There is time yet before the Council meeting."

They followed her in silence through the halls to her tower, where in the grīanan, the sunny room overlooking a garden courtyard, breakfast was already laid out. It was a silent meal, and finally Aeron capitulated.

"Very well! I will give you a *brief* word as to what happened. I will be telling it all at the Council meeting, and I do not wish to go through it twice over." She broke off a piece of bread, dipped it in ale, and smiled at them guilelessly before she bit into it. "It was not so easy for me to judge of them as I thought," she remarked, not looking at anyone's eyes. "But the Terrans are coming here. Aye, they are coming. They are on their way to Inishgall even now, and they will be here at Caerdroia before the week is out. Now do not tell me, any of you, that this is ill thought of or hasty, for I do not wish to hear it from you. There will be enough of that, more than enough, later on . . . But for the Terrans themselves, they seem honorable folk, and I am very glad I went." She set down her ale mether and glanced around the table. "How did the Council take the news?"

"Very badly," said Morwen. "As you knew they would . . . Any road, there were but six of them present; the others were off-planet, and you can surprise them at the joint session. Straloch was furious with you, and I am not sure he was not right to be angry. We did the best we could to smooth things for you, Aeron, but they'll not stay smoothed for long.''

"Aeron," came Rohan's reasonable voice, "if your own Councillors feel you have acted in haste, perhaps you should reconsider. Send the Terrans home to fetch a proper embassy, or delay them in quarantine a little while longer while one is summoned—a fortnight, a month . . ."

"A year," muttered Morwen.

"Not an hour," said Aeron evenly, and left the grianan to prepare herself for the session to come.

Behind her, she left sour silence. Morwen reached for the keeve of ale, poured out a full mether.

"For all of me," she said in honest bewilderment, "I do not understand this sudden passion to entangle ourselves with Earth. We have lived well enough without them all these years; why now must Aeron rush to throw us into their arms?"

Gwydion, who had been silent this long time, looked up at her.

"I think, Lochcarron," he said quietly, "that in truth you do not need that question answered . . . She sees what we have seen, of course. War with the Imperium, war with the Phalanx. And she is praying, as we have prayed, that it will not be war with both of them at the same time. And she fears, as we fear, that that is indeed what will come to pass. So, she buys time for us. An alliance with Earth may well be a naked provocation to battle, as Gavin and some of the others think. Or it may be an effective deterrent. We cannot know. But either way Aeron must be ready. And so must we." He rose from the table, and the others did likewise, for the meeting was almost upon them and they had much to prepare before its start.

"In the meantime," remarked Rohan, "I suggest we begin the ordering of those ceremonies Aeron wishes. If it is to be done at all, let us by all means do it correctly. We have guests coming, and traditions to maintain—as you know."

Joint sessions of the High Council of Keltia and the Privy Council to the Ard-rían were held once a lunar month. Owing to the number of those who were required to attend, such sessions took place in the Hall of Meetings, a large, twelve-sided chamber located on the palace's second floor.

Little ceremony accompanied joint sessions; they were working meetings, and those who attended them were under no illusions about that. Even the Hall itself echoed this workaday slant: It was simply furnished, dominated by a big oblong table of black granite with computerpads inlaid at each place, and benches along the walls also equipped with computer stations. The ceiling was skylighted, the walls faced with cream-colored marble, the ornamentation classically severe. At the northern end of the room, huge windows ran floor to ceiling, framing a spectacular view over Caerdroia, the Great Glen, and, far across the valley, the mountains of the Stair. Aeron's chair was placed with its back to the view; the chair was more elaborate than the others, but her position was not otherwise set apart, and, save for the Tanist's seat on her left, and the Taoiseach's at her right, there were no other formal seating arrangements at the table, and the other members of the Ard-eis sat where they pleased.

The Privy Councillors, who occupied the seats along the wall, had no vote as individuals, only as a body; and if they could not reach a consensus they had no vote at all. That had been made law by the first Aoibhell monarch, Brendan Mór; he it was who had first divided the Keltic Council into the Ard-eis, composed of officeholders and heads of orders such as the Ban-draoi and the Druids; and the Privy Council, which each monarch assembled to suit his or her personal needs, generally choosing kin or friends or recognized experts in specific disciplines.

Aeron's choices for Privy Councillors were no exception: her sister Ríoghnach, next eldest after herself and Rohan; her uncles Estyn and Deian; her cousins Melangell, Shane and Macsen; her childhood friend Sabia ní Dálaigh; and several others. Upon the first anniversary of her accession, lest the royalist party become too unleavened an influence, Aeron had expanded the Privy Council to include the leaders of Keltia's elected and hereditary assemblies as well, a break with tradition that, though widely hailed as a popular victory and a blast of fresh air, had nevertheless made for no little acrimony in joint sessions such as these. Aeron, though, and others, thought that was all to the good; if nothing else, at least the discord of faction fights might serve to keep Councillors awake—though today that, at least, was unlikely to be a problem.

There had been considerable acrimony over Aeron's selections for the High Council. In the first days after her accession, she had decided to carry over many of her father's appointments: older, experienced individuals such as Alun Dyved, the Home Lord, and Kelynen Gwennol, Rechtair of the Keltic treasuries. And that had seemed right and respectful, a most satisfactory attitude. The trouble began when Aeron named to the key positions of Taoiseach and First Lord of War her former sister-in-law Morwen and her future consort Gwydion. The outcry had been loud and bitter; but Aeron, already showing the fabled Aoibhell intransigence, had let the storm break over her with sublime indifference, and in the end nothing had changed. But the resentment among the Council elders had only submerged itself, not dissipated, and it would take very little to bring it to the surface once more.

And such discord, right now, they simply could not afford; therefore did Morwen glance around the Council chamber with such trepidation. She had been one of the earliest arrivals, hoping to test the temper of the hour by observing the others as they came in.

Word of the Terrans' coming had apparently travelled swiftly: The prevailing attitude, as far as Morwen could tell, seemed to be intense annoyance with the Queen and her three chief abettors, and the air was already electric with the expectation of strife.

Not but that Aeron would only enjoy it, thought Morwen. As a rule the Queen could handle her Council with both hands behind her back. But this was a problem of an entirely new order, and Morwen, for all her self-assurance, was for once slightly doubtful of Aeron's abilities.

The room was filled now; with the arrival of Aeron, Rohan a half-step behind her, the tension and excitement shivered down to grim anticipation. Morwen groaned inwardly even as she rose with the rest for the Queen: Aeron was informally dressed, like everyone else, in tunic, trews and boots; but around her neck she wore openly the silver medallion of the Dragon Kinship, and the rod-and-crescent of the Ban-draoi was embroidered in silver around the hem of her tunic. It was not usual for her to make such obvious statements, and Morwen was not alone in wondering why the Ard-rían felt this sudden need to emphasize the source of her powers.

But statements and declarations were thick on the ground today, and Morwen's heart further misgave her as she continued to scan the hall. Gwydion, who sat at the main table a few places down on Aeron's right, had chosen to change his attire since that rather strained morning meal in the royal grianan. As a rule the subtlest of people, he now lounged at the Council table clad in the battle uniform of the Dragon Kinship. Of course he was Pendragon, and entitled to wear the Kinship's garb whenever he pleased, as indeed was any Kelt who was Kin to the Dragon. But Gwydion wore the field uniform, the plain black battle dress seen only in time of war, and few in the room had missed his point. Rohan, across the table, was in the royal green, Morwen was relieved to see, and that was harmless. But all too many of the others, both High Councillors and Privy Councillors alike, wore the dark brown of the Fianna, the military elite of the Keltic armed forces, and that was perhaps even more alarming an indication than Aeron's or Gwydion's displays.

Morwen suddenly felt incredibly unsure, and out of place, and totally unequipped to deal with what was sure to come. Rohan threw her a supportive smile, and farther down the table Douglass frowned slightly.

Aeron noticed all of this, as she noticed most of what went on around her, but she made no sign as she took her seat. Though all in the room had risen when she came in, once the meeting began she would pace back and forth by the windows as often as she would sit, and no one was required to leap up whenever she did.

"This meeting in joint session extraordinary of the Ard-eis Keltannach and the Queen's Privy Council is now open," murmured Morwen dutifully at Aeron's nod, and immediately the room burst into contentious life.

Aeron allowed the uproar to go on for a few moments, then raised a hand and there was instant silence.

"I see most of you have already heard about the situation we are met to discuss. That is well, for it saves me some time. Even so, I would like now to set out in sequence for the rest of you, and for the record, everything that has happened since last night. Uninterrupted," she added with emphasis. "After that, I will allow debate."

"So ordered, Ard-rían." Morwen began recording, and the room settled down to listen.

With that Aeron plunged into a spare narrative that touched upon every aspect of the crisis, from the first reports sent her by the commander of the *Glaistig*, to her middle-night conference with her chief advisors, to her decision to meet the Terrans incognita aboard the *Firedrake*, and what had happened there, to the arrival of the Terrans on the planetoid and their imminent coming to Caerdroia.

Despite what they had gleaned from rumorous sources and from those who had been present at the earlier meeting, most of Aeron's listeners were ignorant of the details of the situation, and now they were reluctantly fascinated by her account, no matter their private opinions of her actions.

Gwydion, to whom this was old news save for the happenings aboard *Firedrake*, was listening to his ruler with only half an ear. The chief part of his not inconsiderable concentration was focused upon her audience. Like Morwen, he had immediately perceived that Aeron was facing a fight. One had only to look at Straloch, for instance, no whit less obstinate than he had been earlier that day. Or Malen Darowen, the Kymric viceroy, who sat as did all the system lords on the Privy Council; or Rollow of Davillaun, Chief Assemblator, the most important elected representative in all Keltia; or any of what Gwydion uneasily concluded was a very fair number dead set against Aeron, and who would, as soon as she had finished speaking, without a doubt make their feelings all too plain. It was not impossible, even, for a vote of censure to be taken against the Queen.

Not that censure would stop Aeron on her own course, or even discommode her to any great extent. The Council had specific, but limited, legal powers; and as sovereign, Aeron had the power to override a vote even if the entire membership of both groups should range itself against her. Though she would be ill-advised indeed to do so; such a thing had happened but rarely in all Keltic history, and was, on balance, unlikely to happen now. Still—

"If you permit, Ard-rían," said Gwydion, coming in smoothly upon her concluding remarks, "I should like to begin that debate you spoke of by outlining our military position for the civilian members of the Councils." He used the bard's voice that, though unraised, resonated authoritatively through the room, and as he looked around he noted with hidden relief that even the most outraged Councillors were prepared at least to listen to him.

That was not always the case. In spite of his royal rank as Prince of Gwynedd, his position on the Council, his personal relationship with Aeron, in spite even of his awesome powers as sorcerer and Pendragon, Gwydion was often viewed—and treated—by the older Councillors as a youth presuming to instruct his betters. This bothered him little for himself; though on occasion it vexed him for Aeron's sake, that they should continue to question her judgment and treat her as a precocious child who just happened, by sheer ill chance, to have become their absolute ruler. But they would learn, as he had known from the first, what manner of Ard-rían they had in truth got themselves.

"I have no objections, First Lord of War," said Aeron, and Gwydion laughed inwardly at her none too subtle stressing of his title and sphere of rule in Council.

Now it was Aeron's turn to assess the room, and from under her lashes she studied the more obvious trouble spots. It was all so very tiresome. Now Gwydion was speaking, with a patience and tact much greater than they deserved, and when he had finished it would be as if they had heard not the smallest word of what he had said, so hot were they upon their own trail. She knew it so well, had seen it so often before. What a waste of precious time, hers, his, everyone's. They should not be talking at all, but getting ready for war on the one hand and alliance on the other, since the latter was what Aeron wanted and the former was what she confidently expected . . .

Abruptly she stood up, startling everyone but Gwydion, whose voice never even wavered, and stalked over to the windows. Below, in the faha, the wide grassy courtyard enclosed by the palace's battlemented walls, a company of Fians was drilling, and Aeron watched them as closely as everyone else in the room watched her.

Gwydion ceased to speak. Without turning, Aeron addressed herself to Morwen.

"I will now hear debate, Taoiseach. You have heard me, and you have heard Gwydion. But before anyone else speaks here, know this: I will open diplomatic relations with Earth, now or later, by royal fiant if you give me no other choice; and I will sign a treaty of alliance also. It is only a matter of time. The Terrans come here in three days, and they will remain here until such time as a treaty *is* signed."

Straloch, face dark with fury, leaped to his feet. "A plague upon your royal father's daughter! Then why discuss it at all? And what of the Protectorates, Aeron? What say have they in all this? And any road, I demand a vote!"

His angry challenge contained one question just about everyone in the room wanted to have answered. Over the past four or five reigns, Keltia had attracted petitions from neighboring star systems, suing for the protection of the Keltic sword against the planet-hungry expansionism of the Imperium and the Phalanx. Keltia's fierce stance of nonalignment seemed the best hope of continued independence for these systems, most of them small, technology-poor, and ill-equipped to beat off the military might of the two chief galactic aggressors; and Keltia had defended her Protectorates militarily many times. Aeron herself had seen active service in that cause.

During the three years of Aeron's reign, however, these petitions had increased dramatically, both in number and in desperation, and each had been duly and carefully considered. And almost all of them had been granted, with the somewhat ironic result that Keltia itself was now an empire of sorts, though the protectorates were regarded rather as friends than vassals. Still, in many of these systems, the sovereigns of Keltia were called by the ancient title first restored by Arthur himself: Imperator, Emperor of the West. And that had not gone unnoticed, either on Alphor or among the Fomori.

"What is that to you? The Protectorates will do as we bid

them," said Rohan crossly, answering Straloch. "You are Lord Extern, you know perfectly well that is part of their bargain with us." He glanced aside at his sister's stony profile, sighed to himself. "We have been down this road with you once today already, Gavin. As to the need for debate on so great a matter, I would think that to be obvious even to you. Though the outcome be already settled by the will of the Ard-rían, there are still many details of the first importance to be determined."

Straloch subsided with an ill grace, and a low mutter of talk ran through the room. Over the muted discussion, Aeron's friend Sabia spoke out from where she sat beside Ríoghnach against the wall.

"I move the Taoiseach take the vote Straloch has asked for. Everyone knew what everyone else thinks a long time ago. More talk might ease hearts but cloud minds, and nothing will be altered."

"Very well so," said Morwen. "Will the Lord Extern put his statement on the record?"

"I am opposed, Taoiseach, to the actions taken last night by the Ard-rían, and to the actions she now purposes to take."

Over at the windows, Aeron's back stiffened, but still she did not turn.

Morwen spoke in a neutral voice. "Who holds with my lord of Straloch?"

Nine people raised their hands, reluctantly or otherwise. Of those, five were members of the Privy Council and had no personal vote. The other four, even though High Councillors, were not enough to make up a majority, and Morwen was deeply relieved.

"The vote is four and five against you, Ard-rían."

At that Aeron did turn round to them. "My sorrow if I have vexed the Council," she said in a cold silky voice.

The Council knew that voice of old, knew what it foreboded. They had heard the Ard-rígh Fionnbarr use it, and the Ard-rígh Lasairían, and some of the eldest of them had even heard the Ard-rían Aoife use it, colder and silkier than anyone except the one who used it now. And Aeron Aoibhell in a temper was a terror they did not care to face. Few dared go up against her in such a mood; Gwydion alone, and sometimes Morwen and Rohan, could coax her out of one. Even so, they were surprised, for unlike the Ard-rían Aoife, not lightly did Aeron give way to anger.

She returned to her place, though she remained standing, and cast a baleful stare around the table.

"I have heard your advice," she said very softly, and they flattened themselves back in their chairs for the blast that was sure to follow.

But again she surprised them. "Taoiseach, dismiss the Councils with our thanks."

It was the customary phrase of royal dismissal, and no one needed to be told twice. The room emptied as if by magic. Morwen, after a hesitant glance at Aeron's thunderous countenance, thought better of what she had intended to say, and instead caught Rohan's eye, jerked her head toward the door, and went out with him.

Gwydion remained unmoving in his seat. Aeron, whose eyes had been fixed on the table directly in front of her, slammed her fists into the black granite, then looked up. She smiled ruefully on seeing him still there, and brushed back her hair with a characteristic gesture.

"Was I so impossible?" she asked, coming to him and putting her arms around his neck.

"Very nearly," he said after a moment, and her arms fell away.

"I am sorry to hear you say it," she said, stung. "We won, did we not? Even Straloch had to bend. And there's an end of it."

Gwydion stood up. "Nay, Aeron, there's *not* the end of it. Because you and you alone are the one who must act on what you have seen and learned and kenned and thought. No matter who throws caltraps in your road, only you have the power and the sacred duty to act. Not I. Not Rohan nor Morwen. Certainly not Straloch. No one else on the Council or off it but you alone."

"Aye so!" she snapped, whirling on him. "And that is why I went out as I did! For all my soul I can *not* understand why everyone is making so great a matter of it. You at least must understand what it is that I do here."

"I understand very well," he said, taking her by the shoulders and pulling her gently backwards, until she leaned against his chest. But her body stiffened at the soothing tones in his voice, and his fingers tightened on her shoulders. "That does not mean I must like it. Aeron, at the end of all counsels, you are Queen and we are your servants. I think you forget that all too often." He looked down with concern at the top of her head, for she had gone very still in his grasp. "And I fear for you," he added, in a lower voice. "More than you know."

At that, she turned in his arms and looked up into his troubled face. She was smiling, though tears sparkled in the green eyes.

"You have spoken two falsehoods, Prince of Gwynedd," she said. "The Ard-rían is the servant of Keltia, not the Kelts hers; and that is the one thing of all things the Ard-rían never forgets."

"And the other falsehood you say I speak?"

"I know too well your fears for me," she said after a hesitation. "Never think I do not know. But, Gwydion, do you know how much I have feared for you? I never thought to admit my care, I did not want to lose you the way I—"

"—the way you lost Roderick," he finished gently and felt her flinch beneath his hands. "Aeronwy, I loved him too. He was my very dear friend, and whatever would have fallen out in the end between you and him, or between you and me, that would not have changed, ever. I knew the choice you had to make three years ago, and I knew the reasons you made it as you did."

They had never before spoken of this so openly, and Gwydion's words were so reasoned and so true that Aeron dropped her eyes before his face. In all truth, it had been her parents rather than she who had been eager for the match with the Douglases, though she herself had hero-worshipped Roderick, the Prince of Scots who was eight years her senior, since she had been a small child. All through her adolescence, it had been assumed by their parents that, one day, Aeron and Rhodri would wed and rule Keltia together. But it had come to be Gwydion who had touched Aeron's deepest soul . . .

Keltic law, uncommonly perceptive and sympathetic among galactic legal canons, allowed for ten sorts of marriage, only three of which were considered permanent; each of them was as lawfully binding as the others, all of them dissolvable, and none of them carried any dishonor. Torn between obedience to her parents and her own wishes, Aeron had given in so far as to make a brehon marriage with Roderick for the usual term of a lunar year. And Gwydion's peace had not been troubled in the slightest. But then Roderick had been slain, with Emer and Fionnbarr, a scant five weeks after the ceremony; and though it was a deeply shaken Aeron who had then turned to Gwydion, both of them knew it was no makeshift second choice but the affirmation of a love each of them had borne the other all along.

He saw her distress, pulled her close against him and spoke soft-voiced into her hair.

"Aeronwy, all is meant. As a Ban-draoi, you know that as surely as do I who am Druid."

Her voice came muffled. "I thought—I feared that you were jealous of my memory."

"That would insult all three of us. But Rhodri is well enough now; we must leave him to work his own dán, and you and I must work our own for ourselves here without him. I am here for you, always; and you for me. What more is there?"

She tightened her arms about him. "No more, lord, than that; except that whatever is coming now to Keltia, I am glad we shall meet it together, you and I, and glad likewise that no one begrudges us our joy."

But in that last Aeron was wrong indeed.

Chapter Five

It was mid-afternoon, and autumn, at Caerdroia as Aeron turned to Gwydion in the Council chamber, but at Caer Ys on the planet of Gwynedd, in the Kymric system, spring and sunrise were only just at hand.

The island castle at the mouth of the Velindre loomed up insubstantial as a phantom in the morning twilight, its lower stories wreathed in the ground-mist that rose steaming from the damp grass, its upper tower-tips already catching the first faint rays that shot from Beli, the giant sun that was this system's primary.

Down on the rocky beach below the castle, a woman walked with two white dogs. She was dressed in white, and the slanting dawnlight glinted silver-gilt sparks off her coiled hair. From time to time, she bent down, scarcely pausing in her long springy stride, to pick up pieces of driftwood and fling them arcing down the strand for the dogs to fetch, but otherwise her eyes were fixed on the surging sea, though her thoughts were far elsewhere. Seeing her easy, unhurried pace, a watcher might have been tempted to join her; seeing her face, no watcher would have dared.

But of late everyone walked in fear around Arianeira of Gwynedd. Ever since her brother Gwydion had been elected to the Pendragonship, and had been appointed by Aeron Aoibhell to be her First Lord of War, people on Gwynedd had not failed to notice that his twin sister, Arianeira, had become increasingly difficult to live with, or to serve under. Where formerly she had been fickle, she had become perverse; where once she had been merely capricious, now she had grown fractious. There was no pleasing her, and no anticipating her, and those who tried either soon wished they had done neither.

In the manner of folk who know when to leave ill enough alone, the Gwyneddans opined quietly to themselves that perhaps their Princess had too little to occupy her time, now that Gwydion spent all his own time at Caerdroia. The governance of the planet, which had formerly been Gwydion's task, had now largely been assumed by the twins' younger brother Elved, who was making a fine and conscientious job of it. Little responsibility was thus left to Arianeira, and much leisure in which to feel herself neglected and aggrieved. But her folk thought all this softly, when they thought it at all, and spoke none of it overloud; the daughters of the House of Dôn were reputed able to hear words upon the winds.

As usual, all of that was only partly true. Arianeira's heart had indeed grown hard with the absence of her favorite brother. But the fox that gnawed the deepest at her vitals, as she felt it, was no simple vixen but the She-wolf herself. Aeron, Morwen and Arianeira had all three been fostered together as children, and the roots of the Princess's present mood went long and deep into that past. When one's spirit craved to rule, hard enough to know that one would not; but when one's foster-sister was a future queen, and one's other foster-sister a future ruling duchess, how much harder to accept for oneself a quiet life.

With the instincts of a twin and a woman, Arianeira knew perhaps even more of the hearts and fates of Gwydion and Aeron than those two knew themselves. And what she knew, she did not love. So she grew, not less lovely, but deeply angrier, and when at last the chance was laid before her, it found her not at all slow to take it.

Up in one horn of the tower nearest the sea, a man leaned against the battlements, his eyes fixed on the distant white-clad figure. He was dark as only the purest Kymry of all Kelts were dark: black hair, thick and curling; black eyes deep-set beneath straight bars of brows; skin ruddier than was the rule among his folk. He was dressed plainly, in a blue tunic of good fabric and gray leather trews and low black boots; his cloak was worn slung over one shoulder and under the opposite arm, fastened by knotted cords across his chest. He looked too common to be a noble, and too arrogant to be a commoner, and no servitor would ever have stared at his mistress as he now stared at the Princess.

Returning up the hill from the strand, Arianeira looked up as she drew near to the castle's outer walls, and saw the man still there against the sky. She raised her arm in a hail, and after a moment his head vanished.

When she entered her solar a few minutes later, he was waiting.

"You are out early, lady."

"And you, Kynon, must have been up betimes as well, to see my going."

He smiled. "I know your mood of late. Besides," he added, watching her narrowly, "there is news this morning, and I thought to tell you before you heard it first from another."

Her head snapped round to him, and upon her face was a look of fearing alarm. "Not Gwydion! Has aught befallen my brother? Tell me quickly!"

"Not as you mean it, lady." He activated the wallscreen. "I recorded this a little while ago; though they are talking of nothing else, and will not for some days, I am sure, I thought you would wish to see the first reports."

The screen was filled with the image of a strangely fashioned starship, and the even tones of a bard came over the transcom link.

"—a Terran probe ship. As announced by the Taoiseach, Morwen of Lochcarron, the Terrans were formally recognized as an embassy with full diplomatic status and privileges. The probe's commander, Captain Theo Haruko, was received aboard the *Firedrake* by Master of Sail and High Admiral Elharn Aoibhell, acting as the personal representative of Her Majesty the Ard-rían. The Terrans, aboard their own ship, have been escorted by the Royal Destroyer *Glaistig* to the out-Wall quarantine station on Inishgall, where they will remain for the next three local days. From Inishgall, they will arrive at Caerdroia to be formally received by the Ard-rían in a—"

With one violent motion Arianeira cut off both screen and voice. She paced the length of the chamber and whirled around, her fists clenching and unclenching stabbing the air.

"Terrans! And my brother sends me no word! I must hear of it like any sea-crofter on the least of the Out Isles . . . But nay, I know well whose doing *that* is, and it is not my brother's—my Gwydion would not so slight his sister . . ." She broke off, suddenly aware that she had said perhaps overmuch in front of one who was after all merely a retainer attached to her household—however close she may have grown to him.

Kynon ignored her abrupt concealment. He knew well enough who it was that Arianeira held responsible for what she perceived as the perfidy done her by her mighty brother— from whose magical powers Kynon devoutly prayed the Princess's own sorcery shielded them both. Perhaps this was the time to put the plan before her, she who would be—if she accepted the plan as fully as she had accepted him—its prime mover. Even to his mind it was a bold and audacious enterprise, and if they were caught—well, best not to think of being caught.

He had waited nearly three years for this moment. When he had first been approached, all those months ago now, in the marketplace on Clero, the out-Wall Keltic trading planet, by a well-dressed Coranian who had turned out to be an Imperial agent, Kynon had been suspicious and skeptical of the plot proposed to him.

So much so, in fact, that at the last it had taken Jaun Akhera himself to persuade Kynon of the possibilities of success—and also the consequences of failure, as Strephon's grandson had taken pains to point out.

Kynon had never known why an Imperial agent had picked him of all Kelts to be the initial instrument in a sequence of treason that would, if it succeeded, begin with the fall of the House of Aoibhell and end with Keltia itself ceasing to exist as a free and sovereign nation. It was true enough, Kynon freely conceded, that some years ago he had been denied preference in the household of Prince Kieran, the Ard-rían's brother—there had been baseless trumped-up charges and fabricated allegations; after that, he had made his way to

Gwynedd and taken service with Arianeira, who had been moping for her brother Gwydion and had cared not at all who entered her service, so long as he was attractive and amusing and could possibly distract her . . . Had Kynon known, subconsciously perhaps, that the Princess Arianeira was no friend to the House of Aoibhell? And had all that somehow been known to the agents of Jaun Akhera? It had been while on an errand for the Princess that Kynon had been accosted by those agents on Clero, and all the dangerous enterprise set into motion . . .

He shook his head. However it had been begun, it was done now. He had taken the Imperial coin, and so was guilty, in deed now as well as in thought, of the worst sin any Kelt could commit: betraying his Chief for gold. For that morning, long before Arianeira had even been awake, Kynon had spread the news of the Terrans' arrival far indeed: He had transmitted it beyond the Curtain Wall, to where an Imperial relay ship picked up his signal and sent it on to Alphor; and so it came about that Jaun Akhera learned that Keltia and Terra had met. And so Kynon had put in train the great Imperial plan; even Arianeira, if she joined him, would do it only for revenge of her imagined slights at the hands of Aeron: And perhaps those grievances were cause enough, Kynon had small knowledge of the ways of queens and their foster-sisters . . .

But Arianeira had this long time been busy with her own thoughts, and now her voice cut coldly across his reverie.

"Gods hear me," she said, "but I would do almost anything to rid myself of Aeron Aoibhell."

Kynon came quietly alert. "Would you indeed, lady?" he asked. "Then perhaps I may be of help to you."

After leaving the lounge of the *Sword*, Haruko had gone straight to his own cabin. There, among all his loved familiar clutter, he flung himself down on the blastcouch, kicked off his boots, and started biting his knuckles. He needed to sleep. He was too overwrought to sleep. Irritably he rolled over and smacked the caller for the medidroid; at least he could get a relaxer shot that would put him out for a couple of hours. Through the tiny port set into the wall beside his head, he saw a blaze of gold moving across stars, a wall of light: the *Firedrake* in turnaround, heading home.

From the preliminary information the *Glaistig* had given them, the big destroyer would complete her duty program in three hours; then they would begin the short sail to Inishgall. Hyperspace would not be needed; at simple lightspeed, the trip would take only two hours of ship-time, putting the Terrans in close orbit around the quarantine planetoid and depositing them on the surface just after sunset local time.

That was fine with him, decided Haruko drowsily, as the medidroid retracted its injector arm from his left bicep and the sedative began to wash over him in lovely warm waves. They'd get there just in time for dinner . . .

Up on the bridge, it was quiet, except for O'Reilly, who was engaged in animated conversation with the pilots of the scout sloop. This conversation was taking place in Latin, much to the disgust of Hathaway and Mikhailova, who had listened for a while, then, bored with waiting for the transla-tions, had gone into the lounge to read or play chess with the computer.

"Sir didn't have too much to say, did he," remarked Hathaway, losing for the fourth consecutive time to the com-puter and packing in the program.

"Well, that Keltic captain wasn't exactly a fountain of information either. I thought the Irish loved to talk; at least that's what O'Reilly's always saying."

"Ahh, she doesn't know any more than we do."

Mikhailova jerked her head in the direction of the bridge. "By the time she's finished chatting with her new friends she will. Did you know she's got a high-speed language-learner hooked into the computer on board the Keltic destroyer? It's all so we can learn their languages before we get to their capital."

"I'm not very good with languages."

"Oh, if you can learn Chja you can learn anything." She stood up, stretching for the ceiling. "I'm *starving* . . . how long till we have to move?"

"Hour and a half," said Hathaway, who carried a clock in his head. "You better eat fast, if you want to run your checks before we get underway."

She waved a hand and vanished in the direction of the galley. Hathaway wandered over to the viewport. The voice of O'Reilly could still be heard; now she was practicing bits and pieces of newly acquired Gaeloch on the communications officer aboard the destroyer.

For all his casually humorous attitude, Warren Hathaway was a disciplined, conscientious person, with a fine perception of the ridiculous and a zero tolerance for fools. He had joined the Navy some twenty years earlier, and still it had not palled. When his exemplary service record and officer's behavior profile had gotten him into the prestigious diplomatic-exploratory corps, that had been even better. So far he had participated in prime contacts with six alien races, but none of them had been a tenth as exciting as this one.

He flopped down on the longchair in front of the viewport, mulling over the scant, tantalizing information the crew had managed to pull out of Haruko and the Keltic captain Chynoweth. These people had been tearing around through space in faster-than-light ships for *three thousand years* . . . Earth herself had had hyperdrive ships, back around the time of the Colonizations, but the technology had been lost during the Wars of Empire, and it was only within the last few hundred years that there had again been Terran ships capable of travelling faster than light. How had the Kelts managed it?

Again he heard O'Reilly chatting in rapidly improving Gaeloch over the ship-to-ship communicator. Well, they'd find out soon enough, he supposed. In the meantime, maybe he should persuade O'Reilly to teach him some of that loopy-sounding language. He just might need it.

When Kynon finished his tale, Arianeira sat silent for a long, long moment. Then, "Jaun Akhera," she breathed. Little was known to her of the Imperial heir save his name and his reputation, but those were enough . . .

"So terrible an undertaking, though, Kynon; do you realize what you ask of me, who am a princess of Gwynedd?"

"Lady," said Kynon gently, "do *you* realize what is here for you to achieve? Not only the ridding yourself of one you hate, but the chance to be more than merely a princess of Gwynedd. And not even a Ruling Princess at that . . . The

Throne of Scone itself will lie within your grasp, and is not that what you have coveted all your life?''

Arianeira went stock-still. ''I had not thought of that,'' she said, and he knew she told the truth. ''I thought only of Aeron removed . . . You are saying that once Aeron falls, *I* could reign here? In Jaun Akhera's name?''

He shrugged. ''What matters it in whose name, so long as you are the one they bend the knee to as Queen? Doubtless you would be allowed to govern here much as you pleased, provided Keltia remained a loyal and biddable vassal state of the Imperium. But we outpace ourselves. I have taken a great risk in speaking of this to you; am I assured, then, of your cooperation?''

She did not answer him immediately but looked down, twisting a ruby ring on her finger and thinking hard. This was such a chance as would never come again, a chance to be *Queen*, herself alone, to be respected and feared and looked up to as she had always felt she ought to be. But could she truly destroy Aeron to achieve it? Perhaps Gwydion too, if it was necessary? With a sudden burst of irritation she realized that the ring she toyed with had itself been a gift from Aeron . . .

''You are,'' she said abruptly. ''And I give you my word on it as a Ban-draoi.''

Kynon was surprised, for he had had no reason to expect so swift or so solemn an assurance, but relieved also; that oath had never been broken by any woman who had so sworn— indeed, to break it would call down upon the oathbreaker the curse of the Goddess. Now in truth they were both committed.

''Then we shall begin,'' he said.

''*How*? My foster-sister may not have seen fit to summon me to her Court, but my absence from Caer Ys at such a time would scarcely go unnoticed. We—or I, at least—cannot go to him, and Jaun Akhera can hardly come here.''

''He cannot come in his own person, of course,'' agreed Kynon. ''But there are ways for him to reach into even so guarded a fortress as Aeron's Keltia—as you shall see.''

''When?'' She was all at once alight with an eagerness edged with fear at the enormity of it all; but now that she had put her hand to treason, best it was to begin at once, delay might cause her to reconsider.

"Presently." He smiled, well aware of her desire for haste. "This coil of the Terrans' arrival may be the best shield we could ever have hoped for. The attention of those who might otherwise be looking in our direction will now be focused otherwhere."

"But how—"

"No more for now, lady, if you please. But if you come to this room an hour past sunset tonight there will be here all the answers that you may require."

And with that Arianeira had to content herself.

When at the appointed hour Arianeira returned to the tower room, she was surprised to see its appearance radically altered by a maze of metal-sheathed instruments covering the top of the table which stood against the wall. Beside the big wallscreen stood a curiously fashioned contrivance; roughly cylindrical in shape, its surface was a cloudy silver covered with a fine wire mesh, into which were set crystals at regular intervals around the cylinder's circumference.

She pointed to it. "What is that, Kynon?"

"A shielder, lady," he said briefly, not looking up from his work. "In a very little time we shall be receiving a signal on a tight-focus beam from a ship far beyond the Curtain Wall. The devices you see here are to amplify and refine that beam so that it is not picked up by anyone other than ourselves. Is anyone else still about in the castle?"

"Scarcely anyone. My courtiers are all in their own chambers or else away from the castle for the evening. I have dismissed the servitors; they have all gone to a ceili in the village. Only the outer-ward guards remain."

"They'll not trouble us here . . ." Kynon rapidly adjusted the calibrations on the tall silver cylinder. "Hard it is with this unlawful gear to maintain a clear signal—which is why so much of it is needed—but we must not miss the transmission. And we have not." He sat back as the wallscreen glowed into life and the room filled with a low eerie hum.

She started a little at the sound. "What does that mean?"

"Naught but good—it means the signal is sent along from

the relay ship. We must stand here now, lady, so that we also can be seen. Look now.''

The crystal screen flared with a blue light that modulated into a remarkably clear picture. It was bright sunlight on some distant planet; they had a confused quick impression of a white-walled room and a hot climate. Then the screen filled with the face of a man: dark, chiselled, hawklike. When he saw them, he smiled.

"I salute Your Royal Highness," he said. When Arianeira remained silent, "I have the honor to address the Princess Arianeira of Gwynedd?"

"My lord," said Arianeira, recovering her poise and inclining her shining head to him, "I am likewise honored to address Jaun Akhera, Prince of Alphor and Imperial Heir."

Jaun Akhera bowed his own head, and when he raised it again his smile was gone and his eyes were keen.

"My compliments, Highness," he said. "And my compliments to you as well, Kynon, on a delicate matter brilliantly handled. At least, I so assume, else we would not be speaking now . . ." He turned his gaze once more on Arianeira. "For obvious reasons, lady, we must be brief, though this communication is as secure as our best techs could make it. Now, Highness, Kynon has told you of my intentions toward Keltia. What is your wish?"

"To be Keltia's Queen," said Arianeira evenly. "I will make this kingdom your loyal tributary nation, so long as I am ruler here."

Jaun Akhera's countenance, ordinarily so mobile, was as guarded now as hers, and he studied her image a moment before he spoke again. She was very beautiful, in a cold way . . .

"And Aeron Aoibhell?"

The answer came back without hesitation. "Her head on a spike above the gates of Caerdroia. Else there is no bargain here, and we but waste each other's time, you and I."

Jaun Akhera leaned back in his stone chair, and in his eyes now was something of the look of his grandfather.

"All this is not a hard asking, but what way do you propose to deliver Keltia to me, so that I may then deliver it to you?"

The sarcasm did not sit well with Arianeira. "My brother,

of whom perhaps you may have heard, is First Lord of War; it should not be beyond my powers to obtain the codes to the navigation of the Curtain Wall. If I cannot, well, there are certain other ways . . . Once I do lower the Wall, your fleets may enter as they please. From then, what you do is your affair, as long as you leave me a kingdom over which to rule.''

Jaun Akhera's expression did not change, but he drummed his fingers once on the arm of his chair.

"So. You will break the Curtain Wall, which all my best information tells me is otherwise impregnable, and my fleets sail in. I destroy Aeron's armies, and Aeron herself, and set you up as Queen. Not an easy task.''

"I did not say it would be easy!'' snapped Arianeira. "I said only that with my help—*my* help, Prince—it will be possible, and it has never been possible before. If you have a better plan, I suggest you set it out before our time runs short.''

Jaun Akhera knew when to move. "I accept your terms, Highness.''

"And I, yours.'' Arianeira drew a deep shaky breath, ruthlessly putting down a faint distant twinge of the same feeling that had assailed her earlier, a protest on so deep a level of her being as to be almost unconscious; she quashed it utterly, and it vanished at once in her growing elation and excitement.

"It is done, then. Do not attempt to speak to me again until you are prepared to lower the Curtain Wall. I will be ready to move within an hour of your word; we will arrange the area of entry, and both of you will be safely with my fleet before battle is joined—and before Aeron learns of your part in what has happened.'' He bowed again, more deeply than before. "Lady, farewell. I look forward to our meeting. Kynon, you have done extremely well, and you shall receive the reward of your efforts. Do not fail now.''

"I will not, lord.'' He saluted Jaun Akhera in the Coranian manner, and the image on the screen flashed to static and then darkness.

In the suddenly silent room, Arianeira and Kynon looked at each other.

"Now it begins," she said, her voice almost a whisper. "Now will all be well."

"Let us pray so, lady," he said, "if it be not too blasphemous a prayer . . . My chiefest concern is that no shadow of this plot be found in our minds by your brother."

"Gwydion sees deep and far," said Arianeira. "But safe it is to say that his sight these days is filled by nearer things than you or I. Never did I think I should have cause to thank Aeron for commanding so completely his attention; but now that will work to our advantage. As to keeping our actions safely hid, I am not so poor a woman of art that I cannot manage a magical veil over what it is that we do. And I rather think Jaun Akhera, who is himself a sorcerer of no mean repute, will be doing likewise. Even Aeron should find that a hard armor to cut through." She pulled open the heavy oak door. "And, Kynon—my very deepest thanks."

"When you are Queen of Kelts, Highness, is soon enough for that. Sleep well."

But Arianeira, for all her sorcery and all her promise of revenge to come, lay not quiet in her bed that night.

Arianeira was not the only one whose sleep was broken. In the round room of the Western Tower, Aeron bolted suddenly awake with a cry, upright in the middle of the great canopied bed. In less time than the thought of it, Gwydion was awake beside her, one arm around her shoulders, the other reaching for his sword.

She was trembling violently; but when he saw no immediate threat, he closed both arms around her and eased her back down onto the pillows.

"Aeronwy, what is it?"

She clutched at the iron-hard arms that held her. "A dream—"

"No dream can come in here, cariad, save that you call it. This chamber is warded, you set the seals yourself."

"I tell you there was a dream!" She flung herself out of his arms, turned her back to him. After a moment he reached out a hand to brush back her tumbled hair, and she flinched at the touch.

"Aeron, nothing can harm you, nothing is here. Tell me."

She twisted onto her back and lay still, staring up unseeing at the constellations of the Keltic sky set in diamonds into the underside of the bed-canopy.

"I do not know," she said bleakly. "But there is great evil coming. From friend or foe, I cannot tell; but we are warned."

His voice was deep and quiet in her ear. "What counsel did the dream give you?"

She slammed her fist into the furs that covered them. "I cannot *see*, I do not *know*! All was blood and fire, Caerdroia fallen, warships in the Bawn, swords on the plain—" She fell silent, drained by the outburst. A dream of war. She had had prophetic dreams before; nearly every Kelt had something of the precognitive gift, and among the Ban-draoi and the Druids and the bards, the talent was highly prized, and actively trained and encouraged. "There was more," she said in a small weary voice, "but I cannot bring it to sight."

Gwydion held her until she had fallen again into fitful sleep. He watched her a little while, then, restless and wide-awake, he slid from the bed and went to the windows that overlooked the City.

The sight that met his eyes was wild and full of portent. The two moons were near setting, the one orb a mellow golden disk and the other a blazing blue-white crescent with sharp horns. Ragged wisps of cloud streamed across their faces, flying fast upon a high cold wind.

No wonder Aeron was dreaming in prophecies. But what else had she seen, to so overset her usual calm? To dream of Caerdroia fallen was perhaps not the best of omens, since Caerdroia had never fallen to an enemy in all the centuries of its being. But it was not like a Ban-draoi to forget a dream of such vivid import, unless it struck so close to the soul of the dreamer that to recall it in waking life was well nigh unendurable . . . Gwydion glanced quickly over his shoulder at a muffled sound from the bed, but she was still asleep.

There were ways, of course, to bring back the dream's entirety: the taghairm, for instance, a Druidic technique that involved deep-trance upon the hide of a sacred bull. For a moment Gwydion considered it, then put the thought aside. Even at the best of times, the taghairm would take too much out of them both, and Aeron especially; and at this moment neither of them, and again Aeron especially, had a scrap of energy or concentration to spare.

No, they would have to do without whatever warning Aeron's dream had brought to her inner mind. Whatever doom was coming—for plainly it was all bound up with the arrival of the Earth ship—would be like no other doom that had been set upon Keltia before.

It was the Queen's custom, and her duty also, to spend several mornings each week hearing grievances brought to her by Kelts of every station. This was according to the brehon law, that every subject had the right to present his case to his ruler; and though in a population numbering in the billions, scattered over many worlds, not every dispute could be laid before the Ard-rían for supreme mediation, many were, in a volume and variety that would greatly surprise the rulers of worlds called democratic.

Gwydion, who had been busy all morning with his own duties, entered the Presence Chamber unchallenged and stood in the shadows just inside the door. Sitting in the high seat beneath a canopy at the far end of the room, Aeron gave no sign that she had noticed him, but went on with the judgment she was giving, the last of the morning's cases. When her speech was concluded, she spoke to the room at large.

"The hearing-court is closed for this day. I will see the First Lord of War alone."

Secretaries, recorders, jurisconsults and litigants all bowed themselves out, and Gwydion came forward.

"What is it?" she asked, smiling. "Has Straloch found some new bogle to fright me with, or has he been suddenly granted the an-da-shalla?"

Gwydion laughed. "The Second Sight? Nay, he sees ill enough only with the first . . . Nothing like that, it was only that I had a thought earlier—have you invited my sister to the ceremonies in honor of the Terrans?"

Aeron looked a little taken aback. "Nay, I never thought to do so. She has been so steadfast in her refusals to come to Court, I had long since fallen out of the way of thinking of her. But you are right, she must at the least be asked. However far apart we have grown, she is still my foster-sister." A sudden memory struck her. "She was in my dream last night—perhaps that is all it was about, guilt for how I have behaved to her." She looked up at him. "I have felt myself much to blame for Ari's unhappiness, and maybe her anger toward me has not been all so unwarranted."

"Meaning?"

"That I have demanded too much of your time—time that formerly was hers. You and she used to be so close, as twins are; I know that from watching my brothers Kieran and Declan. And now that it is you and I—well, I felt Ari blamed me for your absences from her. She is your sister, and she loves you dearly."

An expression of acute discomfort passed over Gwydion's face. "She blames you all unfairly," he said. "Whose choice was it but mine to come here—or to love you? Nay, it goes much deeper and further back than that. And you are not to blame, Ard-rían, though she has made you the focus for her bitter discontent. She has resented you for a long time, though she admits it not, and though perhaps you do not know it."

"Nay, that I did know," said Aeron quietly. "Even as children, when she and Morwen and I were being reared together here at Turusachan and at Kinloch Arnoch and at Caer Dathyl, even then it was always Ari who would throw the future in our faces: that Morwen would have rule as a Duchess, that I would be Ard-rían—and that she would be no more than a prince's sister. When I chose Morwen to be my Taoiseach, Arianeira was jealous, and accused me of stealing Wenna's friendship altogether. When I chose you to be First Lord of War, that angered her far more. We have been unfriends, she and I, a long time now. I did try to make amends to her—I thought, at least, that I had tried my best; clearly it was not enough. But she must come, Gwydion, now. Do you think she will come? It would be good to see her after so long, and to be her friend again."

"If the asking comes from you, I think she will come."

"No more, then. It is done." She smiled, a little shame-faced. "And I shall not tell her it was her brother who had to remind me of my duty. She thinks ill enough of me as it stands. Come, let us speak to her now."

*   *   *

"Aeron! This is a happy surprise." Arianeira's face, sharper than Aeron remembered it, smiled at her from the viewscreen.

"Far too long since we have spoken, Ari. All is well with you?"

"Well enough, Ard-rían. But if you seek my brother Gwydion, he is, as usual, away from his homeworld."

Out of the tail of her eye, Aeron caught the Prince of Gwynedd's expression.

"Nay, he is here with us in Turusachan—but that is not the intention of my call . . . Ari, I would like you to join us here, for the ceremonies that will celebrate the arrival of the Terran embassy."

Something flickered in Arianeira's eyes and was gone before it could be truly seen.

"It is good of you to think of me, Aeron. Yes, I should very much like to come to Court." As if it had been an afterthought, "May I bring a 'tail' with me?"

Aeron frowned, puzzled and a little surprised. It was not like Arianeira to think ahead about bringing a retinue, still less like her to inquire for permission. But it was true enough that no Keltic noble, and few commoners of any consequence, ever travelled without a tail of some kind; certainly no princess of Gwynedd could be expected to come unattended to the Throneworld on an occasion of state.

"Bring whom you will," said Aeron. "The rechtair will have your old rooms prepared for you."

Arianeira's brilliant smile lighted her face, but the blue eyes remained glacial.

"I thank you again, Ard-rían, and I will see you shortly at Caerdroia. Tell Gwydion that I come."

The screen blanked out, and Aeron's face as she turned to look at Gwydion was nearly as blank.

"Did I miss something there?"

But he shook his head. "I am not certain. If you missed it, then I did also. Perhaps it was not there?"

"Nay, it was there." Aeron pondered the screen again, as if the fleeting wrongness she sensed had left some visible mark upon the crystal surface. "It was there. And I think we have not seen the last of it."

*   *   *

Aeron was not the only participant to that conversation who had had a silent witness just beyond the screen's range. In the solar on Gwynedd, Arianeira cast a sidelong glance at Kynon.

"Does that please you, then, that we are invited to Court?"

"It pleases me well, so that Your Grace is pleased," he said, bowing mockingly over her hand.

She pulled the hand sharply out of his grasp. "Save your courtly words for Aeron's ear, they will serve you better so."

"Then I am to go with you to Turusachan?"

"You are; did you not hear me ask if I might bring a tail with me? Certainly you will go with me." She paused a moment. "I do not know what put it into Aeron's mind to summon me to Caerdroia," she said then, "but it is a summoning she will soon have cause to regret."

Chapter Six

*I*t was probably accurate to say that the Terrans had been anticipating something rather different by way of quarantine facilities.

From space, the planetoid Inishgall—Gaeloch for "Isle of the Foreigners"—had looked much the same as any other small, habitable, field-shielded green world. By the time their shuttle touched down on the landing field, at coordinates supplied by the astrogator of the *Glaistig*, it was full dark, and the landscape was obscured by a driving rainstorm.

But a small drone surface car was waiting to convey them to what would be their abode for the next three days, and as it zipped across the mile or so that separated the landing field from their destination, Mikhailova peered out through rain-dappled windows.

"It's a *palace*," she said, her tone one of either delight or acute dismay. "*Look* at it."

They looked; she was right. An indisputable castle, all its windows ablaze for their arrival, raised itself up through night and rain.

Leaving the groundcar at the sheltered entrance, they found themselves in a hall that would have graced an Imperial domicile. All round them was marble and silk and silver wrought in intricate knotwork patterns. They peered shyly around, then looked at each other half in wonder, half in fear, feeling like children in an old story, creeping into the palace of the elf-king.

"Doesn't look much like quarantine," observed Hathaway, breaking the awed silence. Haruko glared at him, but the handsome black face was bland as a baby's. "What now, sir?"

Haruko shook his head. "I haven't the slightest idea."

But before they had time to become really alarmed or doubtful or desperate, their hosts arrived: the embassy Elharn had promised.

It came in the form of a master-bard, a brown-haired giant called Morgan Cairbre, who was, he informed them cheerfully, to instruct them in Keltic history, politics, etiquette; as he put it, "matters which matter much among us." There was also a medical team; and twelve Fians chosen from the Royal Guard itself, for an "honor guard," a euphemism which fooled nobody and which, of course, was not expected to; and most surprising of all, the Queen's own first cousin, the Princess Melangell, as Her Majesty's personal emissary.

The bard Cairbre apologized that no one had been there to greet them, then formally presented the Princess to the Terrans, whose reactions were various. *So this is Keltic royalty,* was the main thought. Haruko, whose business it was as captain and chief diplomatist to think otherwise, reflected that this unknown Queen could hardly have chosen better, if her intent was to flatter them off their guards: The Princess Melangell, besides being of royal blood, was exquisitely lovely and equally exquisitely courteous.

Haruko performed the introductions of his crew to their hosts, and when he had finished Melangell bowed.

"It is my cousin Aeron's wish," she said in a shy soft voice, "that I extend to you her very personal welcome, and that I tell you whatever you may care to know"—here casting a sidelong humorous glance at the tall bard beside her—"and which you may not care to ask Master Morgan. But doubtless you are all fatigued with your voyage, and will wish now to bathe and rest. I look forward to joining you at the nightmeal." She smiled and bowed and left, before the Terrans could complete their own self-conscious bows. Morgan Cairbre looked after her, his face respectful.

"The Princess Melangell is a true cousin to her cousin the Queen," he remarked. "But I delay your rest." He gestured, and half a dozen people appeared in the hall. Each wore a livery of dark green with a small badge sewn to the left breast of the tunic, and they seemed to be retainers of some status. "Go with these," said Morgan. "They will show you to your chambers and attend you while you remain here."

The Terrans followed their guides up the graceful double-spiral stairs to the upper halls of the castle. The suites of rooms to which they were conducted were so luxurious as to elicit a low whistle from Tindal.

"Bit of a change from coldsleep bunks, eh, Captain?"

Haruko had to agree: The rooms were truly palatial, hung with tapestries and arrases of heavy silk, floored with marble and strewn with fur rugs over the stone. Heavy silver wall-sconces set with curiously faceted crystals provided lighting; the heating elements, as Haruko soon discovered when he stripped to bathe, were concealed beneath the floors—the marble was warm to the foot. He wiggled his bare toes luxuriously, and stepped into the bathing-pool.

The stinging hot water, paradoxically, lulled his muscles while clearing his mind, as he sat submerged nearly to the chin in the vast marble pool. His instincts told him all was basically well; no one would have to fret about being slaughtered while asleep. They were being received as honored guests, in the most impeccable traditions of diplomacy as understood and practiced by all polite nations. And that was right and good.

But the quarantine itself puzzled him. Obviously, it was more for the benefit of the Kelts than the Terrans, and not for any trumped-up biological reasons either. Any civilization that could whip up something as technologically terrific as that gold dragon ship could certainly manage some form of decontamination procedure both briefer and subtler than this isolation in splendor. Therefore—Haruko emerged pink and dripping from the bath—it was all to buy time, a delaying tactic. But for what? And for whom?

Perhaps this Queen Aeron was having more difficulty with her people than she might have liked. For the moment, though, Haruko would guard his thoughts, keep his peace, and learn everything he could; indeed, he could do little else. Well, he would pump that bard, and the Queen's cousin, and anybody else who would talk to him. Good job everyone so far spoke passable Englic. Knowledge was power, all right, and often it was found in the unlikeliest places. With that comforting thought, Haruko was asleep on the wide soft bed.

In the other guest chambers, the other Terrans had been occupying themselves similarly, and most of them had reached the same conclusions as their captain.

Down the hall, O'Reilly was still awake. She lay looking up at the figured ceiling high above her bed and listening to the rain with a vast warm contentment. She had not spoken of her true feelings to anyone, fearing Tindal's sharp-tongued sarcasm or Haruko's cold-eyed neutrality. But from the very first exchange of words with the scout ship, O'Reilly felt that she had come home at last. She was of unmixed Irish descent, and extremely proud of it; not many Terrans these days could boast unmixed ancestry of any sort, and those who could, of whatever derivation, rightly bragged about it.

But when those two warriors in the scout sloop had spoken to her in their own language—the Gaeloch, as they called it—which was really *her* own ancestral language too, even though she had never learned it . . . well, it was so strange, but she had felt something leap inside her, something joyous and expectant and incredible, something that made her almost ill with excitement, as if some great and shining present, some wonderful gift that she had always wanted desperately but had never known exactly what it really was that she so longed for, was awaiting her only a few days away . . .

A few doors down, Mikhailova and Hathaway were totally and instantly asleep, not with each other.

Across the hall, Tindal was not even faintly drowsy. As they all had done, he had bathed and changed his clothes, though he with that extra fastidiousness which was part of his character and which had earned him so many extra gibes aboard ship. But he was too preoccupied and overwrought to lie down for a nap as the others had done; and now he paced the room, now stared out the tall windows into the rainy dark.

He was well aware of his reputation aboard the *Sword*, how he appeared in the eyes of his fellow crewmen. They tolerated him merely, suffered his sarcasm and his cynicism and his general attitude, for the sole sake of his brilliance at his job. There were few finer science officers in the Navy, and they knew it; more to the point, *he* knew it. What had always held him back from further promotion or greater responsibilities or awarded honors was a certain tendency to stir things up for the sheer sake of watching them swirl: a kind of joy in malice that no Navy alienist had missed noting in him and that no commanding officer had failed to keep a weather eye on. In Navy parlance, Tindal was a mixer. But much could be forgiven for excellence, and Tindal generally knew to the last fraction exactly how far his brilliance and utility could be made to balance off his perversity.

But what his crewmates on all the many vessels that had seen his service could never manage to forgive was his opportunism. Tindal, in any conceivable set of circumstances, could unfailingly be counted upon to secure Tindal's interests first. It was a trait not so much acquired as inborn, as much a part of his essential nature as his lanky frame or receding hairline or watery blue eyes. It was also a trait guaranteed to win him few friends, and the people who shared the *Sword* with him had been no exception.

Yet here, maybe, was a chance for him like no other chance he had ever had before. This Keltia, now, was a totally unknown quantity, obviously immensely powerful—to hold seven star systems together against all comers for three thousand years, it would have to be—and Tindal had always liked monarchies anyway. The scope here was unparalleled in his experience: for mischief, or for gain. The great thing was that so far, outside the five members of the *Sword*'s crew, no Terran yet knew Keltia even existed. The subspace communique Haruko had ordered sent would not reach the Admiralty for at least a week; until then, they were unique in their knowledge. How that might work to his advantage, Tindal did not yet know. But if it could, he would . . .

Haruko had expected dinner to be something of a strained and formal occasion, but he was both surprised and delighted to be proved wrong. That bored, space-weary crew of his seemed to have come alive—it couldn't have been just the salutary effects of a bath and a nap, he thought; they were all of them, even Tindal, absolutely sparkling—and Haruko found himself responding to their gaiety with a merry mood of his own. What it was, he finally decided, was simply five people giving themselves over to the moment, the spirit of adventure taking the helm at last; though no one except perhaps Hathaway would admit to so frivolous a motivation.

In any event, the Terrans and their hosts were mutually and equally delighted. The food was simple and delicious, the conversation agreeable, the wines and ales and the noble drink called usqueba strong and plentiful.

After dinner, the entire party, save for the medics and guards, adjourned to a drawing room, where a fire burned upon a huge hearth and where the sense of being snug against the storm was conducive to talk. Even Melangell had let down her air of royal reserve, and was chatting animatedly with Hathaway and O'Reilly.

"But I forget," she said at last, with a charming smile, "I am here to answer your questions, not you mine! What is it you might like to know?"

"Everything," said Mikhailova simply.

Melangell laughed. "That would be beyond my telling, I fear." She paused, then continued in a style and attitude rather different from the one she had previously displayed, and Haruko guessed they were seeing the bardic manner at work. "We came from Earth, as you have heard, and as I know Morgan will sing you later. For now, I will say only that we have dwelt here many centuries in peace, and in what passed for peace, and in red war undoubted."

Haruko put to her the question he had asked twice already, to which he had twice received no answer. He expected none now, really, but . . .

"Why haven't we ever heard of you before?"

To his surprise, Melangell answered at once, with a frankness he saw was genuine.

"By policy. About your Earth year 1800, we came upon very bitter times in Keltia. It was the time of the Interregnum, the Druid Theocracy, when the Druid priests, or very many of them, led by the Archdruid Edeyrn, seized power and used it for their own evil ends. There was civil war—for many resisted—and then, at Edeyrn's own instigation, alien invasion, fearful destruction all over our worlds. We were delivered by the arm of King Arthur of glorious memory, he who would become the greatest monarch we ever had. Yet even he fell in time; and when he came to leave us, his sister, Morgan Magistra, resolved that none should ever again find us whom we did not wish to find us.

"Now Morgan was a sorceress, the greatest we have known, mightier even than St. Brendan himself, and she used her sorcery to raise the Curtain Wall, which is our chiefest defense. You will pass through it when we leave here for Caerdroia."

Tindal's professionalism as science officer was aroused. "What does this Curtain Wall actually do?"

"Your people might well call it magic," said Morgan Cairbre. "But to us it is simple science. It is an energy barrier, a force-field that shields all Keltia from entry or observation; it surrounds our systems, hiding suns, planets, people, all. Even energy cannot pass through it, and the Wall cannot be breached in either direction without a ship being keyed to the secret frequencies that permit it to pass. The Wall does not conceal us—from the outside, one knows there is *something* there—but it does effectively mask the space within, the Bawn of Keltia, from without. People know where Keltia is, but they can neither see it nor get into it."

There was an awed little silence. "How can this be possible?" asked O'Reilly then.

"I am no scientist," said Morgan, smiling. "And I could not tell you even were I able to explain such a thing. Call it magic, and let us leave it. But there is much else we may speak of instead." The conversation that had languished flowed smoothly into other channels, and the tension of the moment passed.

Until Tindal brought up politics.

"The Imperium?" repeated Morgan, with a faint frown. "Well, it is far from us, for one thing, and for the rest we have a policy of what you might call hostile noninvolvement, thanks to the work Queen Aeron's father, the Ard-rígh Fionnbarr, did before he was slain. Indeed, it was partly for that policy they killed him and his Queen . . . But it is a difficult peace, uneasy at best, and, I think, not long to last."

"And the Phalanx?"

"Ah. That's very different."

O'Reilly said, slowly and diffidently, "On the *Sword*—the scouts told me a little, they said there was some personal feeling between Queen Aeron and King Bres of Fomor, who is now Archon of the Phalanx?"

Melangell gave a short laugh. "There is indeed. Dearly does each detest the other."

"But why?"

"It was Bres of Fomor ordered the ambush that killed Aeron's parents and consort and about a hundred of our folk beside. They were on an embassy ship, with three escort cursals, sailing outside the Curtain Wall under galactic peace ensigns, and the Fomori fell upon them without warning. All were slaughtered."

"What happened then?" Even Tindal was shaken.

Melangell's lovely face had grown bleak. "Something none of us is greatly proud of. Least of all Aeron . . ." She did not look at any of them. "When Aeron was told what had befallen the embassy ship," she said at last, "she said no word to anyone of her intentions, but took her own ship and went out alone from Tara. She went first of all to the—the wreck of the embassy ship, then she sailed through subspace to—"

"Subspace!" gasped Haruko. "That's the most incredible—" He broke off. Only radio waves, as a rule, ever travelled in subspace; he had never heard of any vessel navigating safely through the weird milky turbulence that lay below normal space as hyperspace lay above it.

"So it is," said Melangell. "But a ship cannot be traced or followed across subspace, and Aeron wanted that security, so that no more Kelts might be lost for this grievance. Also a ship coming out of subspace cannot be detected, and she wanted likewise the element of surprise." She resumed the tale. "Any road, she came out of subspace in the Fomori outskirt system from which the ambush attack had been launched. She announced to them who she was and why she had come; and then she reduced the entire Fomori military outpost, a planetoid known as Bellator, with all its people, down to molten bedrock."

The room had gone totally silent, and only the raging of the storm outside could be heard. Then Hathaway, "Wait a minute . . . I mean, forgive me, Your Highness, but that's just not possible. You'd need at least a dreadnaught, or a fleet of destroyers—"

"Nay, but it happened just so, Hathaway." Melangell smiled bleakly. "Aeron transmitted a broadcast, both sight and sound, of the entire episode as it actually occurred; not only back to us in Keltia but to the Imperial and Fomori capitals as well. You may view the tapes later if you wish, they are horrifying. It was like—I know not *what* it was like, there had never been anything like it before. Any road, the Fomori sued for mercy instantly; there was a treaty waiting for Aeron to sign when she arrived back at Caerdroia. Oh, aye, there was talk of further reprisals on both sides, some blusterings about galactic censures and punishments, but the overall feeling seemed to be that the one horror cancelled the other, and the whole matter was best put behind us. The Fomori evidently thought the same." She looked up at last, at their shocked frozen faces. "I tell you all this not to frighten you into any decision or action, but only so that you may know a little of Aeron when you come to deal with her. You have a right to know."

"Was she—how was she, after?" asked Mikhailova timidly.

But Melangell was silent, and after a swift glance at her Morgan Cairbre picked up the tale.

"The Ard-rían was physically unharmed, but in spirit she was very nearly destroyed by what had happened, and by what she herself had caused to happen. Consider: She had lost her father and mother, who were of course also her King and Queen like anyone else's, a double loss for her there; she lost her consort, Roderick, whom she had wed only five weeks before; and she had lost many loyal friends and subjects also. Add to that the death of Bellator, a whole planet annihilated by her mind and hand, and how many thousands of human souls with it . . . Revenge is a costly business; somtimes the price one pays for it is too high. Even though one may think one can well afford it, too often it turns out not so affordable in the end, and so it was with Aeron. Some folk could kill planets and never think twice about it, so hard are their souls with the usages of evil. Not Aeron; she nearly died of what she had done—more of what she had done, I think, than of what had been done to her. Any road, it was only the soul-healing skills of Her Grace"—here he bowed to Melangell, who sat with bent head, her silky blonde hair veiling her face—"that kept Aeron on life at all, and saved her reason in the end."

Haruko made no attempt to hide his shock; indeed, all in the room were visibly disturbed, even Tindal. Though Haruko's heart had been touched, he had also been somewhat appalled, and slightly staggered at the power apparently commanded by the ruler of this kingdom. *Perhaps by others as well?*

"How did she do it?" he asked presently. "Destroy Bellator?"

"She never told us," said Melangell. "And we never dared ask her. Black magic, undoubtedly."

Haruko gave her a sharp look, but the Princess's expression was utterly serious; plainly she meant just what she had said. *Black magic? What kind of place* is *this?* But all Haruko said aloud was, "The Imperium must have been grateful, then, that it was Fomor to take such a blow, not any Imperial fief."

The bard shrugged. "Perhaps so," he said. "I daresay Strephon found something in it to turn to his own advantage. But how can he be sure that one day Aeron may not have equal cause for fury with the Imperium, and choose to deal with them in like fashion? *We* think she would never do so again, but he has no such certainty."

"You can't just go around melting down planets!" That was O'Reilly, outraged.

"No, of course not," replied Morgan Cairbre in a gentle voice. "That is why Aeron nearly died. There is a terrible price set upon such a use of magical power, even when used in grief or revenge however just or righteous. Aeron broke every rule there is concerning the exercise of her powers, and she paid dearly for it. She knew she would have to pay for her actions, and she chose the price herself. That was why she went alone, so that the punishment would fall upon her alone, and not upon the people. She could easily have declared war; many wars have been fought for far less cause. But she took her own way instead . . . This was three years ago now; and in that time Aeron has learned, and we have learned, and, no doubt, Fomor has learned. Whatever grief she may yet feel, her desire for revenge, at least, is no more, and her hatred diminished.''

"And her power?" asked Mikhailova quietly.

Morgan only shrugged.

"My cousin is young for a queen of ours," volunteered Melangell. "Younger than any monarch we have ever had, in fact, save for Prince Arawn, who was young enough to need a regency set up for him—and that was fifteen hundred years ago. In your Earth reckoning Aeron would be barely of full legal age. And she is young in other ways as well; there is in her still much fire and much emotion that only the years can teach her to control. When she was Crown Princess, Tanista, the people used to call her Aeron Anfa, for that 'anfa' means 'storm' in our tongue.''

Tindal smiled. "And what do they call her now?"

Morgan gave him a long measuring stare before he spoke. " 'Her Majesty,' " he said, and the sting of the cool little rebuke cracked across the room.

Melangell stepped quickly into the jangling pause. "Perhaps Master Morgan would consent to play for us now?" It was not a request, and the bard bowed deeply to her before reaching for his harp.

As the long strong fingers drew a preliminary shower of crystal notes from the instrument, the Terrans, though profoundly grateful for the diversion, sat back (with the exception of O'Reilly) fully prepared to be bored. They were wrong.

Morgan Cairbre was a master for good reason; from the first word his rich deep voice held them enthralled. He had chosen for his chant the epic known as "The Rock Beyond the Billow," which told of the coming of the Milesians to the shores of Ireland, and what welcome they got there from the Danaans who were lords of the land in that time. And the tale told of Amergin, prince and Druid, son of Milesius and that Lady Scota who was the King of Egypt's own daughter: Amergin, who fought the Danaans with their own weapons of magical art, and who won the day and the land for his kindred.

But that was not the end, not then, and Morgan chanted now of Brendan, a thousand years later, son of a Danaan mother and a Milesian father, who grew weary of the suspicious eye, and more than an eye in the end, cast upon the Old Ways by Patrick and his flock of Christers. And so Brendan gathered all those who held as he did, all those skilled in the magical or scientific arts, all the Druids and priestesses and artificers, all those learned in lore or bardship or crafts or crofting—and he built a ship as the Danaans taught him, a ship to sail the stars, and the old man Barinthus stood beside him at the helm, and his own mother Nia of the Golden Hair stood behind him, and Gael and Danaan went out together. In time to come, Patrick would call them snakes and serpents, that the power of the new god had driven from the land.

But that was no longer their concern; they were gone like the snow off the mountain, and from those first starfarers all Keltia was descended. Danaan nobles married royal Milesians, and so the great houses were born. And Brendan—they were beginning to call him *Saint* Brendan even now—did return to Earth, to gather more of his folk to him. He went in secret, in a ship that glimmered like a salmon in a stream, to Scotland, to Wales, to the hidden coves of Cornwall and the Isle of Man behind her rampart of mists and the iron coasts of Brittany across the Narrow Seas—to all the last strongholds of the Keltic race that once had ridden down all Europe. And those strongholds now threw their gates open to a man who talked quietly of a Keltic kingdom out among the stars, of magic green islands outside this world; and those who understood his words were never seen again on Earth . . .

The chant ended on a ringing note that was like one star of hope in a stormy sky, and for long moments no one stirred. In the firelight, the faces of the Terrans reflected their feeling: hearts at odds with minds. The story of Brendan had worked upon them in strange tandem with the tale of Aeron's vengeance upon the Fomori and the interwoven thread of Amergin and his magic.

And doubtless that was entirely what had been intended, thought Haruko cynically, though he had in truth been as enchanted as the rest.

But the room had grown very quiet. Melangell, suddenly

recalling that all the laws of etiquette on all the worlds there were held that no one however diplomatically privileged might leave a room before royalty left it, quickly stood up and bowed to the entire company.

"Until the morning, then. Master Morgan, my thanks. Sirs and ladies, I give you all a very good night." She was gone in a rustle of silks before they could rise or reply.

Haruko got to his feet with an effort. "I don't know about the rest of you," he said, "but I have never been so tired in my life." It was true, too; even more than the voyage, or the *Firedrake*, or the contact itself, even, the last few hours had wrung him of emotions he hadn't known were still there, and now he wanted only to go instantly to sleep.

Apparently the others felt the same, for everyone seemed to be drifting toward the door . . . In a very short time there was left in the room by the fire only Morgan Cairbre. He sat motionless a while, gazing into the leaping flames, then he began to play to himself upon his harp, very softly, a tune that flickered like the fire and ran away into the shadows of the room. It was a sword-dance.

Chapter Seven

All day the stormclouds had been building, forming and shifting and re-forming into great slow billows of air, climbing and massing behind the Loom, until at last their outliers began to move like black towers on the march, a citadel of air that rivaled Caerdroia, a rampart of slate and lead shot through with blue lacings of lightning. Then, in the late afternoon, the clouds began to spill over the mountain barrier that had contained them and surged down the strath toward Caerdroia.

All day in the City, the southeasterly winds had blown, with their heavy ion charges, making everyone fractious and irritable. Those who lived at Caerdroia called that malign wind the Fomor-wind, or the Red Wind of the Hills. It drove everyone a little mad, beasts as well as people. Even An-Lasca, the Whip-wind out of the northwest that whirled down the winter, was better loved, for at least one felt full of energy when it cracked.

After sunset, the evil southeasterlies had given place to a clean, strong, steady east wind that raced down the strath to die in the sea. Then lightning, almost continuous, and an odd sharp thunder that cracked like breaking twigs directly overhead and was immediately silenced, short, sharp, ominous in its abruptness.

Rohan watched from his windows as the storm flared slowly around him. The air was alive with electricity; he could feel it crawl along his skin like ghostly fingers. No lightning, though, could strike even so tempting a target as the towers of Caerdroia; the City was shielded by an antistatic field against just such storms, which were frequent in high summer, though this one was most unseasonal. With each bolt, the field interface grew more intensely ionized, the smarting smell of ozone heavy in the air.

And now at last came the rain, gray sheeted veils of it. Down in the streets it was difficult to breathe; the air was almost solid with water, and what few folk had been still outdoors vanished into shelter as Rohan watched.

Behind him in the room, Ríoghnach extended her quaich for more ale. "I wonder how it is with Melangell."

Morwen's husband, Fergus, filled the quaich with usqueba instead, and she saluted him with the cup in appreciative thanks.

"Did not Aeron send that spy Cairbre with her?" he asked.

Rohan drew the heavy curtains across the windows to shut out the sight of the storm, which he knew Morwen disliked.

"For all that he is the best spy we have, Fergus," he said reprovingly, "he is still a quite genuine and gifted master-bard. I shouldn't like us to use that device too often," he added. "The law that makes sacred the lives of bards is an old and a precious one. If a bard is caught doing spycraft, even on Aeron's command, it will go hard with all bards else."

"Oh, Aeron's wary enough, and if Cairbre is as good as all that, why then, he'll not be caught, will he." Fergus sent the usqueba round again, and leaned back comfortably against his wife's knees. He was a great splendid dark bear of a man, Aeron's second cousin on her father's mother's side, a sailor by avocation and Lord of the Isles by hereditary right, with a nature as open and all-encompassing as the oceans he so loved. He and Morwen saw each other less often than either of them liked, she being in attendance on Aeron at Caerdroia, and he remaining on Caledon to manage their own vast lordships and their two-year-old daughter, Arwenna.

"Well, I for one think Aeron's been injudicious and over-hasty, but all too often has that been her way, and very like will always be so. Little enough we can do about that." That was Ríoghnach's husband, Niall, Duke of Tir-connell, a tall pleasant easygoing individual, as blond as his lady was dark—the only dark one of all the brood of Fionnbarr and Emer.

"Have you told her so?" said Ríoghnach demurely.

Niall laughed. "Nay, not I, anwyl! There are times when the Duke of Tir-connell advises the Ard-rían of Keltia, times when Niall O Kerevan speaks his mind to Aeron Aoibhell, and times when I keep my feelings from my sister-in-law. I try not to confuse the three." On a wave of easy laughter, he stood up, reaching a hand to his wife. "Come, Ríona, it's late." They bade the others good night and left arm in arm.

"Niall had the right of it," said Rohan unexpectedly. "She *was* injudicious and over-hasty, though I'd no sooner be the one to tell her than he."

Morwen gave a low wicked chuckle. "Nay, why should either of you, when Straloch has already done the chore?"

"And we all saw how grateful Aeron was to him for doing it . . . Would she truly turn him off the Council, do you think? My grandmother Gwyneira believes she will, and before very much longer too."

Fergus nodded. "Gavin has been entirely too vocal of late. Aeron welcomes discussion, but only so far; and he has also been entirely too indiscreet in his opinions with regard to all this of Aeron and Gwydion."

Rohan slouched down in his chair and drained a full mether of ale. "He is not the only one troubled by that pairing," he muttered.

Both his remaining listeners sat up at that. Though as of yet the thing was only gossiped of among the people, Aeron's union with the Prince of Gwynedd had been held by her friends and kindred to be in every way a very excellent thing.

"What are you saying, Rohan?" asked Morwen finally. "I know well how you feel about Gwydion—"

"He is as dear to me as any of my brothers, and I know he loves Aeron deeply, and she him. It is that, I think, is the problem. I had hoped she would have by now decided to wed him, make him King. She has gone so far as to admit to me that she wearies of ruling alone; yet she seems unable to take matters any further. It is as if she fears to admit something to herself, and it hurts me to see Gwydion hurt because she cannot, or will not, trust him."

"That is not it at all," said Fergus quietly. "She weds him not yet because she fears to lose him. She lost Rhodri, and she hesitates to open herself to the possibility of another such loss." Morwen made a sudden uncontrollable move, and Fergus reached back to take her hand in a comforting clasp; Roderick had been her much-loved brother. "When Aeron has mastered that fear, then will Gwydion be King, and not before."

There was silence in the room save for the crackling of the fire and Rohan's hounds twitching and moaning in their sleep; outside, the storm had vanished out over the sea, leaving a watery midnight glow and a damp wind as its only traces.

"What do you think she will do?" asked Morwen at last.

Rohan looked up at her, and their gazes held for a long moment. From behind his vast sealike calm, Fergus watched them both.

"I cannot say," said Rohan. "I do not know."

Rohan would not have been much comforted had he known that, even as he and Morwen and Fergus sat silent beneath the weight of their speculations, Aeron herself had been doing much the same. Unlike them, however, she had decided to do something about it.

After the Council meeting, her inner peace had been so roiled that even that tender moment with Gwydion had not helped to settle it. Indeed, that one moment had shaken her even more than all the conflict that had gone before it, and all through the rest of the day and evening she had been cross and ill-balanced. She did not know where to turn for answers, but she did know where to go for peace; and at sunset, therefore, she had gone to her chamber of magic, the twelve-windowed room at the top of her tower, and this was where now she lay in the marana, the thought-trance of Keltic sorcerers.

To all appearances she was as one dead. She lay motionless upon a low stone bench between four torches; her body was naked beneath her black robe, and her hair streamed down over the bench onto the slate floor.

She had made the usual salutes and obeisances upon entering the chamber, her bare feet silent on the stone and her hands carefully cupped around a hollow crystal filled with water. The feeling of peace and power that always came to her in that room surged up to meet her. Like a dancer coming up to the beat of the measure, a seal breasting a wave, or a hawk rising on a tide of the air, Aeron's soul went up with the torches, and she knew how right she had been to come here.

For Aeron was a priestess of the Ban-draoi, the ancient order of sorceresses that had been founded at the very beginning of Keltia itself by Nia, mother of Brendan. Of equal power and lineage with the Druids, the Ban-draoi were servants of the Great Goddess, that Mighty Mother who in Keltia alone had a thousand names, and when a Ban-draoi prayed, she addressed herself directly to that Lady; as Aeron did now.

She had lain down upon the bench, composed herself in the way so familiar after so many years of practice, and felt the trance take hold upon her. All her sight was deep blue shot with sparks; then that opened out and she was through, her body lying on the stone bench still aware of its surroundings, but her inner eye in the soul's body rising above Caerdroia and towering high above the sea, the words of the sacred rann to the Goddess echoing around her, as if spoken in a great voice not her own for all the worlds to hear. *Breastplate of the Gael, Queen of the Danaans, Tear of the Sun* . . .

In that astral immensity, only she was there, she alone was real; until into her vast awareness an unmistakable Presence made itself known. Few words, and insufficient, for such a feeling: The peace that came upon her was as a smile, a touch, a kiss; her doubts and fears were taken from her, and she knew herself safe, wrapped in the mantle of the Mother. *Water of Vision, Wind out of Betelgeuse, Light of the Perfection of Gwynfyd* . . .

For the Goddess she served had many faces: the gentle Maiden Blodeuwedd or the war-red Morrigu, Beira the Queen of Winter or Briginda the Lady of Spring, Rhiannon of the Horses or the Divine Sow that eats Her own farrow. She was the Moon Mother and the Sun Goddess, the Lady of Heaven crowned with stars, whose blue cloak was the deepness of space itself, in whose long hair were caught comets and the burning glow of suns, whose spear stretched across the universe, whose shield blazed with the cold fires of a billion galaxies, whose heart was the heart of everything that lives.

When Aeron returned into herself, it was full morning, and the torches had long since burned themselves out. She lay without moving a moment longer, for her heart was very full, and gladness clung around her like a cloak she was loath to shed.

When at last she quitted the chamber of magic and began to descend the stairs down to her solar, she saw through the windows in the tower wall the little turret walk outside her rooms. Gwydion stood there on the battlements; his head was lifted like a wolf that scents the wind, and the wind off the sea stirred his dark hair. He wore no cloak; at his side hung a sword, his hand upon its hilt. He was looking out over the water, and upon his face was a reflection of the peace and glory that shone from Aeron's own countenance.

She paused on the stairs and thought one thought, one name, that rang clear through the silence. Though he could have heard no sound, for her feet were bare upon the stone steps and she spoke no word aloud, his head came up as at a shouted hail, and he looked up to where she stood. A smile lighted his face, and he seemed to know exactly how she had spent her night.

"It was needed, then."

She nodded once, solemnly, and then came the rest of the way down the steps to him.

"And now you are ready."

Again she nodded.

"Then let us go in. Your presence is required, and there is much to do today. Tomorrow the Terrans arrive; or had you forgotten?"

"Not I," she answered, smiling, and leaned into his side, her arm around his waist. "And I doubt not they neither."

Now indeed did all ways lead to Caerdroia, as the royal fiants went out, summoning peers and senators, assemblators and planetary governors, generals and admirals and captains of the Fianna, poets and bards and those who commanded a more awesome magic—Ban-draoi, Druids, and those who were Kin to the Dragon. All were summoned now to the greatest aonach that had ever been seen in Turusachan's Hall of Heroes.

A very great number who had not been summoned at all came as well. Although all ceremonies would be broadcast on the farviewers to all the Keltic worlds, there were many who preferred to be there in person, sharing perhaps less perfectly in the seeing for the chance to be part of what would be seen. All these came to Caerdroia like arrows to the gold, crowding the houses of their kin and friends and clansfolk, taxing the sacred law of the coire ainsec, the undry cauldron of guestship, and straining the bruideans, those amazing waystations of Keltic hospitality, to the bursting point.

Finally Bronmai of Tallon, Rechtair of the planet of Tara, stepped in at Aeron's reluctant order and closed all ports, making the Throneworld inaccessible to incomers for the first time in centuries.

Except, of course, to the Terrans. When the news of the Earth ship had been announced to Keltia, by Morwen in Aeron's name, the delight of the Kelts had been unbounded—and quite astonishing to most of the Kelts' rulers. Some politicians had even gone so far as to wonder publicly if, judging by the way the news of the probe had been received, Keltia's long isolation had indeed been to Keltia's best advantage.

"It seems a popular decision," remarked Aeron dryly, "this of, ah, *ours* to welcome the Terrans. I knew not I had so many supporters on the Council and in the houses of government; how came I so to miscount at our last meeting?"

She was in her solar with a small group of her intimates. The time was early evening, and the nightmeal was at hand. They had been watching one of the interminable news programs on the farviewer, listening to two assemblators, a senator, an earl and an institutional bard speculate with almost no accuracy—and little information upon which to base any—as to the nature of an alliance with Earth, and what Aeron's next move was likely to be.

"I think they think you mean to lower the Curtain Wall to any galactic trampship that happens by," said Aeron's brother

Kieran, disgusted. He and his pregnant wife, Eiluned, had arrived at Turusachan only an hour before, from their own seat at remote Inver on the planet Caledon.

"Well, more fools they," said Aeron. "That Wall stays up. It was raised for good reason by one who knew well what she was about, and I have seen nothing yet to convince me that the reason for which she raised it has died or changed, or is like to. In fact, quite the contrary."

"Policy is well and good, Aeron, but have you asked us here to starve us?" That was Eiluned, and her sister-in-law laughed.

"Nay, come, let's go down."

The living and working quarters of Turusachan were scattered over the dozens of towers and brughs and courts that constituted the palace, but it was a long-standing and pleasant custom that the evening meal brought the royal household together at the end of the day; as in the most ancient days at Ireland's Tara, it was likewise the monarch's custom to preside over that meal, in Mi-Cuarta, the great royal banqueting hall.

Mi-Cuarta was a huge vaulted chamber, with arches and pillars and walls of topaz-colored marble flecked with gold. Across the width of the hall, over against the far wall from the main doors, was a high table of old iron-oak, in shape of an E without the center-stroke. Midmost at this table, facing the hall, were two high-backed chairs taller than the rest, their cushions of royal green embroidered with gold. At right angles to this center table, forming the top and bottom strokes of the E, were two other tables with seats on both sides; the rest of the hall was filled with long refectory boards and benches, arranged around a big open central space where often the feasting ended in dancing to pipes and harps and fidils.

Mi-Cuarta filled rapidly with those, several hundred in number, of all ranks and positions, whose privilege it was to dine in hall with the Ard-rían; her officers of state, the Fians who guarded Turusachan, members of the royal family, servitors, clerks, guests, friends, any wandering bards who might have been at the palace and claimed hospitality according to the ancient law. All could rightly seek a place at the royal table, and usually did; and most especially tonight.

When the benches of the cross-tables were nearly filled, and the high table's seats also, Aeron came in, unattended as she preferred, and her guests rose as one. She took the left-hand high seat, and indicated to the rechtair that the meal should begin.

It was into the brief quiet before the customary health to the monarch, and Rohan as senior noble present had risen to offer that health, that the doors swung open again.

"Well, Ard-rían," said Arianeira in a clear pleasant carrying voice, "I see that your hall is kept ever faithful to the old rules, and open to the unexpected guest." Kynon stood a little behind her.

"Greetings to you, Arianeira of Gwynedd," said Aeron, after a rather long pause. "And to those who come with you to my halls," she added, with a glance at Kynon and an emphasis on the possessive pronoun that none there missed. "But you, at least, are hardly unexpected. If you would join us?" She gestured, and Arianeira came forward to seat herself at the high table, taking the empty place Aeron had indicated, on the right of Declan, Kieran's twin and the youngest of the Aoibhell princes. Kynon found himself a place on a lower bench, and the room, which had hushed dramatically at Arianeira's sudden appearance, now filled again with talk. Rohan offered the Queen's health, all drank, and he sat down again in his chair on Aeron's left; the high seat at her right hand remained empty, as it had for three years now—the seat of the monarch's consort, it had last been occupied by Emer ní Kerrigan.

Rohan leaned over and spoke into his sister's ear. "Trust Ari to make an entrance."

Aeron laughed. "I wonder if Gwydion knows that she is come," she said, looking around. "He does not dine with us? It was his wish that I ask Arianeira here for all this."

"Was it now." He looked interested. "Who is that who entered with her? Down on the lower bench, the Kymro in the red tunic—"

"I have never seen him before. A friend of Ari's, most

like, or a retainer, part of her tail from Caer Ys. Ask the rechtair for his name, if you are so curious.''

Rohan, still watching Arianeira's dark-visaged escort, shook his head, and his face cleared then of the faint frown that had creased it.

"No matter . . . I just had a strange feeling about him. It is gone now.''

"That you had seen him before, perhaps?'' asked Eiluned from a few places down.

But again Rohan shook his head. "Nay; that I should see him again.''

Down the hall, Kynon was feeling the weight of Rohan's puzzled attention as if it had been a lightsword laid across his back.

"Prince Rohan seems to take an interest in you, stranger,'' observed the lady-in-waiting who sat at his right. "Are you in service with the Princess Arianeira?''

Kynon muttered something that apparently satisfied her curiosity, for she turned back to her plate. He cast a savage glance at Arianeira, who was sitting up at the high table looking cool and confident, either unaware of, or, much more likely, uncaring of, his panic. She would have much to make amends to him for, and he had his own ideas of what form her atonement should take . . . He drained his cup and took hold of himself. There was no way Rohan could suspect him of anything, despite that close scrutiny; the Prince was no sorcerer, and if Aeron herself suspected nothing, as certainly seemed to be the case, then her brother could have no idea at all, and his attention to Kynon was merely curiosity. Besides, had not Arianeira said that her magic, as well as Jaun Akhera's, provided concealment? He would simply have to trust to that, and, in the meantime, enjoy himself.

Arianeira was very well aware of Kynon's trouble, but she had no intention of relieving it, and sat hugging her secret to herself. On her face was a look of icy remove; for if once she smiled, she would laugh, and if once she began to laugh, she would never stop. *Ah, Aeron,* she thought behind her strongest shields, *even your magic has its blind spots; and that is well for me.*

Any road, this very public appearance had been all Arianeira's own idea; Kynon had been dead set against it. But in her mind, it was by way of being a challenge, to Aeron and Gwydion both, and the Princess of Gwynedd was more than a little vexed at her brother's absence from the banqueting hall. And also it was by way of being a test: to learn if the plot she and Kynon and Jaun Akhera had wrought was indeed effectively hidden. And last of all it was by way of being a fair chance for Aeron: If the Ard-rían sensed her foster-sister's treachery, she could move to scotch it. If she did not . . . well, if she did not, she had had her chance and failed at the test and lost the challenge. What would happen then was plainly fated, and as a Ban-draoi, Arianeira put much faith in fate.

At length the meal was over, and in spite of the many friends who implored her to stay for the usual merrymaking, Aeron waved a hand in salute and dismissal, and quitted the banqueting hall. Behind her, the music struck up for the dancing.

Most of those who had been at the high table accompanied her out of Mi-Cuarta, but her wish for solitude was plain, and they made their good-nights quickly.

Aeron climbed the stairs alone to her own apartments, grateful for the tact of Rohan and the rest. It had been a long, tiring day, and quite suddenly she had had enough of people, and tomorrow was sure to be filled with strains and tensions no one had anticipated.

Coming into her solar, she fell fully dressed onto the bed and lay there for a while unmoving. "Sufficient unto the day is the evil thereof," she quoted absently, and all at once she felt cheered. That was something her father had always used to say, a favorite phrase of his from the Christian holy books that had been preserved as literary curiosities in the Bardic Library. Whatever its religious connotations of old, though, it seemed to her to be an entirely appropriate observation on the here and now.

Presently she rose, went into her pool-room, stripped and plunged headfirst into the huge bath. One of the more prosaic glories of Caerdroia was its baths. A network of hot springs lay deep beneath Eryri, fed by the last dying fires of the volcanism that once had covered the entire Northwest Continent in flaming rock. In part, the City had been built to take advantage of this splendid natural resource—cleanliness being an important component of the Keltic ethic of hospitality—and every home in Caerdroia, from Turusachan to the humblest house in the Stonerows, had its hot water and sweat-rooms and heating hypocausts supplied from that tremendous source.

But Aeron's thoughts were far from volcanic geology as she submerged herself in the steaming water. Her hair floated out around her like copper lace, and the warmth relaxed tense muscles and soothed her racing mind into a restful blank. After a while she came up out of the pool, brushed out her hair under the sonic dryer, and wrapped herself in a velvet robe, feeling like her customary self for the first time since the whole coil of the Terrans had begun. She had not done so ill; last night her spiritual tensions banished, tonight her mental and physical tensions: By tomorrow she should be all of a piece to face the demands of the day.

After the pool-room's billows of steam, her solar was shockingly cold, but by now she was too sleepy for it to matter. She slid out of her robe and under the fur coverlets, feeling the silkwool sheets chill against her skin, and was asleep almost at once.

She woke with a start and a cry some nameless timeless time later. For a terrifying moment, confused and disoriented, she was back in her nightmare of two nights ago; then she saw the tall figure standing silhouetted before the dying fire.

"You are late abroad, Prince of Dôn," she murmured, heart still racing from the shock, but comforted by his presence.

Gwydion came to sit on the edge of the bed, and she curled up beside him, her head in his lap. "I thought you asleep, cariad," he said. "My sorrow that I woke you. Tonight of all nights I did not wish you to fall asleep alone."

"No matter; you are here now. Why did you not dine in hall tonight? Your sister was there."

"I know," he said. "I have just now come from her rooms— Well, I did not come to Mi-Cuarta because there was a report from Inishgall that I wished to read. I would repent to you, though, of Ari's conduct. Niall told me the manner of her arrival; it was unnecessarily discourteous, and I said as much to Ari.''

Aeron yawned and snuggled closer. ''Again, no matter. Very likely she believes I deserved the discourtesy, and very likely she is right. Come to bed.''

''Presently.'' He smoothed the clean sweet-smelling tumble of hair that spilled over his knees. ''Aeron, is all truly well with you? The last days have not been easy ones for you, I know, no matter what you may have been able to cozen everyone else into believing.''

She shifted beneath the hypnotic hand upon her hair. ''It has not been easy for any of us, Pendragon. And like to grow less easy as we go along what way we have begun. New and interesting times will take their toll of us all, not the Ard-rían only.'' She kissed the hand she held. ''You have been my main strength to sway the Council and the people.''

''Say you so? I cannot even sway my own sister.''

Aeron looked up into his face; she was fully awake now. ''Has Ari been at you so soon? I thought that at the least her coming here might begin to smooth over her displeasure. I had not much hope of her heart softening in my direction,'' she added, matter-of-factly and without a trace of self-pity, ''but still I did not expect her to continue to hold her grudge against you.''

''Leave it,'' he said curtly. He felt her surprise at his tone, and he kissed the fistful of gleaming hair he had twined in his fingers. ''She is not worth losing your peace over, Ard-rían. I know how hard-won that peace is, and I intend to see that you keep it, for you will need it tomorrow.''

''And you,'' she said, and now she was again on the edge of sleep. ''But after tomorrow, Arianeira will not trouble us, surely?''

''She will trouble all Keltia before she is done.''

But Aeron was asleep.

Chapter Eight

*I*nishgall was a minute bright green dot in their wake, and Keltia not yet there, as the Terrans marked their third hour aboard the *Glaistig*. Their three days in quarantine had passed quickly enough, and that morning, after breakfast, they had been escorted by Melangell and Morgan Cairbre up to the Keltic destroyer for the journey to the throneworld of Tara. The *Sword* followed in tow.

As a captain, Haruko had been accorded the courtesy of an invitation to spend the trip on the bridge. He stood now on the command deck—*a lot smaller than the* Firedrake's, he thought, recalling with awe that spacegoing dragon—and tried to be as unobtrusive as possible. His own crew was ensconced in what passed for luxury aboard a warship, down in the wardroom with off-duty Keltic officers and Morgan Cairbre to keep them company. Melangell was with him on the bridge.

O Davoren, the *Glaistig*'s commander, beckoned to Haruko then, and pointed out the huge front viewports. Haruko looked where the Kelt pointed and felt his skin begin to crawl, and backed a half-step in instinctive terror of what he saw out those ports.

Ahead of the ship lay a nothingness, a lacuna in space even blacker than space itself, a blood-chilling, evil-looking vortex spinning in the void, that no sane captain—no, nor insane either—would dare to steer a ship across. Any ship lost in there was lost forever, in a sea of seething dusty darkness lit from beneath by fires of hell, a giant roiling cloud of electromagnetic chaos such as Haruko for all his travels had never seen before.

"The Morimaruse," said O Davoren. "The Dead Sea of space. It is a horror when first you see it." He seemed cheerfully unconcerned. "We do not take that way."

Haruko tried to feel relieved, but he had been badly shaken by the sight of that—that *nothing* stretching across the galactic horizon like a giant maw, and Melangell gave him a sympathetic smile.

"The first time *I* saw the Morimaruse," she offered, "I was physically ill. It's not meant for folk to see such things, perhaps; our minds cannot absorb the idea of it."

"Has it—has it ever been crossed?" *Oh, surely not . . .*

But Melangell was nodding. "Many centuries ago, Arthur did so, though to our best knowledge no one since. Before we raised the Curtain Wall, the Morimaruse was our chief line of defense."

Haruko could well believe it. Few spacers, however brave or crazy, would care to chance an unknown the scope of *that . . .*

"It was deterrent enough then," said O Davoren. "But we use it now to better purpose. Morgan gave us the key to that."

"Morgan?" said Haruko, taken aback. "The bard—"

"Nay, Morgan Magistra," said Melangell with a little laugh. "Arthur's sister, the Ban-draoi sorceress who raised the Curtain Wall after Arthur went away."

" 'Went away'? You mean died."

Melangell shook her head. "I mean 'went away.' He disappeared during a space battle with the Coranians. His last words to us were that he would return when he was needed."

"But Arthur lived over fifteen hundred years ago!"

"So he did," said O Davoren. "But no one saw him die, or his ship *Prydwen* destroyed either; so according to the brehon law he remains King of Kelts. All monarchs since hold their throne by Arthur's grace and make their laws in Arthur's name."

Haruko blinked. Of all the many things he had learned so

far about the Kelts, this seemed to him the most revealing; except that he wasn't sure just exactly what it revealed . . .

He was spared further painful abstractions by Melangell, who touched his arm lightly. Her face was bright with gladness.

"Look, Theo," she said. "Home."

While they had been speaking, the *Glaistig* had altered her course and increased her speed. Ahead of her now, in place of the Morimaruse, was something very different and in its own way even more alarming. The Morimaruse was a thing of nature's making; but this was not natural, a created artifact; and so, far more terrifying.

Haruko knew without being told that he was looking at the Curtain Wall, the greatest achievement of the Keltic people. It appeared on half a dozen of the viewscreens as a blue shimmer across the stars, a kind of unblinking lightning that remained steady in time and place and did not pass. Haruko stared open-mouthed. *The power that thing must take to maintain*, he thought, numbed. *And, August Personage of Jade, the power of the mind that had raised it . . .*

"I can't see it out the viewports," he heard himself saying in a small tight voice. "Why can't I see it?"

"Only the main screens are equipped to register it," said O Davoren. "It was designed to be invisible to direct view. Any ship that carries uncoded screens will see nothing, and if a ship is not keyed, as we are, to pass through the Wall—"

"What happens then? Are they destroyed? The *Sword* will be all right?"

"Your ship is in tow within our shadow, she will pass easily," Melangell reassured him. "As to your other questions, nothing so crude. That would be a treacherous measure indeed. No, unkeyed ships are simply shunted away, along certain pathways of flux called leys, and they find themselves— somehow—on the other side of the Morimaruse. That was what O Davoren meant when he said that Morgan taught us how to use the sea as a defense. Wait, now—"

There was a vibration, as if something soft and heavy had struck the hull, and the *Glaistig* shook very faintly all along her length. Then she was sailing smooth again, and within the compass of the blue radiance, where no planets or suns had been a moment before, seven stars now burned.

"We have passed the Curtain Wall," said O Davoren formally, "and we are now within the Bawn."

"Welcome, Haruko," said Melangell. "Oh, welcome to Keltia."

Even if it had not been destined to see the events it would soon witness, that day at Caerdroia would have been special. The last rags of the storm of the previous night had blown away, and it was one of those mornings of dizzying clarity that come only in late fall among mountains. The skies above the City were that deep autumnal blue that so often astonishes; high clouds raced past on a strong cold wind out of the north, and blazing color lay on the forested slopes that ran down into the Great Glen.

Caerdroia itself shouted in the sun, every wall hung with banners, every battlement friezed with people in colors as brave as the flags. From the landing field at Mardale Port, where Morwen and Straloch waited as official royal envoys, to the courtyards of Turusachan itself, all Tara seemed waiting to welcome the Terrans.

On a high inconspicuous rampart of the Keep, Aeron stood in the sun and wind, enjoying a last few moments of solitude before her duties fell upon her. She was arrayed for the formal aonach in the Hall of Heroes, several stories below her on the Keep's ground floor, though she had not yet put on the crown she so seldom wore. If she had to become part of an immortal moment, she thought, eyes turned unseeing into the middle distance, this was the way she wished to be remembered. There would be accounts and pictures and remembrances of this day's work for as long as Keltia existed . . .

She lifted her face to the wind, saw her fingers white and strong-looking against the ruddy granite of the battlement. It must be very nearly time; she could hear the people cheering and shouting down in the lower quarters of the City, and from her own tower windows an hour or so ago she had seen a silver needle plummet past the clouds and disappear from sight behind the Loom, over toward Mardale. As if in confirmation, she sensed presences behind her, and she spoke without turning round.

"I am nearly ready."

"I know."

She glanced over her shoulder at them. Rohan, Tanist of Keltia, Prince of Thomond—it was he who had spoken—smiled at her; Gwydion, Prince of Gwynedd, Chief of the House of Dôn, did not. Both men were resplendent in formal attire, Rohan in royal green, jewel-trimmed and gold-embroidered, Gwydion in his usual splendid severity of black and silver. But over the black velvet tunic he wore the white and purple cloak of heavy silk that denoted the Pendragon of Lirias, and the Star and Dragon of the Kinship flashed diamond brilliance upon his breast.

"I shall come presently," said Aeron, and Rohan bowed and was gone. She and Gwydion held each other's glance; then, very deliberately and with great grace of formality, he went to one knee before her and kissed her hand in the traditional gesture of fealty. Keltic royalty exacted such homage from their lieges only once in a reign—at their coronations—and Aeron was moved to tears to see it now, and from him.

Gwydion rose and held out his arm to her, and she placed her hand over his.

"Come, Keltia," he said. "It is time to greet your guests."

As he stepped down from the gilded chariot in which he had ridden all the way from Mardale, Haruko looked around him in hopes of reassurance. The blonde woman who had stood beside him all the way—*Morwen,* he rehearsed to himself, *she's the Prime Minister*—gave him an encouraging smile. The third rider in the chariot, Gavin, Earl of Straloch, gave him only a sour glance. The man seemed intensely irritated with all the Terrans, and Haruko did not have the faintest idea why.

Haruko dismissed the thought and turned again to Morwen. She waved a hand at the many buildings that surrounded them on three sides of the enormous paved square.

"This is Turusachan. That there is the Keep, and, over there, the royal palace—your home while you are with us."

Haruko was glad of the friendly overtures, but it was not until the other chariots drew up, with his crew in them similarly accompanied by Keltic officers of state, that he began to feel a bit easier. A few files back, Melangell waved merrily to him as she jumped down from her own conveyance.

There really was no reason whatsoever to be so stupidly apprehensive, he told himself fiercely. For twelve miles he and the others had been escorted by outriders and banners and cheered like liberating heroes by what he estimated had been several score million Kelts. Nothing in all his experience had prepared him for such a thing, and he was still boggled by the memory of it.

But even their arrival on the planet had been staggering. They had come down in one of the *Glaistig*'s shuttles, arrowing in low over the rolling plain of Moymore, the green gash of the Strath, and then, at last—

O'Reilly had seen it first. "Oh my God—it's not possible!"

Caerdroia had lain below them, fortress-capital of the Keltic nations. It was clearly and pre-eminently a fortification of war; but it was also beautiful as nothing else Haruko had ever seen.

Raised in the days of the Fáinne by the master-builder Gradlon of Ys, it lay along the northern slopes of Eryri— "Abode of Eagles"—as if it had grown there, stretching seven miles from Aeron's tower above the sea to the Fianna garrisons behind the eastern walls. Cut from the volcanic rock of the Loom, the City reached back to the roots of the mountains, and the colors of its stone shone clear and vivid: lime-white, basalt-black, gold-cream and slate-blue and warm ruddy brown. The points of the towers were capped with gold and silver and the softly glowing metal called findruinna, and from every tower floated a standard . . .

"Shall we go in?" repeated Morwen, smiling, and Haruko blushed to realize that his reverie had been keeping everyone waiting.

"Of course," he said, and Morwen led the procession into the Keep.

Haruko had a confused impression of arched ceilings, saluting guards, the glowing crystal eyes of the farviewer cameras. Morwen halted before a set of colossal double doors, perhaps fifty feet high. They were made of solid copper, those doors, hammered into interlaced patterns of knotwork and spirals and fantastical animals, and they were unguarded.

"This is the Hall of Heroes," said Morwen, and now her mien was solemn. "Within, you are awaited by the highest in the land. It is no ordeal, but welcome; you are guests here, and you will learn, in days to come, what honor that state carries among us. Are you ready?"

Haruko did not trust himself to speak, but queried each member of his crew with his eyes. He was satisfied with what he saw there. Interest, excitement, a not unacceptable degree of awe and impressed respect, even a faint amusement in the face of the cynic Tindal—but all was well. He took a deep breath and nodded to Morwen, and then in the last remaining seconds he composed his own self, his emotions and his countenance and his *hara*, as the doors swung open into the Hall of Heroes.

The size of the chamber hit him with all the force of a blow. It was bigger than a starship's hangar bay, marble-floored and marble-walled, pillared and cruciform and colossal. Two hundred feet above his head, heraldic banners hung down from the stone ribbing that supported the giant cross-vaults of the ceiling, the armorial devices indistinguishable at that distance, even in the brilliant glow of the crystal sconces set into the walls.

He had little leisure to study the decor. Several thousand people—the rulers both noble and common of seven star systems, the entire royal family, Kelts all—had risen to their feet at the entrance of the visitors from Earth. The courtesy rocked Haruko for an instant, then he recalled the bard Morgan telling them, back beyond the Curtain Wall on Inishgall, that this was Keltic custom when guests entered the hall, no matter how high or noble the host or how low-born the guest.

There was a fanfare salute of trumpets, silvery and sweet, echoing off the marble walls and sounding in the roof, and then, at a tiny nod from Morwen, Haruko began the long, long walk down the green-carpeted aisle.

It was a walk the likes of which Haruko had never before experienced: He would not care to repeat it, and he would not ever forget it, and he dared not think of the effect it must be having on his crew, for if he started worrying about them his own composure would slip its tenuous moorings and that would be that. The whole of the enormous chamber was silent; only the music still sounded, and as he paced down the length of the room, Haruko kept his eyes straight ahead, fixed upon the one person in the Hall of Heroes who had not risen when the doors opened.

Directly behind her captain, O'Reilly was looking around her at every step. Her lips were parted in a half-smile and her eyes were shining, and any Kelt who caught her eye smiled back at her, and everyone who saw her that day remembered her happiness forever.

But for her as for the rest of them, it was the occupant of the great carved-stone throne that commanded all attention. Alone of her folk, she remained seated as the Terrans drew near, and as he approached her, Haruko found that he could not look her in the face just yet, could not raise his eyes above the topmost of the seven steps that led up to the throne.

As the procession reached the wide carpeted space between the dais and the first rows of seats, Morwen, Melangell, Cairbre and the other Kelts who had escorted the Terrans from the port turned aside to their own seats, leaving the Terrans to go on alone. As they covered the last little distance, the woman in green slowly and gracefully rose to her feet, timing the movement perfectly, so that she stood and the Terrans halted before her in the same instant.

Haruko, standing forward of the others, bowed deeply in the Japanasian manner, holding the bow for the full ten seconds required for a reigning monarch, then straightened up to look her directly in the face. It was the shock of his life, before which all the other shocks they had met with paled to nothing: He had seen her before, for she was the red-haired girl who had stood upon the bridge of the *Firedrake*.

He had a few minutes' grace to cushion his shock, for the musicians instantly struck up the Federacy's anthem and then went smoothly into the Keltic anthem. But he heard neither, and, if challenged later, could not even have said what it was that the musicians had played.

At the anthems' conclusion, Aeron, by the grace of the gods Ard-rían of Keltia, Empress of the West and Domina Bellorum, inclined her head gravely to the Terrans and seated herself again upon the Throne of Scone. There was a rustling as the rest of the aonach took their own seats, leaving only the Terrans still standing; but Haruko correctly surmised that the Queen would not keep them so long.

Aeron had dressed with care for this first official encounter. She was clad in a long plain tight-fitting gúna of the royal green, her only jewels the two rings she wore always: the big emerald that was the Great Seal of Keltia, and the black and silver Unicorn Seal, personal signet of the Aoibhell monarchs. Her hair was unbound, streaming down over the purple cushions of the throne, except where it was caught back by the curiously fashioned crown that so nearly matched it in color and gleam: the ancient Copper Crown of Keltia. The crown's origins were lost in myth: Some loremasters held that it had been brought from Ireland by St. Brendan's mother in the first great immram, while others said it was older by far, that it had been forged in Atlantis by Gavida, Smith of the Gods. But whatever the truth of its making, the Copper Crown held the soul of the Kelts within it, and no monarch ever placed it lightly upon his brow.

"I welcome you to Keltia, friends from Earth," said Aeron.

Haruko bowed again, less deeply and more briefly than before.

"Your Majesty's welcome is more than welcome to us," he replied, blessing O'Reilly for all those language tapes she had stuffed into his head, for the Queen had, of course, spoken to them in the formal speech, the High Gaeloch. But the diplomatic platitude had rippled off his tongue before he could think about it. The truth was that he was still totally confounded at seeing her, and he knew she knew it, and she gave him a smile that echoed that knowledge.

"You at least I know already, Captain Haruko," she said. "Though I fear I have yet to make the acquaintance of your companions."

Steadied at once by this graceful reminder, Haruko threw her a glance of thanks and turned to present the others to her. They, of course, had not been aboard the *Firedrake*; he had not mentioned the enigmatic red-haired woman to them, and they had been more than a little puzzled by both their captain's astonishment and the Keltic Queen's words. Aeron, however, had a courteous speech and a smile for each Terran, and won O'Reilly completely by greeting her as a distant kinswoman. Then the Queen rose, descended the steps, and began to present the Kelts to the Terrans.

It had been decided in Council, in the interests of time and confusion, and in the face of the probable fatigue, emotional as well as physical, of the Terrans, that Aeron would present at the aonach only the immediate members of the royal family, the members of the High Council, and the heads of the three houses of government—still a daunting number of new faces for strangers to deal with. As she moved down the front rows of chairs, she could see the Terrans making visible efforts to memorize everything, and she smiled inwardly. *I shall like these folk,* she thought.

Haruko's fleeting impression was of a lot of very tall and very attractive people, all of whom were much more richly and impressively clad than their Queen, who had obviously opted for understatement. Of all the Terrans, Haruko was the only one accustomed to formal diplomatic presentations, though not many of his experience had been quite so grand as this one, and by rights he should have been the first to recover his self-possession. But he was just as bedazzled as the diplomatic novice O'Reilly . . . In all the bewilderment of strange faces and stranger names, two images stood out clear and vivid in his mind's eye: the calm blonde beauty of Morwen Lochcarron, and the enigmatic bearded countenance of Gwydion Prince of Dôn . . .

With a start, Haruko realized that Aeron was speaking again, and he had missed most of what she had said. One does not ask enthroned sovereigns to repeat themselves, so when she paused and looked expectantly at him he could only leap boldly and blindly into the breach.

"We are most honored, Your Majesty, by your kindness and that of your people, and may we express the hope that, ah, that our two nations will soon be joined in the bond of friendship and alliance, renewing our kinship from of old." *And Kuan-yin, Mother of Mercy, let that make sense to her. . .*

But Aeron appeared satisfied with the sentiment, and turned to face the hall, lifting her chin a little and standing quite still. That seemed to be the signal for the end of the audience, for everyone immediately stood up and began to talk informally to those in neighboring seats.

For one panic-stricken moment Haruko wondered what on all the earths he was expected to do next, but he need not have worried. Aeron took his arm, surprising him considerably, and, nodding to the others to follow, she led him through a small door set in the wall to the right of the throne-dais.

Looking quickly behind him, Haruko saw his crew following after, escorted by other members of the royal family with an apparent total disregard for precedence, the Councillors and various other Kelts trailing along behind. This sequel had not been discussed in advance; neither Melangell nor Morwen had mentioned it, and Haruko's misgivings returned in force. He was not alone, though, in wondering what the Queen had in mind. Every Kelt in the room was wondering right along with him.

Chapter Nine

Within the presence-chamber adjoining the Hall of Heroes, however, nothing more alarming awaited than a small informal reception ordered by Aeron for the Terrans. Considerably relieved, though perhaps a little annoyed that the Queen had not seen fit to inform them of her plans, her advisors relaxed, and devoted themselves to easing the social tensions of the moment, for Kelts and Terrans alike.

Having spoken briefly and privately to each of her guests, Aeron had singled out Haruko for special attention—he was, after all, the one holding ambassadorial rank, and thus, as a representative of a foreign power, technically her equal—and was now talking to him animatedly in a corner of the room. Language, she was beginning to realize, was indeed going to be a problem, though not in the way she had anticipated.

She had addressed the Terrans from the throne in the High Gaeloch, knowing that her subjects would have resented the use of any other tongue in such a moment; but when first she began to chat informally with the visitors, she did so in word-perfect Englic.

Haruko, however, out of some perverse wish not to be outdone in courtesy, and O'Reilly, whose professional honor was at stake, stubbornly elected to speak to their hosts only in Gaeloch, which they had sleep-studied until their very dreams rang with its cadences; and when on occasion this difficult new acquisition failed them, though they were by far the most proficient of the *Sword*'s crew, they used Latin, which had

131

come to all five Terrans more readily than had the Keltic tongue.

It was rapidly evolving into something of a comic problem, and Aeron finally put a laughing stop to it.

"Of your grace, Captain Haruko," she said, "allow us to be the ones to do battle with the language of the stranger; at least for the time being, and those of us who can. You will grow facile in our tongue sooner than you think. Are we agreed?"

"As Your Majesty wishes," he replied in Englic, bowing. The faintest of pained expressions flickered across Aeron's mobile face and was as swiftly gone.

After the Queen had moved away, Ríoghnach took Haruko by the arm and smiled at him winningly.

"I know your Earth custom," she said. "But did no one instruct you as to how we address our monarchs here?"

Haruko stared, a little discomfited. "Your Highness—I mean, then all that was *true*? We are expected to address the Queen's Majesty as—'Aeron'?" He seemed to have difficulty getting out the unadorned name.

"Not only expected, but encouraged, and assured by law as well as custom. Of course, you may wish to do as we do, and by your courtesy call her 'Lady' or 'Ard-rían.' But, yes, it is surely 'Aeron,' to prince and crofter alike, and no one's feathers are ruffled—least of all Aeron's. It is more pleasant so, don't you think?"

Haruko wasn't quite sure. Any monarchy that tried that sort of thing anyplace else he had ever heard of would not long keep the respectful submission of its subjects. But perhaps the Kelts, though they certainly seemed believers in respect, held no brief for submission.

"It seems very—democratic," he said.

The Queen's sister laughed. "By out-Wall standards I daresay it is," she said. "There is no keeping of great state here to distance the folk from their rulers; that is not our way. The great love and respect the people bear the Ard-rían is the only kind of distancer we care for. But royalty here is otherwise little different from royalty elsewhere. And nor is it our only hereditary profession. Among others, we have hereditary poets and jurisconsults and warriors as well."

"Suppose the hereditary poet can't rhyme to save his life?"

"Most unlikely," said Ríoghnach firmly. "But so long as someone of the name carried on what you might call the family business, no sanction would be taken."

"Sanction?"

"Oh yes, our law provides fine and sanctions for an amazing number of offenses, from insult to murder . . . As you no doubt know, hospitality is a sacred obligation with us, and anyone who transgresses the law of the coire ainsec is subject to a fine. Or if I should take it into my head to insult you, and you could not answer in kind, I would be obliged to pay you a blush-fine—in proportion to your honor-price, of course, which is also set by law. An ambassador's is equal to a king's," she added teasingly.

"Such a law must be hard on your satirists."

"Oh, they are exempt." They both laughed, and Ríoghnach added, "But for the sake of that exemption, they can claim insult from no one. Still, it doesn't seem to blunt their tongues—as you will doubtless learn."

Over in the center of the room, Mikhailova was studying a large three-dimensional construct worked in gold, silver and various jewels. She looked up as she was joined by Melangell and a tall man with red-brown hair and mustache that she vaguely remembered being presented to, one of the Queen's cousins or Council lords or something . . . She smiled shyly at Melangell.

"I'm not very used to this sort of thing," she confided, indicating the room as a whole.

"No more are we," said Melangell. "No, truly; never before have we had such guests. You do very well, Ensign. But I think you have met Prince Rohan?"

Mikhailova blushed; Rohan was the heir-presumptive to the throne, and she should certainly have remembered *him* . . .

"You'll be kind enough to forgive me, Highness," she said. "I haven't got everybody's name and face fixed yet."

"Many times I feel the same way myself," said Rohan with a smile. "You will learn very quickly; look how you have done with our language. The Ard-rían tells me you are an artificer-specialist, most skilled too."

Mikhailova could think of nothing to say in reply to that, so she pointed to the construct instead.

"What is this, my lord?"

"A representation of Keltia. See, this globe is Tara; and here, this marks Caerdroia." He touched an emerald set into a rock-crystal sphere; the crystal itself was etched with the outlines of oceans and continents, and ringed with two flat gold planes representing the Criosanna. "Here you see the other star systems of our realm—the construct is not astronomically accurate for distance, of course, but it is correct for direction and relative size."

Mikhailova, looking at the seven interlocked gold spheres that represented the seven suns of Keltia, felt the reality, and the immensity, of Aeron's kingdom as she had not done before. Then she yawned.

"Your pardon," she stammered, appalled. "I didn't mean to be so rude. I'm just—all of a sudden I am just so *tired*—"

"And no surprise," said Rohan sympathetically. He caught Aeron's eye, where she stood on the other side of the room talking with Tindal and Morwen, and she nodded.

Mikhailova stared. "What—what did you *do*?"

"Did your Captain not tell you? We have some skill as short-range telepaths, and some among us who are trained to it can send their thought lightyears. Any road, it can often save a great deal of time and explanation. I simply suggested the thought to the Queen that you be allowed to go to your rooms and settle in. There will be a ceili tonight—a party— and you will need to rest yourselves for it. See, she is saying as much now to Captain Haruko."

As soon as the double doors shut behind the green-liveried page, O'Reilly ran to the window and jumped on the cushioned seat. Directly below her, as she knelt leaning on the wide sill, were the royal gardens, and beyond the walls of Turusachan all Caerdroia fell away down the mountainside, spread out in the golden afternoon light. Something absolutely enormous to the north and east, which she suddenly realized was the Wolf Gate seen from behind; on the other side, the view glimpsed through the sitting-room windows was over the sea.

O'Reilly roamed around idly. The chambers were elegant without being intimidating—a Keltic commonplace, as she was coming to learn. The furniture was of goldenwood, carved and inlaid; there were tapestries on the walls, a few portraits—ancestors of Aeron's, perhaps, cold of eye and arrogant of mouth—but nothing abstract. Melangell had told them that Keltic art was almost purely representational, running to portraits and landscapes and illuminations. But there were beautiful hand-embroidered oak-leaf borders on the silkwool sheets, and a fur bedspread that had apparently been knitted, or knotted, into a striking diamond pattern, and books bound in leather and enamelwork, and one of the ubiquitous computer-pads beside the bed—and, neatly hung in a big carved wardrobe, all her own things brought down from the *Sword*.

The same feeling of homecoming that she had experienced on Inishgall came over her again, many times stronger, almost buckling her knees with the strength of delight it brought her. What *unbelievable* luck that she had been chosen for this particular exploratory . . . or maybe luck had nothing to do with it? O'Reilly did a little sideways vault and landed full-length on the bed, legs crossed at the ankles and arms flung out to the side. Whatever the diplomatic upshot of all this, she had a feeling that she was going to be very, very happy here.

That night saw Caerdroia aglow with the lights of a thousand festive meetings; on such an auspicious occasion, and with so many visitors in the City, that was not to be wondered at. But chiefest of all, and the most fiercely aspired-to, was the royal ceili given by the Queen for the Terrans. Held in the seldom-used State Apartments, the party was enormous; Aeron had invited only the barest minimum of politically-dictated guests, and had filled the halls instead with the merriest Kelts she could find: nobles and commons alike, poets, artists, bards, warriors, musicians, dancers, and the entire royal family, even the youngest and shyest Aoibhell of all, the Princess Fionnuala.

And most of that family was in a line at the doors to greet their guests . . . the Queen included, noted Haruko with some surprise; he had expected her at least to follow universal royal custom and enter ceremonially once the ball was well under way. But here again the Kelts, or perhaps just Aeron, were a law unto themselves, and Aeron was standing in the middle of the line, smiling and greeting everyone with real warmth and a personal word, passing each guest down the line to her brothers and sisters and cousins and uncles and aunts.

Once he had leisure to look around him, Haruko's breath was taken away by the beauty of the setting: a series of huge airy chambers opening into each other, walled and floored with gold-veined creamy marble, gilt flowerets spangling the arched ceilings. Dull gold hangings of some unfamiliar figured cloth draped floor-to-ceiling windows, some of which led out into a garden pleasaunce with fountains. At one end of the main room was a low dais occupied by apparently indefatigable musicians, and in other rooms long tables were laden with all manner of food and drink. There were easily a thousand people present.

An access of timidity had overcome all the Terrans at first, even the suave Hathaway, but that soon vanished as a Keltic escort attached to each one of them—*out of courtesy, surely*, Haruko thought, and not to spy on them as Tindal so plainly suspected. These escorts, or protectors, or guides, changed several times over the course of the evening, so that never was a Terran left alone, and to all except Tindal their presence was never other than welcome. Haruko found himself on the arm of the Princess Ríoghnach, while across the room her husband, the Duke of Tir-connell, was teaching the shy Mikhailova the steps of an incredibly vigorous Keltic dance.

"Do *you* care to dance, Highness?" asked Haruko gallantly.

Ríoghnach's face flashed into laughter. "That is a most noble offer, my lord Captain," she said. "But I think perhaps you might better enjoy yourself in talk?"

"I would," he confessed with frank gratitude. "There is so much to learn . . . If you could begin by telling me who some of these people are? The bard who instructed us on Inishgall, and your lady cousin, taught us as much as we could remember, but it was all so new, and so confusing—"

"I doubt it not," said Ríoghnach with a smile. "But come,

I think by now you know all my brothers and sisters? And Morwen and Gwydion . . .''

Haruko scanned the room. "*Who* is *that*?"

The Princess's huge dark eyes grew cold. "That's Arianeira," she muttered. Then, recollecting her manners, "The *Princess* Arianeira . . . Gwydion's sister. They were born at the one birth, though you'd not think it to look at them—or to know them. Also she is Aeron's foster-sister—and among us that bond is as sacred as blood-kinship or marriage-kinship."

Haruko was enchanted by the streaming silver-gilt hair, the magnificent figure clad in the white, silver-girdled gown, the moon-paleness of the finely drawn face.

"She's very lovely."

"Oh aye, she's beautiful, right enough—at least on the outside." With the air of one leaving a distasteful subject for a pleasanter, Ríoghnach nodded over to the opposite corner of the room, leaving Haruko intensely curious about Prince Gwydion's lovely sister. "But over there, my grandmother the Dowager Queen Gwyneira, now I shall present you to her—'

O'Reilly giggled to see the staid Haruko dragged off by the dainty black-haired Princess, and drained her third cup of ale.

Her companion smiled down at her: Aeron's cousin Desmond, tall, black-haired, blue-eyed, a Fian general and Elharn's eldest son.

"You enjoy yourself, then, Lieutenant?"

"Oh, I *do*—"

"Glad I am to hear it. Still, I think perhaps not all of your compatriots share your feeling?" He directed her gaze to where Tindal, arms folded, stood leaning against the wall, contemplating the entire assembly in a vaguely offensive manner. Tindal's escort of the moment—Morwen—looked more than a little helpless. As they watched, they saw Tindal speak briefly to her and then wander off alone in the direction of the banquet tables. Morwen, noticing their attention on her, came over to them with some relief.

"I mean no insult, O'Reilly," she remarked, "but is Tindal always so?"

O'Reilly nodded happily and maliciously. "Always."

Over across the room, Arianeira sipped warmed wine from

a silver cup and watched her brother with the eyes of a nesting hawk. Kynon, who attended her, shifted restlessly at her side, but dared not speak.

Arianeira was greatly interested in the Terrans, all of whom had been presented to her over the course of the evening. She had dismissed most of them immediately as unsuitable to her purposes: The captain who led the embassy was too unshakably righteous; the tall black man seemed too perceptive; and the Irishwoman, whom she had at first appraised as the most promising candidate, was all too clearly already too infatuated with the established order—by which Arianeira meant Aeron. That left a pair of possibilities: the rather weedy-looking Tindal, and the small dark woman, Mikhailova. Either would do very well, if Arianeira had been correctly informed: Tindal was science and engineering officer, Mikhailova technical and weapons officer; and there were suitable strategies to be employed with both.

A smile flowed across Arianeira's lovely features. This was an opportunity she had not expected—and one of which she intended to take fullest advantage.

In a pause in the dancing, Aeron withdrew laughing from the last wild reel and retired to a seat, attended by a small group of courtiers. She had dressed for once in full court panoply, and the effect was considerable: Her gown of heavy violet silk was edged with pearls and silver embroidery, and a small crown of amethysts and diamonds held the golden-red hair in thick braided swags. She was set to charm as well, not only the Terran visitors but her own folk also; for she would need all the allies she could muster for her future course. But tonight, at least, everyone seemed intent on nothing more serious than having a merry time, and by and large they were all succeeding. Across the room, she saw her grandmother talking with Douglass Graham and Douglass's brother Wolf. She threaded her way among the throng, swept up her grandmother and went out with her, arm in arm, to the gardens.

The Dowager Queen Gwyneira was a lovely woman still, her charm and intelligence undimmed by the years. The famous violet eyes were pale lilac now; the red hair her royal grandchildren had inherited proved her name—"Whitesnow"—

at last. But the mind and will that had ruled Keltia—and, some said, the Ard-rígh Lasairían—were sharp as ever.

"What is it, child?"

Aeron laughed. "Never could I keep anything from your Majesty—The Terrans, to be sure."

"What of them?"

"That is just my difficulty. I cannot put my swordpoint to it yet, but there is something, something for which they shall be the crux, and I feel too that I can do naught to stop it, or turn it aside."

"Surely no more than what we all must feel, now that we have made contact with Earth again, and great changes are toward? Or, *is* it more?"

"More, I think, and worse." She recounted to her grand-mother the dream she had had, and Gwydion's reaction.

"What does Morwen say?"

Aeron gave a short laugh. "She suggested the taghairm. But she is no sorcerer, and Gwydion forbade me to try."

"I agree with Gwydion. It seems a desperate measure for so early times. Better perhaps to wait."

"Until desperate times are full upon me? By then we might well be at war."

"Nothing seems more probable, Ard-rían," said her grand-mother gently. "And not just for reason of the Terrans' coming. That you know . . . Can you deal with it?"

"I shall have to." Aeron stabbed moodily at a dead leaf that had lodged in a cracked corner of the bench on which they sat. "But upon my soul, when I opened the Curtain Wall to the Terrans, it was not my chiefest thought."

"Three years ago it was your only thought."

Aeron's head came up at that, and she stared at her grand-mother's serene face, green eyes into violet.

"Three years ago I had great cause to be thinking so. Interstellar war has been made for less."

Gwyneira nodded. "True; but you took your own éraic for the deaths of your kin. It was a creagh-rígh, a royal reiving, and you did not take Keltia with you when you went out against the Fomori."

"It seemed the best and only way," said Aeron in a low voice. "Was I wrong, then, grandmother?"

"Not to my mind! I'd have done no different, had I been in your boots, or even but fifty years younger. Nay, child, what you did was fearful, but it was *your* doing. Rest sure in that."

"And now?"

"We must all wait upon the time. You most of all."

"Ah! Waiting is worst. I'd sooner be doing."

Gwyneira laughed and put her arm around her granddaughter's waist. "Now *there* spoke your great-grandmother Aoife . . . let us go back in."

When Aeron had at last bidden good night to her guests, and left hand in hand with Gwydion to walk through the palace corridors back to her own apartments, it was very late, and very quiet in that part of the royal residence, though behind them the ball went on unchecked.

They entered the round bedchamber, where a fire burned on the hearth, and Aeron dismissed the attendants who had been waiting on her retiring.

"Aeronwy, you are sleepwalking," said Gwydion, half teasing, half solicitous.

She smiled. "Then so must you be, else could I not be speaking with you." She pulled off the little crown and tossed it onto the bed. "A long and weary day, Prince of Gwynedd."

"Sit, then."

Aeron obeyed, and he began to unpin the heavy plaits, thick as a spear-haft, unbraiding the knee-length strands with gentle fingers. She relaxed visibly, closing her eyes; her hair was a living extension of herself, as much so as an arm or leg, and sometimes it seemed to those who knew her best that her very nerves lived in the network of red-gold tresses.

"What do you think of our new friends?" she asked after a while.

The silver brush did not alter its steady rhythm upon her hair.

"Early days to say. They seemed well enough, fair-spoken certainly, and I think as wishful of peaceful alliance between our nations as are we." Gwydion ran his hands under the heavy hair and began to massage neck and shoulder muscles stiff with strain. "And there will be more trouble with Straloch, I think."

"Peace between *us* is not the question. It is the Imperium that concerns me most. And as for Gavin, if he goes at such a gait very much longer I shall replace him on the Council. Mac Diarmada of Rannoch would be a good choice . . ." She leaned back against the strong swordsman's hands that pressed against her neck—it felt so good—and veered off at a tangent. "Ari looked lovely tonight, did she not? I have asked her to stay on here as long as she likes, in the palace if she wishes, or perhaps she will go to Llys Dôn. Any road, it may help to make us better friends again."

"What did she say to that?"

Aeron shrugged. "She seemed delighted that I asked."

"But?"

"No buts." She shivered a little, and the hands stopped at once.

"You are chilled—" Gwydion turned away, intending to fetch her robe, but she caught the hem of his tunic.

"Nay, we will be warm enough."

For all his nervous exhaustion, Tindal was not in the least sleepy, and after returning to his rooms from the ceili, he read for a while, then pulled on a robe and went to the window. Located near O'Reilly's in the Rose Tower, his rooms faced east with a view past the Keep and Seren Beirdd, the Star of the Bards, down over the Stonerows to the plain.

He pushed the casement open to the night, and the stillness struck him like a blow. It was so quiet, even for so late an hour; no drone or hum of machinery, Keltic technology was beyond that. From far below, a voice raised in laughing challenge floated up to him; then silence again. The air was cold and fresh, and the breeze that blew along the Strath carried the pungent smell of burning autumn leaves.

Tindal reflected on the events of the day. No doubt about it, Keltia was an impressive place, and it had an impressive ruler. But the person who stood foremost in his thoughts was a lady he had not met until the evening had been well advanced. She had smiled at him, beckoning him over, and had herself introduced to him—the Princess Arianeira of Gwynedd, sister to the formidable Gwydion.

A smile on his face, Tindal returned to bed, as inexplicably happy as O'Reilly had been earlier that day, though his reasons were rather different. He allowed himself the hope that Queen Aeron would take her time about alliance; the longer the delay, the better it would be for him. He would get something out of this kingdom and this situation if it was the last thing he ever did. And if he could not, he would make such trouble that the whole kingdom would wish he had . . .

He had no way of knowing that Arianeira, alone and equally wakeful in her own rooms, looking out on the same moon-washed middle-night quiet, shared his thought, and, moreover, planned to do all she could to bring that end about.

"Christ," muttered Hathaway, a little daunted. "Isn't anyone here just a humble peasant?"

He and Haruko, on an impulse and for lack of anything required of them to do or anywhere they were required to be, had risen early on the morning after their arrival to take advantage of the freedom of the City that Aeron had conferred upon them, and now, after breakfast, they were making their leisurely way down from Turusachan to the marketing streets and squares of the lower City. They were accompanied at a respectful and discreet distance by two Fians, two lords of the royal household, and two of Aeron's personal pages.

Haruko knew very well what his officer meant. Even the babies carried themselves like princes, and as for the princes— *not to mention the Queen*, he thought, *whom we won't mention*—well, they carried themselves more like your minor gods. Yet no one was arrogant or condescending; on the contrary, as aboard the *Firedrake*, Haruko was aware only of an open, warm, exquisitely polite interest in himself and his companion as people first, Earth people second, and he felt it from every Kelt they met: kilted warriors, merchants wearing rich figured cloaks fringed with gold, ladies tall as spears and graceful as osiers, fearless children who spoke to them frankly and unselfconsciously.

The other thing that impressed Haruko most vividly, as it had Tindal some six hours earlier, was how quiet it all was.

Even in daytime, in the stone streets of this fortress-city, capital of seven star systems, the stillness was incredible. It had a curious quality all its own, making both Terrans feel oddly elated, as if a great joy were dancing somewhere in the air, just out of reach of their senses.

Hathaway was eager to purchase something, anything, and Melangell had recommended a visit to a certain shop in the Street of the Metalworkers, in the craftsmen's quarter that spread out around the Market Square.

"You can't send it home, you know," Haruko pointed out, as they emerged from the little shop after a half-hour during which not only had the jewelsmith refused to accept payment, claiming the not inconsiderable honor of being the first to serve the Terrans, but had introduced them to his sons and drunk a welcome-cup with them besides.

"Then I'll wear it myself." Hathaway affixed the silver and enamel brooch to his uniform breast, noting with a start an ancient painted sign hanging outside another tiny shop: LICENSED TO SELL WEASELS AND JADE EARRINGS. Having no need of either commodity, they spent another pleasant couple of hours in the huge Market Square and the nearby public gardens, then began to stroll back up the stepped streets to the palace.

Halfway there, Hathaway surprised a strange look on his captain's face.

"What's the matter?"

Haruko smiled, a little embarrassed. "I've never before known anyone personally who had her picture on coins."

Delighted, Hathaway immediately dug into his belt-pouch, coming up with a handful of Keltic coinage which the palace rechtair had given them in exchange for their own trading currency—a needless courtesy, since so far no one had allowed them to pay for a thing. About half the coins—small gold crossics, large silver coroins—bore Aeron's crowned likeness, full-face, not profile; recognizably herself, but imperious, and very cold. They examined the other coins curiously. The bearded, kind-eyed man of middle age was Aeron's father and immediate predecessor, the late and genuinely lamented Fionnbarr; while, on the more worn coins, the considerably older-looking individual was apparently Lasairían,

Gwyneira's husband, and the woman wearing a flowing veil and wimple beneath her crown could only be Aoife, Aeron's redoubtable great-grandmother.

"I see what you mean," remarked Hathaway at length. He stuffed the coins back into the pouch. "Sir," he said hesitantly, "everything *is* all right? I mean, with the mission and all?"

"Why do you ask, Warren?" Haruko, very much aware of the Kelts a few paces behind them, was praying that their Englic was on a par with the Terrans' skill-sketchy Gaeloch.

"I don't know," said Hathaway after a troubled pause. "Just this—this *feeling* I have."

"Only what we all feel," said Haruko, unknowingly echoing Gwyneira's reassurances to Aeron. "That it's all so new, so unexpected . . . It'll get better." His voice trailed off into uncertain silence as they passed through the gate-arch of the palace, and he glanced up, almost guiltily, to where he knew the royal apartments to be located. He wasn't about to admit to his officer that he felt every bit as unsure as Hathaway did; but he wondered suddenly if, just possibly, the Queen of Kelts felt the tiniest bit the same.

Chapter Ten

Sunlight streaming through the round windows made white glowing pools on the walls of the Painted Chamber. In the Imperial capital of Escal-dun, the day promised to be exquisitely hot, more so even than usual, all under a cloudless sky as blue as milk.

Around the long stone table in the cool center of the room were assembled perhaps forty people, men and women of a dozen different races from a score of different stars. All had made the long journey to Alphor and the Painted Chamber at the behest of the Cabiri Emperor.

To some, Strephon's invitation was an order, and they had had neither choice nor inclination to do anything but obey. To others, it was a suggestion carrying all the force of command, and to others still, a courteously worded request sent through proper diplomatic channels. But all Strephon's guests shared without reservation a consuming curiosity as to the message they had been summoned to hear.

Most of them, however, had a pretty shrewd idea of the nature of what was afoot, if not the identity of the target, and that went far toward explaining the presence of so many out-of-uniform generals and starfleet commanders—though their untranslatable military bearing gave the game away.

Whatever Jaun Akhera thought, it did not show on his face as he entered the room. He was immaculate in white linen, intricately pleated and belted at the waist; a flat wide collar of beaten gold partly covered his chest, half-bared by the open

145

jacket, and his black hair was held off his face by a thin gold band.

A very gratifying turnout, he thought, *however wary its constituents* . . . At one and the same table sat, among others, the kings of Shoke, Felire, Dhanas and Thelen; the queens of Bor and Jalchi; and, surprisingly, the war-leader of the Yamazai, that matriarchy of warrior-women that held half a galactic sector under its sway. The remaining seats at the table were occupied by minor kings, Imperial and Phalanx vassal lords, and Jaun Akhera's own people, including his brother Sanchoniathon and his captain-general Hanno.

But best of all was the presence, at the opposite end of the table, of the newly elected Archon of the Phalanx worlds: Bres, King of Fomor. He was flanked by his heir, the Crown Prince Elathan, and Talorcan, his firstborn by his legal concubine, and he looked to be in no mood for social backchat.

It was Jaun Akhera's moment, and he savored it to the fullest; then he seated himself in the white marble chair with the eagle's-head arms and turned a dazzling smile on his guests.

"Princes all," he began in an easy voice, "doubtless your various spies have already given you a good idea as to why this council has been summoned. Therefore I shall waste neither your time nor my own. His Imperial Majesty the Cabiri Emperor, long may he reign, has seen fit to initiate a state of war against the kingdom of Keltia. My beloved grandsire sees fit, further, to make me his general-in-chief against the Kelts. I assure you my plans are well under way for the commencement of hostilities, and I invite you now to join with me in this endeavor."

He allowed the murmur of comment, astonished or knowing as was the case, to continue a while, calculating from under half-hooded lids the true level of consternation. *It was like watching a riverhawk in a school of sunmice*, he thought, amused, even while another part of his brain was busily assessing the room: who stood with him, who against; who could be swayed and who would remain aloof to the end; all the eddies of power and fortune, the undercurrents and overtones of the prospect of war.

"An invasion of Keltia," the king of Felire mused aloud,

stroking the beard that came, four-forked and plaited, to the center of his chest. "That one will be a hard seed to crack."

"I agree," said Jaun Akhera evenly. "That is why I have arranged that the main cracking shall be done from within." Swiftly he outlined the plans that had been made with Arianeira and Kynon, though the Princess's identity was not disclosed. Not even Strephon yet knew who the high-placed Keltic traitor was to be . . .

His revelations changed some minds, but not enough, and not the one mind Jaun Akhera most wanted changed: Down the length of the stone table, Bres remained silent and would not even lift his eyes to meet Jaun Akhera's.

But it was Bres's own heir who, all unwitting, gave the Emperor's grandson the opening he needed.

"We have lived in a state of armed truce with Keltia for many years," began the Fomorian prince. "Or, at least, we have done so for the most part," he corrected himself, flushing and glancing at his father. "Why now does the Cabiri Emperor choose war?"

"The Queen of Kelts is on the point of making alliance with Terra," replied Jaun Akhera in a matter-of-fact tone. "I need not describe to this company how extremely undesirable such an alliance would be from our point of view. It was the Emperor's perception that now, before they are joined together and so grow too strong for any of us, now is the time to strike—at Keltia first, then, if necessary, at Terra also. The Keltic Protectorates, too, give us good reason to attack: Over the past hundred years they have grown from nine star systems outside the Keltic Curtain Wall to forty-two. Not many, you may think. But in the three years of Aeron Aoibhell's reign, the status of protectorate has been granted to nearly as many systems again, bringing the total to seventy-eight—some with many planets and settled moons, some critically important in trade, or of military value because of their galactic locations."

The queen of Bor let out a long impressed breath. "If they continue to expand at such a rate—"

Jaun Akhera smiled. "Exactly, madam. The Emperor, as I have said, perceives this danger, and I have been ordered to act on it. Keltia—"

"A kingdom of vipers ruled by a headstrong child!" The outburst came from Bres.

Jaun Akhera raised an eyebrow, but said merely, "Aeron Aoibhell is hardly a child. Though she is also not, it would appear, the sweetest-tempered monarch in the galaxy. No doubt you would know that far better than I."

A sudden intake of breath went round at the table at this unsubtle reminder of Bres's ambush at Bellator and its aftermath. But Bres was hot on his own trail and did not appear to take Jaun Akhera's meaning.

"A willful obstreperous brat! When Fionnbarr died she was only just old enough to hold her throne unregented. But they're *all* children! That damned logician Morwen Douglas, and that thrice-damned sorcerer Gwydion—and they're all related to each other!" He stood up, face black with rage. "If we do not get the life of these worms chirted out of them, the reproach of it will stick upon us forever. No more! Emperor's heir, Fomor stands with you in this quarrel."

Jaun Akhera's face reflected only sober approval, but he was screaming with laughter within. Aeron Aoibhell! So that red-haired harpy was the pin to winkle Bres out of his obdurate isolationism; even if the rest of the Phalanx refused to follow its Archon into vendetta, Fomor alone could shoulder a good part of the military burden—and expense—of the coming campaign. *I must remember to thank you, Aeron, when we meet*, he thought, *for you have done what I could not have done without your help . . .*

"The Imperium thanks the King of Fomor for such a promise," he said. "But what do the others say? Panthissera, War Leader of the Yamazai, what is your people's will?"

A few seats away on Jaun Akhera's right, the black-haired woman with the slanting eyes and the crescent-moon tattoo upon her forehead looked up. Her dark eyes were cold with contempt.

"We fight as pleases us best, and when," said Panthissera. "Neither to Bres's grudge nor Strephon's order; but three times never so against any woman. No, lord, we will draw no sword against Aeron Aoibhell."

"But you will not hinder us who do?" That was Talorcan, leaning forward intent on her answer.

"No," said the Yamazai heavily. "We do not approve, and we will not help; but neither will we hinder, and that word I shall take back with me to Aojun."

After several hours' discussion, the patterns were clearly set, and Jaun Akhera called for a final tally. One by one, those at the table rose and avowed their support, or else respectfully gave their reasons for refusing. In the end, Jaun Akhera came off not so badly: He had had no real expectations of the Phalanx lords, save for Bres, and so he could not be disappointed by their all but universal declining of his invitation. After all the hours of talk, still only Bres had declared for the Imperium; and he could only try to persuade his fellow monarchs, not command them. But several of the small independent allies were swayed by Fomor's public espousal of the Imperial cause, and sided with Jaun Akhera, motivated chiefly, for all their rhetoric, by the hope of picking up a few of the Keltic protectorate worlds, once Keltia was no more.

"But *why*, in the name of all the gods, do you insist on involving the Terrans?" Kynon was angry, and his anger was rooted in fear. If he could not argue Arianeira out of this— "You seem to be as eager as Aeron, lady, to throw yourself into the Terrans' embrace."

They were in Arianeira's gríanan at Llys Dôn, he standing by the hearth, she stretched indolently on a cushioned longchair near the windows. Rain was beating against the glass.

"I *insist*, as you put it, on involving them because it will be to our advantage if we do. You were lamenting only the other day the necessity for using relay ships to communicate with Jaun Akhera. The Terrans have goleor of combanks aboard their ship; if we could use those to make our next contact, it would be both easier and safer for us. Their booster gear can hide all trace of any signal we send, which your equipment, good as it is, cannot. Also, if by some ill chance the signal is intercepted, we shall have someone else upon whom the blame would fall."

Kynon scowled. That was clever thinking on Arianeira's part, and perhaps that was not such a good thing—though certainly she had a point. But this sudden, and alarming, taste for initiative could well bode trouble for the future. Still, her reasons made good sense, and also made life considerably easier for him . . .

"Have you decided on the Terran who might most easily be persuaded?"

Arianeira nodded, twirling the stem of the golden goblet she held. "There are two possibilities, so if we fail in our first attempt we have yet another string to our bow. I have decided to try first with Athwenna." That was Mikhailova; so the Kelts turned her name *Athenée*.

"Why her?"

"Various reasons. Chiefest for that she is the Terrans' technical officer; very suitable to our purposes. And she is shy, as the others are not, and so would be perhaps the more grateful for the friendship of a princess—and the attentions of a Keltic warrior."

Kynon cast his eyes up in exasperation. He had suspected that was coming—Arianeira's finicking distaste for doing any of the spadework herself—and seducing Mikhailova, literally or figuratively, did not accord with the plan he himself had in mind. And doubtless Arianeira knew about that too.

"It is possible," he said at last. "But if she does not prove so grateful as we might wish?"

She shrugged. "Then we try with Tindal," she said. "His skills lie in science and enginery, I am told, and he would be equally useful."

"And, presumably, equally grateful for the attentions of a princess?"

Anger flared on Arianeira's face, then she laughed unwillingly and drank off her wine.

"Aye so . . . if there is need. Did I not say there was little I would not do to rid myself of Aeron Aoibhell?"

"That you did, lady. But how do you plan to start with Athwenna?"

"I do not plan. You will—and you will also do the starting."

The white sun-pools had left the walls and crept down onto the tiled floors by the time Jaun Akhera's business was concluded to his satisfaction and the visitors dismissed with his thanks. Quitting the Painted Chamber, he paced thoughtfully down the gallery to the Imperial family's private quarters, and entered the white-columned stoa.

Strephon seemed not to have stirred from his longchair beside the pool since his grandson had last seen him there—as perhaps he had not. But he greeted Jaun Akhera warmly, gesturing him to sit upon cushions beside the jewel-encrusted chair.

"Went it well?"

"Very well, lord." He explained at length and in detail.

Strephon sighed when his heir had finished, and tossed a breadcrust to the goggling carp in the pool.

"It is done, then. Well, and a good thing too, before Keltia becomes too strong altogether. We have delayed our enterprise nearly a month as it is. As for Fomor, I am not at all surprised that he was so swift to join our venture. He has no moderation, and has long felt the Keltic thorn in his side. He would be easy to sway as a sandwillow."

"The rest of the Phalanx stood like oaks, not willows, and not to our cause."

"No great matter. If we are victorious against the Kelts, we may deal with the Phalanx at our leisure. If we are defeated, it will matter still less, for they shall then deal with us at theirs . . . Though, naturally, I prefer that if anyone is to pick up the shards of an empire, it be my own hand that does the gathering. Keltia itself, and all its Protectorates—now, that would be a gratifying handful."

"I will do what I can, or may, to give it you, lord."

Strephon's water-pale eyes gleamed in the light. "I know that." He dropped a bejeweled hand on his grandson's shoulder, an almost casual touch that could have been either approval or dismissal.

Jaun Akhera chose to take it as both.

Another nightmeal over; at the high table in Mi-Cuarta, where she and the other Terrans now had their regular seats at the high table, not many places away from the Ard-rían, Mikhailova stood up with the rest as Aeron left the table, then sat down again to enjoy the music and dancing that invariably followed the meal.

She wished she were a little bolder, a little less constrained by shyness—it looked like such fun, that dancing, and there were O'Reilly and Hathaway right in the middle of it. But she had always been shy, diffident of putting herself forward; it was one of the reasons she'd gone into the Navy. A certain reserve was a very good thing on a small ship, and she had been able to make a solid asset of a trait that might otherwise have proved a grave disadvantage. It was only at times like this that she wished— Again she looked at the laughing dancers on the floor, and her hand kept time on the table.

"Would you care to join the dance, lady?" said a voice from behind her. "My honor if you would partner me."

She felt the familiar hot and cold rush, then looked up and over her shoulder. "I'm sorry—were you talking to me?"

The man's easy smile flashed down at her. "So I thought! I am called Kynon ap Accolon."

"A pleasure to meet you, my lord. I am Athenée Mikhailova."

"I know . . . doubtless you remember it not, but we met briefly at the Queen's ceili, the night of your arrival. And I am no lord, but only a retainer of the Princess Arianeira of Gwynedd. So, since I am no stranger, Athwenna, will you not dance with me?"

She looked her question.

" 'Athwenna'—you do not care for it? It is but your own name, more or less, in our own tongue. It comes easier to our lips than 'Athenée,' and I think—yes, I think it suits you better."

Mikhailova blushed, and he led her out onto the floor.

Turusachan was not all buildings. Round about three sides of the royal palace spilled a large and lovely park. Formal gardens occupied one end; along the seaward front was a magical garden of herbs and the thirteen types of trees held sacred by the Kelts; and, at the end nearest the royal family's quarters, a ragged and charming little wood that stretched up the side of Eagle, mostly birches and oaks below, pines farther up. Aeron loved the peace and tranquillity of the place, and escaped into it whenever she could, to refresh her mind and ease her soul—though not for long and not often, for she had many more pressing calls upon her time.

O'Reilly had discovered the wood the first week of her residence in the palace, and made frequent use of it for reasons much the same as the Queen's. Like the rest of the *Sword*'s crew, she was finding things a little daunting, being no more accustomed than they to seeing the likenesses of people she knew on coins and seals and scrolls, in the journals and on the farviewers, displayed reverentially in public places and lovingly in private ones. But she had been in Keltia three weeks now, and the strangeness, for her not great to begin with, was wearing off almost by the hour.

Aeron herself was largely to thank for that, O'Reilly acknowledged with grateful wonder, as she sat leaning comfortably against a giant oak-trunk silvery with age and moss. She had given them more of her time and attention and, yes, friendship than anyone had any right to expect; even Theo was surprised, and he was an ambassador, entitled to expect courtesies from queens . . .

"May we join you, or is this private?"

O'Reilly jumped—she had heard no one approach—then looked up to see Melangell smiling down at her. The Princess was accompanied by another young woman, brown-haired, blue-eyed, with fine sharp features and an elegant carriage.

"Of course—have a seat. Both of you."

Melangell settled herself comfortably against the oak, and, after a moment, so did the other newcomer.

"I am sorry we startled you," said Melangell. "But this is my cousin Slaine. Aeron's cousin too, of course; there are rather a lot of us. Slaine, Lieutenant Sarah O'Reilly."

"Just O'Reilly," said that individual hastily.

"Your name in our language would be Sorcha," said Slaine in a crisp pleasant voice. "The names are not translations, but the sound is close enough."

"I should not presume," said O'Reilly with a certain diffidence, "but I do like the sound of it."

Melangell laughed. "Enough, Slaine, you are embarrassing her . . . We have spoke but little together, you and I, since our time on Inishgall. How is it with you, truly?"

"Oh—" O'Reilly's heart filled, and words failed. She spread her hands helplessly, and shook her head, and the face she turned to Melangell was one of shy and shining joy.

The face told Melangell all she needed to know. The three sat for a while without speaking further, listening to the sea far below, the light wind in the oak-leaves, the sounds of early evening drifting up from the palace.

O'Reilly stifled a string of violent sneezes; her damned allergies had tracked her even to Keltia, and she would have to see a medic about it. The quality of the silence was marvelous, and she did not wish to disturb it with sneezes. Then, from the open windows of a nearby tower, a sound so beautiful rose up that she instantly forgot both her sneezing and her self-consciousness. Someone was playing a clarsa, and the clear ringing loveliness floated out over the palace gardens and up the slope to where the women sat. Slow it was, and fair it was, and freighted with that long-familiar lonely longing that O'Reilly knew could never be explained to any who had not already felt it in their own hearts.

So, she thought, *they know that here too. I rather thought they might* . . . ''Tell me about Aeron,'' she said into the silence, when the music had died away at last into a final magical shimmer.

''What would you wish to know?''

''Anything. She is so—so different.''

''Certainly she is that. She was born to be Ard-rían, O'Reilly; ever since her earliest childhood, her education and her training have been geared to that knowledge. The real tragedy is that no one ever expected her to succeed her father so young. She should not, in the ordinary way, have become Queen until she was at least eighty years old. Our average lifespan is longer than you Terrans', and most monarchs are in mid-age, the full flower of their years, at their accessions. But Fionnbarr wed late, and Emer did not conceive for some years. She was exceptionally young when they married, and they delayed— some thought irresponsibly, some thought wisely—in ensuring the direct succession.''

''What kind of training did Aeron have?''

''Everything Fionnbarr and his advisors thought she might someday stand in need of,'' said Slaine. ''Though all those near to the throne are given such training as might befit a possible future monarch. But Aeron had some years first of all at the Ban-draoi schools; then the Fianna training academy, the Bardic Colleges and the Hill of Laws—the brehon school. Then back to the Ban-draoi to finish her magical schooling. Even for a Queen she is well-educated, though as a child she was naturally shy. A princess and future Ard-rían cannot be permitted shyness, so Emer pounded social graces into her. Now, Ríoghnach and Kieran were pests of hell when small, and that is not permitted either.'' She and Melangell exchanged amused glances.

"Who are—does she have many friends? I mean, not royal or noble, but—'' Unaccountably, O'Reilly blushed deeply.

Melangell heard the behind-thought. "She is already very fond of you and Theo both. I have noticed that before now, and I think it very good. Well, she has a great number of folk full eager to claim her as friend—as all rulers must have—but in truth, outside her own family and foster-kin and childhood companions, she is close to relatively few. And those few, you may well imagine, guard that friendship as a treasure and a trust. And nay, by no means are they all noble! Bar Morwen, her closest woman friend is Sabia ní Dálaigh, who met Aeron when they were students at the Ban-draoi school at Scartanore. Sabia's family have been horse-breeders on Erinna, farmers, for longer than the Aoibhells have ruled Keltia. Aeron's black mare, Brónach, was a coronation gift from Sabia, in fact—a magnificent creature, the O Dálaigh raise fine beasts. Aeron is great friends also with several other families, the Drummonds and the Camerons and the O Fortyn— old families, all of them, and courtiers for many generations, but none of them noble. True, most of her High Council is of titled rank, but that is plain politics. Look rather at the Privy Council; save for various Aoibhells and Kerrigans, it is all untitled.''

Emboldened by such candor, O'Reilly dared to press on to satisfy her consuming curiosity.

"She seems to have more of a—personal life than I thought a Queen could manage to have.''

Slaine gave a delicate snort. "Very like! In nothing was *that* more clearly seen than in her marriage with Roderick.''

"How is that?''

"Her parents pushed very hard—and gods, that Emer knew how to push—for a formal religious ceremony, so that Roderick would in the fullness of time become King-Consort. Aeron dug in her heels and refused to contract anything other than a brehon union for the traditional lunar year—perfectly honorable, and dissolvable upon either party's public declaration. Royal heirs often contract such marriages, chiefly for the protection of any issue born of the union. But kings-consort of Keltia are not wedded so, and her parents were ill pleased.''

"But she loved Roderick?"

"That's an odd thing," said Melangell reflectively. "I for one believe she did, and very much. She hero-worshipped him, certainly; he was eight years older than she, and she had known him since her childhood.''

"What was he like?"

"Rhodri? He was Morwen's eldest brother, the Prince of Scots and Chief of the Name of Douglas, a master-bard, a poet and a chaunter; he made songs and poems that will some of them be sung for a thousand years. But—how to say this—he lived almost entirely in the 'here'. He was neither Druid nor Dragon, and, save for that which all bards must learn, magic seemed to play but small part in his life. Aeron is made otherwise, and for that reason I and others have ever thought it was Gwydion who was her true soul's soul, and I think Aeron knew that also. Yet Gwydion and Rhodri were dear friends.''

"But Rhodri—Roderick—died."

"And you have heard, I am sure, what éraic Aeron took as payment from those who wrought his death. But she never spoke his name again, not openly, once the state funerals were done; not unless she has done so to Morwen or Gwydion or Rohan. Certainly no one else has ever heard her speak of him." Melangell fell briefly silent. "Roderick, for all his virtues, was like the rest of us, or the most of us. Gwydion and Aeron, for all their faults, are two of a kind unlike nearly all of us. If they do choose to wed, and I think they shall . . . it will be either triumph or calamity, for the realm as well as for themselves. There is no middle ground for those two.''

Chapter Eleven

Kynon had for two weeks been involved in the whirlwind courtship of Athenée Mikhailova. Arianeira had been correct in her assessment: Once coaxed past her initial reticence, Athenée had been eagerly, almost pathetically, grateful for Kynon's attentions, and had responded to the Kymro's overtures with a sort of half-disbelieving, half-astonished delight.

So Kynon led her the sorry little dance, day after day, night after night. Not, he admitted, that it was in truth so great a hardship; Athwenna was young enough, certainly pretty enough, and hardly stupid or dour either. In fact, over the past fortnight, she had bloomed into real radiance, and had let down her guard to confide in him all sorts of fears and hopes and memories. In spite of himself, he had come to be genuinely fond of her, and at certain moments had felt true regret for the part she was being unwittingly groomed to play in his and Arianeira's schemes. And she came to trust him; so that when at last he touched upon the questions which were for him the object of the exercise, she did not at first understand what he meant.

"Go aboard the *Sword*?" she repeated, as amused as she was amazed by the suggestion. "I'm afraid that's fairly impossible; the ship is in starharbor, even we don't go out to her. Why would you even want to?"

"Only to see it," said Kynon smoothly, covering his annoyance. "After all, it is part of our history now; but more than that, it is part of your life. It is what brought you to Keltia, Athwenna—and to me.'' He kissed the hand he held, one part of his mind coldly noting her blush at the caress. "Any road, I know little about such matters,'' he went on. "Even about your own duties—what *is* it, now, that a technical officer does when she is away from her ship?''

Mikhailova laughed. "Not very much, I'm sorry to say. My main job, as I think I've told you, is artificer—keeping the computers and the other machines aboard ship in good repair. I'm just a sort of fixer-general.''

"You are over-modest about it, I am sure. But during these enforced holidays, do you not keep your hand in at all? You might find our own computers of interest; they are living crystals, and some of them are capable of original thought processes.''

That caught her interest, and she began to speak enthusiastically of the capabilities of Terran computers in general and her own charges on the *Sword* in particular.

"Well,'' said Kynon at last, "glad am I to know that Keltia is not behind the times, for all that she stands so far apart from the out-Wall worlds . . . Have you been in touch with your home, since you came here?''

Mikhailova felt a small, though definite, tug of unease. He had never before paid such pointed attention to her work, had in fact given her instead the distinct impression that he was unversed in technological matters. But if he was, she mused, could it really matter if she answered . . .

"I certainly have not, and I don't think the others have either; though I believe that your Queen has been in communication with our government.'' She took a long swallow of her drink. "Anyway, we'd need help to get through that Curtain Wall with any messages we sent from here.''

"So? But how if you sent them by way of your ship?''

The fire of the usqueba shuddered down inside her. "Oh, that too, probably—do we have to talk about this?''

"Nay, surely not, if you do not wish it. It is only that I know so little, and I am curious. You it is who interest me, Athwenna, you know that; your work only for that it is a part of you. You are weapons officer also, I hear.''

Her unease mushroomed into alarm, and she disengaged

her hand from his, sitting forward, away from the arm that encircled her shoulders; suddenly it seemed more confining than comforting. But he was smiling into her eyes, and she felt herself melting, as happened every time . . .

"Well, not officially, and only because we lost one of our crew in coldsleep." She leaned back again into his arm. "There isn't much call for a weapons officer on an exploratory, but you never know. Even the officer who died, Ensign Gro, had other duties; Tindal took on those—" Mikhailova held out her cup imperiously to be refilled, and Kynon attended to it at once. She knew perfectly well she was becoming dangerously tipsy, but all at once she did not care, and when he persisted in his questions about her work she allowed herself to react with angry annoyance.

"Will you stop asking those things! I've told you before—"

Kynon tilted her face up to his. "Do you not trust me?"

"I—no—I don't know, damn you!" She pulled away from him, tears of panic beginning to glitter in the corners of her eyes. "You're just—different tonight."

"I! Nay, anwyl, no different."

"You are, you are!" She could not say how, exactly—the drink seemed to have made her hyperaware, had given her a sort of heightened telepathy, a psychic radar that was picking up all these nuances she really didn't want to know about . . . "You've never asked me questions like this before—"

"What, because I ask a few questions, you lose all faith in my motives? Silly one, I ask about your work because it is important to you. I have no knowledge of my own concerning such things; all found knowledge is worth having. You first intrigued me for that you were a Terran, an out-worlder, that is true enough; but it has since come to be much more than that. Athwenna—say you not so?"

The charm and force of personality Kynon exerted here was almost irresistible; but Mikhailova, whether it was indeed by grace of telepathy or simply because there was truth in whiskey as well as in wine, was suddenly certain of her disquiet's cause. . .

"No," she said. "No, I do not say so."

Even then he continued trying to persuade her, to gloze over the situation, but when it became plain that she would not, or could not, be placated, he stood up, his expression coldly contemptuous. There was obviously no point in prolonging the charade . . .

"It is your right to say so, of course. But, Athwenna, it appears to me that it is you who have changed, not I. My sorrow that it should be so. But if you trust me so little, after having come so close—well, I will trouble you no more with my attentions. I had not thought you believed them so unfounded—or so unwelcome." He bowed with icy gallantry and was gone.

Alone in the grínan, Mikhailova stared unhappily at the door. Could she really have been mistaken? It had certainly felt to her that she was being used, but— She had driven people away before with her own inner insufficiencies, imagining rebuffs and rejections where none was meant; perhaps she done the same thing here?

After a while, stunned silence gave way to a dull wave of hurt and confusion and embarrassment. Her soul closed up like a clenched fist, and she turned her face away from the door; and presently, without any sound at all, Athenée began to weep.

Having left his grandfather feeding the gluttonous carp, Jaun Akhera passed once more between the guards and headed down the wide corridor that led to his own wing of the palace. As he passed a cloister arch that opened onto a fountain court, a glimpse of color caught his eye. He glanced aside to see Elathan, unattended.

The Prince of Fomor sat in one of the cloister's broad open arches, his back against the curve of the carved spandrel and his attention fixed on the fountain. Plainly he had neither seen nor heard anyone pass by.

Jaun Akhera paused in the cloister entrance, strangely drawn and also strangely diffident. He had few friends, was closest of all to his brother Sanchoniathon, and here was one who was not only his own age but an equal in rank and expectations as well. Still he hesitated to approach, to intrude upon the other's obvious desire for solitude. *Perhaps Sancho would be a more welcome visitor?*

He was spared the decision, for Elathan, growing aware of

the covert scrutiny, had twisted in the window and was now looking straight at him. The Fomori's face was polite, but no more.

"Were you seeking me, lord?" he asked.

Jaun Akhera came forward. "No," he said honestly, "I was not, but I am glad to have found you here." He nodded toward a stone seat in the courtyard, and Elathan, with some reluctance, slid from his seat and followed.

"We had no chance to speak privily in the Painted Chamber," said Jaun Akhera when they were sitting side by side on the bench. A blossoming pear arched its snowy boughs above their heads. "What is Fomor's true thought about this war?"

Elathan shrugged. "You heard the words of Fomor's King."

"I heard Bres's opinion," corrected Jaun Akhera. "I have heard neither what yours is nor what your people's is likely to be."

"My people will do as my father bids them. In any event, they are not over-fond of Keltia, and my father is not the only one in whom the memory of Bellator rankles. I am his heir, and so I support his decision. No more to it than that. Did Strephon send you?" he asked suddenly, turning to fix his companion with unexpectedly direct dark brown eyes.

Jaun Akhera shook his head, spoke with shyness. "No—I only thought . . . perhaps you and I should be better acquainted, for the future if for no other reason."

Elathan's laugh was mirthless. "The future! What is the future your grandfather and my father will bring about between them but more of the past?" He rose, and Jaun Akhera rose with him. "I do not know what protocol obtains between two princes of the blood, but I am a guest here, and very weary, and I would withdraw. Until later, then." He gave Jaun Akhera the nod customarily exchanged between royal equals and left the cloister.

Jaun Akhera sat down again, losing himself in thought and the music of the fountain. Silks stirred behind him like soft wind, and a shower of pear blossoms fell into his lap. He reached out a hand without looking around, and after a moment a slim honey-colored hand slid into his, wrapping long thin jewelled fingers around his own.

"I grow jealous of this Aeron Aoibhell," said Tinao. "Of late she is more in your thoughts than I." Her voice was cool and melodious, with just a touch of reproach, and, far below, annoyance.

He laughed, brushing her hand with his lips, and leaned his head back against her waist as she stood behind the bench.

"Even you, my leopardess, must give place a time now to the She-wolf. But I shall tame her presently."

The beautiful almond eyes grew narrower. "I misdoubt that one will ever make a lapdog. She bites, does she not?"

His smile vanished. "She does indeed," he said shortly. "But I shall blunt her fangs soon enough. Perhaps you would then care to have her as your personal slave?"

She leaned over him, smiling, the blue-black hair rippling as she moved, swinging forward to veil him in two smooth dark wings.

"Whyfor? I have you, do I not?"

He twined his fingers in the thick glossy hair, pulling her head down to him, and did not trouble to answer.

"Is that all you have to tell me?"

"I have said ten times over that the woman will not suit our purposes! Hu mawr! How many times more must I say so?" Kynon, pacing back and forth between windows and fireplace in Arianeira's grían, ran his hand through his hair and threw the room's owner a glance of purest venom. How dared she sit there and look at him so— "Well, I have tried. We were wrong. Now it is your turn, lady."

Arianeira's expression of smiling scorn grew deeper. "And now you shall see how it is that puppets are to be handled . . . I hope for all our sakes, Kynon, that Athwenna speaks not of your wooing—and your questions—to her Captain . . . or to anyone else, for that matter."

He shook his head impatiently. "Nay, she is too timid for that. She thinks herself at fault for that she insulted me by being suspicious, and now she feels a fool. She will not advertise that to her friends."

"Like as not; but we might be wiser to prevent the chance altogether."

Kynon turned sharply to stare at her. "To kill her? I say no!"

She laughed in his face. "Scruples, son of Accolon? Who would have guessed it? —Well, no doubt it would raise more questions than it would silence, if Athwenna were to meet with some accident or other. There would be inquiries, for one thing, and you would certainly have to face a truth-senser—it being known that you have spent time with her." Arianeira's beautiful face hardened. "But, Kynon, let there be no mistake here. If I see or sense that she is about to betray us, she dies, and that is that . . . Any road, it is in my mind that Tindal will serve my designs—our designs—to far better result."

"And if he does not?"

"We are no worse off than before. It will mean only delay and some difficulty, a little risk; the which we had already been prepared to deal with. But I do not think Tindal will prove so delicate of sensibility as your Athwenna."

"You have a plan, then."

Arianeira's lips curved in a smile. "Always."

When the beautifully lettered invitation arrived, delivered to his rooms by a retainer clad in the blue and silver livery of Gwynedd, Tindal was flattered and excited, but not, truth to tell, completely surprised. He had had a feeling that it was only a matter of time before the Princess Arianeira sent for him, and he had been right—as usual; though he was never to know he had been but her second choice.

In the weeks since his arrival in Keltia, Tindal had kept a profile lower even than usual. Except for the command appearance at the royal ceili, he had consistently declined the hundreds of social invitations with which all the Terrans had been inundated. He rather thought, however, that this particular one would be well worth accepting.

"Thank Her Highness for me," he said, on being assured that a verbal reply would be both sufficient and correct. "And tell her that I accept with very great pleasure the honor of her invitation."

On the night appointed, the page returned to Turusachan, to convey Tindal by closed chariot to the Gwyneddan palace.

The high-rent district, thought Tindal, impressed, peering out the coach's windows as the silver and blue chariot rolled silently past exquisite brughs, the town-palaces of some of Keltia's oldest and wealthiest families, each in its own gardens.

Arriving at Llys Dôn, the Court of Dôn, maenor of the Princes of Gwynedd since the City was built, Tindal was flustered to see that a sizable crowd had gathered to watch for him.

"They heard that you would be the Princess's guest this night," explained the page, "and they wished to greet you suitably. It is a very great honor for Gwynedd that you have come," he added shyly.

Tindal nodded, distracted. He had not bargained on the omnipresent public curiosity, did not enjoy it, and would prefer not to have it generally gossiped that he had been Arianeira's guest.

Nothing to do, however, but brazen it out. He stepped down out of the chariot's upholstered innards, smiling and acknowledging the cheers, and disappeared into the palace.

The entire household had assembled in the lower hall, and Tindal found himself being addressed by a white-haired old man with a proud military bearing and a warm smile.

"The greeting of the gods to you, stranger," he said in a surprisingly strong voice. "I am Pendaran, rechtair to the Prince. I welcome you in his name to his house."

"And I add my welcome to Pendaran's," said Arianeira, coming down the sweeping stone staircase. She had taken particular pains over her appearance tonight, and she knew that she was looking her best.

Tindal, bowing deeply to her, took in at one admiring glance the long sinuous line revealed by the clinging blue velvet gúna, set off by wide jewelled bands at her wrists and hips. A sapphire-studded fillet circled her wide forehead, and against it her silver-blonde hair burned like gilt flame.

"Highness."

Arianeira smiled, well pleased by his reaction. "Shall we go up?"

Tindal followed her up the stairs to the Great Hall, noting the luxury all around him: gold-threaded tapestries on the marble walls, light-sconces cast in solid silver, priceless

Kutheran carpets, five hundred years old, strewn on the stone floors. Gwydion's family were apparently not impoverished royalty, whatever else they might be . . .

They entered a huge stone-walled room, its hammerbeam ceiling gilded and painted, arrases covering the ashlar and a fire blazing in the head-high hearth on the far wall.

Arianeira gestured him to the place on her right at the long polished table in front of the fireplace, where gold dishes and goblets were laid out for two.

"Am I to be your only guest, Princess?"

"For dinner, aye," said Arianeira with a dazzling smile "I wished, selfishly, perhaps, to keep the pleasure of your company to myself alone. But afterwards, we may be joined by one I think you will be interested to meet. We shall see." She nodded to an attendant to begin serving, and from a gallery high overhead came the music of a telyn, the little lap harp of the Gwynedd mountains.

Arianeira's purpose was to intrigue as well as to captivate, and soon she and Tindal were in animated conversation over the lavish meal.

"We have not visited Earth for a very long time," she said in answer to one of his questions—a question Tindal had in fact asked numerous times before, all in vain. "Not since your years of the twentieth century, when your folk first developed instruments that could detect our presence and craft that could pursue us in air. Therefore we know almost nothing of your recent history . . . But even before that, it was dangerous to go back, and unpleasant; though we were by no means the only ones who did so."

"Why go back at all, then?" Tindal held out his goblet to be refilled.

Arianeira had dismissed the servitors and was pouring the wine herself.

"At first, only to make sure the way out was still there, for folk to find who could; and to take away with us those who made contact. After that, we returned at long intervals only for ideas—some were good ideas, others less good—and we took the good ones back with us, things like thoroughbred horses or the principles of symphonic music. We stole a great deal from you before our voyages ceased, I am sorry to say."

"That is all you thought worth the taking?" Tindal, by no means a planetary chauvinist, was nevertheless obscurely insulted on Earth's behalf: Surely there was much more worth stealing from Terra than horses and music. "Not electricity or atomic theory or medicine or philosophy?"

Before she replied, Arianeira rose from the table. "If you have no objections, Lieutenant, perhaps we might withdraw to my grianan? It is rather more comfortable than this great barn of a room."

As they walked down the corridors of the Llys, she returned to his unanswered question.

"Well, you forget, we share your own heritage of Greek and Roman classical thought, and we built our own philosophical edifices on the same foundation, even as did you. Why trouble, then, to take your later philosophies? Yours has grown with Terra as ours has grown with Keltia. As for medicine, most Kelts can heal themselves of minor things, small fevers and illnesses, and our trained healers can often cure by what you seem to consider magical means. Our science does not operate according to the laws of accepted electrical theory, as you, a scientist, have surely noticed; and atomic power is to us, as it is to most interstellar civilizations, an unnecessary and dangerous crudeness. For us, magic is the way."

"Magic," said Tindal gloomily, settling himself in a comfortable chair in Arianeira's grianan. "Yes, I was forgetting magic."

"In our midst, you would do well not to forget it. We have sorcerers among us of such might that if they wished it so, this planet could be blown to powder beneath our feet. The measure of their control is that the planet remains; those who wield that kind of power have also a system of checks and reins upon that power you cannot begin to imagine."

"Those reins did not halt Aeron, one time I have heard tell of."

She looked up, half-frowning; his tone had been bland, but his eyes sparkled with malice.

"Aye so, though she paid dearly for her lapse—she is perhaps something soft-hearted for a High Queen."

"What about wars? I'm sure I give away no state secrets

when I say that war seems to be a major preoccupation of quite a few people just about now.''

''That does not surprise me,'' said Arianeira. ''And yes, we have certainly had wars, civil wars as well as out-Wall conflicts. We are less remote than Earth from other civilizations, though still well off the main trade routes. But for the past fifteen hundred years we have had the protection of the Curtain Wall—though I, for one, have ever thought the Wall was more to keep us in than to keep you others out. Nay, we have had our full share of conflict, and doubtless we shall have other conflicts in time to come. Perhaps sooner than any of us think.''

Tindal leaned back in his chair, suddenly sure. ''We seem to understand each other very well, Princess. May I speak freely?''

''Of course. Was that not why I asked you to come, and why you chose to accept? We are much alike, Tindal. I perceived that the first night, at the ceili; why else do you think I have stayed all these weeks at Caerdroia?'' She filled a silver quaich with usqueba and passed it to him. ''You were, even then, looking to find a way to make Keltia do something for your personal benefit, not so?''

He smiled, a little twistedly. ''You are indeed perceptive as well as lovely. Was I just being incredibly obvious, or are you simply an uncommonly good telepath?''

''Obvious only to one whose thoughts tended in the same direction—but I have proved before now that I can conceal my thoughts even from Aeron and my own brother, and they are two uncommon telepaths indeed . . . You have naught to fear, and much to gain, if you throw in with me.''

''How may this be?''

She took a deep breath. Now they had come to it. ''I have your word of secrecy? I could, of course, use my art to compel you to silence, but I think you might prefer to arrange your own censorship.''

''Quite. Well, you have my word, then.''

Arianeira smiled, as much with relief as with excitement. ''Kynon, you may enter now.''

The hangings were pushed aside, and a man came in. In his

hand he carried a telyn, and he rippled a little chord on it as he bowed first to Arianeira, then to Tindal.

"Lady, lord, your servant." He dropped into a chair without waiting for the Princess's permission, and grinned knowingly at Tindal. "I have heard much of you, Terran."

"Then you have the advantage of me, sir," said Tindal coolly, and Arianeira laughed.

"Peace here! You are two who must be friends if our plan is to work to all our good . . . Lieutenant, I present to you Kynon ap Accolon, of Ruabon on my home planet of Gwynedd. He can tell you best of the plan that we have made."

Kynon, leaning forward, took the silver quaich from Tindal, and, holding it between his hands, all trace of levity gone now, trained his dark glance on the Terran and began to talk.

"But how can you be so sure of Jaun Akhera?" asked Tindal. They had been discussing Kynon's plan for two hours now, and this was the point to which they kept returning. "Or is there actually honor among thieves? Or among traitors and would-be regicides, as the case may be."

Arianeira flushed angrily. "Call me what names you please, Terran, but my bargains are not lightly broken, and no more are the Prince of Alphor's. Here, they will not be broken at all. There will be no betrayal here."

"Only Aeron's." Tindal drummed his fingers on the side of the empty quaich. "I am in it," he said with sudden decision.

Beneath the fillet's sapphires, Arianeira's eyes blazed with equal blue brilliance.

"You will? Oh, Tindal, you will not rue the bargain, and we need you sorely."

Tindal looked once into those eyes and could not look away again. From a very great distance he heard Kynon's voice, slow with amused scorn.

"The Princess means, Lieutenant, that your help will make things a great deal simpler for us. As science officer, you have access to your ship's combanks and computers and power sources. If you assist us, we can use that equipment to transmit to Jaun Akhera."

"You've transmitted to him before," said Tindal, his eyes

still on Arianeira. "Aren't your own facilities better and more extensive than the ship's?"

"They are good enough, for illicit equipment, and I have transmitted to him more than once. But always through a relay ship hookup: inefficient, and very dangerous, but the best I could manage. Now we need to contact Jaun Akhera one more time only: to fix the time and place of the invasion. You can imagine we wish to take no chances with *that* message . . . It will be harder to intercept, and impossible to trace, if you send it for us, by way of the *Sword*. You can do this?" Kynon shot the question at him, and Tindal blinked.

"Yes—yes, of course, nothing easier, really."

"And you *will* do this?" murmured Arianeira, in a voice like slow honey. Her eyes seemed to Tindal to be growing larger, silver-blue mountain pools where the ice had frozen clear as crystal, the moving water plain beneath the surface. Tindal was falling into those pools, numbed by the cold and frozen by her beauty. . .

He did not notice that Kynon had left them, only that Arianeira had twined her arms around his neck, was leading him to a curtained recess, warm and firelit and richly hung with silken curtains over a wide soft bed.

In the morning she was gone, the silkwool sheets cold with her absence, the fur coverlets rumpled as she had left them. Servitors with carefully expressionless faces came to help him bathe and dress, then served him breakfast and conveyed him back to Turusachan in the same chariot in which he had ridden the night before. It was all so remote and weird now, a dream of too much usqueba compounded with his own fantasies.

That afternoon, a royal page with Aeron's badge sewn to his tunic breast knocked on Tindal's door.

"From the Princess Arianeira, lord."

After the page had gone, Tindal opened the blue leather box with the Gwynedd arms stamped in gold on the lid. It had been no dream, then . . .

Pinned to the box's white velvet lining was a silver cloak brooch, shaped like a sword.

Chapter Twelve

*T*he King of Fomor and his only legitimate son had fought all the way from Alphor back to their homeworld. Starship crewmen from commanders to cadets had kept well clear of the cabin on the bridge deck where their royal family was engaged in such wrathful disputation, and now that the ship's shuttle had landed, that contention was being carried undiminished into the palace itself.

Guards flattened themselves against the walls as Bres stormed into the family quarters with Elathan only a few steps behind him. The King's face was all lowering brow and blazing eye, his heir's scarcely less full of furious passion.

"Enough!" roared Bres. "My heir you may be—though at this moment, by all the gods, I'd alter *that* if I could—but you are not yet master here! I have heard your arguments, and I find them unacceptable and insupportable. Were you twenty times my son, I would yet think this sudden desire for peace with Keltia the thought of a coward, and a treasonous coward at that!"

Elathan's own anger blazed higher still. "Lord and Father—"

"Leave us! No, *I* shall leave—I have matters of state to discuss, and I would do so with those who are still loyal to their King and servant to his wishes!"

With a straight-armed shove he flung the doors wide, nearly knocking over the lady who stood on the other side of them, and without another word passed from the room.

Basilea the Queen recovered her balance and stared fearfully after her husband, then cast a reproachful mute look at her son and hurried out into the corridor, leaving Elathan balked and furious.

In the Queen's train, a sweet-faced lady, very dark of hair and very fair of skin, had curtsied with the others as Bres strode past. She remained dipped until Elathan, turning and seeing the bowed head, raised her and drew apart with her.

Wide blue flower-petal eyes, dark now with alarm and loving concern, sought his face.

"What is Keltia to your father, my lord, that it should sow such anger between you?" Camissa of Broighter, for all her long experience at Court, was shaken enough to forget royal protocol, addressing her betrothed before he addressed her.

Elathan, who cared little enough for protocol and still less for its practice in private, sighed wearily and put his arm around the delicate shoulders.

"You may well ask, beloved."

Mindful of the glances—most approving, some envious— cast their way by the Queen's ladies, Camissa led him out onto the wide terrace that overlooked the city of Tory a thousand feet below.

"Do you wish to speak of it?" she murmured, leaning her head against his shoulder.

As ever when he was with her, Elathan felt his tensions lessening, the adrenalin murderousness he had felt against his own father ebbing away to be replaced by something like tired peace. He buried his face in the masses of flower-scented hair, his dark blond head the more golden by contrast to its shadows.

"I have *no* wish to speak of it," he said. "But it is a thing you must hear, and I had rather you heard it from me than some other." Briefly he recounted the events on Alphor, and the history of the Fomor-Keltia feud, and Camissa listened with growing horror.

"And such," he concluded bitterly, "is the family grudge into which you shall be marrying, and why my father now allies with Strephon, a man he hates, against the Kelts, whom he hates still more."

"But that is a terrible thing! I remember Bellator, of course," she said, her voice faltering a little. "Who among our people does not . . . but I had not known the rest of it—your father's long quarrel with Queen Aeron's father. Surely equal wrong has been done on both sides—cannot she and my lord Bres let it rest there?''

"You would think so, wouldn't you. And Aeron well might, from all that I have heard. It seems she was as sickened by Bellator, in the end, as any of us— Yes, Aeron well might. And I certainly would. But I am not King here.''

"At least, not yet, my brother.'' Enjoying the effect of a perfect cue, Talorcan stood in the doorway. "Leave us, lady,'' he added, not looking at Camissa.

Elathan nodded, and only then did she move to obey, drawing in her silk skirts as she passed Talorcan, as if she feared to sully them by brushing against him. She turned in the door to drop a deep respectful curtsy to Elathan, gave Talorcan an unsmiling two-second stare, and was gone.

Talorcan grinned and came forward to lounge by the parapet in a low marble seat.

"Your so charming betrothed seems to stand in need of further instruction in Court manners. I am, after all, demiroyal, and the next male heir of line after yourself.''

"The Princess Rauni precedes you in the line of succession,'' said Elathan with some heat, "and as for the Lady Camissa—''

"—who will be the Crown Princess Camissa by year's end . . . and in the fullness of time should become Queen Camissa. I hope, Elathan, that by then she will have altered her bearing towards me, and have come to love me as a brother.''

"Then see to it you bear yourself to her like one!'' snapped Elathan. "No brother looks so at his sister-to-be.''

Talorcan laughed, not offended. "Never fear, I have no designs on your little ladyship. She'll make a most decorative Princess. But enough talk of women, I would far liefer hear your thought on Bres's plan for alliance with the Imperium and the war with Keltia.''

"I thought you wearied of talk of women,'' said Elathan pettishly. "If we speak of Keltia, we must speak of Aeron Aoibhell.''

"Oh, that one. She is a royal ruffian, and I am not surprised by what I hear about her.'' He stretched his legs out in front of him, admiring the slashed and jeweled leather of his boot-tops. "No, what *does* surprise me is you, brother. I listened to you most of the way from Alphor, and I confess I am still confounded. This sudden longing of yours to hold out a hand to Keltia—a hand without a sword in it—seems greatly to displease the King our father . . . and to be something out of character for you as well."

Elathan studied his half-brother, seeing the traces of their mutual sire in the lines of mouth and chin, though Talorcan's dark hair and light eyes were rather a legacy from the Lady Thona, Bres's legal concubine since before his marriage to Elathan's mother, Basilea, and so Talorcan was a year the legitimate prince's senior.

"You know perhaps not so much of what is either in or out of my character as you seem to think," he said at last. "I fear that my father will not rest until he has made the scars of yesterday to be tomorrow's bleeding wounds. By the time I *am* King here, there will be no smallest hope of peace—the Kelts will have hated us too much and too long for it."

"And Aeron?"

Elathan's laugh was short and bitter. "Aeron! If she does not slay my father in combat, or he her— I could have been her friend, Talorcan, and she mine; I know that she would have been full willing to call halt to this madness if—" He gave his half-brother a twisted smile. "Do you know, the Kelts even gave us our name? They called us Fomori with such insistence over the past three thousand years that we took the name for our own . . . No, of course I shall support my father. I shall ride beside him in battle and stand beside him in council—and that is all that you, or he, or anyone else, need be concerned with. What I may or may not feel about the matter—that, son of Thona, is a matter for myself alone."

"For the present," said Talorcan.

He did not look round as Elathan went back into the palace, but turned in his seat to lean his chin on the parapet and look down over the city.

"For the present," he repeated, smiling. "But, my royal brother, I shall not forget it for the future."

* * *

"Are there no temples here?" asked Haruko one morning.

"Temples?" said Morwen, puzzled.

"Churches, holy places. For formal public worship?"

"Oh, you mean the nemetons. You have seen pictures of them, I am sure—they are great stone circles, located all over Keltia in the sacred places."

"Could I go there, do you think? I'd like to meditate in some place a little more conducive to it than Turusachan."

"Anyone may go to the stones at any time, of course, for any reason or no reason. The chief nemeton is on Mount Keltia, the Holy Mountain, where almost nobody ever feels brave enough to go. Aeron went, one time, before her coronation—all our kings and queens must do so, before they may be crowned—but even she was terrified. That circle is called Caer-na-gael, and is the place of most awe in all our worlds." She eyed him with some amusement. "It is said that if you pass a night there and survive, by sunrise you will be either a poet or a madman . . . though I think myself there is little differ."

"Ah. Well, perhaps some other time—"

"Nay, nay," she said laughing, "there is a circle much closer to hand, and far less perilous, though still of course very holy: Ni-Maen, the personal nemeton of the royal house. It is up on the mountain behind Turusachan, along the Way of Souls. There it is that all the sainings and handfastings and passing rites of the House of Aoibhell are held. There all our dead rulers are barrowed, and there it is also that Aeron leads the services, on the eight hallowdays of our faith."

"She does? Why not Ffaleira or Teilo?"

"The sovereign is also our Chief Priest or Priestess; it has been so with us ever since the days of Brendan. Some monarchs make more of their sacred duties than others: The Ard-rígh Fionnbarr cared but little for it, and did only what the law required, while the Ard-rían Keina, of my own Clann Douglas, has been venerated as a saint these thousand years."

"You have monasteries of Druids, I am told, and convents of the Ban-draoi. Is it they who take care of the poor, do works of charity and such?"

Morwen looked sideways at him, startled. "Poor! What poor?"

"Well, surely everyone in Keltia can't be as—comfortable as the folk here in the palace?"

"Nay, you are right there, some families are certainly wealthier than the Aoibhells, or even the Douglases." She laughed outright at the look on his face. "Forgive me, Theo, I know what you wish to learn. Well, we have no poor. The brehon laws are so structured that if any poverty or want or lack occurs under any lord's jurisdiction, and that lord does not alleviate it, he—or she—is held personally liable; subject to a fine, and loss of honor-price too. It is so instinctive a thing with us that we seldom think of it; it works of itself."

Haruko said slowly, "You mean you have—no poor people."

"Not one, in the sense you mean. All Kelts, from the highest rank to the lowest, have their basic needs assured by law: food, shelter, employment and the like. Of course, there is no law forcing anyone to take advantage of any of this— though I for one have met very few who wished to be hungry or homeless or idle—but in Keltia, the fear at least of these things is nonexistent. That is the reality of the clann system. Widows and orphans do not suffer hardship, old folk do not starve or die alone, victims of disaster need not fear lack. Their clanns care for each of them, under the authority of the clann chief. If for some extraordinary reason the system should go awry, any Kelt may then appeal directly to the Crown, as Chief of Chiefs, and the petition must then be met at that level. In practice, it fails so seldom—I cannot call to mind the last instance, but it was certainly no more recent than the reign of Aeron's great-great-grandfather—that such appeals are almost never necessary."

Haruko thought, with indescribable feelings of bitterness and envy, of the hungry billions still afflicting Earth, the wretched children of excess still being born and still dying like flies. Presently he shook his head.

"You shame us," he said quietly.

"Ah, no shame, only bad management. Do not forget, we have been at this for a very long time. Even though our numbers have increased many thousandfold since our earliest days, the laws still hold, and still work. If your own Earth governors were subject to a few stiff brehon corp-díras, you would see a difference very swiftly, I am certain."

"And the Queen? Suppose the monarch refused to honor the law?"

"In Keltia no one is above the law or beyond it, not even the sovereign. Especially not the sovereign . . . Aeron can be fasted against, or overruled by the Chief Brehon, or even challenged to personal combat either magical or military, though she is némed, sacred of person, and may not be otherwise declared against in any court of justice, Low, Middle, or High. Indeed, under our law, the people even have the power to depose her at any time for sufficient cause."

But Haruko was still a few thoughts back. "Combat! You mean she would have to *fight*?"

Morwen nodded, very serious now. "She has done so, and won, two times already. Even though the Fianna has the right to supply the monarch's military champion, and the Dragon Kinship the like right to furnish a magical champion, and both posts are currently filled by most worthy individuals, like the Ard-rían Jenóvefa before her, Aeron prefers to be her own champion in both forms of combat."

"But to risk her so!"

"It is Aeron's concept of her duty as Ard-rían," said Morwen quietly. "Though if she were any less skilled either as warrior or sorceress we would never permit it— But it is the fíor-comlainn, the truth-of-combat: to defend in her own person the reality of Keltia. And if it should come to war, Theo—well, that would be the ultimate fíor-comlainn. Aeron would not stand away from that fight, not while the life was in her."

"I do this against my resolution quite," remarked Arianeira, watching Tindal's long slender fingers assembling steel and crystal into a makeshift, though powerful, communicator.

"Resolution or not," said Tindal through his teeth, pulling a laser-cone into position, "you have no choice. Before I take any more chances I may regret, tapping into the combanks of the *Sword* like this, by God I want to know who I'm dealing with. This"—he indicated the miniaturized communicator— "should be able to poke through the Curtain Wall without leaving an overly noticeable hole, as it were. I want to make sure everything is as you claim it is, and to do that I intend to have a chat with your Imperial friend. I'm a cautious person, as you will see.'' He tightened a final fitting and stood up. ''There. Call him, Kynon.''

Five minutes later Jaun Akhera's image formed in the viewscreen. His appearance was immaculate as ever, though a faint overlay of displeasure darkened his countenance.

''I permitted this communication, Princess, because I thought it better to complete it once it had been begun. But I do not like it, and I thought I had given orders against it, and I expect it to be both very brief and very important.''

Arianeira reddened under the sting of his words, but replied with equal crispness.

''A new associate of ours, lord, one essential to our plan's success, has demanded this contact. May I make known to you Hugh Tindal, Lieutenant of the Terran Navy, science and enginery officer of the FSS *Sword*. Tindal, His Royal Highness Jaun Akhera, the Imperial Heir, Prince of Alphor and Lord of the Cabiri.'' She explained swiftly about the decision that had been made to involve Tindal in the plot.

Jaun Akhera nodded when she finished. ''Well,'' he said at last, ''this does not displease me, and may prove to be better thought of than you knew. Certainly it is safer to transmit by way of your ship, Tindal . . . well met, then, and how may I help you further?''

Tindal laughed shortly. ''Nice of you to offer, Highness. If I am to involve myself, as I seem to have done, in this, ah, enterprise, I'd like some sort of assurances that, afterwards, I shall receive appropriate consideration for my services. I'm giving up a lot to throw in with you on this.''

''That is understood. Well, you have our royal word, if that means anything to you. More concrete assurances must wait upon our meeting. What more?''

''You *will* be able to pull this off, militarily speaking? The risks—''

Jaun Akhera's patience snapped. ''If you are so unsure of me—''

''Not at all,'' said Tindal with an equal sharpness. ''But cast what Your Highness is pleased to call your mind back about three years, to the last time some misguided royal idiot raised a hand against Keltia.''

"The point being?"

"The point being that anyone who messes with the Kelts—and more particularly with Aeron, or with anyone Aeron is fond of—might get what Bellator got, and maybe worse. Are you prepared for the possibility, at least, that history could repeat itself?"

In spite of his annoyance, Jaun Akhera grinned. "If you are as talented in matters technological as you are rude to princes, Tindal, your future with the Imperium is well assured . . . But, to answer your question, all this had been factored into our plans, and you will have nothing to worry about on that account. Do you stand with us, then?"

Tindal nodded. "Oh yes."

"Good. Then let me not hear from you again—any of you—until such time as you have the word of invasion to give me." The picture blurred to interstellar static, and Tindal rocked back onto his heels and expelled a long breath.

"Well then?" demanded Arianeira. "Was it worth such a risk, merely for you to be able to insult him?"

"Worth it to me, absolutely." Tindal had begun to disconnect the equipment from the link-up to the *Sword*. "Anyway, I don't think he was all that insulted, and, as I said, I wouldn't have gone through with our plans without having spoken to him first. He's not what I expected."

"Not?" Arianeira's voice was sour.

"Not. But maybe I'm not what he expected either."

"Not hard," observed Kynon, "since the Prince of Alphor expected you not at all."

Tindal let that pass, and completed his work. Arianeira, after a glance at him, indicated that Kynon should take his leave. The Kymro seemed at first disinclined to obey this order, but he appeared to think better of it, and, bowing perfunctorily to them both, went out, closing the doors behind him.

Arianeira poured herself a cup of wine from the golden bowl kept by the fire, then reclined on her favorite longchair, lolling back luxuriously with a fur rug over her lap.

"May I stay?" asked Tindal uncertainly, after a long silence.

For answer she pulled a cushion out from behind her and tossed it to the floor beside her chair. After a moment, Tindal seated himself upon it, leaning his back against the carved gold frame of the chair; and neither said any more.

Arianeira sipped her wine and was content, though that seemed a poor word for the state of mind in which she now existed. All was well for her; this evening could have spelled utter disaster for her and Kynon and the plan they had made between them. But she had succeeded with Tindal, where Kynon had failed with Mikhailova; and Jaun Akhera had gone along with the allowing of a Terran into the plot. All was very well indeed; and as yet Kynon and Tindal had not the smallest idea, nor would they, of the true value Arianeira placed upon them, or the reward she intended to give them both in the end. And by the time they did learn, it would be far too late . . . She hid her smile behind the rim of the gold cup, and smoothed the fur of the lap rug.

But if she had bestirred herself to ken the true state of the Terran's mind, she would have been not only unpleasantly surprised, but alarmed also.

Hugh Tindal was very well aware that Arianeira was using him; and that was fine with him, for the moment. The love of mischief-making was with him almost a passion, and here was an unparalleled chance to make trouble on an interstellar scale. So of course it was acceptable that the Princess was making a cat's-paw of him; it suited his own plans exactly to be used so. And the longer she thought she was using him, the longer she would be ignorant of the fact that in truth he was using her. And by the time she became aware of *that*, he'd be safely beyond her reach . . .

Tindal smiled and reached out to pour a cup of wine for himself, then leaned his head back against the soft, dense furs.

Taught by Haruko, Aeron was learning the Terran style of dueling, with thin whippy sword and hilted dagger. Having learned of his interest in, and skill at, swordfighting, she had instructed him in the use of the glaive, the long-bladed Keltic laser sword, and now he was returning the favor.

Rohan and Slaine, passing the fencing hall in search of her, detoured at the sounds of combat and leaned over the gallery rail, looking down on the action with professional interest.

The two duelists below seemed to move in step, advance and retreat, dodge and weave, the click of their blades a constant counterpoint to their muffled footfalls. It ended in a flurry of blurred motion—lunge, parry, counterparry—and Aeron's laughing cry of triumph as she scored the final touch.

"You are too quick for me," complained Haruko, but he was laughing too. They had fought unmasked and unshielded, a mutual compliment to the accuracy of their swordsmanship, and their faces were flushed with exertion. "You pick up the style as a swordsman born," he added, mopping his brow with a towel.

"And you not only swordsman but teacher of swordsmen, which is to my mind much the harder feat." She saluted him with her weapons held crosswise above her head before laying them down. "It is a strange change from the glaive, the rhythms are so different. My brother Rohan must teach you the way of the claymore, he is my master there . . . But see who has been watching." She waved up at the two in the gallery; their heads disappeared, and a few moments later all four were together on the practice floor.

"Gwydion sends us with news you must hear, Ard-rían," said Rohan. "And Theo also—will you come?"

"We are all of a sweat from the bout. Come and tell us while we bathe."

Haruko, certain he had misheard her, followed the others to the pool-room that adjoined the fencing hall. No, he realized, blushing furiously, he had *not* misheard her . . . Aeron had stripped off her practice tunic and was now removing the skin-tight trews and low boots, talking all the while to her brother and her cousin. None of them seemed to think this the least bit unusual, and clearly they considered him enough one of them to find it as natural as they did.

Hastily he removed his own practice suit—Aeron had dived into the pool by now, and that made it considerably easier for him—and slipped into the water himself. Once submerged to the chin, he regained his self-possession enough to listen to what Rohan was saying.

"—and detected what appears to be a tremendous buildup of Fomori forces."

"They have a standing army even as do we," said Aeron,

twisting onto her back and lazily propelling herself through the water. "Gwydion knows that; the explanation could well be a simple one."

"True, but the activity came immediately after Bres and Elathan returned from a visit to Alphor. They were not Strephon's only guests," he said after a pause.

"Indeed. Who else, then?"

"Perhaps forty assorted heads of government and ministers—kings, queens, war-leaders—from the Phalanx as well as the Imperium, and from a fair number of unallied worlds as well; chiefly of note among those last being Panthissera of the Yamazai."

There was a tremendous splash from Aeron's direction. "Could Gwydion's spies learn no more than that?"

"What more than that do we need to know ?" asked Slaine from where she lounged at the pool's edge, carefully out of range of errant splashes. "It comes so pat on the heels of Theo's arrival here—I think perhaps word should be sent to Earth also, lest they shortly receive a less pleasant surprise than merely the simple news of our existence."

"Theo? What do you say?"

Haruko, unprepared, snorted in hot water. "I think the Lady Slaine's idea is well taken," he said, when he was again able to speak. "May I send such a message, Ard-rían?"

"You may." Aeron had hoisted herself, sleek and streaming, out of the pool and dried herself off. "But, Theo, do not make more of this than the facts might warrant. A simple alert should suffice." She had pulled on her everyday attire as she spoke, and now paused in the doorway. "My thanks for the match, and the lesson—I'd not cross swords with you in anything but friendship."

She went out attended by Slaine, and Haruko collapsed gently back into the water. Through the wet black hair plastering his face, he saw Rohan watching him quizzically.

He decided to be honest about it. "People here seem to be pretty casual about—well—"

"Nakedness?" Rohan smiled. "Theo, in the *very* old days, we used to go naked into battle; in fact, some of the more old-fashioned Fians still do . . . But no one here bothers about skin."

When Rohan too had gone, Haruko finally emerged from the pool, very pink still from more than just the heat of the water.

"Well, it certainly bothers *me*," he said aloud, drying himself vigorously. It had bothered him profoundly, and obscurely, and not least because he couldn't verbalize exactly what it had been about the sight of Aeron unclothed—a very beautiful woman, after all—that had so bothered him. Just prudery, no doubt; the Kelts present had obviously thought it entirely usual, and Rohan was her own brother.

With a final headshake he buttoned himself firmly into his clothes, glad that the steam of the pool-room had hid his blushes. Keltia was going to take more getting used to than he had thought.

The swordsmanship lesson had had more purpose to it than instruction or even simple exercise. Aeron had spoken of it to no one, not even Gwydion, but ever since the Terrans' arrival she had continued to have prescient dreams: not so vivid nor so immediately alarming as the one from which Gwydion had comforted her, but steady and unsettling and always on the same themes—war, the fall of the City, invasion, betrayal. Waking too, now, she was beginning to be haunted by dim feelings of impending disaster.

To combat it, she had thrown herself into her work, both political and social, had ridden herself and her horse to exhaustion with furious gallops at all hours, had drugged herself to where dreams should not have been able to reach her—but all to no avail. The dreams continued. Therefore, the only course left to her was the one she was about to undertake.

That night she went up the outside staircase to her chamber of magic and, closing the bronze doors behind her, leaned back against them and soberly surveyed the room.

She was not unfamiliar with what awaited her. Trance was no new thing to so experienced a sorceress, and there were several trance techniques taught in the Druid and Ban-draoi schools, the marana being the lightest and the least of them. But to learn what Aeron now needed to know—the source of her dreams, the reason for her unease—she would have to go deeper and farther into trance than ever she had done before. She would have to dare the trance called taghairm.

For all her powers, she was nevertheless a touch apprehensive, and mindful of the peril. Even Gwydion would have thought twice about such an undertaking, and after her first horrific dream he had in fact forbidden her to attempt a taghairm. He was naturally concerned for her, of course; as she would have been for him. But she was Ard-rían, and she was Ban-draoi, and she was Aeron; and above all else she needed to know. She had not resolved lightly upon such a course of action; it would be exhausting and it would be dangerous—sorcerers had died before now trying it—and only her great need and greater desperation had decided her in the end to take the risk.

So she had spent the early evening in preparation: fasting, light meditation, a ritual purifying bath; and now she was as ready as was necessary, or possible.

She lighted the four torches that marked the four compass points of the room, stripped off her black robe, and, veiled only in her unbound hair, stepped into the center of the inlaid circle. In her hands she carried a rolled-up white bullhide, which now she unfolded and spread out upon the slate floor.

She took up the great ritual sword from where it lay upon the stone altar in the north of the circle, then stretched out upon the bullhide and rested the sword upon her body, its blade cold between her breasts and its point touching her throat. Extending her arms to either side, she cast the Circle in her mind and fell at once into trance.

She was sinking, sinking like a stone into a dark pool, her consciousness a hard bright pebble turning over and over as it fell down through the black cold water. The marana trance was inwards, then out upon the astral; but the taghairm lay only inward, deeper and deeper. Then suddenly her dreams were there, just as she had dreamed them, clear and complete in all details: war and fire and blood, swift vivid pictures that blinked in her mind and were as swiftly gone—Gwydion in his scarlet cloak, with rain upon his face; herself with her sword in her hand in a strange battle-choked courtyard; Morwen floundering through a snowdrift; Theo looking up at her, then falling forward . . .

And then she was past the dreams and the pictures, and here there was only a cold slick blankness, smooth and featureless as a glacier. She came up against it with such speed and force that the impact was physical; her head jerked backward as if she had been struck a blow. Again she flung her mind against the wall, and yet again, and each time she was thrown back, until at last she lay there with her mind bruised and battered, without the strength to go on. Either there was truly nothing to learn behind the dreams, or else— she began to come back up out of the pool, rising gradually back to everyday consciousness—or else someone very powerful indeed—more than one person, almost certainly—was blocking certain knowledge from her by sorcerous means; and even she could not break their power.

Aeron emerged from the trance and sat up slowly and carefully, setting the sword to one side and grimacing at the headache that splintered her temples. With surprise, she saw that the sky outside the tower's windows was gray with dawn. And she was cold, and her muscles were stiff and cramped, and her head hurt abominably, and she was no closer to knowledge than she had been before.

Well, that was not entirely true. She did know, now, that she was being blocked—maybe. And that was as alarming an indication as the dreams, perhaps more so; and she could do as little about it . . .

In all modesty, she thought, wrapping herself in her robe, *it would take a stupendous amount of power to keep me out, and with a taghairm too . . .* Few there were in Keltia who could manage it, and surely she would be aware of anyone possessing that measure of magical strength? Sudden misgiving seized her, and she shivered, not entirely with the chill.

"Next time I shall listen to Gwydion," she said aloud, and began to extinguish the torches. But in truth there was no more she could do. She had tried, and she had failed; and now she must bide the issue, will she or nill she. Still, she rather thought she would not tell Gwydion, or anyone else for that matter, what she feared and what she had attempted. There was little to be gained save a scolding. Better it was to keep her failure and her fears—and her unrelenting dreams—to herself.

Chapter Thirteen

The Terrans had been in Keltia nearly two months now. According to their orders, they were required to remain until the arrival of a duly constituted formal embassy, if their hosts permitted it, and neither Kelts nor Terrans seemed to think it any hardship at all that the Terrans stayed. Quite the contrary: The visitors from Earth had become social lions—a fact to which each of them had reacted in his own particular way.

Of them all, only Mikhailova could be said to remain truly aloof, and the others did not understand it. She was shy by nature, of course, but she had always tried to compensate for it, and she had started off as eager as the rest of them. Then for no reason they could see she had withdrawn into a shell that no amount of friendly overtures or coaxing or teasing seemed able to pierce. Tindal continued to devote all his attentions to the Princess Arianeira; and though his colleagues thought it extremely uncharacteristic, to say the least, they also had a tacit understanding to make nothing of it, among themselves as well as to outsiders. Hathaway saw no reason whatsoever not to have a very good time, and he was enjoying himself immensely; while O'Reilly had simply capitulated with a sigh of wonder, merging into Keltia like a young stream into a deep and mighty river: She had come home and she was happy.

Yet oddly enough it was Haruko who had come closest of them all to the Keltic Queen. The others often saw them

185

walking together absorbed in talk, Aeron tall and vivid, Theo serious, chunky, strangely exotic on a world that had seen since the days of its founding few indeed of any race other than its own.

That afternoon was gray with the threat of cold rain; Aeron, who had recovered entirely from the effects of the taghairm some nights before, though not from the reason for it, had spent the day in an unending succession of audiences, councils and meetings. At last she had rebelled and fled to the gardens, taking Haruko with her. Once there, she did not speak for some time, and Haruko knew her well enough by now to know that such shared silence was a sign that she felt truly at ease with someone, that the usual Court backchat was not necessary between them; and the compliment thrilled him.

"If you were back on Earth, Theo?" she asked after a while. She plucked a handful of wild fraughans from a bush and offered him some. "What would you choose to be doing?"

Haruko nibbled on the luscious dark-red berries and recounted his fantasy of luxury starliners. "And you? If you were not Queen in Keltia?"

"I think I should like to be a nun," said Aeron dreamily. "To go into a Ban-draoi convent—there's a beautiful old one on Vannin, on a little island in a sea-loch—and spend the rest of my life in prayer and contemplation."

He laughed, not unsympathetically. "The oldest dream of all the rulers of all the earths, Lady: to put off the crown and take the vows."

"Not very original, I admit. But few better."

They walked a while longer in the same companionable silence, through the gardens along the edge of the cliffs overlooking the sea.

"What is the teaching of your folk, Theo, about life and death and the life again after?"

So Haruko explained about karma, and the way of the Tao, and she listened, nodding in agreement.

"That is a good and worthy Path."

He glanced curiously at her. "What do *your* people believe, Lady, about such matters?"

She was silent again, and he respected her silence. "The Great Wheel," she said then. "And the Three Circles that all mortal life must traverse and may aspire to: Annwn, the Abyss of the Unformed; Abred, the Path of Changes; and Gwynfyd, the Circle of Perfection.''

"And God?"

"Inhabits alone the circle of Keugant . . . You know that all Druids are priests, and all Ban-draoi priestesses? Well, then, in the Mystery Schools we are instructed in matters not commonly taught to the rest of the folk. Of how we may choose our next lives; of how the future is and is not fated, and how it may be lawfully altered; of the things of power. This is where my authority originates; the heart of all true sovereignty and right order.''

Haruko was seized by a sudden inexplicable resentment and distaste. "You rule by divine right, then.''

"Nay, I rule by the will of the people,'' said Aeron, mildly surprised by his abrupt coldness. "Keltia elects its monarchs, though I admit the choice is a limited one.''

"What limits are these?"

"What we call the rígh-domhna, all eligible kin of the previous sovereign. For instance, the election that made me Ard-rían could have fallen upon any of my brothers or sisters; my father's brother or sister and their children; or my grandfather's brothers, their children and grandchildren. It is a sort of royal pool of possible monarchs.''

"Yet you were chosen.''

"In actual practice, it has been well over a thousand years since any other than the firstborn heir of the sovereign has been elected to the Crown. Yet, lest that should make us firstborn complacent, or the accident of birth order be regarded as a *right* to the Copper Crown, we have the ríghdomhna and the election. It has been so here for three thousand years, and longer than that on Earth.''

"That is impressive,'' said Haruko, whose ill disposition seemed to have vanished as quickly as it had arisen. "But suppose tradition held, and the firstborn, though chosen, was not the best choice for the job?"

She shrugged. "Doubtless that has happened many times. Perhaps even this time,'' she added with a smile. "How are we to know? In theory, and even in law, the Sovereign in Keltia is all-powerful, yet how much can one lord make or mar in one reign? We have fenced ourselves such a scaffolding—the brehon laws, the Senate and Assembly and House of Peers, the Fáinne, custom itself—that even a monarch deliberately bent to evil can accomplish little of such an intent.''

''Evil? Have you ever had a truly evil leader?''

''We have had our full share,'' she said quietly. ''And the worst of them was Edeyrn; for when a sorcerer turns his might to evil he is the worst of all men . . . Yet I think even your own Way would say that evil in this world is as necessary as good. Any road, so do we believe. The Dark, as it now is, is the greatest evil that we know; and our teaching is that our true work here in this circle of Abred—yours, mine, everyone's—is not to fight to resist the Dark, for that is a vain struggle doomed from the start, but rather to take the evil from it, to absorb it as a right and natural part of ourselves, our Shadow, and in so doing, to restore it to its natural balance. Without the Light, the Darkness within us becomes malevolence; without the Darkness, the Light within us becomes forceless virtue, weak and ineffectual. Without the one, no other; for the Dark was not evil in the beginning, and it will not be evil in the end. On Earth, one of the myths in which this great truth was clothed was that of the fallen archangel, that Prince of Darkness who was called Lucifer.''

''Yet, in the Latin tongue, 'Lucifer' means 'Light-bearer.' ''

Aeron smiled, her whole face bright with the paradox. ''Even so. That is a Mystery only the wisest among us can hope to attain knowledge of on this plane, and I am not one of them. To us, that lord was no angel but a god; his seat was among the Mighty Ones. He was a Prince of the Air, and his fall shook all the worlds. We—the Druids and the Ban-draoi—are taught that mankind's great work is to restore that Prince to his former place, to the bright throne in Gwynfyd that once was his. And it shall be done,'' she said, in a voice half prayer, half promise. ''For in restoring him we do restore ourselves . . .''

''But you say 'gods,' and you spoke before of one God?''

''We worship above all others the One—Kelu, the Crown, that Highest God who is above all gods forever. It is our teaching that the One, whom we call as those of Atland did,

Artzan Janco, the Shepherd of Heaven, cannot be truly known to us while we remain upon this plane of enlightenment. Such knowing would destroy us; we are not prepared to know, and our minds have no place to hold his reality. We say 'he,' but he is neither male nor female, or both male and female together, or beyond male and female alike. As for our other gods, they are closer to us, they can be spoken to as friends or kin, and they answer us in the same degree: the Goddess, the Mother, of whom I and all Ban-draoi are servants; the Lord-father, to whom the Druids owe their service; various Powers who rule certain spheres—gods and goddesses of peace and war, lore and literature, farming and smithcraft and bardery and the like.'' Her smile held a touch of irony, and more than a touch of self-mockery. ''There are even stories that my House, the House of Dâna, and several other of the old houses, are descended from certain of those gods. But I for one would not care to count upon it.''

The next morning Haruko went early to Tindal's rooms in the Rose Tower. He had delayed sending that message to the Admiralty for nearly a week now, but today he would do it, before he forgot about it altogether, or, God forbid, it became academic. Important as it was, somehow he never seemed able to remember, or something came up, or he was otherwise prevented. But now he would do it.

He knocked twice on the heavy oak door. Receiving no answer, he knocked again, louder, then cautiously lifted the latch and pushed the door ajar.

''Lieutenant Tindal? Hugh?''

Still no answer; Haruko stepped round the door into the sun-laced grÍanan. Not since their arrival at Turusachan had he had occasion to seek out Tindal in his quarters; and for that matter he had seen very little of him elsewhere, unlike his other crewmen, with whom he spent a great deal of time. O'Reilly, he remembered now, had made some snide observations about Tindal spending all his own time with Gwydion's sister Arianeira . . . distinctly odd, if true, but all the rest of them had Keltic friends by now, and why shouldn't Hugh.

The rooms made a pleasant suite, facing east over the City, as luxuriously furnished as those of the other Terrans, and

Tindal's personal effects were scarcely to be seen; *typical*, thought Haruko.

But the rooms, however devoid of their occupant's personality, were also obviously empty at the moment. Haruko was turning to go when the thought occurred to him that he might leave a message for his officer. He peered around the bedroom door; yes, as he had expected, there was the computerpad, angled across the bedside table.

Haruko sat down on the edge of the bed, took the pad in his lap and activated it. Instantly the small screen was filled with complex calculations; Tindal had apparently forgotten to command the pad to clear and store his work in the big wall computer. Haruko was about to do this for him—nobody liked losing their work in one of the little pads—when something about the numbers caught his attention.

He tapped his fingers over the touchboard, frowning slightly. The screen blinked, then cleared to a sequence Haruko knew by heart: the combank codes of the *Sword*. Tindal, it seemed, had already hooked into the ship's computers.

Haruko stared down at the little screen, nonplussed and more than a bit puzzled. There was absolutely no reason for those codes to be here; why had Hugh bothered to work them out? Unless he had come into possession of the Second Sight, as the Kelts might say, and knew Haruko would be coming round to ask him to assist with the transmission to Earth—But that seemed, on the face of it, extremely unlikely.

So—what then? Haruko began to bite absently on the first knuckle of his left hand. This was all *very* strange. Judging by the calculations—he recalled the first display to the screen—Tindal was planning on making some very long-distance transmissions indeed. But where, and to whom?

"That is the question . . ." For once in his life Haruko felt utterly at a loss. He leaned back against the pillows and prepared to impose some sort of order on the ill-assorted facts.

Item: Tindal, knowing nothing of his captain's orders, had nevertheless gone to the considerable trouble of setting up a remote link between the *Sword*'s combanks and some other computer. Item: In spite of the fact that he could contact anyone he pleased through the Kelts' own very excellent communications network, Tindal had chosen instead to fashion his own clandestine means of transmission.

Well, Haruko reluctantly concluded, there weren't too many licit reasons for such activity. Therefore, he must now begin to consider illicit ones . . . If the hookup was in fact not meant for Earth, then for where was it intended? Someplace outside the Curtain Wall, obviously. But what circumstances could possibly require such secrecy, save something utterly unlawful— Tindal was, certainly, an opportunist; but surely no more than that?

Haruko sat forward slowly, trying to deny the dawning of a possibility too dreadful to contemplate. But it would not be denied, small though it was, and it was also his sworn duty to consider *every* possibility, however unlikely and however unpleasant . . .

Very well. Assume for the sake of argument that Tindal, for whatever reasons, was planning contact with someone beyond the Curtain Wall. With that as the unpalatable given, then, who might it logically be? Aeron's enemies the Fomori? That was certainly logical, but how would Tindal know to get in touch with them, or, for that matter, they with him?

The answer to that, of course, was that they wouldn't; not unless—

He carefully cleared the screen to its former blankness, decided against leaving any message, and came out again into the grianan, thinking hard.

—Not unless some other party had told them. Told them, and then set it up with Tindal. The logic was as terrible— *though still totally speculative*, Haruko carefully reminded himself—as it was inescapable: If Tindal was in truth planning to get in touch with outside powers for nefarious purposes, and had to sneak around using the ship's combanks to do it, then someone here in Keltia would have to be acting as intermediary. And that intermediary would have to be a Kelt.

Haruko was almost physically sick at the idea. A Kelt. Someone whose entire culture was geared to loyalty, to whom betrayal would be, or should be, the one unforgivable sin. Someone outwardly loyal to Aeron, perhaps someone she knew personally; someone highly placed in her councils or in her household; someone she trusted, maybe even someone she loved . . .

With a mighty effort, he turned his mind to fairness. Conjecture as he might, none of this was proved; all of it was possible, sure, but was it likely? Even now, could he not find some logical, innocent explanation—

As he stood there rocked with intolerable alternatives, the outer door opened and Tindal came into the room. He was more gaily cheerful than Haruko could recall ever having seen him, and when he saw he had a visitor, far from flinching with guilt, he brightened still further and looked Haruko straight in the eye.

"Ah, Captain! Were you looking for me?"

"What are these Shining Ones?"

Slaine, who was with O'Reilly in the bardic archives at Seren Beirdd, where they were doing research to verify the Terran's pedigree, looked up with a quizzical frown.

"Why do you ask?"

"Oh, well, nothing really—but I was out riding the other day, over Miremoss with Eiluned and Kieran and a few other people, and we met a woman walking with her child. Naturally we all stopped to talk, and the oddest thing happened then. It was like—like walking light, or ribbons of air, all silvery and glowing with iridescent colors. It came down the face of a hill like a sailboat. You'll probably think I'm crazy"—here she glanced apologetically at Slaine—"but it seemed to *bow* to us."

"And then?"

"Well, the woman bowed back, and said something to it, I couldn't make out what. And then she told her child—and this I *did* hear, very clearly—to make a curtsy to the Shining One. Whatever a Shining One might be. Kieran and Eiluned just sort of nodded to it—but a very polite nod, if you know what I mean. It was very interesting," concluded O'Reilly lamely, "and I thought you might know. I mean, I know *all* of you *know*; I thought *you* would *tell* me, and I was afraid to ask Aeron or Gwydion, in case they told me too much."

"Truly, I—or they, for that matter—can tell you but little,'' began Slaine, ''for little enough is known. Still, for what it is worth—''

''Yes, well, as a matter of fact, I *was* looking for you, Lieutenant.'' Haruko took a firmer grip on himself. Though much might be suspected, nothing was yet proved; and who was the Captain here, anyway?

''I will be sending a message to the Admiralty in the next local day or so,'' he continued, ''and I want you to fix it so that it's transmitted by way of the ship's combanks. I've already spoken to O'Reilly and Mikhailova about it, and they say they'll need your help.''

''Probably will,'' agreed Tindal easily. Not by an eyelash's flicker did he give any indication to Haruko, who was watching him as a cat watches a sparrow, of the shock he had felt at finding the Captain in his rooms. ''But the Kelts will have to do something too, sir. It's a long way to Earth even for the subspace boosters, and we can't get through that Curtain Wall without some help.''

''Since the Queen has given permission for us to transmit, I'm sure she'll also see to it that you get whatever assistance you need.'' Haruko hesitated, on the point of asking Tindal straight out what the hell was going on here. But his officer's cheerful frankness put him off: How could Hugh stand there and chat, and all the time be guilty of what Haruko thought he might be guilty of? Unless, of course, he wasn't . . . *Really*, he thought, *when am I going to learn to give people the benefit of the doubt?*

''Well, then, I'll—just let you know, then, shall I? Yes,'' said Haruko helplessly, ''I'll just—do that.''

When Haruko had gone, Tindal flew into the bedroom as if the Cwn Annwn themselves were on his track. He snatched up the computer-pad from the table, activated it, then sat down hard on the bed, weak-kneed with relief. No, his calculations were still there, and nothing else was there that should not have been, like a message from the Captain . . .

Even so—Haruko might not have left a message on the pad, but perhaps he had been about to? And if so, might he not have seen what he should not have?

On the whole, Tindal thought not; the Captain was as a rule

not good at dissembling. If he had indeed stumbled across the figures and the codes, no way he would not have at least guessed at Tindal's purposes. And if he *had* guessed, no way he could have stood there and been so casual.

Still, it had been unbelievably careless to have left the stuff so easily accessible. If Arianeira came to learn of it, she'd have his guts for garters . . .

Whistling tunelessly, Tindal triple-coded the information for belated security and stored it in the wall-computer, then lay back on the bed with his hands behind his head. If that message Haruko wanted to send to Earth tomorrow was as important as Tindal thought it might be, those figures wouldn't be staying in storage very long at all.

Profoundly confused and unsettled by the interview with Tindal—the thought that an officer of his was possibly up to no good was no easy one—Haruko went to his rooms to lie down. Upset and brooding, finally he fell into a fitful doze, and when he woke it was nearly time for the nightmeal. He felt an overwhelming desire to get out into the open air, and went out into the gardens to clear his mind and think what to do next.

It was just past sunset, and the afterglow was pale gold in the west. He could see for miles in the low light, everything around him brightened to an unnatural clarity by the strange brightness that seemed to hang in the cold air.

Away up on the hillside, a flicker of movement caught his eye, and he instinctively glanced after it. Aeron was walking on the edge of the little pine-wood. She was cloaked in black, and pacing not six feet from her side was the biggest animal Haruko had ever seen.

For an instant he thought it was her wolfhound Cabal—one or the other of her two giant hounds was never far from her—then his eye measured out the true proportion: This animal was more than half again Cabal's enormous size. It became aware of him in that moment, and Haruko's voice died away in his throat as he saw that the beast was a wolf.

He stood absolutely motionless under the animal's cool, almost amused regard; there seemed to be a human intelligence behind those jade-colored eyes. A magnificent male it was, with thick shaggy fur brindled in bars of gray and black, a milky silver star upon its chest, and Haruko estimated uneasily that it would stand over ten feet tall on its hind legs.

Then Aeron herself caught sight of him, and as she lifted her arm in greeting his blood froze within him, for the wolf was no longer there.

She came down the hill, her smile of welcome changing to a puzzled frown as she drew near.

"Theo? Is something amiss?"

He knew what his face must look like, knew also that only the truth would serve, with her.

"Just now—before you waved—there was a wolf with you. Then it was gone. It just—vanished." To his intense annoyance, he was shaking.

"Ah." She slipped her arm through his, turning him from the hill back to the palace. "I am not surprised that you of all your folk should see what you have seen," she began. "But you saw him, truly? Did you see my fetch?"

Haruko felt himself recovering from the shock, grateful for the warm, steady hand upon his arm.

"It was so huge—and it *looked* at me . . . But where did it go? It just wasn't—wasn't *there* anymore."

"It was never there, Theo, not in the same way that you and I are *here*."

"It was a vision? A—ghost?"

"In a way. You know that the House of Aoibhell has as its sign and token a wolf's head? That is no accident, nor herald's whim neither: The tutelary spirit of our kindred, when it comes to us in physical guise, takes the form of a wolf. What you saw was the fetch of the Aoibhells—a spirit-wolf, the protector of our fortunes and the guide of our souls, and only those very wise in such matters, or very favored of the gods, or very much in need of guidance and warning, are privileged to behold him. Even I do not often see him, though I frequently sense his presence, and I am Chief of the Name of Aoibhell."

"Do the other houses have such—friends?"

She laughed, relieved to see him restored to the point of sarcasm. "Oh aye. Gwydion's family's fetch is a white stag with golden antlers, and the Clann Drummond have a serpent that speaks to them in dreams. There are many dozens of others.''

Oh great, a status symbol . . . "But this is pure magic, Lady.''

Aeron shook her head. "Nay; the fetch cannot be invoked nor yet commanded. It comes of its own will, choosing its own time and place. There was a fetch once in form of a winter hare that stopped a battle, and another in shape of a master-otter that caused one . . . 'Her wolf,' you think; but you would be more nearly correct to call me his mortal. Sometimes have I been named the She-wolf of Keltia by my enemies, who think they insult me thereby. No insult to me, but a very great honor, to be called so.''

"Well, why did *I* see him, then?" Haruko burst out passionately. "I'm no Aoibhell, certainly not a sorcerer, not even a Kelt!''

Aeron shook her head again, more gravely. "I know not, Theo,'' she said. "But the fetch often comes to give warning where warning is most needed. Is there aught you know of, that might merit such a cautioning?''

Haruko did not answer.

Chapter Fourteen

Whatever warning the fetch may have portended, the event seemed unthinkably distant. At Turusachan, the business of governing went imperturbably on, and only the most pessimistic, or the most prescient, could have had cause to predict calamity.

It had rained earlier that day, but now golden sunlight alternated with the last black wisps of rainclouds chased by a freshening breeze. Haruko walked with Aeron across the wet paving-stones of the Great Square, arm in arm and both of them giggling helplessly.

They were returning from a meeting of influential members of the Royal Senate and Assembly. Morwen had warned them to be on their best behavior for the audience, and they had gravely obeyed her, comporting themselves with immense dignity and diplomacy; so much so that now they felt well entitled to play the fool a little, and they had told jokes, jested, and roared with laughter all the way across the square, composing themselves only when they saw the grinning faces of the Fian guards at the palace gates.

As they walked down the corridor leading to Aeron's office, Haruko reflected on the audience they had just attended.

"Are they usually so—"

"So truculent?" Aeron grinned again. "Nay; usually they are much worse. They were so biddable today only because they desperately want you to think well of them."

"I!"

"Surely." She gave him a sidelong glance. "You may know the elected houses—Senate and Assembly—are as keen for an alliance with Earth as the House of Peers and the High Council are averse to it. That is why the Chief Assemblator, Rollow of Davillaun, who held forth so eloquently just now, has so featly changed his cloak. He was originally set as iron against your even coming to Caerdroia, until he heard to the contrary from those who elected him to his position."

"I hadn't realized."

"Nay, well, it matters little enough in the long run; only for that having the elected bodies with me rather than against makes my life that much easier . . . But look, what is this here?"

They had turned a corner in the corridor and come upon O'Reilly and Melangell.

"Do you like it, Lady?" O'Reilly rotated shyly, arms held out from her sides. She was experimenting for the first time with Keltic dress, and she was nervous—and acutely aware of Haruko's owlish disapproving eye fixed on her from over Aeron's shoulder.

"Very fine," said Aeron. "You wear our costume as if born to it."

"Melangell picked them out." O'Reilly blushed with pleasure and threw a smile over her shoulder at Melangell. And she did look far more natural and at ease in the Keltic style than in the Terran civilian garb she had brought down with her from the *Sword*. Melangell had chosen for the brown-haired O'Reilly a crimson tunic, black leather trews, a full-sleeved white shirt and sand-colored boots of sueded leather, with a furred cloak over all.

"Very fine," repeated Aeron. "Still, it needs something—" She unclasped the necklace she was wearing at her own throat—little linked gold shields enamelled with her sword-and-crown badge—and fastened it upon O'Reilly, who hardly dared even to breathe. "There, then. Keep it for welcome-gift, if it pleases you."

After Aeron, pursued by O'Reilly's stammering thanks, had gone on her way to yet another audience, taking Melangell with her, O'Reilly still stood unmoving, boggled with dazzlement. Haruko's voice cut harshly across her transport.

"Going native, Lieutenant?" Even he was appalled by the waspish snap of his tone.

"Sir?" O'Reilly seemed about to burst into tears, and he repented instantly.

"I'm sorry, Sally," he muttered. "I don't know what the hell I'm saying anymore. Here, let me see that. It's quite an honor, I should think."

O'Reilly lifted her chin as Haruko peered at the necklace, taking the moment to study the face so close to hers.

"What's the matter with you anyway?" she demanded, still hurt. "You've been acting extremely weird the past few days. Tell me."

Haruko pursed his lips. "I don't have anything really solid to go on just yet," he said at last. "And if I told you what I suspected, that might color your judgment just when I need it to be really objective."

"As you wish, Captain."

"Oh, *don't* do that, *please* . . . Anyway, when we go home—"

"Go home!" O'Reilly stared at him. "I—haven't thought about it."

"Apparently." Haruko had guessed right, then, as to how his communications officer really felt about Keltia . . . "You seem to have forgotten you're still a Terran serving officer. Would you desert your commission, never see Earth again? All just to stay here?"

"Yes!" she flung at him. "You bet I would, Theo, in a *minute*, and so would you! And don't try to tell me you wouldn't, because I know better! Anyway," she continued in a calmer voice, "Aeron could probably fix it so we could stay and not get into trouble for it. She could ask the Admiralty to have us seconded here on an advisory basis or something, they'd do that for a queen."

"Maybe. Just don't count on anything. And while I think of it, you and Tindal and Mikhailova have clearance to make that transmission tomorrow to the Admiralty. Morwen says you can send it from the Fianna communications room."

"Whatever you say, sir." A speculative smile softened her face. "Just imagine, maybe by spring we could have some more people here from Earth."

"We'll see. Anything could happen by then." If his suspicions turned out to be as well-grounded as he thought, he reflected gloomily, Terrans could very soon be Aeron's least favorite aliens to have around.

"Ever so good of you both to help me out with this."

O'Reilly looked skeptically at Tindal, then over at Mikhailova, who cast up her eyes to heaven. The three of them were in the communications room of the Fianna Commandery, across the square from the palace, preparing to send Haruko's message to the Admiralty. As ordered, it was being sent by way of the *Sword,* with the help of the Fianna computers.

"We didn't seem to have much of a choice," remarked O'Reilly. "And anyway, you told Sir you couldn't do it alone."

"Oh, well, maybe I did say something like that . . . Not that I couldn't, you understand; it's just so much easier when you—Oh, Christ, Athenée! Don't touch those!"

Mikhailova, who had been on the point of transmitting a long list of codes up to the *Sword* to activate the combanks, froze, staring at Tindal in astonishment.

"I'm sorry! They're only verification codes—"

"I know perfectly well what they are! I mean, I sequenced them myself, I know how they go. I'll do it." He wiped the list from Mikhailova's screen and onto his own, which faced the wall and could not be overlooked by wandering eyes.

"All right, Hugh, there's no need to get shirty. Athenée didn't mean to profane your sacred sequencing." O'Reilly made a little grimace of exasperation to herself and a little face at Tindal's averted back, and sat down beside Mikhailova. The two worked together in silence while Tindal executed his own program in privacy on the other side of the console.

After a while O'Reilly glanced up. "Are you ready, Your Ubiquity? Or would you like to do this whole thing yourself after all?"

"No, no, Sally, as I said, I'm grateful for the help . . . I'll just take it back now, thanks so very much."

O'Reilly took advantage of the momentary respite in her chores to have a good close look at Mikhailova. She was disconcerted to see her fellow crewman's face thinner and paler than it ought to have been, with dark smudges under the hazel eyes.

"Athenée? Are you all right? I mean, if something was wrong, you would tell me? Or Sir?"

Mikhailova would not meet her gaze. "I'm *fine,* Sally. There's nothing wrong. I'm just a little tired, maybe. Why do you ask?"

"Well, it's just that—you've been so reclusive lately, I thought . . . well, I was a little worried, and so was the Captain. You weren't so antisocial when we first got here, and I wondered if something might have happened that you hadn't told us about."

"No. Nothing happened. Nothing at all, I'm just tired, can we not talk about it, please?"

"Well—sure." O'Reilly shrugged, defeated. "What's to say about nothing, anyway?"

"Quite."

"On the mark, O'Reilly," called Tindal over the top of the console. "Time to do your stuff."

This was O'Reilly's specialty, and she was very good at it indeed. She riffled through the program at top speed, but somehow only the robot was working on the job. The real O'Reilly was analyzing very different data: data to do with why the woman sitting beside her seemed so very unhappy. But it did not compute, and after a while she gave it up, and put it away for future consideration.

Tindal had reclaimed the program again, she realized. Strange that he seemed not to want anyone else to handle those codes. . .

She leaned forward and craned upward, resting her chin on the top of the console housing and peering down at Tindal. He was intent on his work, oblivious to her scrutiny, and smiling—*no, smirking,* she corrected herself—smirking with a kind of buttery self-satisfaction that one would have thought entirely inappropriate to the job at hand.

He finished with a flourish and looked up at O'Reilly with a broad grin.

"Logged, coded, scrambled, dispatched and stored. Sir will be pleased. A job well done, Lieutenant."

O'Reilly continued to look soberly down at him. "If you say so," she said then.

Two days later Aeron summoned Gwydion to her formal office on the palace's ground floor. Unlike the solar, where she did her real work, the huge chamber was the sort of imposing, elegant setting popular opinion imagined a queen would work in: walls of polished rose marble, high ceilings frescoed with historical scenes, an enormous goldenwood desk backed by priceless tapestries, windows opening on a view over the sea. Aeron did not love the room, and used it only because her father and grandfather had done so.

Gwydion was nearly at the door when the formidable Elharn emerged from the office into the corridor. The Master of Sail's face was white and his expression dazed, and he did not seem to recognize his friend.

"And they said the King was dead," he muttered, and went on down the hall, shaking his head.

Gwydion looked after him a moment, then pushed the door open and went in. Aeron was standing behind her desk, the aftermath of her anger still vivid on her face. Gwydion nodded to Aeron's secretary Robat, who bowed and withdrew.

"What happened here?" he asked mildly.

"Some slight brangle. My uncle Ironbrow and my cousin Macsen had an idea I liked but little. I'll mention it to Macsen later," she added darkly. "But come with me to my tower, if you would. I have asked a few others to come in a while also. There is something I have to say." The flash of a rueful smile. "And perhaps you would fetch your telyn? I should like to improve my mood before they arrive."

"Who is that *singing*?"

"Aeron and Gwydion, I should think," said Morwen, who preceded Haruko on the stairs from the faha up to Aeron's rooms. "That is certainly his hand upon the harp."

"So beautiful."

"Oh aye, they sing like the Sidhe, those two, when it suits them."

Haruko couldn't say about the Sidhe, but the two in the room above sang like angels: Gwydion's deep bass and Aeron's unexpectedly crystalline soprano. Somehow Haruko hadn't thought Aeron would have so high and soaring a singing voice; it rang true and clear on the notes, like a bell over water.

"Most harmonious," he said, and Morwen snorted.

By now they had reached the level of Aeron's rooms. Much to Haruko's surprise, the door that led from the staircase into the tower was unguarded, though there had been Fians posted below in the faha. Morwen noticed, and laughed.

"Nay, Aeron is not so trusting as that. Put out your hand."

Haruko extended his right hand directly beneath the carven stone lintel of the doorway. Sudden cold gripped his hand in a net of invisible ice-crystals, holding it frozen and immobile. He tried to withdraw it, but his struggles only caused his arm to be drawn in up to the elbow. He looked at Morwen in mute panic.

"It is well. Stand quiet." With perfect equanimity she stepped entirely into the strange cold field, spoke in a clear, even voice. "Morwen, with Haruko." The iciness vibrated around them, and then it was gone.

Haruko reached a careful finger behind him. There it was, as cold as before. "Ve-ry neat," he said, much impressed.

"Aeron prefers as few guards as possible near her private quarters," said Morwen. "This is much more effective."

"How does it work?"

"In non-technical terms, it is a modified restraint field, keyed to voice in combination with known personal auras."

"Oh. Magic." Haruko thought about it for a moment. "You mean if I stepped into it and said I was Prince Rohan, it wouldn't believe me?"

"Not only would it not believe you, Theo, it would knock you senseless and hold you there until the guards, or Aeron herself, came to release you. I'd not advise the experiment . . . But here we are."

They could hear no music now. They had come to a heavy oak door, iron-studded, with the winged-unicorn device wrought in silver and onyx upon it. Morwen touched a flat silver plate inset shoulder-high in the stone to the right of the door, and the door swung silently open.

*　　*　　*

In O'Reilly's chamber, where she had gone early to bed for once, the transcom buzzed discreetly, and she groaned as she rolled over to answer it.

"The Ard-rían's compliments to Lieutenant O'Reilly, and would you attend her directly in the Western Tower."

"Me! The Queen wants to see *me*? *Now*? Oh, *yes*!" She leaped out of bed and began to scramble into her clothes.

The interior approach to Aeron's chambers ran along a gallery overlooking the sea, and O'Reilly saw no one in all her long walk from her own rooms in the Rose Tower. When she arrived, the doors stood open, though this entrance, unlike the one used by Morwen and Haruko, was guarded by impassive Fians. The wolfhounds Cabal and Ardattin lay across the threshold, and they thumped their tails to see her, though they did not otherwise bestir themselves.

Aeron was not alone in the inmost chamber. She was wearing another of her old ragged robes, her feet bare as usual; and again as usual, she looked no whit the less regal for it. Haruko, sitting in a cushioned chair by the fire, appeared remarkably at his ease, and he smiled warmly at his officer. Morwen, also shoeless, was stretched out on her stomach on the furs by the hearth, and across the room, in the shadows of the window embrasure, Gwydion was a dark quiet presence. A small gold harp lay in his lap.

"Am I in trouble?" muttered O'Reilly to her captain in Japannic, and he shook his head almost imperceptibly.

"You come too late to join our singing," Aeron was saying, sitting cross-legged in the middle of the bed. She was unbraiding her hair as she spoke, her temper much improved from that of an hour before. "Rohan would also be here, but for that he is away from the City tonight . . . Well, all of you know by now that Theo's messages to the Federacy, and the ones we ourselves have sent, have been received. And now have I received an answer, and I wished you to hear it. Terra will be sending an embassy ship to us, to leave Earth in advance of the *Sword*'s scheduled departure from here. But, since I knew that the arrival of the formal embassy ship would relieve you, the exploratory crew, of your diplomatic duties, I also made formal petition that you be permitted to remain with us as military liaison, if you so choose." O'Reilly's face lighted, and Aeron smiled. "I have received no word on that as yet, though I think they will be full willing to grant my request." She pushed her unbound hair back over her shoulders and looked at each of them in turn. "Whatever, the ship will soon be on its way to us. And I intend to send Terra an embassy of my own, before I am many days older."

"You have decided, Lady?" asked Haruko. *It had to be; she'd made up her mind, then . . .*

"I have. I decided long ago, truly; it was only that everyone else needed to grow accustomed to the idea. But it will be formal alliance, a sealed and signed treaty. It will not be a totally popular decision, and almost certainly it will involve one or both of our nations in war. Indeed, the mere hint of alliance was apparently cause enough for the Fomori to arm against us. Very like, too, it will be a treaty years in the working-out; but I wish to grow oaks, not dayflowers . . . Any road, I shall announce this in Council tomorrow, but I wished you to hear it in private first. Is there any other thing I should know before I make known my decision?"

Haruko thrust any least tiniest wisp of a thought of Tindal firmly behind a wall of steel in his mind, and kept that wall solid against her as her glance touched on him, though his heart ached to do it.

Apparently she sensed nothing amiss. "Does *no* one have anything to say, then?" she demanded, half-laughing. "I can hardly believe it . . . Taoiseach?"

"None, Ard-rían," said Morwen. "You know all my thought."

"First Lord of War?"

Gwydion drew a soft chord from the telyn in his lap before answering. "You know my thought as well, Ard-rían. Whatever dán your decision brings, I shall find you the swords to deal with it."

Aeron sighed. "Be it so, then." She leaned back against the solid brindled flank of Ardattin, who had crept, one huge paw at a time, onto the bed during the conversation, and who now lolled on the pillows, imagining herself undetected. "Well, has no one a song to give us?"

*   *   *

Sleet scratched on the windows of O'Reilly's room. She had crawled gratefully back into her bed some three hours after having been so peremptorily summoned out of it, her head now dizzy with ale fumes and buzzing with song and talk. She had reached the toppling edge of sleep when the door opened. As she sat up, startled, in the big bed, Haruko came warily in.

"I hate to bother you, Sally," he said, "but can I talk to you?"

The grave look on his usually cheerful face pierced her sleepiness and surprise, and she nodded.

"Sure. What's the matter?" In spite of herself, she yawned.

Haruko hesitated only briefly. "Treachery. Well, I think so anyway. Maybe. I'm still not sure. Certainly not sure enough to tell Aeron or Morwen. But it's been bothering me, and I needed to tell *some*one."

O'Reilly laughed incredulously. "*Treachery*! Oh sir, you're joking." But she quickly sobered at the sight of his eyes. "You're serious—but whose?"

He looked at her for a few minutes before he spoke. "Tindal."

Tindal! O'Reilly bounced full upright in the bed, wide awake now, the ale haze miraculously dispelled.

"How strange that you should think that," she said. "I believe you. In fact, I have something to tell you . . . But you first."

Haruko recounted his accidental discovery of the combank calculations on Tindal's computer-pad. "And that's why I've been in such a bad mood over the past couple of days," he concluded. "But what I wanted to ask you was if there was any way—any reason . . ."

"You mean any way those figures could have been legitimate? Any good honest reason for them being there, before you even asked for them? Not a chance," said O'Reilly flatly. "And that's what I wanted to tell you. When he and Athenée and I were working together, he insisted on being the one who did all the coding—as if he were afraid to let anyone else see the communications log. As if there were something in the log he'd rather keep to himself. Since he coded it himself, of course, nobody else could get at it." She related in her turn what had transpired. "I just had a feeling there was something going on, but I couldn't imagine what. And at the moment I was more concerned about Athenée."

"Athenée? What about her?"

"She wouldn't tell me. But you've seen yourself how depressed she's been lately. I think it's to do with some man, personally, and nothing to do with Hugh. But he's been acting weird too. A lot more secretive, and a *very* lot more obnoxiously self-satisfied than he usually is. You know how he can be. But if you think something's going on, sir, why *don't* you tell Aeron—or Morwen, if you'd rather not tell Aeron just yet?"

Haruko spread his hands helplessly. "What could I tell them? I haven't any hard evidence, just suspicions and feelings. He'd only be sent home, under a cloud at best or under arrest at worst, and we'd be no closer to discovering his accomplices."

"Which you think he has."

"Which I *know* he has . . . I just don't know who. No, this way, you and I, maybe Warren and Athenée, we can all keep an eye on him. Now that we know what to look for, maybe we can come up with something more substantial than just weird feelings. Maybe. I hope."

O'Reilly studied her toes under the coverlet. "You are aware, of course, of how—cozy Hugh's been lately with Arianeira."

"Sure. She was the first person I thought of."

"And?"

"Well—do *you* think Gwydion's own sister would have anything to do with treason?"

"Well, I don't *want* to think so, no! No more than you want to think what you're obviously thinking—which is why you're here in the first place. Besides—" she drew her knees up to her chin, hugging them like a child being told a bedtime story—"Arianeira is foster-sister to Aeron and Morwen both. That's as sacred as blood-kinship to Kelts. She'd never betray a bond like that . . . do you think?"

"She might, if she thought she had reason to—or had the right sort of persuasion. Do you think Hugh would really mutiny?"

She shrugged. ''Maybe he had the right kind of persuasion too. He's been spending all his time at Llys Dôn lately—and I mean, *all* his time. If he really is in league with a Keltic traitor, or traitors, it stands to reason Arianeira would be somehow involved. Either he's using her for cover, and she doesn't know it, or else she's the traitor herself. But even supposing all this is true, what could they be planning to pull?''

''I haven't the slighest idea. And I think we'll just have to leave it there. Well, at least for the next few days, anyway. Just think about it, maybe talk about it to Warren and Mikhailova—and then we'll tell Morwen, even if we still have nothing new to go on.''

O'Reilly looked doubtful. ''Can we afford to wait like that?''

''Given our position? I think we can't afford not to.''

After the Terrans had been affectionately dismissed, and, a little later, Morwen too had taken warm leave, Aeron lay on the bed watching Gwydion, who now lounged before the fire, idly picking out a Vanx dance on his telyn.

''Shall I stay?'' he asked presently. When she made no reply, he said with a smile, ''I will, of course, if you wish it, Aeronwy, but I think you may have more need tonight of time to yourself.''

She smiled in answer, a lovely warm slow smile that seemed to light all their past as well as the present.

''How comes it you know me so well?''

''Long years' practice, Ard-rían.''

Aeron nodded thoughtfully, almost absently, then slipped from the bed and sank down beside him on the furs by the hearth, leaning her elbow on the seat of a chair and staring into the flames.

They sat awhile thus in silence, and Gwydion continued to play softly. At last Aeron stirred, face flushed from the fire's heat, and pushed back her hair with both hands.

''Have you seen aught of Arianeira lately? She stayed on in the City as I invited her to, but I have not heard anything of her since the night of the ceili.''

''Nay—she keeps to herself at Llys Dôn; I myself have

seen her only once or twice, when I was there on household matters. Though I have heard that she sees much of the Terran Tindal. My rechtair at the Llys, old Pendaran, tells me Tindal comes to dine with her almost every night, and very often leaves not until morning.''

"Tindal with Ari?'' she said, surprised. "How very strange . . . I would not have thought him a likely choice of hers.''

"Ari has ever been easily caught by novelty; and just as easily uncaught.'' Gwydion seemed unconcerned. "I doubt it will last . . . I am told also that the other Terrans find it just as surprising for him. But since Ari does stay on in Caerdroia,'' he added, "I should make more time for her. She has been here some weeks, and I have scarcely spoken to her. And yet . . .'' He struck a deliberately jangled chord. "And yet when we did speak, she and I, I did feel something cold and hostile from her that I, at least, have never felt before. I would alter that, if I can.''

"If you spent more of your time at Llys Dôn you might find that easier.''

He laughed. "Perhaps I should go there now, then.''

"It is a cold dark ride to the Llys this time of night,'' said Aeron judicially. "A long walk back to your tower, even.''

"So it is.'' Gwydion drew from the telyn a chord so exquisite that she closed her eyes, letting the beauty of the sound flow over her. Then she reached out and took the harp from his hands, leaning back against him without a word, and he closed his arms around her. They sat so without moving, without speaking, for many long minutes; both knowing, as clearly as if it had been spoken, that this night could well be one of the last such they might share for many nights to come.

"Play again,'' said Aeron suddenly. He did not let her go, but took up the telyn and steadied it upon her lap. As he began to play her favorite Erinnach air, she could feel the flex and pull of the muscles of his arms as his fingers moved upon the harpstrings, felt the absorption that enfolded him: that total engrossment of the true musician playing true music, so within himself he was in fact utterly outside himself.

She thought with deep humility how very graced they were to have come to each other so, after all that had befallen, in the face of all the demands of duty and of rank: Many men there were in Keltia fit to be the Ard-rían's consort, some few fit to have been Aeron's lover; but for *her*, for Queen and woman together, of all men else there was now none but he. She was filled with a fierce fearing desire only to hold him, to have him hold her, to cling together though the stars went out around them . . .

She twisted in his arms and looked up into his face, and the golden harp fell silent.

"I have loved thee, Gwynedd," she said softly in Kymric. "Oh, but I have loved thee . . ."

Chapter Fifteen

"As the Councils are aware," said Aeron, standing at her place at the head of the table, "I have been in preliminary communication with the Terran President and Senate regarding a formal embassy. Now that we have had these weeks to consider in full what this might mean both to us and to Earth, I would hear some last brief remarks before I announce to you my decision on the matter. You may speak as you please; this is far too important to leave any thought unsaid." She seated herself in her chair as Straloch leaned forward in his, and all round the room they steeled themselves for renewed hostilities.

"We know from Gwydion's spies"—his voice gave a contemptuous twist to the word, but Gwydion only smiled—"that there has been a meeting on Alphor, high officers and heads of state from Imperium and Phalanx both. This being followed by an invasion-level buildup of the Fomori forces, we must presume a similar weapontake by the Imperials—not to mention the levies they can draw upon from their vassal systems. We would be fools indeed, Ard-rían, to think this was pointed anywhere save square at our own throats. As soon as we move to ally formally with Earth, we shall feel the prick of that sword."

"And we still do not have sufficient strength to resist such a double onslaught," said the brehon Auster. "Our First Lord of War has admitted as much himself . . . Ard-rían, not one of us here is opposed in principle to eventual alliance with

Earth, but can it not be done more—temperately, so as not to inflame the situation any more than must be?''

Aeron jumped up and stalked over to the windows. "True it is I said you may speak as you please, but by the gods I do grow weary of this milk-mouthed whining: how we dare not offend or anger the Imperium or the Phalanx. What of how *they* dare not offend or anger *us*?''

"If you wish for that sort of certainty you must make a bid yourself for empire.'' That was Gwydion, and she turned on him, but Douglass Graham cut in adroitly.

"That may be no wild thought, Ard-rían. You are already Empress of the West, by right descent from Arthur. And your rule is over out-Wall systems now as well as over our own: This war, when it comes, will be for that reason as much as for the other, make no mistake about that. If you were to declare yourself Empress in law as well as in fact, in opposition to the Cabiri, no Kelt or Protectorate citizen would fail to recognize you as such, and a thousand other systems would be eager to offer you allegiance. More, very like. Strephon could not begin to challenge such sway, not for a very long time. Perhaps not ever.''

Aeron's face was set and hard. "I do not wish for Imperial sovereignty. I have never sought that kind of power.''

"Yet it might be forced upon you, will you or nill you,'' said Gwydion quietly. She turned a cold glare upon him, but he continued, "Bres and Strephon must be stopped. You are the only one who has both the will and the means to do so. That is why the out-Wall systems sue for Keltia's protection in such numbers: They know Keltia cannot be moved, and that they know because of what you have shown them these past three years.''

There was a long heart-freezing silence, then Aeron slowly returned to her seat.

"That's as may be,'' she said, "but it makes no odds. Imperial sway is not one of my options at this time; indeed, I pray not ever, and I pray likewise it never becomes no longer option only, but necessity . . . But I will not delay you further: I have decided to ally formally with the Terran Federacy, and I have already sent their leaders a message to that effect. Their embassy ship will leave there upon arrival of my offer. There will be no discussion and no more debate. My decision is by royal fiant, and so unalterable; and it will not be subject to review by the Senate, the Assembly, or the House of Peers. Taoiseach, let it be so set down."

The only sound in the room was that of Straloch's fists slamming down upon the table.

"Then by all the gods there ever were, Aeron, take some wit and wisdom along with your folly! Declare yourself Empress, raise the Protectorates, do anything but sit idly and wait for Strephon to act! You're as obstinate as ever your father was, and gods know *he* was always as stubborn as a moscra—"

Gwydion made as if to speak, and Straloch rounded on him. "And as for you, Prince of Gwynedd—I have not been the only one in this kingdom, or even on this Council, to question your fitness to hold the offices you hold."

"They who are Kin to the Dragon bestowed upon me the one," said Gwydion evenly, though his eyes glinted dangerously. "And she who sits upon the Throne of Scone raised me to the other. Do you, then, question Queen and Kinship both?"

"Certainly I question whether Aeron's personal affections have not interfered with the Ard-rían's judgment! Someone of greater age and prudence—"

"Such as yourself, my lord?" snapped Rohan.

"Such as any who has seen and done and managed more than you or your sister or your friends! This Council, this entire *kingdom*, is run by intractable bairns who have not the sense to appoint their elders and betters to the places that age and wisdom merit. I warned you, Aeron, what any alliance with Terra would cost us, and you insisted on ignoring my advice, even though I am Lord Extern and presumably know somewhat about dealings with the world outside the Curtain Wall. I tell you now, if your stupidity brings war upon us, the guilt of it be upon you alone!"

Aeron had listened to this tirade with bent head, only her fingers flexing and unflexing around her lightpen giving evidence of her anger, but now she looked up at Straloch, and her eyes blazed pure green in a white face.

"Then upon my head be it," she said softly, in a voice that

chilled them all. "You for one, my lord of Straloch, shall share it not, for you are dismissed from this Council from this moment, and you are much to thank me I do not banish you from this kingdom as well."

"That will need a vote, Ard-rían!"

"I need *no* vote!" Aeron was on her feet now. "Am I not Ard-rían—even to your distaste? You have already thrown it in my face how like I am to my father—go, Straloch, before I show you how like I can be to my ten-times-great-grandsir Brendan Mór, and take off your head for this!"

"Aeron—"

"Go!"

Straloch bowed with frigid courtesy and paced from the room. Aeron flung herself into her chair, one hand shading her eyes.

Into the screaming silence, only Elharn dared to speak.

"May one ask, Ard-rían, how you came to your decision for alliance?"

"One may *ask,* certainly!"

He caught her glance and held it—not for nothing was he the son of the Ard-rían Aoife—and after a tense moment she relented.

"We cannot keep the universe out forever, uncle. Despite the obvious preferences of my lord of Straloch . . . We have stood removed from the rest of the worlds these fifteen hundred years gone by. We need not drop the Curtain Wall to do so, but to stand more in the stream of events can only be to the good of Keltia. If we deny it now, this fair and excellent chance, then the next time the outside world comes to our gates may be far less to our liking. I for one would sooner make common cause with the rest of the galaxy when *I* please to do so, not at the pleasure of others." She pushed back her hair with her familiar gesture. "As for Straloch's accusations, they have been made before now, and perhaps true enough as far as they go. Some of us here, myself not least, *are* full young by comparison. I say it does not signify. Young or old, I am your Ard-rían; I have chosen my Councils to suit my needs and the changing needs of this kingdom, and I have appointed all of you, novice or veteran, as I have seen fit. I loved the Ard-rígh my father most dearly, but this is my reign, no longer his; and things will be done in my reign that would not have been done in his had he lived two hundred years and died in his bed. And if, like Gavin, any of the rest of you have any smallest difficulty with that, I give you leave and blessing to withdraw now.'' She paused for the space of ten heartbeats, and did not look at them. No one moved. "Well, then.''

Morwen glanced anxiously at the pale profile to her left. After the unprecedented violence of the last few minutes, Aeron seemed suddenly fragile, too fine to bear the weight of the queenship's decisions and demands.

And this was a decision that would reverberate through all Keltic history, ever after from this moment, would stand alone beside St. Brendan's command to forsake Earth and the sword-dance that Arthur of Arvon had led against the Theocracy: the Ard-rían Aeron's decision to pull aside the Curtain Wall. She would be damned or sainted, would rise or fall, by what she had chosen in this moment for her people and herself. And, meeting Aeron's eyes, Morwen saw that Aeron knew it too . . .

In the corridor after the Councillors had dispersed, Rohan, looking harried, caught Morwen up.

"She's dancing on the skirtedge of disaster,'' he said bluntly.

Morwen felt her heart lurch within her. "She has always been a very neat-footed dancer—even with such a partner as that.''

Aeron's heir shook his head. "So far. Pray this time she treads not upon its toes.''

"May I speak with you, Taoiseach?''

Morwen looked up at the sound of the familiar voice. It was late afternoon of the day of the Council meeting. O'Reilly stood in Morwen's office doorway, plainly hesitant, yet equally plainly resolved to speak her mind to the First Minister of Keltia.

"Always. Come in, then.'' She waited courteously while O'Reilly seated herself on the far side of the big marble table, but when the Terran finally began to speak the topic could not have been more unexpected.

"What is this omen they're all talking about?"

Morwen snorted. "Oh, the kingdom is forever full of omens, people seeing prodigies in bowls of milk— It comes of having a sorcerous population. If Aeron gave heed to a hundredth part of them she would not be able to stir nor hand nor foot."

"But do people take it seriously? And what *was* it, anyway? Nobody would actually tell me."

"True it is that many put faith in such things . . . Well, they say that last night at sunset, in the uplands of Moymore, a great black hand crawled down from Mount Keltia and shadowed all the Great Glen, reaching its fingers toward Caerdroia. There have been other portents as well, on other worlds. The Mari Llwyd, the Ghost Mare, has been seen galloping in the night on Dyved. On Erinna, the river called Destroyer ran red with blood, and the sun shone at midnight over the plain of the Leha on Kernow."

"Does it all mean anything?" O'Reilly, consumed with guilt, could not look the other woman in the eye.

Morwen's shrug was eloquent. "Who can say for certain? It all depends on who does the interpreting, and not even the sorcerers are in agreement. When such portents have appeared in times past, sometimes they meant one thing and sometimes another, and very often nothing at all. Aeron does not seem over-fretted by any of them, and she is a Ban-draoi, a most skilled one too, and she would surely know if any evil were toward."

"She doesn't seem exactly over-full of good cheer lately, either."

"No . . . no, she does not. What is it you would say to me, O'Reilly?"

"Treachery," she said at last, and the word came out a whisper. "The Captain and I, we think there is some kind of plot." She halted, then finished up all in a rush. "We think it's Tindal, that he might be up to something. But we don't know what. He could be working alone, but we think he's got Keltic accomplices. Just a lot of little things that add up to—well, to possibility . . . the Captain found some suspicious codes in Tindal's computer, Tindal doesn't know he found them. We think—Sir and I—that Tindal was using the combanks aboard the *Sword* as a booster, sending secret messages to someone outside the Curtain Wall.''

Morwen's expression had grown progressively graver during the Terran's speech, and now she tapped on the marble desktop with the tip of her lightpen.

''That is a serious charge, Lieutenant. I would put much in your word and Theo's, but—is there any more solid proof of this?''

''No,'' said O'Reilly with reluctance. ''Tindal left no record of the transmission—if there even *was* a transmission. He would have erased the computer's memory after using the codes—he could do that, he's very good with computers, a lot better than I am. So unless your own tracking stations logged the transmission, or somehow traced it back . . .'' She shrugged.

''I see.''

''Will you tell the Queen?''

''I do not know just yet. Does Theo know you have come to me?''

O'Reilly nodded. ''Oh yes. He and I discussed this last night after we left you and Aeron and Gwydion, and we thought we'd wait a while before we told you, in hopes of having something more concrete to go on. Then, after seeing what went on this morning in the Council meeting, we—changed our minds. Even so, Sir asked me if I'd be the one to tell you. He sort of was afraid you might blame him.''

''Blame him!''

''For not telling you sooner.''

''What, when he had no proof of anything amiss? He thought to be blamed for that? Oh, he can be such an amadaun!''

''Well, he said he'd be happy to talk to you, if you ever even wanted to speak to him again after this.''

In spite of her growing disquiet, Morwen laughed. ''Then let us fetch him here at once.''

When Haruko joined them, head high despite his guilty conscience, Morwen wasted neither time nor words.

''No apologies, Theo, for you are not at fault here, but I must know everything that you know. I am no truth-senser to say for certain, but I feel—I cannot say how—that you may well be right. If you think Tindal does betray us, do you think he acts alone?''

He met her gaze with steady dark eyes. "I do not."

"With whom, then?"

"Arianeira. But I can't prove that either. If I could, Aeron would have heard from me five minutes later."

Morwen's face, at first unchanged in the surprise of the name, which was somehow no surprise at all, turned white, then red, then flooded with stunned comprehension.

"Oh gods, but I think that you are right." It would explain so much that had gone unexplained in the last few weeks: Arianeira's attitude, her closeness with Tindal, even her presence at Court. *And Mighty Mother,* thought Morwen, *how do I tell Aeron—or* Gwydion . . .

She stood up. "Will you both come with me now to Gwydion?"

O'Reilly blanched at the thought of telling the Prince of Dôn of his sister's possible treason. But Haruko was firm.

"We will, Taoiseach, if you think it good."

"I do so, and I think also we will not speak of it yet to Aeron. But let us find Gwydion."

They did not find him for some time. They went first to his rooms in the palace, but he was not there. Nor was he at Llys Dôn, or the Fianna Commandery, or any other of the places he was likely to be, and he had left no word with anyone as to his whereabouts.

At last they met him returning from a solitary ride in the fells to the east of the City, and they went back with him to his rooms, there to deliver the matter to him in private.

Like Morwen before him, Gwydion gave no immediate sign that he had even heard. Haruko lapsed into uncertain silence, but O'Reilly was by now in the grip of outraged emotion.

"This is your sister we're talking about! Doesn't that mean anything to you?"

He looked at her then, and she wished she had emulated Haruko's silence, for the gray eyes were terrifying.

"It means a very great deal to me, O'Reilly," he said. "Not only is Ari my sister, but she is Aeron's foster-sister, and Morwen's also, and you two know by now what that means to a Kelt.''

Haruko's face was full of all the helplessness he felt. "I am sorry, lord, to be the one to carry this suspicion to you. And desperately sorry that I didn't do so sooner."

"Better you than another, Theo. You did right to come to us, and later or sooner, I think, will make but little differ here. Any road, I too have had suspicions about Ari of late. I have sensed—well, I thought my suspicions unworthy of either her or me." His laugh was short and unamused. "The reality seems to be a thousand times unworthier than aught I could have imagined."

"Will you tell Aeron, then?" murmured Morwen. "Or shall I?"

"When time is, I shall tell her. But not yet. She has much upon her shoulders at the moment. If we tell her now, the first thing she will demand is proof, and we have none to speak of. Neither of Tindal's guilt nor—nor of Ari's."

"We have some pretty good circumstantial evidence, at least."

"We do, and very like Aeron would honor our judgment by accepting that evidence as fact, since it was presented in good faith by us whose word she values. But it is not fact, and no brehon in the kingdom would sentence a pig upon such evidence. We have not even convinced ourselves yet; how are we to convince the Ard-rían?"

"But suppose we're too late!" O'Reilly's anguish broke through at last.

"Then is it dán, fated so," said Gwydion, "and certainly no fault of yours." His voice was soft, full of concern for her distress. "You did not delay out of any reasons but good ones: justice and love. And now must I do no less. But I feel it will not be very long until we know."

"One way or another," said Haruko heavily.

Gwydion nodded as their eyes met and held. "As you say."

"So Aeron is expecting real ambassadors." Kynon swirled the ale in his cup and looked up at Arianeira, who stood, flushed from the outdoors, beside the fire in the Great Hall at Llys Dôn.

"She has just informed her Councils so this morning. That old bodach Straloch told me all about it. He was in a rage over it, and that was why he was so eager to talk to someone; and I have always been a favorite of his. He opposed Aeron most bitterly, and the upshot of it was that she dismissed him from the Council on the spot. How long before that embassy ship should arrive?" she threw over her shoulder.

Tindal shrugged. "Depending on when they leave—maybe a month, two months at most. I respectfully suggest Your Highness notify our Coranian colleague."

"I agree, lady," said Kynon, in response to the questioning look Arianeira gave him.

She took a deep breath. "Well then, tonight. Tindal, you will make the necessary preparations."

"One moment," said Tindal. "Once I *have* sent the message, how will you let down the Curtain Wall to fulfill your part of the bargain? You've been rather vague about the details, and you did tell us you couldn't manage to winkle the clearance codes out of your brother's office."

"There are more ways than one to shear this particular sheep," said Arianeira, unruffled. "And it is in my mind that Aeron, of all people, shall show me that way." She ignored the massive doubt registered on the faces of the two men. "You have the escape plan to hand. Once the message is sent, you will leave Caerdroia separately and head for Gwynedd. Go to Caer Ys, where you will be expected, and be prepared to take ship from there when I send word that the Curtain Wall has been breached. That should be in no more than a day and a night. By then I shall be aboard Jaun Akhera's flagship, and I will send you sailing instructions. You shall be kept well away from the fighting, I assure you," she added scornfully, for Tindal's face had filled with alarm. It was surely the sarcasm of the gods that she had to rely on such a one for such a matter—but the end was surely worth even so contemptible a means . . .

Kynon had divined something of her intent. "You will use magic, then," he said gruffly. "True it is that you are a renowned sorceress, and I am no magician of any skill, lady, but do you know what you do?''

Her blue eyes flashed displeasure. "I know very well what I do, son of Accolon, and better it will be for you if you do not question it.''

When her two accomplices had withdrawn, leaving her alone in the high-ceilinged hall, she put her hands to her mouth to still her excited trembling and turned a passionate unseeing gaze on the room.

"Ah, Aeron,'' she breathed, "how easy you have made it for me to destroy you . . .'' Of course, it would not be truly easy, what Arianeira had it in mind to do. After all, Aeron had used the same method at Bellator; it had worked, right enough, beyond all expectation—but its aftermath had also nearly killed her.

Arianeira scowled at that thought. It would be tedious indeed to be so—inconvenienced. But Aeron had always had a core of conscience far too easily pierced for one who would be High Queen. She herself would not be so afflicted.

Arianeira had little difficulty that night in obtaining a ship at Mardale Port. Few would refuse the Princess of Gwynedd transport in her brother's name, and once the ship stood well out from Tara, it was a simple enough matter to control its crew. Some died in resisting her magic, their minds torn apart even as their bodies ended in torment. But to her way of thinking, better it was for them that they perished now than in what was to come when the ship docked at the Curtain Wall station of Murias.

Jaun Akhera himself had specified this station, in his conversation with Arianeira earlier that night. Of the four Curtain Wall power outposts, it was the one nearest to the Keltic Throneworld system, and also the one most convenient to the Imperial armadas, which even now were assembling outside the Wall, their ranks reaching back for many thousands of star-miles.

The personnel at Murias station never knew what killed them—it happpened much too quickly for that, so there was some small mercy even at the end. One minute they were welcoming the sister of the First Lord of War, the next they were dead or dying.

. . . Arianeira lowered her arms, breathing hard after her exertions, as if she had run a race or fought a bout. *And it was Aeron who showed the way,* she thought exultantly. It was somehow fitting that the same sorcery Aeron had used against Bellator to avenge a wrong should now be used against her for the same reason. But it was truly a fearful spell. It had taken more out of her than any magic she had ever worked, though she had studied it ever since she and Jaun Akhera had first made their hell-wrought bargain, knowing she would undoubtedly be obliged to use it in the end and steeling herself to master it.

But it had not been so difficult after all, merely tiring; or else perhaps she had grown stronger for her months of discipline. Pity it was, though, that the Curtain Wall was too far distant from Tara for even Aeron to sense the backwash of the magic; though she would hear of it soon enough.

She looked around triumphantly at the carnage she had wrought. And that was only the first step, the clearing of the way for the real work now to begin. And as for Kynon and Tindal . . .

Arianeira permitted herself a small smile. Those two would find at Caer Ys neither ship nor sanctuary, but only a rather abrupt passing into their next lives. She had set there a telesm, a kind of magical time bomb keyed to the personal auras of the two men. It wanted only their arrival to activate itself, and would not do so until that moment, even though all the rest of the kingdom should crowd into the castle. The resultant implosion would bring down the castle, and perhaps even the entire island upon which it stood, upon their unsuspecting heads.

She turned her attention to the next phase of her magic: the destruction of the Curtain Wall. Before granting him the mercy of death, Arianeira had subjected the station captain to the full force of her kenning powers; and the information she had ripped from his mind—how *could* the Fianna assign such weak vessels to such critical posts—had revealed to her the station's points of greatest vulnerability. Destroy that, and this entire section of Wall would billow inwards like a tapestry in a draft. It remained only to do it. And beyond the Wall's thin blue glow, though Arianeira could not see them, nor they her, waited the Imperial fleets.

She drew three deep breaths and raised her arms above her head, joining her palms together, for the final phase of the spell of destruction, then closed her eyes and summoned all her power. As the sparkling vortex began to build around her, she smiled again, for nothing could stop it now.

"Aeron," she whispered, "you are undone." And the evil radiance began to stream outward from her hands.

Chapter Sixteen

*F*ull winter now on Tara. At Caerdroia, the prevailing winds had backed round into the north, blasting down through the high passes of the Stair, snow-laden, blue with chill from out of Northplain.

Up in the seaward tower, snow hissed against the windows. In the tapestry-curtained bed, it was warm and snug as a walled pleasaunce, and the last of the firelight flickered over a man and woman deep asleep.

Gwydion's arm even in sleep was laid protectively over Aeron, tanned skin contrasting with blue-veined ivory. But his sword arm was unencumbered, ready to reach at need for the weapon that lay on the chest beside the bed.

Aeron slept profoundly, totally trusting for once to another's strength rather than her own. The news of the coming Terran embassy, and the ensuing brangle with the Council, and above all the passage-of-arms with Straloch, had wearied and upset her, and even before that her dreams had been troubled with renewed prescience. So that Gwydion, coming to her from his own council with Morwen and the Terrans, had not the heart to waken her when at last she seemed peacefully asleep; he would tell her of the Terrans' suspicions in the morning.

In the dark cold predawn hours, everything seemed to happen at once. The automatic viewscreens lit with a sudden blaze of urgency, alarms sounded, and two cloaked people burst unceremoniously into the chamber.

Gwydion was awake with his sword in his hand before Aeron even moved, so great was the speed of his warrior's reflexes—and the measure of his protectiveness. When he saw that the intruders were Rohan and Morwen, he relaxed, but even so he was slow to lower the point of the sword.

Aeron, whose own instinct had told her almost as swiftly that only three people in the universe could enter her rooms unannounced and unchallenged—and one of those three was already beside her—was less startled, though a good deal angrier.

"Do not ever do so again . . . do not. But tell us quickly."

Morwen wasted no words. "The Curtain Wall has been breached, and an Imperial armada is on its way here. Get dressed at once, both of you are needed in the Commandery."

Without a word Gwydion began putting on trews and boots, and Aeron caught the black Dragon uniform that Morwen took from its peg in the wardrobe.

"What other word?"

"None as yet," admitted Rohan, holding boots and cloak ready for his sister like one of the royal dressers. "The verified signal has only just come through, as you heard; we were in the Commandery on other business when the preliminary alarms sounded from Murias station on the Wall, and we came here at once, thinking to warn you. We were something late . . . Also the Terran Tindal goes missing."

Aeron pulled the tunic over her head and came up shaking her hair from her eyes. "Declare a state of war, effective immediately."

"Already done, Ard-rían, and the order awaits only your sign-manual to be official."

"You say Tindal is missing?" Aeron sat on the bed to pull on her boots. "Where has he gone, could he be in danger? Did no one see him go?"

Morwen shook her head. "We do not know where he is, and we fear the worst; if he has dared to venture off-planet, he could be in very great peril. But we have sent some to search for him . . . Meantimes, the Fianna generals and the Dragon commanders are now assembling in the War Room; the Earl-Marischal and the Earl-Guardian have been summoned also."

"Good." Aeron stood up and flung her cloak about her. "Now fetch the other Terrans to the War Room, and for the sake of all the gods find Tindal!"

When the knock came at his door, Haruko, awake at once, was not at all surprised, and he opened the door fully prepared for the worst.

A tall warrior in the black Dragon Kinship uniform stood there, and saluted Haruko smartly. "I am Grelun, lord," he said. "Lieutenant to the Pendragon."

Confused for a moment, Haruko remembered that that was Gwydion's Dragon title, and he nodded. "Yes, Lieutenant?"

"You are summoned by the Ard-rían, lord, to the War Room, you and the others who came with you. They are coming here now." He gestured. "If you will?"

"Of course." He grabbed up his uniform from the chair where he had thrown it and pulled it on hastily. "Is it war?"

"That is not for me to say, lord," said Grelun, and Haruko finished dressing in silence.

In the tower courtyard they met O'Reilly, Mikhailova and Hathaway, each with a Dragon escort and each looking apprehensive. Haruko peered around.

"Where's Tindal?"

"Lieutenant Tindal is apparently not in Caerdroia," said Grelun.

Haruko and O'Reilly instantly sought each other's eyes, shattered by the same thought: They had been right about Tindal after all, and now it was too late.

"Captain?"

Haruko turned his head with an effort. Mikhailova stood at his elbow, looking white and frightened in the light of the torches.

"What is it, Ensign?"

"I have something to tell you, sir," she said all in a rush, as if in fear she would lose her courage before she could say what she must.

"May we have a moment?" said Haruko to Grelun, and the Kelt nodded. Haruko drew Mikhailova to one side and put a hand on her shoulder.

"Tell me, Athenée. It's all right, I promise you."

"Well—I don't know if this is the best time to bring this up—it probably isn't—but it's been bothering me a long time, sir, and I'd just as soon tell you, if that's all right with you."

"Of course." Haruko felt a chill breath pass over him, as if somehow he already knew what it was she wished to tell him.

"You remember the party, the night we arrived here? Well, a man came up to me at dinner a couple of weeks later and said that he'd met me at the party and that he—he wanted to be friends with me."

"What man?"

"His name was—is Kynon. He's a retainer of the Princess Arianeira—you know, Prince Gwydion's sister."

Haruko felt his blood flood cold to his feet, and he leaned back against the tower wall, a little faint. This, then, was the link he had sought all this time in vain, the proof he had needed for Morwen and Gwydion. It wasn't the whole story, but it was enough for Haruko to see where it had to be going and where it had begun. Only now it was too late to stop it—

But Mikhailova was intent on her own thought, and did not notice her Captain's reaction. "It was so strange, sir. He was very attentive for a few weeks, and I must admit I felt very flattered. And then, all of a sudden, he turned so cold—it was like flipping a relay switch—and I never saw him again. Well, I did once or twice, actually, from a distance, with Tindal . . . I was just hurt and confused, and I didn't know what to think, so I just withdrew from everything. That's why I've been so out of things lately." She looked up at him at last, heartened by his hand squeezing her shoulder. "I thought I'd been stupid and naive, making a fool of myself, and I didn't want to think about it, and I didn't want to risk doing it again. I know it probably doesn't have very much to do with whatever's going on tonight, but I should have told you sooner, and I just wanted to tell you now, so you'd know."

Haruko chose his words carefully, not wishing to give the appearance of blaming her, which, God knew, he most certainly did not . . .

"Athenée—I don't think you were either foolish or naive, I think you were being used. Tell me now, honestly, do you remember this Kynon asking you things, maybe he hadn't any business asking about?''

She looked up at him sharply. "Oh, but he did! And it made me feel so uncomfortable. He would ask about my duties on the *Sword*, what a tech officer could and couldn't do, what kind of computer facilities we had, things like that. I didn't tell him anything, sir; I swear it.''

"I know you didn't," said Haruko. "And when he realized you weren't going to tell him, Athenée, that was when he dropped you, and found somebody else who would.''

"Who would?" she repeated blankly. Then, with dawning horrified comprehension, "Not—not *Hugh*!''

"I'm afraid so. I haven't time to go into it all now, but Sally and I think that's exactly what's happened. And if we're right, that's why we're being summoned now by the Queen.''

"To the War Room, they said. *Is* it war?''

Haruko nodded, and across the courtyard Grelun gestured to him. "We have to go now. I'll tell you the rest on the way.''

The Fianna Commandery occupied a brugh of its own across the Great Square from the palace, and could be reached from there by means of underground passageways. The War Room, nerve center of the huge complex, was located in a tower of its own; by the time Aeron arrived there, Gwydion and the others close behind, it was ablaze with lights and roaring with activity.

At her entrance the frenzy redoubled, and the captain-general of the Fianna dashed over to her.

"Hail, athiarna," he said, saluting in the Fian manner.

Aeron acknowledged the salute, moving to the hologram star display in the room's enormous two-story center well.

"Well met in ill time, Donal. What is our current state?''

"Ill enough, Lady. An Imperial armada has entered through a deliberately created breach in the Curtain Wall. Murias station has been completely destroyed, as yet we know not how or by whom. Fleets have been sent against all our systems, but the main strength of the invasion is coming in along Ullin's Straight Way, headed for Tara.''

Aeron was studying the shifting lights of the display. "If I were leading them in, I would bring them rather by hyperspace on the sunside of Droma's orbit. Far closer to Tara, and shorter, than the path they now take.''

Donal mac Avera's grin was wolf-fierce. ''I would say they do not care to risk entangling themselves in the Answerer.'' That was Fragarach, a sun-gun emplacement, a laser-cannon battery about the size of a small moon, and Aeron smiled grimly in response.

''I daresay they do not, and that proves their intelligence sources limited. Someone obviously warned them about Fragarach, but—''

''Exactly, Ard-rían—but could not tell them about military navigation for hyperspace, once they had actually penetrated the Bawn. That is why they sail straight-space, and so we shall have sufficient time, thank gods, to prepare for them.''

''Mm. Doubtless they realize that, too . . . What of our own fleets?''

''Called up at the first alarm. Elharn has gone to the *Firedrake*, and Rohan will join him later. Gwennan Chynoweth has already taken the ship out of starharbor, with a full escort of cursals and heavy destroyers. The main fleet is assembling at the Roads of Grannos, the system navies are mobilizing to defend their own space, and the advance wings go even now to Murias—or what was Murias.''

''Has any trace been found of the Terran Tindal? Where in all the hells could he have got to?''

''The portmaster at Mardale informed me a few minutes before you came in that Tindal left last night for Gwynedd, in a hired vessel.''

Aeron stared at him. ''And the portmaster did not think to inform *me*?''

''The Terrans have the freedom of their diplomatic status,'' said mac Avera, somewhat stung at her implication of neglect. ''Which Your Majesty confirmed them in—''

''Aye, I know, I know. I meant no criticism. Still—why Gwynedd, I wonder? And why last night of all nights?''

''Do you think he has some connection with the invasion?''

''It seems not possible, but it is surely beginning to look so. Though how it could be so—'' She broke off as Morwen, who had been busy with the generals across the room, came up to them.

"The declaration of war, Ard-rían. Not though the formality matters now, but just so all is done seemly."

"It matters, right enough." She seized the diptych from Morwen's hands, signed swiftly *Arigna Regina,* and slammed both signets into the matrix. "War they have sought of me, therefore red war shall I give them. The terms are as you please, Taoiseach. And in the name of the sainted Brendan, bring in Tindal!" She turned again to mac Avera, who anticipated her next question.

"All Fian commands are on full battle footing. Douglass Graham is overseeing the alert of the catha on the outlying worlds. On this planet, the Pillars of Tara have been mobilized. Elharn requests orders. We have been at war for fully an hour, athiarna."

"So it seems, my friend." She gripped his shoulder for an instant, turned to Morwen. "Get me an open farviewer link, and blanket all signals save military ones. Sound the Crann Tarith on every planet so that no one sleeps. I will speak to the people, and I care not if the enemy hears me."

Within the hour, every farviewer, every viewscreen in Keltia, carried the same image: Aeron, face pale but completely composed, clad in the black battle dress of the Dragon Kinship and seated behind a table in the Commandery. Her voice was grave but confident, and, knowing as she did that the signal would almost certainly be picked up by the invading fleet, cold with menace.

Mac Avera and Gwydion, among many others, stood outside camera range along the wall, watching her.

"She does very well," whispered the Fianna leader. "Her father, gods rest him, would be proud of her."

Gwydion nodded, but made no other response. Twenty minutes ago he had received the first authenticated information about the breaching of the Curtain Wall; as yet only he and Morwen, of all those in the War Room, were privy to it, and they had agreed that he should be the one to tell Aeron, but not until after the broadcast.

Aeron concluded her brief address; the camera crystals went dark, and she sat motionless at the table for a moment.

When Gwydion approached, she looked up at him as if she did not recognize him, then ran a hand over her face and stood up.

"Aeronwy, there is a thing you must hear," he said quietly. "We have had news of the plan and manner of the invasion."

"What news?"

He glanced around the thronged room. "Not here. Come aside a moment." He led her to the windows that formed a great bay in the eastern wall, overlooking Caerdroia, and turned her gently to face him.

In spite of his precautions, every eye in the War Room, save only Morwen's, who deliberately turned away, was nailed to them even in this poor privacy. None could hear what Gwydion said to her, but all could see the effect of his words.

Aeron spun away from him to stare out the windows into the dark, unable for the moment to trust her self-control.

"May the High God Artzan Janco hear me," she said at last, and her voice shook with her anger. "That I may be face to face with Jaun Akhera, and nothing between his throat and my hands—unless it be my sword. Chriesta tighearna! To suborn Tindal was a deed black enough, but to cause a Kelt to betray his own folk—" Her head came up as one more piece of the puzzle fell into place. "Then *that* was why I could not see—"

"Not see?"

"I told you not, but I underwent the taghairm some time ago. I was still being plagued by dreams, and I tried to find out their cause."

Even in that moment of utter horror, Gwydion was shocked. "You did *what?*"

Aeron lifted her chin like a child hoping to brazen out a scolding. "It was no use in any case—and now I see why. Jaun Akhera is a sorcerer fully capable of shielding his cat's-paws from discovery."

"He was not the only sorcerer in it," said Gwydion grimly. "I had hoped to spare you a while longer. But there is more, and worse."

"Then say it!"

"Three there were who contracted Keltia's fall with Jaun Akhera: Tindal, the Kymro Kynon ap Accolon, and—and one other, who used black sorcery to break the Curtain Wall."

She had caught an inkling of what he was about to tell her, and had gone very still. "And that one?"

"My sister. Arianeira."

All the fury, and all the blood, drained from Aeron's face, and Gwydion caught her elbow to support her. But she shook off his hand.

"Oh gods . . . Nay, it cannot be true, surely?"

He nodded, carefully keeping all feeling out of his face and voice, for emotion now would undo them both.

"True enough, Ard-rían. There is proof incontrovertible. The delay is fault of mine: Haruko and O'Reilly came to Morwen, and then to me, with suspicions of Tindal. But I decided not to speak of it yet to you, for that the information was still doubtful. This"—he indicated the War Room, and, by inference, the war itself—"came all too soon. But now it is certain."

Aeron's expression had not altered, but there was about her an air of entirely arrested movement, as if her whole being had been checked abruptly in its tracks.

"What proof is this you speak of?"

"One survived the attack upon Murias station, and managed to escape in a lifeship before the station was destroyed. She had seen what happened, and who had caused it to happen, and when she reached Caerdroia she summoned Morwen and me to hear her testimony. We have just come from speaking with her."

" 'Summoned,' by the gods! And this one was so certain, was she, of her facts? That it was Ari destroyed the Wall, and Tindal and Kynon her accomplices?"

"Certain enough, for she swore it to a truth-senser and a robed brehon before she died," said Gwydion with deliberate harshness, and Aeron's eyes fell. "As to Kynon and Tindal's involvement, she said Ari boasted of it to the captain of the station before she killed him . . . And we have the additional word of Haruko and O'Reilly. Or shall you doubt them too?"

Aeron shook her head wearily. "Nay, not those two. Have they come, then?"

Gwydion signaled to Grelun, who stood by the War Room door. Ushered in by the tall Dragon, almost unnoticed by the others in the room, Haruko and O'Reilly came timidly across the floor, followed by Mikhailova, white and shaken, and Hathaway, who was trying hard to maintain his usual imperturbable demeanor.

Haruko had eyes only for Aeron. He came straight across the room to her and proceeded to ignore all the diplomatic etiquette he had ever learned, by presuming to address her first.

"Majesty, we have been told of Tindal's part in the treachery. I ask your forgiveness that we didn't tell you sooner what we suspected. Perhaps if we had—"

"It would have changed nothing, my friend. Do not torture yourself."

"I too ask Your Majesty's pardon." The small voice was Mikhailova's, and Aeron turned to her in surprise.

"You, Athwenna? But why?"

"I will explain." In a low quick voice Mikhailova repeated to Aeron and Gwydion what she had told Theo in the tower yard. When she finished, Aeron said no word but laid a gentle hand on the Terran's shoulder. Mikhailova looked up, startled, and then a tremulous smile came over her face.

"No blame to you," said Aeron. "To any of you . . . But I am sending you home at once, all of you. If you leave the planet now, we will be able to get you back aboard your ship in good time, and you should find it possible to evade the Imperial fleet and get safely away. Though you will have to take your chance there—as will we all."

"Your pardon again, Ard-rían," said Haruko, "but Tindal, however much an alleged traitor, is still my officer, under my command. Has he been found?"

"He has not. Last night, I am told, he left Tara, reportedly headed for the planet Gwynedd. A squadron of cursals has been dispatched in that area to look for him. And, given his part in all this, Captain Haruko, I am very much afraid that I must usurp your authority over him. If he has committed an act of treason against Keltia, his diplomatic immunity must be forfeit, and he be punished appropriately when he is taken."

"I accept Your Majesty's judgment," said Haruko after a short silence, and bowed to her.

"That is as it will be—but as to your own escape, we will drop a section of the Curtain Wall opposite the breach, so that you may slip out without need of a tow. Fetch what gear you have, and quickly; you must be at Mardale within the hour. Grelun will take you there in an aircar, and put you aboard a sloop of war to bring you to the *Sword*."

In spite of his woe, Haruko's heart swelled. Home! For a brief instant he allowed himself to think of all that home meant to him. Then to his own astonishment not least, he heard himself saying firmly, "Ard-rían, I am not leaving."

He had the rare satisfaction of seeing Aeron brought up short with surprise.

"Again, Theo, I did not hear you aright?"

"I said I'm not going." He met without flinching the full blast of her angry stare. "Aeron, I want to stay. I choose to stay. If you send me back to the *Sword*, I swear I'll take one of the lifeboats and come straight back, right through the middle of the Imperial fleet if I have to. I haven't wanted anything so much in a very long time. Please don't send me away." And he went to one knee before her.

Aeron had listened to this speech with her expression growing gradually more and more astounded, and when at last Haruko knelt she reached him both her hands and raised him at once.

"Send you away! Oh my dear friend, that is my will, not my wish . . . But think well before you throw in your lot with ours. It is a dangerous decision at best, perhaps a fatal one. You might never again be able to return to Earth."

Haruko was unswayed. "I don't care. I want to stay."

Aeron surrendered with a laugh. "Stay then!" Looking past Haruko's dazzled face, she saw O'Reilly's alight with the same mute plea. "Aye, and you also," she said quickly, to forestall yet another impassioned entreaty. "But the others, I think, will wish now to be gone."

Hathaway and Mikhailova looked relieved.

"Do you wish us to take any message back with us, Lady?" asked Hathaway, suddenly realizing how much he would miss this place, these people . . .

Aeron nodded, her attention already back on the big hollow map of the threatened star systems.

"I have both written and recorded a message to the President and Senate of your Federacy, which I had intended to send them in less desperate time," she said. "In the past hour, I have amended that message, and I pray you both to see it delivered; nay, I charge you to see it so. And, if Captain Haruko consents, I would ask you to take with you my ambassadors—not perhaps the ones I should have chosen later, but now . . . Well, I would send my sister the Princess Fionnuala, and as chief ambassador—Gavin Earl of Straloch. Also your old friend Morgan Cairbre, and, if the Pendragon permits, the Dragon Emrys Penmarc'h."

Her eyes met Gwydion's, and they shared the same thought: Fionnuala was the youngest of the immediate royal family; not only would she be better off out of the coming battles, but as youngest she was the one best able to assure the direct succession. As for Straloch, for all his difficult nature he was a matchless negotiator. The bard Cairbre would be Aeron's eyes, and the Dragon Emrys Gwydion's arm.

"If, of course," she continued, "your ship can carry the extra people?"

Surprised, Hathaway turned to his captain, and Haruko nodded.

"The *Sword* can certainly carry them, and so she will. You will do as Her Majesty asks, Lieutenant. I will supply you a formal entry for the ship's log to save trouble with the Admiralty."

"And I will do what I can to spare similar difficulty for you who remain," added Aeron. "In the message pouch there shall also be a word to the effect that it was I who held Haruko and O'Reilly there by royal prerogative. The last thing I would have you two face is court-martial in absentia." She straightened, and a more formal air fell upon her. "Then to you, Warren Hathaway and Athenée Mikhailova, who have been our guests and friends in Keltia, I say fare very well. We will meet again, doubt it not. Gods with you." She embraced each of them in turn.

Hathaway started to reply, then bowed deeply instead, and turned away to bid a warmly affectionate farewell to O'Reilly and a proudly formal one to his captain. Mikhailova made her goodbyes also, hugging the other two long and wordlessly, and then she and Hathaway were gone with Grelun.

Aeron watched them out of the room, then sighed and looked upon the pair who remained expectantly before her.

"If I may ask you two," she said, a smile touching the corners of her mouth, "what is the nature of your present allegiance? We are on a war footing here, and I cannot afford to carry noncombatants even if I would."

"Give me a sword, Aeron," said O'Reilly, "and you shall see."

"Accepted," said Aeron, and O'Reilly kissed her hand. "Enough. Go to Slaine, she will see you fitted out. And you, Theo?" she asked, as O'Reilly, transported, left them for the moment. "O'Reilly was Kelt from the first, but she was born so, it is in her blood. You have chosen to be of us, and for us, and that is a very different matter."

He bowed in the formal Japanasian manner, the bow of a vassal to his lord. "My hand is for you, Lady, though it hasn't struck very many blows lately. And also—it's sort of by way of reparation. I should have warned you sooner."

She understood his pain, and did not smile. "And that is the last we shall say of that . . . But I need you for a thing more important to me than your sword arm. We shall be meeting many alien minds and thoughts in the days to come, and I shall need all the non-Keltic insight I can get to help me deal with them. The Curtain Wall keeps out more than invading warships; it keeps out ideas. Time, perhaps, to rejoin the galaxy; I have staked my throne, and many lives, on that thought." She touched his arm in a gesture of affection rare with her. "Tell Desmond I wish you armed and outfitted as a Fian, give your log entry to Hathaway, and then return here in an hour's time. I must take further counsel of my commanders—but first I must bid my ambassadors farewell."

On the small landing-pad behind the Fianna brugh, tucked away in the sheltered ground between the tower and the wall, an aircar waited. It was painted green and gold, as a craft of the Royal Flight, and Grelun already sat at its controls. Alongside the ship, shivering a little with cold and anxiety equally, were Hathaway and Mikhailova; a few paces off, the bard Morgan Cairbre and the Dragon-warrior Emrys Penmarc'h spoke quietly together as they waited.

Just within the shelter of the arched tower doorway, Aeron stood with Fionnuala and Straloch. Behind them were Morwen and Gwydion.

"Time runs short," Aeron was saying, "and the *Sword* is waiting at the starharbor. What gear you will need has already been stored in the aircar. Nuala—" She took her youngest sister by the shoulders, looked long and searchingly into the clear violet eyes. "Until now you have had little to do with the politics of our kingdom, and your royal duties have fallen but lightly upon you. That is all changed now: You know my will, and my mind, and my love. You are an Aoibhell and a princess, and a child no longer. Do not forget."

Fionnuala smiled, brushing the strawberry-blonde hair out of her eyes with the same gesture Aeron favored.

"Nay, I am the Ard-rían's sister, and her servant also," she corrected proudly. "I will not forget." She kissed Aeron, embraced Morwen and Gwydion, then suddenly hugged her sister one last time and ran quickly to the aircar.

Straloch alone remained. Aeron and he looked silently at each other, and what each read in the other's eyes and mind was not hard to ken. Aeron began to laugh.

"I shall say it out if it gives you pleasure, Gavin—"

A rare grin split the Earl's gaunt countenance. "To hear you admit I told you thus? Nay, no pleasure, Aeron; the pleasure, and the honor, comes in my duty: that you have made me your ambassador. I too am the Ard-rían's servant, and I shall follow your orders." He added in a lower voice, "And I shall look after Fionnuala well; you need not worry about that."

"That I know, and the other too," said Aeron. "Else had I not chosen you . . ." He bent to kiss her hand, and she embraced him. "Go now."

The doors of the aircar shut seamlessly behind the little group, and Grelun had the craft airborne in the same moment. It rose straight up above the tower, then arrowed away east over Seren Beirdd and the falling ground where Turusachan sloped down to the lower city. They watched it until it was no longer visible, and even then they stood there a few moments longer.

Chapter Seventeen

When Haruko returned to the War Room as he had been bidden, clad now in the Fianna brown and feeling intensely proud, O'Reilly was waiting for him. She too was dressed in the brown uniform, and when she saw him, she smiled and ran forward to meet him.

"There is a meeting of the High Command in the Salt Tower," she told him. "Aeron told me to wait for you."

"Have they found Tindal yet?"

She shook her head, not looking at him, and he sighed.

"*God*, I wish—" he began, with an almost savage remorse. "Ah well, too late now."

"Do you think Hugh's dead?" she asked in a small voice.

"I don't know, Sally, but I think I almost hope so . . . Where is this meeting?"

They left the room together, going down a flight of stone steps and along long cloistered passages, to a guarded door at the end of a corridor. The Fian sentries each side of the door saluted and stood aside to allow them to pass. They returned the salute, feeling shy and more than a little awkward, and went in.

The large bright room was packed; of those there, the Terrans recognized many of the highest-ranking officers of the Fianna, Starfleet, Dragon Kinship and other military divisions. Aeron, seeing them hesitate just inside the door, waved them to seats in the row behind her.

At the front of the room, Gwydion was standing before a

huge projection screen upon which was displayed a hologram section of the Great Glen.

"He will land here," Gwydion was saying, his lightwand stabbing the map where the Strath widened out into the beginnings of Moymore, some fifty leagues east of Caerdroia as the hawk flies. "There is no other place. Closer to the City, the Strath is too narrow for a landing in force, and also too heavily defended. He would never attempt a sea landing, and Armoy and the plains of the south are too distant. Northplain would allow him to assemble his forces within striking distance of Caerdroia, but it is full winter there now and the snow and wind very bad, and soon to grow worse."

"So we meet him at the entrance to the Strath," said Douglass Graham.

Gwydion nodded. "If we cannot defeat him there, we shall still be able to fall back on the line of fortresses along the Avon Dia; and so, in the end, upon Caerdroia itself—if we must. If we beat him beside the Cliffs of Fhola, so much the better."

"But you think we shall not." That was Aeron.

"I do not think we can hold him." He spoke to them all, but his eyes were upon her. "And further, we must prepare ourselves for the very real possibility that Caerdroia may fall."

"Never!" snapped Desmond.

"Peace, lion," murmured Aeron, who sat beside him, laying a hand over his. "Hear him out."

"In space, and on the other planets," continued Gwydion, "we can be certain of victory, or so near certain as to make no differ to our overall strategy. Here on Tara it is another, graver matter, for here it is that his attack shall come with greatest force."

"Caerdroia has never fallen to an enemy, not even in the time of the Druids' Wars and the Theocracy," objected a tall woman in the uniform of the Fianna.

"We have never before faced such an enemy," countered Gwydion. "Oh aye, I know you are all thinking we have defeated Coranians before now, and that is true enough. But never before have we fought the full might of the united

Imperium—and far less both our ancient foes together, for the Fomori come against us also, as Imperial allies.''

That last was a piece of news Gwydion had been saving, though Aeron and a few others were privy to the knowledge, and he was grimly amused to see the consternation that swept the room.

"Fomori!" muttered O'Reilly, dismayed, to Morwen. "Did you know about them?"

Morwen nodded. "The word came from Gwennan aboard the *Firedrake*, a little while ago. A scout sloop far in advance of the fleet intercepted an enemy transmission, and the bards on the flagship managed to decode it. The Fomori are in it without a doubt, though it seems the other Phalanx worlds chose rather to hide the issue. Nay,'' she added quickly, perceiving O'Reilly's reluctant thought of Bellator, "it goes back many years before that. This revenge has long been sought by Bres—though not, I think, by Bres's heir.'' That was said so low and so distractedly that O'Reilly was not sure she had even heard it. But Gwydion was speaking once more.

"These are the immediate dispositions for the Throneworld," he said, and his hearers straightened unconsciously in their seats, for what the First Lord of War said now carried the weight of an order for the coming fight.

"The Ard-rían will make her base for the initial defense at Rath na Ríogh. That is the royal fortress most distant from Caerdroia, as you know, and closest to the ground upon which we have chosen to make our stand.'' His hand described a half-arc over the lighted map. "Eight of the Pillars of Tara will be stationed here; the others remain to guard the City, and doubtless they will see action soon enough. Attached foot-soldiery will be under supreme command of Tanwen of Marsco.'' The room filled with approving murmurs, and Tanwen, the tall, dark-haired woman who had spoken earlier, acknowledged the order with a salute.

"The cavalry forces, both chariot and horse, will be ordered in three wings,'' Gwydion continued. "Commanding the left, Denzil Cameron; on the right, Fedelma ní Garra; and Maravaun of Cashel will hold the center. The marca-sluagh, the guard of horse and foot around the Ard-rían, will be commanded by Struan Cameron. I myself, with Niall Tir-connell, will accompany the Ard-rían as her captains-general. Mac Avera will direct the Fianna; Illoc mac Nectan and Douglass Graham will order the out-planet defenses; in space, Rohan and Elharn command the fleets. Has anyone any question?''

"Only a suggestion, First Lord," said Morwen. "Too many of the rígh-domhna in one place may make that place—and themselves—too much a target. The noncombatant members of the royal family should be dispersed as widely as possible."

"To increase the chances of an Aoibhell surviving to the succession, should the Ard-rían fall," remarked Aeron, but she was laughing. "Very well, Taoiseach; I leave it to you to get my family on the move." She rose, and all stood with her.

"Now, sirs and ladies," she said, and her face was alight with an iron grimness. "To our work. Too long have we been anvil. Now let us be hammer."

She left the room without a backward glance, and Gwydion went with her.

"Bravely spoken," said Gwydion, as they quitted the Commandery and headed back to the palace across the huge, deserted Great Square.

Aeron shrugged. "Perhaps so. But did they believe it?"

"They believed as much as was good for them to believe," he said after a while. "Most important of all, what does the Ard-rían of Keltia believe?"

She gave a gentle laugh. "Everything, and nothing . . . Let us not go in just yet." They passed the palace gates, taking the startled salutes of the guards, and she linked her arm through his and turned him toward the gardens.

Little now was left of the summer's glories, but among the fallen drifted red leaves poked the shaggy heads of white asters, and thickets of gold chrysanthemums, and the little hardy autumn rose that grows wild along that coast. Dawn had come while the work of war went on within the Commandery, and now a red-streaked yellow sky hung like a dome over the City; though the night's snow still patched the ground, the wintry air had grown soft as the upper winds shifted.

Aeron spoke no word as they walked slowly through a little birch-grove to the archway that led to her tower, but when they came to the stone fountain in the middle of the wood, she plucked an aster from a nearby cluster and sat on the fountain's rim. When the flower was white shreds in her lap, she looked up at Gwydion, and spoke hesitantly.

"This may well be the end of all, for us."

Gwydion shook his head, smiling, and gently gathered up the ruined aster from her hands, scattering the petals in the bubbling fountain.

"Even if Keltia itself should cease to be," he corrected her, "naught to do with us, Domina, can ever end."

The sudden sound of her Ban-draoi title steadied her, and decided her . . .

"Then let us place such bonds upon ourselves as to confirm that, in trust for the future. We have spoken of it often enough before now, after all." When he made no answer, she added innocently, "And too, 'King' is a title somewhat less frequently encountered than 'Prince'."

He laughed. "That has never been the problem, and fine you know it."

"Fine you taught it me— But what is your answer?"

"I will gladly; you know that too. But is now the time?"

"The only time, I think," she said, and over her face came the look he knew so well, a grave look almost of listening, alert, as if she hearkened to something just beyond the range of sensing that only she could hear. "The only time," she repeated, more confidently, and he smiled.

"As the Queen commands, then."

"The Queen cannot command here. She dare not . . . Only, Aeron asks now, as you have asked her in time past."

He took her hands in both of his and gently kissed the cold thin fingers. "Aeronwy, whatever oath you please, in whatever time and place you choose, that will I take. I have told you so before, and I tell you so again."

"And now I am ready at last to hear it . . . I have already spoken to Teilo and Ffaleira, and they as heads of our Orders will solemnize what bonds we take upon us, and serve as witnesses before the law.''

"Then let us do so," he said, kissing her hands again. "And there let it rest, cariad. Until the battle is won or lost, as the gods will have it."

When Aeron entered Mi-Cuarta that night, all rose to their feet and shouted wild greeting, drumming on the tables with the hilts of sgians and swords. She returned the hails with a radiant smile, and stood in her usual place at table, gesturing futilely for seated silence. When the tumult died away at last, she spoke; her countenance was high and glad and shining, and she seemed not at all like an embattled ruler whose realm had just been invaded.

"This has been a long day of evil tidings. Yet tonight would I share with you here, first of all in Keltia to hear them, tidings of a different nature. At sunset this day, in the circle of Ni-Maen, in the presence of Rohan Prince of Thomond, Morwen Duchess of Lochcarron, Auster, Lord Chief Brehon, Ffaleira, Magistra of the Ban-draoi, and Teilo Archdruid, Gwydion ap Arawn and I have been set handfast each to the other. Although we think it wisest not to wed under the shadow of war, it seemed good to us that we pledge ourselves to each other, and to you, for the future. And so I, Aeron Queen of Kelts, present you your King that is to be."

She turned to Gwydion, who had stood slightly behind her, and reached him her hand. He came forward, kissed first her hand and then her lips, lightly and lovingly, and bowed in acknowledgment of the thunderous cheers. Then he and Aeron sat down together, and the great chair beside her own, which had stood empty since the death of Emer ní Kerrigan, was occupied once more.

"Well, that is some surprise," remarked O'Reilly to Haruko, as they seated themselves farther down the high table. "And a very nice one too. Did you know about it?"

He shook his head. "No, but I thought it not unlikely. Aeron is right, it's not the appropriate time for a royal wedding, but this gesture was very well thought-of, both for those two and for the people. I'm very happy for them," he added.

"That's nice," said O'Reilly demurely, not looking at him. "I sort of had this feeling you were in love with Aeron yourself."

Haruko stared at her. *"What?* Don't be ridiculous! Nothing has *ever* passed between the Queen and me of an improper nature, the idea is—"

"I never thought it had." O'Reilly continued to attend steadily to her plate. "I only thought you felt for her—how shall I put it—more than the usual affection that a loyal subject bears his monarch."

Haruko was silent. Well, he had never felt called upon to put it into words, but now that O'Reilly had been so grossly insensitive as to mention it— Yes, he supposed he did love Aeron; but not the sort of love O'Reilly thought. With sudden insight, he realized he had worked past his initial infatuation and had come to love Aeron as a teacher loves a brilliant pupil; or even, yes, as a father loves a daughter. More wonderful still, that feeling was returned; she loved him too—as a mentor, as an uncle, as her first friend from Earth— and that was more than enough for him.

And he was profoundly grateful for it, and more thankful than ever that he had been allowed to remain in Keltia. He had made the right decision after all . . . *I'm happy,* he thought, with a thrill of joy that brought sudden tears to his eyes. *When was the last time I was really happy?*

"Never you mind," he told O'Reilly cheerfully. "Just never you mind at all."

On the Imperial flagship *Marro,* Jaun Akhera and his officers were convened in the common-room. A map was projected on all viewers, and it was this which was at present commanding the Imperial Heir's full attention.

"It's a hundred years out of date!" he snapped to Hanno.

"Still, lord, it is more recent than the maps we had to work with on Alphor," replied his captain-general. "And as you see, it is close scale for the lands around Caedroia. Things change very little, if at all, on Tara; I doubt a hundred years will have altered much that matters, as far as we are concerned."

"Hmm. How if we sent a column over these mountains—the Loom—and came at the City from the rear?"

His generals looked surreptitiously at each other.

"There are no passes that lead into Caerdroia from the south," said Sanchoniathon, as no one else seemed willing to speak. This was his first campaign with his elder brother, and he was not afraid to speak his mind. "Those dales are impassable for armies—there is probably deep snow by now in any case—and we must also assume that the lateral passes, even, will most likely be mined."

"Mined!"

"Oh, psionic trip-mines, if anything; that is sheep-ranching country. Still, we could not hope to get through with fewer than, say, fifty per cent casualties."

Jaun Akhera scowled. "Too many. Yet the Kelts may go and come as they please through the hills . . . Station a strong force at the southern entrances to this Pass of the Arrows" —his lightpen touched the map at a green expanse also marked "Bwlch-y-Saethau"—"to cut off anything, or anyone, they might think to send that way—especially fugitive royalty. And see to it that part of the force is Fomorian; let Bres have a share in the chores as well. For the rest, we proceed as planned to the landing in Strath Mór."

"Lord—" began Hanno.

He was silenced by a look. "As planned, gentlemen. That is no peasant general or simple brigand who commands the Keltic forces. That is a queen; I suggest you remember it."

There was a small stir at the door, and he looked around, frowning, at the interruption. A young ensign burst in, saluting, breathless with his haste.

"Pardon, lord, but the Princess Arianeira has just come on board. She *demands* to see you," he added, indignant.

Jaun Akhera's dark face lighted with a smile. "I will be very happy indeed to attend Her Royal Highness. Tell her that I come directly. No, escort her to the bridge. I will meet her there."

Arianeira walked down the main corridor of the *Marro,* skirts frothing with the vehemence of her stride, oblivious to the whispers and sidelong glances which attended upon her passing. The young Coranian officer escorting her, though as dazzled as any by her beauty and her charm, was nevertheless very much mindful of her powers—not to mention her recent deeds. This was not only a Keltic princess, sister of the mightiest warlord her kingdom could at present boast, but she was herself the one person who had made this invasion possible at all. She had succeeded where all others for fifteen hundred years had failed: She had breached the Curtain Wall; and the fear that prompted the stares and whispers was very real indeed.

Striding onto the bridge, pleased at the sudden dramatic hush, she swept her glance around.

"But where is my lord Jaun Akhera? Should he not be here to greet me?"

"He sends word that he will join you presently, Your Highness. He has been much occupied with the planning of the land battles— Look, he comes now."

Arianeira turned as Jaun Akhera came onto the bridge, noting with concealed approval the subtle tensions his presence brought to the *Marro*'s crew, and noting with approval not concealed at all his considerable attractiveness.

"Well met at last, lady," he said, kissing the hand she held out to him. "I have much to thank you for, and, now that I see you, honoring our bargain—and repaying my debt of gratitude—will be no duty, but pleasure."

Arianeira smiled, coolly reclaiming her hand. "You do me grace to say so, lord," she murmured. "At least, so I take your meaning—" She looked around the bridge, observing what the many viewscreens showed: fierce ship-to-ship combat, blue-white laser trails crawling away among the stars, blasted hulks and crippled vessels. "How goes the battle?"

"Why, as we had expected: hard. You gave us an unprecedented opportunity, lady, but we never thought the Queen of Kelts would give us anything but hell's own fight. Still, we do not do too badly, and we shall make our scheduled landfall on the planet of Tara in six days' local time."

"Aeron will be ready for you."

"I don't doubt it . . . But where are your colleagues? I understood they would be joining you here on the *Marro*. Or am I mistaken?"

Arianeira's lovely face was bland as cream. "No mistake. But they appear to have encountered some—difficulties in escaping."

"Yes, I can see that they might have." His voice was amused. "Well, for us, lady, difficulties lie behind. I said just now I did not doubt Aeron's readiness. Do not you, Arianeira, doubt mine."

She looked long into the golden eyes, then swept him a deep curtsy, her hand to her breast, and all over the bridge eyes slid furtively in their direction.

"Your Highness's servant," she said, smiling.

At Aeron's order, no public announcement had as yet been made of the part played by Arianeira, Kynon and Tindal, though rumor of the treason had run like flame, like the Solas Sidhe itself, among the folk.

When word came, later that next day, that Kynon had been taken trying to escape from Gwynedd, Aeron ordered him brought to the Presence Chamber, and summoned the High Council to witness her judgment.

Gwydion, still cloaked from his interrupted duties in the field, where the armies were already assembling, met her in the chamber.

"They found him in the ruins of Caer Ys," he said quietly, taking his seat beside her under the canopy that overhung the dais and the two high chairs. "The island where the castle stood is sunk beneath the water—Arianeira had set a telesm there, to destroy the castle with her fellow traitors yet within . . . though no trace of Tindal has yet been found, I am sorry to say." No sign of the emotion he must surely have felt was visible upon his face; Caer Ys had been Arianeira's favorite of their family's castles, they had spent many happy hours of their childhood there together, he and she, and their brother Elved with them, later, and their parents before their father had died . . .

Aeron held her face as immobile as his. "Bring Kynon in."

A very wretched Kynon came into the chamber, within a square of Desmond's Fians. His tunic was bloody and muddy, his hair disheveled, but his eyes remained sly.

Beside Aeron's chair, Rohan started violently as he got his first good look at the prisoner's face, and his memory fled back to Mi-Cuarta, the night before the Terrans came, and a black-haired stranger in red standing in the doorway behind Arianeira . . .

"I knew I should see that one again," he said, half to himself, as Aeron looked up at him curiously. "And yet once more, I think, before the end . . ."

Kynon, unaware of any of this, walked steadily enough to the foot of the thrones, then broke past his guards and flung himself prostrate at Aeron's feet.

"I know nothing of this, Ard-rían! I am unjustly accused, and I swear to your presence that it is so!"

"That you shall do indeed," said Aeron, and the peculiar note to her voice caused Kynon to look up suddenly fearing. She raised a hand, spoke to Teilo, who stood by. "So grave a matter may not be left to lesser proofs. Fetch in the Cremave."

The Cremave . . . Aeron's Councillors turned and looked at each other, troubled. Kynon, who had little interest in magic and less skill, had heard only wild rumors of the Cremave, the magical clearing-stone of the House of Brendan. It had the power, reputedly, to tell truth from falsehood, so that the hand of the one to be cleared was placed upon the stone's center when the oath was taken.

"If I may ask, Ard-rían—"

"You may *not* ask, Kymro. We shall wait upon Teilo's return."

There followed many minutes of deathly silence. Kynon crouched miserably on the carpet before the high seat; the others stood in small huddled groups. Aeron remained seated, hand to chin, Gwydion sat unmoving beside her, and no one spoke at all.

At last Teilo returned, and in his hands he carried something covered by a black cloth. Aeron rose, and pointed to the center of the carpeted space before the thrones.

"Place it there, Archdruid, and then do you withdraw."

Teilo set the object down, bowed to Aeron and stepped back. Aeron knelt on the carpet, spread her hands for a moment above the cloth-swathed bundle, then slowly removed its black silk wrappings. As one, everyone else in the room, save for Gwydion, flinched a little. Kynon, seeing what lay there, backed to flee.

Before the Fians could seize him, however, Aeron raised her right hand, sketched a quick interweaving gesture, and then flicked her fingers as if gently tossing something for Kynon to catch. Instantly he stood rigid, unable to lift his feet from the floor. He stared incredulously at Aeron, and gradually his expression of scorn turned to one of panic.

"He is earthfast," whispered Ríoghnach to the pop-eyed Haruko. "A spell even children can perform; but he cannot now move until she releases him."

Aeron turned her attention again to what lay before her on the faded Kutheran carpet. A rough stone it was, all unpolished, perhaps the size of a loaf of bread, shapen only by the chippings of flint adzes in a time, or by a folk, that knew not iron, its blue-gray surface glinting darkly, laced with twisting veins of crystal and flakes of gold. It seemed somehow ominous, possessed of sentience, even, as if it had a plane of existence all its own. Kynon, as he stared at it, was suddenly filled with nameless dread, a mortal terror of the stone.

Aeron rose from her knees, and her eyes now carried some of the stone's own ominousness.

"Kynon ap Accolon," she said in the High Gaeloch, "come thou forward."

And he moved slowly to her as through deep water.

"Kneel, and place thy hand to the Cremave. I would know, Kymro, the truth of the betrayal thou hast wrought against me and against Keltia. Was it Arianeira daughter of Gwenedour and Arawn, Princess of the House of Dôn, or thou thyself, first compounded with the enemies of thy Queen?"

He collapsed, shivering. "I cannot . . ."

Teilo said severely, "You have been brought before the High Justice to be judged. You face the Cremave to be cleared or damned, according to your acts. If you refuse to swear, the guilt is upon you and the iron-death is yours."

"And if I do swear? What then, Druid?"

"If you are innocent, the Cremave will clear you for all time, and right and proper reparation will be made according to your honor-price. If you are guilty, a mark will be set upon you. You will be declared fudir, and daer-fudir, nameless and rankless and clan-broken; and though your life will not be taken from you it will be a life that is no life, with the hand of man and god alike against you. The choice is yours.''

Kynon looked up at Aeron. "Must I swear, Lady?"

Her face was no less hard than the stone itself. "You have heard the words of the Archdruid, which are as my words. Choose you, Kynon."

He dragged himself up on his knees. The curse of the gods on that slut Arianeira—by this time she was well away out of it, safe with Jaun Akhera, no doubt, aboard the Imperial flagship. All along she had had it planned so, had planned to trap him in Caer Ys with the Terran, slaughtering them both from a clean, safe distance—though as to Tindal's fate, Kynon neither knew nor cared; once the stones of the castle had begun to crack around them, it had been each for himself, and he had not seen Tindal again.

He looked down at the Cremave. It seemed larger now, its darkness almost pulsing. It would know his falseness as soon as he touched it—maybe. Even so, it would not kill him; the Archdruid had said so, and perhaps he could fool it after all. What was it but a chunk of rock . . .

"As the Cremave is my witness," he said in a voice to be heard throughout the room, "it was Arianeira of Gwynedd lured me into treason." He laid his right hand to the slight hollow at the heart of the stone. "So swear I."

A piercing shriek cut the silence, and even Gwydion shuddered. When the echo of the scream had died away, Kynon lay curled up on the carpet, his right arm clapped to his side and his hand hidden in his breast.

"The Cremave has judged him," said Teilo. "Let the truth now be made known to the people."

Aeron took in her right hand the scepter of findruinna that Rohan silently extended to her.

"For that you yourself have been the means by which Keltia has been betrayed, and for that you have sought to further that betrayal by falsely blaming another who already carries her own guilt and her own doom, this is the judgment of the High Justice to which you have appealed.

"Kynon of Ruabon, we name you fudir and daer-fudir; you have no place and no hearth, no name and no folk; your honor-price is set at naught, and you may claim none from man nor woman from this moment forward. All this have you forfeited by your treason, and the holy Cremave sets this doom upon you.''

Kynon, whose fearful writhing had ceased, had not looked at Aeron as she spoke, but now he lifted his head and bent upon her a stare of such malignant hatred as caused every warrior in the chamber to start forward, hand to swordhilt.

"And in fair return, I set this doom upon you, Aeron Aoibhell," he said, his voice deadly soft. "The stars' wandering between you and the brother of the one who betrayed me. Your crown from your head, your lord from your bed, and may the Shining Ones themselves ride forth to war before you return again as Queen to Caerdroia. Let that be your doom and your dán." He stared balefully at her, then at Gwydion, then slowly removed his hand from the concealment of his tunic.

It had been shriveled as if drawn by some terrible disease, or by the flame, wasted and skeletal from fingertips to elbow, curved and scarred and hooked inward like the desiccated limb of a corpse long dead.

"See now the justice of the Cremave," he said mockingly. "Yet I too shall see justice done in time."

Aeron gestured to Desmond, and the Fians closed in around Kynon and began to march him from the room to begin his long punishment. But his voice came back clear to those who remained.

"Remember, Aeron! Gwydion, remember! The Cremave has doomed you both as surely as it has doomed me!"

Aeron had spoken to no one in the Presence Chamber after Kynon's departure, but had left the room, quickly and alone, by a different door. No word had come from her for some hours when Gwydion himself went in search of her; no other, even in the face of war, dared trouble her solitude.

He found her, as he had expected, in her chamber of magic. The four great torches were unkindled, and there was no power in the chamber; it was only a room of stone, cold, with the last light of day dim behind the windows.

She was huddled upon the floor against the stone bench.

Her hands were pressed to her mouth, and her streaming hair and bare feet struck Gwydion to the heart. After a moment, he crossed the floor to her, sat upon the bench, and gathered her up into his arms.

"They ask too much of you," he said, savagely angry, then tilted her face up to him with sudden concern, for she was weeping. "Cariad, what is it?"

Her voice came choked and broken, half to herself, like a child's that has cried too long uncomforted.

"—*I*, to dare to call justice to answer? When I myself have done evil a thousand times worse than his? Nay, I deserve such a dán as the one was laid upon me! I have used magic to unlawful ends, have slain for vengeance's sake, have brought war upon my folk by my arrogance . . ." She was trembling uncontrollably now, and he took her face between his hands, spoke with quiet urgency.

"And you have paid in full for it, if evil it was . . . Hear me, Queen of Kelts: The weave of this war was laid down a thousand generations ago, on the last day of Amnael, when Telchine betrayed Danaan in Atland itself, and framed the pattern of the ages."

"If I had not wrought the death of Bellator—"

"Bellator was but your answer to a strike of injustice undoubted from Bres's hand," he said. "And that but a response to a word of Fionnbarr your father's, spoken seventy years ago in who now can know what justice or injustice, and he too had his reasons . . ." He took her hand that bore the Great Seal of Keltia, turned it so that she could see the knot of the Six Nations carved into the big emerald. "Where does the knot begin?"

She had ceased to weep, though tears still glittered on her cheek.

"What then do you really say to me?"

"No words that you have not already said a hundred times over to yourself. But I say them yet again, in the hope you may hear them more clearly in another's voice."

"And who but a prince of bards to say them," she said, with a small weary smile, and pulled herself to her feet. He rose also, and she clung to him a moment, then stood away, and already she was once again the High Queen.

"And now?" he asked. "You are needed in many places, Ard-rían."

"Then do you come with me and we shall attend those needs. We ride in the morning for Rath na Ríogh."

Chapter Eighteen

The next morning dawned clear, though snow still streaked the frozen ground. The armies of Keltia, the catha, led by the twelve Fian battalions known as the Pillars of Tara, were assembled on the plain below Caerdroia. A strong east wind blew down the Strath, snapping cloaks and banners, and the bright winter sunlight was broken by high cloud.

The banners in the wind spoke of ancient days and hallowed power: in the van, the flags of the Six Nations: the crown-collared wolfhound of Erinna, the red dragon of Kymry, the Scotic lion, the Kernish choughs, Brytaned's rose and Vannin's triskele. Behind these, in ordered ranks, the banners of the noble houses and the standards of the clanns: among them the sun-cross of the House of Dâna and the unicorn of the Dôniad, the Camerons' sword-fret and the black Douglas lion and the sword and serpent of Clann Drummond. And, finally, the personal battle standards of the commanders: Gwydion's gold-antlered stag, Desmond's black bull, the hawk in flight of Fedelma ní Garra and Niall O Kerevan's blue and white counterchanged boar. But highest of all floated two huge banners, one black and silver, the other gold and green: the winged-unicorn Royal Standard, indicating the presence of the sovereign, and the Keltic knot that symbolized the Six Nations.

Before the sun stood very much higher, the hai atton sounded from the City walls, and was answered from the plain below; then the Wolf Gate opened, and Aeron rode out upon her black mare Brónach at the head of a small company of perhaps forty horse. She was wearing a light lorica of highly polished findruinna—as did most of those who rode with her—and the black Dragon uniform under a fur-collared green cloak. At her right stirrup rode Gwydion on a big gray stallion, and on her left Rohan, who would leave the riding at Mardale to join his escort and sail out to the *Firedrake;* others of her household who were in the party included Sabia, Melangell, Haruko and O'Reilly.

The standard-bearers fell in, the pipers skirled on before, and the ride to the plain began. This marchra, which would last six days and cover nearly sixty leagues, was intended chiefly to hearten the folk. The main body of troops committed to the defense of the Throneworld, horse and foot alike, was already being transported to the chosen battleground by troop carrier. Aeron had elected to ride the full distance herself, with a strong escort of her personal guard in addition to those of the royal household; she was only thankful there was time enough to do so.

Haruko, somewhat ill at ease in the saddle, though mounted on the smallest and placidest charger in the royal stables, was a few files to the rear of the banners, riding beside Desmond, and after a while he expressed some doubts as to the leisurely progress of the royal cavalcade in the face of the incoming armada.

"We will be there two days before them all the same," Desmond assured him. "And the armies will be fully assembled in camp by this time tomorrow. As you know, the invaders dare not sail in through hyperspace, and normal space is, of course, heavily mined. Elharn predicts forty to fifty per cent Imperial ship losses by the time their vanguard reaches Tara." He looked pleased.

Fifty per cent! Haruko privately thought the estimate a bit on the high side, but said only, "That's very encouraging, but do we really have the time to waste in riding to the end of the Glen?"

"I do not think that the Ard-rían thinks of it as time wasted. In addition to reassuring the people by her presence— for you must remember they have never seen anything like this on Tara before—the marchra will also allow the officers and troops to refresh their memories of the Strath's terrain, should it come to land battle all along the Glen and we be forced in the end to fall back upon Caerdroia.''

Haruko glanced at him, but the blue eyes under the black brows were staring straight ahead.

"Do you think that likely?''

"Likeliness seems to have little to do with this whole coil. Who among us ever thought it likely the Curtain Wall could be breached? Or that a princess of Gwynedd could betray her Queen?''

The bitterness in Desmond's voice was deep and plain, and Haruko did not know how to answer it.

"When will the armada arrive at Tara?'' he asked at length.

"No more than a sevennight tomorrow, Haruko. You will see action in Keltia's service sooner than might have been expected.''

Haruko thought about that for a while. Well, he could not say he was sorry, not really; if truth be known, all this made him feel young again. He had been a Terran serving officer all of his adult life, and during the course of that career there had been battles aplenty, in space and on worlds alike. Yet none of those engagements—some of which had earned him medals—had filled him with the kind of anticipation he felt at this moment. War was never fun; but sometimes it could be—well, satisfying in a righteous kind of way, and there was no question whatsoever here as to who was in the right. Keltia had been invaded, laid open by treason to invasion; the only thing to be done was fight back. Nothing war-mongering about that, and he was glad to be able to be a part of it.

But he wondered all the same if he could get out another message to the Admiralty on coded frequencies. Such a message would reach Earth long before the *Sword*. It might well have occurred to Jaun Akhera and his stooges to send a few legions in that direction as well, since the news of the alliance seemed to be the prime cause of the present hostilities. Or at least the *avowed* cause, he corrected himself. The prime cause of Imperial irritation rode a few ranks ahead of him, on a black mare under the Royal Standard.

*   *   *

The marchra rode dawn to dusk, making perhaps thirty miles a day, with stops for the noonmeal and frequent brief halts to rest both horses and riders. The first night from Caerdroia saw them at Blair Drummond, guests of David Drummond's family, who held the castle from the Earl of Rannoch and who had been friends and courtiers to the Aoibhells for five hundred years; and the night after that at the royal hunting lodge of Nancarrow.

On the third day, Haruko found himself riding beside Desmond's brother Macsen, and they passed the hours agreeably, swapping tales of battles past, for Macsen, along with Gwydion and Desmond and the late Roderick Prince of Scots, had seen much active service outside the Curtain Wall in defense of the Protectorates. Finally Haruko worked up the courage to speak of what was troubling him.

"What use can the Ard-rían really *have* for us? Your own methods of communication—not to mention telepathy—are far superior to any we could offer, you have great skill with language, and so O'Reilly is not needed. Your own warriors— well, we are no Fians, as you have seen, and not needed there either. I haven't been in real combat in years, and even when I was, it was mostly from the deck of a ship."

Macsen listened sympathetically, but in the end shook his head with a smile.

"It is nothing to fret yourself over, Theo," he said. "Aeron keeps no hounds that cannot hunt. She has good use for both of you, doubt it not."

"My cousin spoke truly," said Aeron, later that day, when she had dropped back in the line to ride beside Haruko herself. "Did you not listen, Theo, when I said I would need the benefit of an out-Wall point of view, and that you would be for me those eyes? And, too, you and O'Reilly are my friends. You gave up much to stay here with us, and I do not forget it."

All along the route of march, they had been greeted by folk flocking to the Royal Standard, who came to cheer their passage and kiss Aeron's hand. Haruko, who was by now able to read her fairly well, saw what torment she was suffering, but he could think of nothing to do for it, and realized that if he noticed, those closer to her must have seen it long ago. So he said nothing, and did nothing, but it troubled him that it had to be so.

By the fourth nightfall, when they came to Ath-na-forair, Aeron was weary beyond speech, in body and in mind, and she retired almost immediately to the hastily refurbished rooms at the top of the keep. Gwydion made as if to go after her, but Melangell shook her head, and followed Aeron herself.

But even in the privacy of the solar Aeron did not seem disposed to deliver herself of her cares, and finally Melangell broke the long uneasy silence.

"Aeron, speak and be solaced. What so troubles you?"

"I can endure betrayal, invasion, war," said Aeron after another long pause. "What I think I shall never learn to endure is being beloved of my people. They ask for *nothing*, cousin, except the simple fact of my existence." She laughed. "Simple!" she repeated with savage irony. "Whatever I do is right in their eyes, so long as it is I that do it. They come to kiss my hand no matter what it has of late been set to, and if not my hand . . . Did you see, some today actually kissed my boot in the stirrup, or my sword in its scabbard, or the hem of my cloak—whatever was nearest to their grasp. And when it comes at last to battle, they will die shouting my name for their ros-catha." She stood up, on the verge of losing the iron grip of self-control that she had closed, like a gauntlet, around her emotions ever since that hour in her chamber of magic with Gwydion.

Melangell had never seen her so unstrung; not even when Rohan, ashen-faced, had brought Aeron the news of her terrible accession to the throne, had gone to his knee before his own sister, not even then had Aeron been so openly anguished as now. But—

"You are the Ard-rían, Aeron," she said quietly, all the soul-soothers at her command in her voice. "There is no higher nor more worshipful calling in Keltia. If the people are to be strong enough to throw back the invader, where then are they to find that strength save from their Queen?"

"So Gwydion says, too," said Aeron almost indifferently.

"Well, then! Do you doubt us both?"

"I doubt only myself, Meleni," she said, using the diminutive Melangell had not heard since the days of their childhood. "And I wonder how my father would have dealt with this . . ."

Melangell said desperately, "Of the two of you, Aeron, it is he, not you, would have been the more like to torment himself with what-ifs. Or so at least all of us have thought . . . until now."

Aeron's mouth quivered as if her cousin had struck her, then she looked sideways at Melangell and laughed.

"That was a near hit, kinswoman. And a shrewd touch . . . doubtless inherited from *your* father." Suddenly fired with mercurial cheer, she spun about, hair whipping after her like a sparkling comet. "Enough! I need not fight myself as well as Jaun Akhera . . . is the company yet in the hall? Then let us go down again to join them."

It was during the course of the marchra that O'Reilly, who had for some time been performing various small services for Aeron, was formally asked to become the Queen's personal squire. O'Reilly leaped at the offer, but the development was not viewed with equal delight by all observers.

"O'Reilly is much attached to the Ard-rían," remarked Sabia to Haruko, at the nightmeal next evening at Dundrum.

"A bad case of hero-worship," muttered Haruko. "I'd thought she was old enough to have outgrown that sort of thing."

"Nay, most of us feel the same, you know; even those of us Aeron honors with her friendship. It is natural and right to look up to the Queen simply for that she *is*, after all, the Queen, but the more so for that she is Aeron."

On the sixth day they came at last to Rath na Ríogh, farthest from Caerdroia of all the line of fortresses that stood like an iron rampart along the Great Glen.

"Rath na Ríogh," said O'Reilly dreamily, looking up at the towering walls of honey-colored stone. "That means Fort of the Kings. Look, there's the camp."

Haruko followed the direction of her pointing hand, but the camp would have been hard to miss . . .

At the mouth of the tributary glen where the castle stood guard was broken land leveling off to high moors, and in other times the empty sweep of the bracken-covered uplands would have been bleak indeed.

It was not empty now. For as far as Haruko could see, the plain was thick with tents and the dome-like structures called clóchans favored by the Fianna. Horse-lines snaked in and out around the perimeters, and he could see the quartz-hearths set up for evening. It was staggering, and he said as much.

O'Reilly nodded agreement. "And these are just the troops for the first battles; not the reserves, even, or the forces that remained to defend the City, or the battalions in the other cities on this planet—not to mention the other planets. Everybody's a warrior here, men, women, probably children, too . . . But we have to go up there." She jerked her chin up toward the castle; the gates had been opened, and the first riders of the marchra were already passing between.

Rath na Ríogh, like most of the castles along the line of the Avon Dia, royal or otherwise, had been built in the early days of Keltia, long centuries before the raising of the Curtain Wall, when civil war and alien attack had been all too familiar realities to the folk who lived in Strath Mór.

There had been more people on the Throneworld then than now. In those earliest years, only Tara itself, then later Erinna and Gwynedd, had been settled by the first emigrants from Earth. But nowadays, the greatest part of the Keltic population lived on the other worlds to which they had spread so long ago, and Tara's present inhabitants numbered perhaps only a hundred million. Caerdroia itself was home to fewer than a quarter million.

The Rath itself was by far the largest of the Strath fortresses also; and in all Keltia only Ardturach, on Erinna, Turusachan itself and Gwydion's own seat of Caer Dathyl on Gwynedd were of greater size. Laid out in the classic four-towered pattern, with concentric walls around a faha and central keep, Rath na Ríogh, Fort of the Kings, commanded the entrance to the Great Glen, and therefore it had been chosen by Aeron and her generals to anchor the first defense of the Keltic throneworld in seven hundred years.

"What a great place to put a castle!"
O'Reilly draped herself precariously over the crenellations.

From here at the top of the keep, she could see far downplain to where the Avon Dia, in its descent from its sources high up on the slopes of Mount Keltia many miles to the east, began to broaden from an upland stream to a real river, flinging itself over the Lithend to pass between the huge double scarp of the Cliffs of Fhola. Those cliffs, sheer and fluted, formed an east-west running palisade for twelve miles on both sides of the river that long ago had carved them through the volcanic plain. Beyond cliffs and river alike, lost in blue distance, the mountains of the Stair rose up, snow-crowned giants forty miles away, and, far northeast on the very edge of sight, the outliers of the elf-haunted Hollow Mountains.

"Some view." Haruko had joined her, and he was still more than a little breathless from the long climb. "And good ground for a fight." He handed her a leather-covered flask. "Here, I brought us some shakla."

O'Reilly sipped gratefully at the bitter, chocolate-tasting beverage.

"Thanks—I could use the caffeine." She cupped cold fingers around the warm flask. "Now what?"

He shrugged. "Now we wait. Not for long, though. The armada is only a day away, probably less. Desmond told me the Imperials should lose forty per cent or more of their ships before they got here, and so far they say that estimate's holding. But we've lost a lot, too."

"But—"

"I know, I know. You don't have to tell me." Any soldier knew it: Nobody invaded anybody else unless they were absolutely sure of any of three things—surprise, superiority of weapons, or numerical advantage. The first was out now, of course, but that still left the other two up for grabs.

Haruko thought about the coming battle. Hand-to-hand combat had been the rule in interstellar warfare for more than a millennium now; planetary governments had learned, after some appallingly harsh lessons, to limit their warfare so, since there was apparently as little hope as ever of ceasing it altogether. All nuclears, all laser weaponry save laser swords and long-range siege guns, *any* kind of remote-control slaughter, even simple blastguns, were strictly proscribed by galactic covenant in combat situations, and the penalty for flouting that law was planetary annihilation. *Keep the gore in war*, he thought bitterly, *it might even help to keep the peace*.

But even the Imperium and the Phalanx dared not break the convention, and so the coming engagements would be fought in the ancient, accepted style, with the remove of bloodshed limited to the distance between one sword and another.

"Now that you're the royal squire," he heard himself saying, "I presume you'll be fighting beside Aeron."

"*Beside* Aeron? What are you talking about?"

It was his turn to be surprised. "She will be fighting personally—you mean you didn't know?" Judging by the shocked face O'Reilly turned to him, she had indeed not known, and he was instantly repentant.

"You're kidding."

"I'm sorry—but no, I'm not kidding, and I was appalled too. Morwen told me about it, a long time ago. It's a matter of Keltic law: Aeron cannot legally ask of her people anything she's not prepared to do herself. She can't be Queen otherwise." He shook her arm lightly. "It's not so unusual, really. And you don't imagine for one minute they'd ever let anything happen to her, do you? Morwen? *Gwydion?*"

"I have never heard of any monarch of any world in the known universe going personally into battle," said O'Reilly flatly. "And Aeron's not likely to let anybody keep her out of anything she wants to get into."

Too true, he thought; but he hardly needed, or wanted, to say so.

Gwydion stepped out onto the rampart and looked up at the sky. The day was burning itself to death. The sun, only a few minutes from setting, was balanced on the horizon; but the splendor, far from dimming, was spreading even as he watched. Even around into the east, the sky was rose and gold and opal, while the west was so bright he could not gaze directly into it, and the light it cast upon the fortress walls was clear and hard as crystal.

It seemed to cast a silence as well as a light; he could hear the horses nickering down in the lines, and the thud of a siege engine far out upon the plain.

O'Reilly had come up beside him, and Slaine also, but

neither woman spoke in the enormous hush, and as he looked around the battlements he could see against the glow other dark figures silhouetted, all looking west as they were.

Up on the keep's central tower, there was one that was not dark but blazed like a torch. Aeron's hair, loose around her, was a cloak of flame to her knees, and the huge crimson cloud-wings that spread north and south from out of that heart of burning light cast a glory over her face.

Her mind was not on the sunset, though, but rather closer: about ten light-seconds out from Tara, where the Keltic fleets fought the invaders for the space around the Throneworld. *And fighting them magnificently, too,* she thought, though her heart contracted at the thought of the staggering losses already incurred. So soon in the fight, and already she had had news of the deaths of many known to her—

A shout went up, and she turned her back on the sunset to look east, into the huge blue-gray dimness that veiled the plain off to her right. Then came her first sight of that which they had all foregathered upon the battlements to see: a faint wildfire trail, arcing down through the amethystine sky to disappear many miles away behind a swell of the rolling uplands. She knew well what it was: the first of the Imperial landing craft plummeting in free-fall to earth, from the troop carriers in parabolic orbit around the planet.

We came to meet them, she thought, *and now they are here* . . . Still, they came not so easy, for all that; she could see blue-white lances beginning to rise from the plain, volleys from the long-range laser-cannon batteries sited by the Fianna to shoot down the troop shells as soon as they entered atmosphere. Yet for every gliding sliver that was blown into flaming sparks, five more came safely to land.

She had earlier consulted with Gwydion and the other commanders, with the result that the Keltic dispositions had been somewhat altered; so that most of the key detachments were now spread out in a mighty arc across the Strath entrance, one point of the iron sickle anchored upon Rath na Ríogh, the other at the Cliffs of Fhola.

As soon as the invaders were well entrenched, she knew, they would send her an embassy to arrange a parley, and then she and Jaun Akhera would come face to face at last. What would he be like? As he himself had done some months before, she had studied all available information on her royal adversary. Eight years older than herself—*the same age as Rhodri,* came the inescapable computation—Jaun Akhera had been named Strephon's official heir and successor only a year ago. *Truly, he had used that year to good advantage,* she thought somewhat sourly. She would wager crossics to cheese the invasion had not had origin in the brain of Strephon, devious though that brain surely was . . .

She spun on her heel, so sharply that her spur grated on the stone, and went down the tower stairs to the rooms she had taken for her own use. There was no point remaining to watch: Soon enough would she see for herself what those falling sparks had brought to Tara.

At first light the next morning Aeron rode to the front with her commanders and her guard. Their path lay through the heart of the miles-deep encampment, and, man or woman, galloglass or general, every warrior who could manage a few moments away from duties came down to cheer their progress. O'Reilly, who as squire rode directly behind Aeron, beside Rialobran who bore the Royal Standard, was nearly ill with excitement, and, as Aeron halted often to greet many warriors known to her and many more who were not, nearly deafened by the tumult.

At last they came to the far edge of the camp, where, across five or six miles of gently sweeping moor, the enemy's own tents were clearly visible. Here on a little rise of ground a pavilion had been erected, and Aeron retired within, accompanied by her officers, to await the Imperial embassy.

She did not stay within for long, though, and the sun was not yet high when a small party of riders approached from the far camp. Aeron, who had watched through a field-glass since the group was first sighted, lowered the instrument and straightened, still gazing out across the plain.

"My purple cloak," she said, not turning, and behind her O'Reilly vanished into the tent. When she returned with a darkly gleaming armful of imperial purple, Aeron pulled a thin black surcoat embroidered with the royal arms over her lorica and raised her hands to her shoulders. O'Reilly laid the cloak edges into her fingers, and Aeron buckled the jewelled clasp at her throat. Thus attired, she waited.

Under the eons-honored ensign of the white flag, the riders halted at the base of the little hill, and their leader, with his flagbearer, approached on foot to where Aeron stood with her commanders about her.

"Hail, Queen of Kelts!" he called. "I am called Garallaz, and I bring Your Majesty the salutations of my Lord Jaun Akhera, Prince of Alphor, Heir to the Throne of the Cabiri. May I come?"

At a curt nod from Aeron, he covered the remaining distance to the top of the knoll, dropped to one knee and extended to her a silver-bound diptych. Aeron made no move to take it, and it was Gwydion who instantly reached out a gauntleted hand. After a moment's hesitation, Garallaz relinquished it to him.

Gesturing Garallaz to rise, Gwydion broke the seal of wafer-thin gold, scanned the tablet's contents, then held it for Aeron to read.

"It seems we are bidden to a parley," said Aeron pleasantly. "According to what is set down here, I may bring with me six companions to a spot I choose myself. All negotiations will be conducted in Englic as a neutral tongue, and Jaun Akhera will ride to meet me with six companions also."

"You must come yourself, Majesty," said the envoy, nervously, for he had heard tales of the Keltic queen's chancy temper. "Not send any deputy in your place. My master shall do likewise."

"I will come."

But Garallaz, more nervous still, spoke again. "Forgive me, Majesty, but you must leave all weapons behind. Your escort may remain armed, of course. But you may not. My lord insists on this, and he too will be unarmed."

That troubled Aeron not at all, who had learned long since that if the power is not in the arm that wields the sword, it will never be in the sword itself. But her friends were vexed. She cut them off with a warning glance, then unhooked her glaive from its battered, silver-studded baldric and handed it, together with the sgian from her boot-top, to Struan Cameron;

the huge claymore from the saddle scabbard she gave to Grelun, who stood by, holding the reins of her horse.

She swung up into the saddle, saying over her shoulder, "I name to accompany me: Gwydion Prince of Dôn; Slaine Countess of Ralland; Lord Wolf Graham; Sabia ní Dálaigh; David Drummond, who will bear my Standard; and Sorcha ní Reille."

With a shock O'Reilly realized that the last-named personage was herself; she had not yet grown accustomed to hearing her name in the Gaeloch. But had Aeron really meant her? She caught Sabia's eye questioningly, and Aeron's friend nodded, smiling. O'Reilly hurried to mount.

"In the absence of the Ard-rían and the First Lord of War," Aeron was saying, "Niall Duke of Tir-connell is Chief here, and Tanwen of Marsco is War Leader." She looked approvingly over the little party, all now horsed, then turned her attention back to the waiting Garallaz.

Wheeling her horse in a half-rearing circle, she pointed to a small rise in the land crowned by a cluster of goldenbirch, more or less equidistant from each camp.

"We will meet your lord by the knoll of birches. Tell him so. Nor do I think we shall cumber ourselves with hostages, not in the midst of this. So I shall set my royal word against his own that no treachery is toward. You may tell him that, also." She touched one green leather boot-heel to the black mare's flank, and the others followed.

A hundred yards from the little stand of birches she drew rein, and her companions did likewise. Garallaz and his escort swept past at a gallop, and a very few minutes after they reached the Imperial camp, another knot of riders detached itself from the main host and headed at an easy canter for the little hill.

When they were perhaps thirty feet from the Kelts, they halted. Aeron contemplated them for a moment—Bres was among them, and her mouth went down at one corner—then raised a gloved hand. David Drummond, who was nearest, leaned forward in his saddle.

"Ard-rían?"

"Behind Jaun Akhera—what man is that who rides the bay?"

He followed her glance. "That is Elathan, Crown Prince of Fomor."

Aeron felt a small unpleasant shock. It seemed hardly right for the son of Fomor, an ancient enemy to her blood, to look so: a face of almost impossible beauty, dark blond hair and eyes as brown as bracken. It was as if he was aware of her shock, and the cause of it too, for he met her gaze and smiled, and his smile was a friendly one.

With an effort she looked away, moving her horse forward, as at the same instant Jaun Akhera did also, for the terms of parley had called for the two of them to speak alone, though still within earshot of their companies.

Brónach danced sideways under the pressure of Aeron's leg, and Jaun Akhera, when he came up to join her, turned his own mount likewise, so that the faces of the two leaders might be visible to both entourages. It was the first time they had ever seen each other in the flesh, and they faced each other with almost as much curiosity as antagonism.

Jaun Akhera was resplendent in white and gold, with a heavy gold coronet set upon his brow. She studied him openly. He seemed taller as he stood forth from his companions; in his battle armor, confident and assured and expectant of victory. Her frank stare did not appear to discomfit him. He was tall and lithe of build, though not so tall nor yet so lean of line as most Keltic men, and his frame beneath the gilded breastplate seemed well-muscled enough for any warrior. His hair was black, his eyes gold, and there was a gold-dusted look to his tanned skin. Strangely attractive, though it annoyed her to think it, and his eyes possessed a power of compulsion like to a snake's fascination of glance over a bird.

Well, she thought, *let him try to charm a hawk* . . .

By comparison, Aeron looked almost austere. She wore no crown, the only outward mark of her rank the cloak of heavy purple silk that fell over her horse's quarters—and the hue of which, she was amused to see, plainly irritated her royal opposite. But her mail glittered like water in the sun, and against the deep purple, color of emperors, her hair blazed with the fire of a meteor.

He reined his horse back, and bowed deeply to her from

the saddle. Aeron inclined her head, as one sovereign to another, but spoke first, as a sovereign to a subject.

"Hail, Prince of Alphor."

"Hail Keltia," he answered at once, smiling, and his voice was light and pleasant.

"We have each suffered much loss, lord; many of my folk are dead, many more of your own. Allow me to save you words and time. This war is to the death only, and though I may well lose, you shall take my City only over my blood upon its stones."

"That may be, Aeron," he said. "Though now I have seen you, I say in all truth I could wish for a less costly victory. I take it you will not consider any—accommodation?"

Aeron smiled. "Who has been advising you, Emperor's Heir? You have been listening to ignorant counselors; have they told you nothing of me at all? Even my onetime foster-sister knows me far better than that . . . But no, Jaun Akhera, I will consider *no* 'accommodation' save that of your immediate and total withdrawal from every foot of Keltic earth and every parsec of Keltic space. There shall be left within the Bawn of Keltia not one Coranian or Fomori or spawn of any other race you may have among you—except in death if that is the way you choose. Further, you will take the most solemn of oaths never again to come against us in arms. Or perhaps the Coranians do not have quite so vivid a memory as do the Fomori—of Bellator?"

Taken aback, he recovered himself with a little laugh. "Ah, Aeron, you do not disappoint me. They told me that the tongue was as sharp as the face was lovely, and on both counts they were right. I fear I cannot meet your conditions, memories or no. But I say this to you: After the battle, if I have won, and if both of us live to speak again, I shall ask you to consider a different offer."

"And that?" she asked, off her guard for an instant.

"A throne beside me. My grandfather is old, as you know, and has not many more years left to him. If you would wed me, join your Crown to mine, you could rule with me over Kelts and Coranians alike, and we could together bring this ancient strife to peace at last. Both our peoples would bless you for it."

The Wolf Gate itself could not have closed more completely against the invaders than Aeron's face shut now against the words of Jaun Akhera. Of those who watched and listened with fascinated horror, those who knew her only by reputation thought the beautiful pale face expressionless. Those closest to her beheld an anger such as they had never before seen upon any human countenance.

That is the look that destroyed Bellator, thought O'Reilly, numbed by it. —*that destroyed Atland of old,* thought Gwydion, even as he fought to retain his own composure.

Nearly half a minute passed before Aeron trusted herself to speak; only to speak, and not to strike, though even then she still felt fury at her back. Even Jaun Akhera felt it, and he shifted in his saddle.

"I think neither your folk nor my own would set their seal to that duergar's bargain," she said at last. "Any road, the throne beside *me* already has one to fill it—Gwydion Prince of Gwynedd."

"You would be an empress, Aeron," said Jaun Akhera, concealing his astonishment at the news she had just given him, and wondering even as he spoke what lunacy made him persist. *Surely she could not hold such anger in check very much longer?*

But her words came now with coldness. "By the grace of Arthur of old, Marbh-draoi, I am already an empress. And that would I prove upon your own body, should you care to take this quarrel to the sword between us two alone?"

His smile was twisted. "Nay, Majesty, that is one challenge I must decline, interesting though it might prove."

"So I thought. Very well then, Strephon's heir, there shall be rather fewer of you to carry my words home to your aging grandfather." She saluted him contemptuously, spun her horse on its haunches and spurred back to her waiting escort.

Jaun Akhera watched her go, then turned his own horse's head to the Imperial camp. *Hathor of the Horns,* he thought, *that is a most worthy opponent.*

Chapter Nineteen

*B*y the time Haruko returned from his tour of the camp, in the company of Denzil Cameron and the Princess Ríoghnach, it had gone full dark. *Except that it was seldom full dark on this planet*, thought Haruko, looking up at the Criosanna. That sight never failed to fill him with wonder, and tonight it was more than usually brilliant, for the aurora was streaming down out of the north, a cloak of light, rippling like silk in the solar wind.

"It is what we call a white night," said Denzil, "though it is every color *but* white."

Haruko agreed absently, but his mind was elsewhere, running over the events of earlier that day. O'Reilly had told him all the details of the encounter between Aeron and Jaun Akhera, and he had been alternately outraged and proud. He was only half-hearing the idle conversation that followed, until a word of Ríoghnach's jarred him sharply into full attention.

"You mean—" Both Kelts turned courteously to him, and he mastered his surprise. "You just said, Princess, I think, that the cavalry and the chariots are the heaviest force we have?"

Ríoghnach nodded. "That is so, Theo; what of it?"

He couldn't believe it. "Highness, the Imperials will have hoverplanes, low-level bombers . . ."

"And they will find within ten seconds of launch, if not before, that their aircraft are totally useless," said Denzil.

"But why? *How?*"

For answer, Ríoghnach took his arm and turned him to face the Hollow Mountains, plain in the ghostly aurora-light, a low black frieze many miles away to the northeast.

"There, see you those? They are solid lachna; I do not know the word for it in your tongue, or even if you know its properties. But it has a very strange and very certain effect on any kind of flight motor. Why have you never seen anything bigger than an aircar or small personal ship in atmosphere on this planet?"

"I hadn't really noticed," admitted Haruko. "I suppose I must have thought they were simply prohibited?"

"And for good reason! The field of force those mountains put out knocks them out of the sky all over Tara. Though some of us believe it is not the lachna, but the power of the Shining Ones, whose home is in those hills—" Her eyes sparkled. "The invaders will learn the harsh way. Oh, they may well capture a few of our aircars, maybe even some of our troop transports, which are powered differently and so come not under the ban. And we will shoot them down. And then they shall see what Keltic cavalry and war-chariots can do."

"And if they capture horses and chariots as well, or bring their own? Suppose they have mechanized armor?"

Denzil smiled. "As to your first question, I could wish them luck of it and not rue the wishing. Fighting from the back of a war horse is chancier than it looks, and the Coranians are not accustomed to it—though I hear more and more out-Wall folk are taking to our style of warfare. And driving a chariot is harder still. They will not be able to use mechanical chariots because the land is too broken even for tortoises— what you call tanks. I do not think the cavalry commanders— myself included—are over-fretted about that side of it."

"Is Aeron?"

Before Aeron's sister could answer, a page came up to her, spoke quietly, and was as quietly gone.

"Well, the Dancers of the North may hear a merry measure," said Ríoghnach, casting a last longing glance upward at the trembling veils of color, "but I fear there is little tunefulness within. My sister and her commanders are just now having a small disagreement over means, and we have been ordered to join them at once. So, my lords—''

They heard the council of war long before they reached the hall in which it was being held. At least four or five voices were raised in acrimonious dispute, judged Haruko uneasily, but none of them was Aeron's. At least, not yet . . .

Almost no notice was taken of their entrance, all those present being too taken up with their debate. At the moment, the action appeared centered on the violent disagreement of Desmond, the cavalry commanders Fedelma and Maravaun, and a tall, pleasant-looking man Haruko had never seen before.

"That is Rhain," whispered Ríoghnach, noting the direction of his glance. "Melangell's eldest brother. He is a Druid scientist on loan to the Fianna, and his duties concern the maintenance of the Curtain Wall. If he is here now, it is at Aeron's order, and there must be some problem with the Wall. Perhaps—'' She listened intently for a moment. "Yes, it is as I thought: Rhain says it is impossible for the Wall to be repaired at the present time and in the present straits. The undamaged sectors remain intact, but the gap Arianeira created remains also. We are still open to the outside, and various courses have been urged upon Aeron."

Haruko tried to follow the debate, but his Gaeloch, though improved a thousandfold in the past months, could not handle the swift colloquial broadsides blasting back and forth across the room, and he had a feeling that telepathy was coming into it as well.

"They want Aeron to use more sweeping strategies, and more immediately, against Jaun Akhera," said Denzil, leaning over and speaking into Haruko's ear. "She will not commit further troops to the first battles, and I think she is right to hold back—for the moment."

In a sudden lull came unexpected advice from an unexpected quarter.

"If you won't use logic, Aeron, then use magic!"

The speaker was Morwen, who ought to have known better, and Aeron grew very still.

"Is this all your best counsel?" she asked, raking her glance over the room that had suddenly gone deathly quiet. "All of you? —Yes, I can see that it is. Well then, in your wisdom, what do you suggest may be my best and surest course? The Faery Fire? Nay, for too many of our own folk would take hurt from it. The sea-magic, perhaps? Shall I raise a wave like to the one that drowned Atland? Or shall I rather call upon the earth itself to shake our enemy off, as a horse twitches a fly from its shoulder?'' She stood up, waving them angrily back into their seats. ''Counselors you are called—by *my* grace! Come to me again when you have somewhat worthier counsel to give me.'' She strode from the room, and no one dared to follow.

No one, that is, save Haruko. If he had stopped to think he would not have dared, any more than the others, and so he just went. Outside, he lost sight of her for a moment, then saw her, two levels above him and moving upward, and he dashed up the tower stairs after her. *Why does she always have to walk so damned fast . . .* In his haste to catch her, he lunged up the remaining few steps, and, too out of breath for the moment to speak, gave an unmannerly tug to her cloak. Aeron swung round on him with a swart oath, and before the look on her face Haruko flinched in terror.

Her expression changed at once. ''Theo! You! Why didn't you say?'' But she was still very angry, even if not at him, and he watched from a wary distance as she paced the turret walk.

Far below, in the mouth of the glen, a siege crew was still at work, setting in place the last redoubts against the morning's battle. They sang as they worked, and their song floated, faint but very clear, up to Haruko's ears. Heavily accented, melodic, rhythmic, it was obviously a work song—one voice sang the verse, all voices together on the refrain—yet it held a primitive solemn something that made Haruko's skin crawl, as if a chill finger had just brushed his cheek. It was beautiful, and its counterpoint was menace. It rang against the valley walls like the hollow boom of a battering-ram.

''Long time since last we sang that song in this glen.'' Aeron, calmer now, had come up quietly while the song had held him rapt, and now she leaned beside him, her elbows propped on the crenellations. She did not look at him, but far down the plain, at the small bright smudges that were the quartz-fires of the invading army.

"There are a hundred legions, Gwydion says," he remarked after a while. "Jaun Akhera called in all his markers for this one."

"All his *what?*" she asked, half-laughing. "I do not know your idiom, Theo, but I take your meaning plain . . . Are you sorry, then?"

"Sorry?"

"Now that your life too is tied into the sword-knot." Her voice was uncharacteristically bitter.

Much moved, and greatly daring, Haruko laid a hand upon her arm. "I chose for myself, Aeron. So did O'Reilly. So did the others. They left—or fled. We stayed. We wouldn't be here—violating, I might add, all the best rules of diplomatic practice—if we didn't dearly want to be."

As he had hoped, she smiled. "That's as well, then. They'd probably never have given you another embassy."

"Yes, well, landing in the middle of an interstellar grudge match isn't exactly good diplomacy either."

"Oh, but that is hardly your fault. Kelts hate Fomori, Fomori hate Kelts—that is a feud of but two generations' standing. Kelts hate Coranians, Coranians hate Kelts—and *that* is a feud of a thousand generations' standing. Besides, war is the final argument of kings. No diplomacy ever practiced has ever altered that."

Haruko voiced the fear of many hearts. "But if the City should fall?"

"It falls! But Caerdroia is not Keltia . . . Its fall, though very evil, would not be the worst fate to come upon us." She fell silent, staring upward as he had done earlier at the glory of the aurora. "We do not love war, Theo. Even in self-defense and unassailable righteousness of cause, it is a low form of possession, to be avoided or averted whenever possible."

"But surely to prevent a greater conflict—"

"I see nothing *but* conflict." She turned her back on Jaun Akhera's campfires. "Suppose we succeed in smashing the Imperial armies, and their Fomori friends too," she offered. "The rest of the Phalanx overlords even now watch and wait, and will, very like, fall upon us in force just when we are least able to turn them aside. We are alone, Theo. Earth cannot send to help us in time even if they would, and we have no right even to ask. For all we know, Earth too could be under attack . . . I look for our only real aid from the Protectorates, if my cousin Kerensa came there in time, or, indeed, at all; but even so they cannot send much for they cannot spare much to send. In this, then, we stand alone, and perhaps that is best after all.''

Haruko took a deep breath to face the royal wrath sure to come. ''I am sorry to ask this, Lady, having heard you in council just now and knowing how you feel—though not *why* you feel so—but what of magic, and why not?''

But Aeron did not explode as he had expected. Instead, she was silent for long moments, then sighed and spoke with gentle patience.

''I know this will be most difficult for you to understand— yet you yourself are not unacquainted with reasons not of the material sort . . . Theo, I would sooner perish, and see Keltia perish with me, before I would use the magical arts against Jaun Akhera without he had cast the first spell. This is war, surely, but whosoever first brings magic into this quarrel—be that magic Low or High; Dark or Light; Old or Wild or Cold; Sun or Moon or Star; Fire or Sea or Earth; Keltic or Coranian, Danaan or Telchine, or whatever magic there may be yet unmastered and unknown—then is that one's cause lost forever, though the day be won.''

The passion that had grown in her voice during this speech astonished her hearer; once more she was silent, and when next she spoke her voice was gentle again, more human.

''I know you and O'Reilly think this perverse and ill-done of me. Some of my own folk—some of my own kin, even— think the same . . . But my power and Jaun Akhera's power derive from the same root. The Coranians and the Kelts both are children of the children of Atlantis; the same pattern lies upon us both. Use magic against Jaun Akhera, you say. I and he, his people and my people, are kin from of old, and for that reason I may not. My power and his power are kin also, and for that reason I dare not. I could become such a one as he so very easily; for I have felt it in myself before now, and I would not feel like that again. Else has Bellator taught me nothing indeed.''

"But could you destroy him? If you wanted to?"

She smiled, a little coldly, a little sadly. "I, Gwydion, perhaps a thousand others, any one of us could destroy him in a matter of minutes, if we had no care for method or aftermath, using such means as Telchine used against Danaan on the last day of Amnael, and so Atland perished . . . But that day would be a Beltain revel compared to what destruction would be here if I used magic in Keltia in unlawful time. Before I would call such a day into being, rather would I throw wide the gates of Caerdroia with my own hand, and bid Jaun Akhera enter." She took his arm and steered him toward the stairs. "Let us speak no more of this tonight."

His soul in turmoil, Haruko was only too happy to oblige.

In the silk-draped tent at the center of the Imperial encampment, Jaun Akhera pulled his chamber robe around his lithe figure and studied his visitor's face, pale and impassioned in the lamplight.

"I receive you at this hour, King of Fomor, only to avoid an open scene. Battle begins at dawn. What is your trouble?"

Bres seated himself at the ivory table without waiting for an invitation, and Jaun Akhera's mouth went down at the corners.

"I come at this hour, Prince of Alphor, only because you avoided receiving me all day . . . Unless my perception was dulled by distance, Jaun Akhera, you seemed most cordial this morning toward Aeron Aoibhell. Has your policy altered, perhaps, since we spoke on Alphor?"

Jaun Akhera was suddenly alert, like a wild thing that hears a stick snap in a silent thicket.

"If it has, that is *my* concern. *I* lead the armies in this fight. And, Bres, a word in your ear, lest you take too much upon yourself in our mutual interests: Remember that the Keltic queen is reputed wondrous quick with a sword, and you are not. And a further word: Inform the armies, especially your own, that whoever harms Aeron, or Gwydion, or Morwen of Lochcarron, will pay dearly in return, be he soldier or be he king. I say this once only. I want those three, and Aeron most particularly, alive and unhurt. Is that clear?"

"Oh, very clear! So you were in earnest, then, when you

asked her to consider an alliance of state . . . I could hardly believe it, and I'm sure your Imperial grandfather will share my disbelief. Or does he already know that you would have Aeron to be the next Cabiri Empress?"

Before Jaun Akhera could reply, the silk curtains over the tent's inner door were flung back. Arianeira stood there, her silver-gilt hair unbound and rippling to the floor, a white velvet robe clutched close around her.

"Empress Aeron, is it?" she said coolly.

Bres, who had risen hastily at her entrance, now bowed with exaggerated courtliness. "Forgive my intrusion, Highness. I shall leave you to yourselves." With an ill-concealed grin, he left the tent as abruptly as he had come, and Jaun Akhera turned to face his angry ally.

"That was not meant for you to hear."

"Plainly not! Did you think you could truly keep such a thing from me? It was all over the camp within an hour after your return this morning. I waited only, and vainly, to hear it from your own mouth."

"A policy of statecraft, no more. Our agreement stands."

"Oh, cozen me not, my lord! You forget to whom you speak!" She spun away in fury from the conciliatory hand upon her arm.

"As do you, Princess of Gwynedd," snapped Jaun Akhera, angry in his turn. "Or perhaps your informants have merely censored your information. Have you not heard that Aeron has wedded your brother?"

Arianeira smiled thinly. "A greater surprise to you, lord, I think, than to me. But nay, I had indeed heard. As to 'wedded,' well, true it is that they are handfast, but according to our succession law they must still confirm that bond formally at a future time. Though," she added reluctantly, "that law also provides that now he may act in advance of such a formal ceremony."

"Meaning?"

She shrugged, enjoying his discomfiture. "King Gwydion," she said. "In all but name, at least, and you would do best to account him as such."

"And you did not think to inform me of that possibility, back when first we laid our plans, and set our terms, for this war! Was that oversight merely, or did you simply think it politic not to mention? I had not allowed for a surprise warlord consort at Aeron's side—she does far too well on her own without one." He sat back, steepling his fingers and watching her closely. "Aeron has raised your brother high indeed—from Prince of Gwynedd to First Lord of War to King of Keltia. Small wonder he has had so little time for his own sister."

A slow flush stained Arianeira's cheeks. "That is as it is. But do not make overmuch of this. Gwydion will be king, right enough, but king-consort only; never High King—never Ard-rígh. Aeron remains Ard-rían; she cannot give over her power into another's hand, and she would not if she could."

"No, I can see that—and that is why I must take it from her. And *will* take it, Arianeira, if I have to take her hand along with it . . . either in alliance, or off at the wrist."

"And what of our bargain, then? You swore that I alone should reign in Keltia after Aeron had been destroyed. Had I not opened the Curtain Wall to you upon that assurance, you would not now be here at all."

"Very true. Well, you need have no fear on that score. Your wish was to be Queen in Keltia, to supplant your foster-sister and revenge yourself upon her for all her supposed sins and misdeeds to you. I was the only way you could achieve it—as you were the only way I could achieve my own ends—and I shall honor the bargain we made."

But she was still not entirely pacified. "All its terms?"

"You shall have everything that you have earned," said Jaun Akhera at last, but there was a glint to the gold of his eyes that Arianeira rather marked than liked.

She studied his face for some other clue to give meaning to his words, but she found nothing, and the faint narrowing of his eyes told her he knew she had failed. Her fury redoubled, and she would have let it have full rein if only she had dared. But she could not dare, not yet, and perhaps not ever . . . Balked and angry, she dropped him the smallest of curtsies and vanished behind the silken draperies.

Alone again, sleep now the thing farthest from his rattled mind, Jaun Akhera sat down at the ivory table and poured out a cup of wine with a shaking hand. They had all warned him, everyone from his grandfather on down, that in this war he would walk an exceeding narrow edge; and they had been so right. Traitors were kittle cattle, always very chancy to handle; and one who had turned her cloak once could turn it back again just as easily. He would have to keep a close eye on Arianeira; it was beginning to seem that he might have to make war on two fronts at once: with Aeron, and with her new sister-in-law as well.

Yet it was something he could not have anticipated, for all the warnings. When first his plan had begun to take shape, when he had so blithely promised the Keltic throne, and Aeron's head, to the Princess of Gwynedd, it had been very remote from any reality, purely a military and political expediency. But now it had become very personal indeed, and the only thing he was sure of at this moment was that if he won the war, Aeron should not suffer for it.

But what troubled him most was that he could not put his finger on the moment when this change had occurred. When he had ridden out that morning to the parley, there had not been the smallest thought in his mind of offering Aeron peace on any terms whatsoever. But once there, speaking with her face to face at last, peace had seemed the most logical thing in the world, and a state alliance, of kingdoms and rulers both, the perfect solution for all concerned.

Obviously not. He called to mind how Aeron's face had looked at the suggestion: a marble mask, with only the faintest hint of disgust playing around the corners of the lovely mouth. The only thing worse had been Gwydion, who had sat his horse twenty feet away looking like an intransigent god.

Jaun Akhera tilted his winecup from side to side, watching the amber liquid swirl within. Gwydion. He would have to revise policy with regard to him, now that he was, as Arianeira had implied, for all practical purposes Aeron's legal consort . . . Outside the tent, he heard the quiet challenge and response as his bodyguard changed the watch, and the faint chink of their weapons recalled to his attention the more immediate matter of the battle only a few hours away. Perhaps that battle would decide for him more than a merely military victory.

"And perhaps not," he said aloud, and set the empty cup down hard upon the ivory table.

Aeron had moved her personal base of operations from Rath na Ríogh to a tent down in the camp; as much from her wish to be in the midst of the army as from an instinct that it was better not to be pent up in a castle during a fight—too easily could one's refuge become one's prison.

She had had a late-night conference with a few of her commanders, smoothing over the feathers ruffled earlier, then, weary though she was, stalked sleep without success. After a vain hour's tossing, she rose, borrowed a dark cloak of Slaine, and went to walk the encampment in the middle watch, putting a fith-fath upon herself so that her face might not make shy her warriors' speech. Few took any special note of the brown-haired Kymri in the Dragon uniform who wandered quietly among the clochans, and after a while she sat down at one quartz-fire where a harper sang to a small circle of warriors.

When his song was done, the harper turned courteously to her. "Be welcome to our fire, mistress. I am Garrack of Chyvellan, and all we here are in the chariotry of Hollin Macdonald. Whose name do you ride?"

She laid fist to shoulder, including them all in her smile. "I am called Lassarina, my masters," she said with perfect truth. "I fight in Struan Cameron's horse."

Amused, approving murmurs. "Oh, *Struan!*" "He is the púca's own whelp—" "Nay, his brother Denzil is worse still, from all we hear!"

"If you ride with the Cameron, mistress," said the harper, "he is master of horse in the marca-sluagh, and surely you must have seen the Ard-rían close to."

Aeron took the wooden quaich of ale that a friendly hand passed to her, drinking deep before replying.

"I have so, many times. Have you not met her yourselves, then?"

"Nay, mistress," said another, older veteran. "Not but that we would dearly like to. But it is a big army, and Aeron has many calls upon her. You could not expect her to come among us."

"She is the loser by it," murmured Aeron, then louder, "But what word would you have for her, if she came?"

The harper Garrack smiled. "Only that we love her dearly, and, gods willing, we will win her this fight."

"But if the fight was not born in righteousness? What then? Even queens must doubt."

"That is nothing to us," said the veteran. "Who has no doubts about his acts, be they great or small? Any road, not a warrior in this army but thinks Aeron is in the right. War was made upon her, and she has made the only answer she could. Nay, mistress, we have no quarrel with that, and perhaps, if you should yourself have speech with the Queen, you will of your goodness tell her so."

Aeron nodded slowly, and rose to her feet more slowly still.

"Gods with you, sirs, and strength to your arms," she said quietly. They gave her the same, and then she was walking back to her tent through the dark camp.

But many others were also wakeful in the last hours of peace.

In his own tent, Haruko lay staring up at the roof, gnawing his knuckles and struggling to overcome the numbness that seemed to have frozen his entire body. It was not fear; that he knew well from previous encounters, and this appeared to be something entirely new. A premonition, then? That felt more like it—but the real premonition had come long since, when he had looked at the viewscreens of the *Sword* and beheld a gold dragon coming toward him from stars no one had seen for more than a thousand years. No, that warning had been timely given and serenely accepted. Sure, he could have tried to thwart it—he could have left with Hathaway and Mikhailova. But he had known that true fate cannot be thwarted, and if karma, or dán, or whatever you wanted to call it, had caught up with him at last, he was only glad it had done so here, now, in Keltia, and grateful that it had given him a few months of joy before calling for the payoff. All in all, not a bad trade . . .

In another tent not very distant, Gwydion lay neither waking nor sleeping, but collected and very much aware in the marana trance. His present purpose was not magical nor even divinatory, but rather to allow himself to assimilate the many and diverse patterns of the past weeks, to weave the strands into an unbroken front of the spirit that he might present for battle in the morning . . .

In Aeron's tent, O'Reilly sat up in the little anteroom, sleepy and worried sick. Aeron had been gone nearly two hours, and she had looked so troubled—maybe O'Reilly should go out herself in search of her? With that fith-fath on her, nobody would know her as Aeron if anything happened to her, not until it was too late—and even the Fianna had so far not managed to find Tindal. Suppose he had sneaked into the camp and was even now lurking about outside, waiting for the chance to do Aeron a mischief, or worse? Then she heard the sound of spears striking ground in salute, outside in the faha, and she knew Aeron had returned at last . . .

And in the tent at the center of the Imperial camp, Arianeira had not ceased her agitated pacing. Presumably Jaun Akhera slept untroubled, in his own chamber beyond the silk and tapestry walls, for no sound came through to her ears.

Her anger had not abated; she had tried to sleep it away, to drug it into calmness, but it had resisted all strategems, and had even grown stronger, as if it were some living thing contemptuous of her feeble efforts to put it down. So now she paced, and in the blazing heart of her wrath an old seed of doubt began to blossom.

In the weeks since she had first made her bargain with Jaun Akhera, Arianeira had maintained a hold of findruinna on both her motivation and her conscience, and she had had no reason to expect that her grip on either would ever diminish. Jaun Akhera was for her, Gwydion and Aeron against; to her mind it was as simple as that. And so she had betrayed the two, and pledged to the one, and he to her.

And that was what now fed the secret root of doubt, what nourished all her fear and fury: the perceived possibility that Jaun Akhera might betray her in turn and pledge to Aeron. Indeed, had not such a thought already crossed his mind, and had not all heard it? Even Bres had been apprehensive for it . . .

Yet the root as she followed it went deeper still. All that day, Arianeira had had much leisure for thought, for memory and pondering of both present and past, and what had come recurrently and unerringly to her mind over those hours was in fact the far past. Days of her childhood with her parents and her brothers at Caer Ys—*by now destroyed,* she thought, the pang of loss striking curiously deep even through her anger. She had destroyed that past as surely as she had destroyed the castle, and with the same hand. Days too at Turusachan and Kinloch Arnoch, with Aeron and Morwen, and all the other Aoibhells and Douglases—

Yet the festering resentment held firm as the doubt began to grow. Aeron had preferred Gwydion to her, had preferred Morwen to her, had preferred Rohan and Roderick to her, had even, now, preferred Terrans to her . . . Arianeira had always been the least and the last of Aeron's intimates, had not been chosen to either of Aeron's councils, and—could never *be* Aeron.

Sick and dizzy with the struggle, she fell onto the rumpled bed, a huddled shape of white silk in the dimness, her hair covering her face and her hands to her mouth.

Oh gods, she thought, and a little whimpering sound, half moan, half protest, escaped her, *have I been wrong after all? Is this truly the only way it could have gone?*

So Arianeira, in the Imperial camp, waited as the others waited for the dawn, her soul no less a battlefield than the one that would be contested at the rising of the sun.

Chapter Twenty

Tindal saw the cloud-veiled surface of the planet Gwynedd sink below him as the little ship darted out into space. Well, that was that, then . . .

"Put not your trust in princes," he muttered. "Or their sisters, either." But Christ, he had been lucky to get away at all from that little magical firecracker Arianeira had planted in the castle of Caer Ys. Unless he was much mistaken, their other co-conspirator, the ineffable Kynon, had been caught in the wreckage. The same fate had been planned for Tindal, of course; Arianeira's little way of hedging her bets. She had never had the slightest intention of honoring her part of the bargain, the royal slut. She had used them both, him and Kynon alike, and when she had what she wanted fast within her little grasping hands, she had coolly sent them off to Gwynedd and their deaths.

Well, he hated to disappoint her, but by God, he was not about to roll over and play dead, even to oblige a princess. He consulted the coordinates she had given him. They seemed perfectly accurate; knowing he was a starship science officer, no doubt she had feared to fob him off with bogus starcharts. He had no intention now, naturally, of venturing near the sailing route indicated here for the *Marro*, Jaun Akhera's flagship. They might spot him and decide to blow him out of the spacelanes, for one thing; for another, the *Marro* might have already engaged the *Firedrake*, and recalling only too well what the Keltic flagship had looked capable of, he wasn't going anywhere near it.

No, he would sail quietly around behind the action, and with any luck at all manage to hide behind some moon until he could make his break for the nice big rip Arianeira had by now obligingly torn in the Curtain Wall. He had lain doggo on Gwynedd for a few days, after crawling out of the wreck of Caer Ys; then he had managed to steal this little ship. He was glad to be getting out at last. After that—well, he'd see. Earth somehow didn't seem to be in the picture at all. But there were plenty of other places he could go; they'd be only too pleased to see him on—

The singleship rocked alarmingly, and Tindal, startled, turned his attention to the controls. Again the terrific jolt, and he realized with horror that he was under attack.

He threw the ship into a roll, trying to see his enemy. Who the hell was it, Kelts or Imperials, or both? Did they know who he was? No ships of any stripe had appeared on his screens; where had it come from? Another blast on the portside and, almost simultaneously, one directly astern. No matter who was firing, he was in very big trouble.

With a heartfelt curse flung in the general direction of Arianeira, Tindal laid back his ears and headed off into deep space.

The sun of another system had risen over a scene of battle unimaginable. Aeron and her generals had not waited for full day, but in the cold gray half-light of the hour before dawn had flung the Keltic armies at the Imperial camp.

They kept the advantage that they so rashly reached for. True to Denzil's prediction, the Imperials watched with stupefaction and dismay as every single one of their first-launch winged craft plunged to earth like shot swans, and the remnant of their air arm remained firmly on the ground.

Hard upon that shock came the first wave of the Keltic chariotry, two- and three-horse vehicles, light and incredibly maneuverable, each bearing a driver and a warrior. They closed on the half-formed enemy ranks like moving steel walls, and the high yell of the great war-pipes rose chillingly over all.

To Jaun Akhera's credit, he had anticipated something of the sort, and had positioned his forces in near-deployment the previous night; and so he, at least, was not in such bad case as might have been. As Fomor undoubtedly was: The Keltic chariots, and the horsemen that came after, went through Bres's disarrayed troops like scythes through dry grass.

For all that, the counterattack, when it came, was considerable. On the right, Imperial infantry succeeded beyond all hope in turning the Keltic flank, and Gwydion recalled several squadrons of cavalry, hurling the horsemen against the unprotected Coranian foot.

In several places, the Imperials had broken the Keltic schiltron formations, and the fighting swirled up the rising ground to engulf the marca-sluagh itself. Under her standard, Aeron fought methodically and with deadly efficiency, and when the foot nearby were hard-pressed by Fomor's horse— *they knew enough about how we fight to bring their own cavalry arm,* a cold little voice said in her mind, *though the Imperials did not*—she led the knights of her own guard down the slope to relieve them.

In a lull, she reined in her horse and relaxed in the saddle to catch her breath.

"We like it not, Aeron, your fighting so," muttered a very weary galloglass who paused beside her.

Aeron grinned and pushed back the escaped strands of hair under her helm. "I like it no better to see *you* fighting so, my friend. But shall we both sit out such a ceili?"

"Nay, Lady," she laughed in answer. "A few reels more for us both."

"I hope longer yet—but see that Struan knows the need of horse here, and tell him I myself send you. Go now."

"It is done, Lady," she said, saluting, and vanished into the press.

Through all the long day the balance swayed back and forth, until at last all was brought to a halt late in the afternoon by a blinding rainstorm that leaped down the Strath like a hunting wolf. The Kelts held their sickle formation across the glen mouth massively unbroken, though sadly battered. The Imperial lines could not be seen through the rainy gloom, but as Keltic captains and lieutenants reported to their commanders, it became apparent that Jaun Akhera had come away a good deal more badly mauled than Aeron from their first encounter.

Rain drenched the camp as Aeron returned to her tent, and the Fians who saluted her as she walked slowly up through the faha noted privately, and with deep concern, how haggard she looked.

Inside the tent, O'Reilly thought the same, and wondered aloud if Aeron were sickening for something, or had been injured in the fighting.

"Nay, truly, I am well enough." She held out her arms, and O'Reilly divested her of cloak and surcoat, so wet their royal green looked black in the light from the crystals. "I went to visit some of the wounded in the healers' tents," she added, as O'Reilly unfastened the lorica. "Then Teilo felt the need to plague me—crammed full, a little after the fact, with Druidical portents and woe."

O'Reilly, hanging up the sodden cloak, remembered a conversation with Morwen, something about omens—

"Do you believe in portents, Lady?"

Aeron shook her head, and water flew from the ends of her hair in a crystal arc.

"Only when they portend what I wish them to . . ." Enveloped by O'Reilly in a fur-lined robe, she sat as close as she could get to the crystal brazier. More than her body seemed to have taken chill tonight . . .

To the Terran, it seemed that the austerity that had frozen Aeron's beauty for the past sevennight had thawed somewhat in the face of disaster. The loveliness of the fine-featured face was not diminished, but it was also somehow more human again. She began to brush dry the curling damp hair, darkened by the rain to the color of rubies—or old blood. With an effort, Aeron schooled herself to relax; after a few minutes O'Reilly pulled the shining masses of hair back over Aeron's shoulders, set a torse of gold-wound silk around her forehead to keep the hair from her face, and stepped back.

"Is there anything else I may do for you, Ard-rían?"

Aeron nodded, eyes half-closed. "Send for some to join us here; I would not be alone just yet."

O'Reilly withdrew, then, after a moment's thought, put on her cloak and went out to inform certain people of the Queen's wish for companionship . . .

By the time O'Reilly returned, chilled and wet, from her errand, most of those she had summoned had already arrived in the royal tent. She paused just outside the entrance, caught by the sound of music from within. Someone was playing a telyn, playing it beautifully; the little Kymric dance rang upon the harpstrings like crystal snowflakes pattering on a bell, like silver leaves falling from their branch onto a frozen stream. She was not at all surprised to see, when she entered the tent's spacious central chamber, that the harper was Gwydion.

Voices hailed her cheerfully, and O'Reilly blushed, suddenly shy. Which was very silly: There was no one there but that she knew well, and had herself invited here in Aeron's name—Morwen, Ríoghnach and Niall, Sabia, a few others, all casually strewn about on low camp-chairs or heaped cushions.

From his seat on the floor, leaning comfortably against Aeron's knees, Gwydion, smiling, motioned O'Reilly to dispose herself nearby on a pile of soft furs.

"For you are a Kelt now, Sorcha, and you must do as we do." And that was the first time any had called her that so easily . . .

Sinking gratefully into the furs, O'Reilly was emboldened by the teasing note in Gwydion's voice.

"Maybe, lord, but I don't think too many of the Ard-rían's other subjects have the chance to sit so, in her own tent—and in such company too."

Aeron laughed, and pushed Gwydion with her foot. "She has you there, Gwynedd."

Before Gwydion could reply, the outer door billowed open again on a gust of cold air; the inner curtains parted, and Rohan came in, his cloak dripping and his hair wet with wind-whipped rain.

He waved away their pleased surprise. "I shall tell you all presently—The storm grows," he added, warming cold hands at the crystal brazier. "The Shining Folk fight with their own weapons, maybe."

"They fight a different war than ours," murmured Sabia, and he shot her a quizzical look.

"That's as may be," he said, "but there is news, Ard-rían, and I thought to be the bearer."

"Tell it, then. No soul here but will not know of it within the hour, so they may as well hear now with me."

"Tidings both fair and ill. We have routed the combined fleets from the systems of Vannin, Kernow and Brytaned; admittedly, great force was not sent against those systems, but what was sent is now either fled or destroyed. Mostly destroyed . . . Of the other systems, Scota is three parts cleared, and our fleets now are ordered to Erinna and Kymry, where the fighting is very heavy, and to this system, where it is worst."

"What then is the ill news?"

Rohan met his sister's eyes. "Elharn is slain. I have put Caradoc Llassar in his place as High Admiral, and brought his body here."

Sudden silence fell over the chamber. Elharn Aoibhell had been kin, friend, or commander to every person there, save O'Reilly only. To Aeron, he had been more: a trusted and valued advisor; in age he was contemporary with her parents, though he was in fact her father's uncle, and she had thought of him—and loved him—as a second father.

She stood up. "I shall go to him. He is the first of our kindred to fall in this fight, and I shall speed him myself. Those of you who wish to do him honor, join me in the tent of the Fianna in half an hour's time. And bid someone fetch Teilo to him, that the rites be observed with greatest honor."

In the enormous clochan of the Fianna field command, Aeron stood silent, looking down on Elharn as he lay in the torchlight upon the wicker bier, a Fian's war-cloak drawn over him to his chin and the narrow gold fillet denoting his princely rank set about his iron-gray hair. Teilo, as Archdruid, had spoken the brief Keltic death ceremonial over him, and Ríoghnach, a high priestess, had taken the Ban-draoi's part in the rites.

"No red for Ironbrow," said Aeron. "He would not wish it, and we will speed him in the way of the Fianna."

The huge tent was packed; as many high-ranking officers as could be crammed decently into the chamber were present, for Elharn had been a First-rank Fian, a teacher at the War College and a field commander in out-Wall actions, as well as High Admiral and Master of Sail, and his passing was deeply mourned. Desmond and Slaine stood at the head and foot of their father's bier, their other brother, Macsen, beside Aeron.

Teilo, on Aeron's other side, was ready when at last she turned to him. He placed in her hands an unusually large and curiously faceted crystal, and all near the bier drew back several paces. Aeron cupped it in her hands until it began to glow, its light spilling like water through her fingers, then knelt to set it upon Elharn's breast above the folded hands. The glow spread to envelop Elharn's body in blue flame, though no heat was felt by even the nearest of the onlookers, and the blaze held motionless for many moments. Then came a burst of cool white brilliance, and when the afterimage cleared from the eyes of those who watched, both bier and body had vanished. Only the crystal, dark and cold, now remained.

"His sign shall be set on the stones of Ni-Maen," said Aeron. "As befits a prince of Keltia fallen in battle. And we will not forget to remember the name of Ironbrow. Gods with him."

"Gods with him," came the answering murmur, and Aeron went out with Rohan.

Back in the royal tent after the ceremony, the visitors gone, O'Reilly tidied up somewhat aimlessly, all the while casting covert glances at Aeron's averted profile. How did you comfort someone who had just lost a close and dear relative? Then she remembered that Aeron was by no means unfamiliar with such sudden griefs, and she wanted to weep.

But Aeron turned as if she had heard, and gave her the flash of a smile in understanding and apology.

"I would be alone, O'Reilly. I am too troubled to trouble anyone else—except that if Gwydion should return, he and he alone may come in. Tell the guards so, and then go you and rest yourself."

When Gwydion did come, much later, he found her still

wide awake, and the face she raised to his kiss was troubled and unsmiling.

"What is it? Elharn? He made a fine Fian's end, Aeronwy, and Caradoc Llassar will make a fine High Admiral to follow him."

"Not Elharn only . . . How many others were lost today, with less ceremony though no less honor to mark their going? Yet all we sat here at our ease, drinking ale and listening to you play the harp. Is that the way for the Queen to spend the first night of battle?"

"Would you feel any easier, Ard-rían, if you were out there dead in the rain—or even just alive and freezing? Aeron, the dead are sped, the wounded are cared for, and the rest of the army is just as comfortable as you are. More so," he added, exasperated, "for *they* do not spend their time torturing themselves when they should be sleeping. No one is cold or alone or neglected, I promise you."

She laughed unwillingly, more than a little shamefaced. "I had thought I had this overmastered. Apparently I was mistaken."

He smiled then, more relieved than he allowed her to sense. "It is but your first real battle, cariad. For one so new to war, you do very well."

"Ah, praise from the First Lord of War for my poor martial talents! That is praise indeed." Aeron curled up gracefully on the field-couch, one foot tucked beneath her. "Prince of Dôn, how is it you can endure me? I must vex you very much."

"Very much indeed, Ard-rían; yet would I have it no other way. Try to sleep now."

Gwydion came suddenly out of a fitful doze to complete, alert wakefulness. He had planned to return to his own tent once Aeron was settled and sleeping; but, weary from the demands of the day, he had drowsed off in the camp-chair. But now— Some sound, some lack of sound; something was not as it had been, or should be. Yet the woman asleep on the field-couch had not stirred, and her senses were notoriously acute. Perhaps it was nothing?

But his sense of wrongness grew. He put out a hand for his

sword, and it slid silently into his grip. He glanced again at
Aeron's tranquil sleeping face; it seemed incredible that she
did not wake, for the feeling of cold pervasive danger grew
ever stronger.

In the corner of the sleeping-chamber nearest the outside
wall of the tent, a dim blue mist began to swirl. As Gwydion
watched, it trembled, eddied, then thickened and resolved
itself into the image of his sister Arianeira. Though it was a
projection only, of the sort known to sorcerers as a taish, she
appeared to look directly at him, and she spoke to him; but
her lips did not move, and the words that came only to him in
her own voice he heard within his mind.

"I send this taish to you, my brother," she said. "I would
speak with you before battle is joined again. There is a place
near the glen mouth, you will know it when you see it"—into
Gwydion's mind flashed a brief clear picture of a certain
place out on the high moor—"and I would have you meet me
there, with Aeron, before the sun is full up."

Gwydion nodded slowly. "I shall be there, Ari," he said
aloud, and the image's mouth curved in a smile. Then the
blue mist shivered and was gone. Gwydion leaned back in his
chair, and kept his sword across his knees, and slept lightly,
if at all, the remainder of the night.

In the daffodil dawnlight, Aeron, scrambling over a low
gorse hedge, reached up for Gwydion's hand. He pulled her
up to stand beside him on top of the slope, and she paused a
moment to look around doubtfully at the scorched desolation.
There had been heavy bombardment here, and the ground was
torn up for many hundreds of yards, still smoking and warm
where the long-range siege lasers had struck.

"Are you sure this is where she showed you she would be?
It could be but a trap . . ."

Gwydion shook his head, abstracted, as one who is only
half-listening. "I think not . . . But the time and the place are
right, and—and she is here."

"Alone?"

"So it seems."

With a deep indrawn breath, Aeron turned resolutely to

face, for the first time since the war began, the author of Keltia's afflictions.

Arianeira was coming toward them steadily over the broken ground, with her usual long elegant stride. She was muffled in a voluminous blue cloak, and when she saw them, she halted, putting the hood back from her face.

"Hail, Gwydion my brother! And my Queen also—hail Aeron." Her voice carried clear across the little stream that separated her from them. "May I cross?"

Gwydion hesitated a moment, then nodded. But as his sister ran lightly across the flat stones of the fording-place, and came up the hill, he thrust Aeron behind him and raised the point of his drawn sword.

"That is hardly a safeguard, Gwydion," said Arianeira teasingly. "Any one of us three could destroy the others without recourse to steel . . . as you know. But if it makes you feel safer on Aeron's behalf, well enough."

"What is it you would say to us, Ari?" asked Aeron quietly. "Gwydion has told me you sent a taish to him to ask for this meeting. You must have wanted it sore."

Arianeira shrugged. "Doubtless you would have done the same yourself before very much longer. Your curiosity, if naught else, would have compelled you to it—for you *are* curious, Aeron, are you not? But you did come, as I asked. Surely that must prove you still trust me—a little?"

"It proves nothing but that I trust your brother," said Aeron shortly. "But is it forgiveness you seek?" She was puzzled; try as she might, she could ken nothing of the state of mood or mind behind Arianeira's smiling mocking face.

The Princess's peal of laughter was eerie to hear in that torn and blackened landscape.

"Nay, Aeron, not that! I neither wish it nor hope for it, save to hope that you will not afflict me with it . . . But as to why I am come, there are several reasons, not the least of them being to thank you."

"To thank me?"

"How else but by following your example did I manage to tear the Curtain Wall like a worn gúna? You yourself showed me the way—at Bellator." Aeron's face blanched to the hair-roots as realization struck home at last, and Arianeira smiled. "But that is not my chief reason. Say rather that I am come as a friendly emissary from Jaun Akhera, with new terms you may care to accept once you have heard them—and their alternative. Still, I fear they will be little to your liking, Aeron. But I pray you listen, and try not to allow your guilt, or your grief for your uncle Ironbrow, to cloud your royal judgment. — Oh, aye, we heard all about Elharn. You will find there is little goes on in your camp we do not know of."

Aeron had mastered herself once again. "If that is so, Ari," she said and now there was only cool reproof in her voice, "I wonder that you seem not to know that I will never accept any terms of Jaun Akhera's devising, still less when they are brought to me by a Keltic traitor."

Arianeira scowled, and turned instead to Gwydion. His swordpoint had wavered not an inch, and his eyes upon her face were more watchful than before.

"Say the terms, then, Ari."

"They are so: That this planet shall be ceded up to him immediately, without let or further contest of arms, and the fleets and armies of Keltia shall on the instant cease hostilities. Jaun Akhera will accept the submission of the Six Nations, and spare the folk in return; and he will leave here to rule in his name a Regent."

"You," said Aeron, not surprised in the least.

"So he has promised."

"And what of the Ard-rían?" asked Gwydion, intent on the answer.

"My lord Jaun Akhera has also promised," said Arianeira, after a moment, "to spare her life, so that she will make submission of fealty to him, and she must then remain a prisoner of state on Alphor for the rest of her life. That is his mercy, Aeron, not mine; my terms called for your head atop the Wolf Gate."

Aeron's smile was small and cold. "Then if he has offered my head to you, Ari, how comes it that two days ago he offered his hand—and his throne—to me?"

"It is no real offer," replied the Princess calmly, though anger flicked her anew at the memory. "Besides, he has since reconsidered; else I had not been here making this offer. And any road, are you not pledged already?'' This time the note of jealous hatred in her voice was unmistakable.

"Kynon of Ruabon was put to the Cremave," put in Gwydion smoothly, and his sister's eyes dropped. "Did you know that also?"

"What is such a one to me? He and the Terran had barely the wit to carry out my bidding."

"Such is the quality of loyalty among traitors," replied her brother. "Well, for his part, he tried to cast all blame upon you, said it was you made first overture to the Imperials and led both him and Tindal into treason. But the Cremave proved the truth of that was otherwise; of that much, at least, are you guiltless."

But Aeron could curb her pain no longer. "How came you to hate me so much and so hardly? Ari!" It was a cry from the soul, and it pierced even Arianeira's armor. "I know we have been unfriends of late, and for that I shall ever be sorry; but why did you not come to me and speak of what was in your heart? I would have listened, and having listened surely I would have acted. You and I have known each other all our lives; did you not know that at least of me?"

"Oh, what do you know of what was in my heart— *Majesty?*'' snarled Arianeira, her voice venomous on the title. The face she turned to Aeron was white and pinched with hatred revealed at last. "You were born with your life's task assured, none greater or more honorable: to rule Keltia. There was nothing left for me, nothing! You took my friend from me, and my brother, and then you cut me from you. Do you wonder, foster-sister''—again her voice hissed like a nathair— "that I chose in the end to turn elsewhere? The Queen of Kelts had failed me, and Keltia herself had failed me. Keltia! The Gwrach-y-Ribyn, the Blue Hag, the Sacred Sow that devours her own young! Me she devoured early on; do not wonder, then, Aeron, at what I did in the end."

"You might have done as the rest of us," said Aeron steadily, though her heart bled within her. "Refused to be eaten . . . Ari, you had only to speak—"

"To *you?* To Aeron Aoibhell? Nay, Queen of Kelts, when I did come to speak, I spoke to those with whom my speech carried most weight, and did me most weal."

"To Jaun Akhera," said Gwydion, who had kept silent while his lady and his sister spoke. "For that I loved Aeron, and she me, you chose to sell us all to the Marbh-draoi."

The contempt in his face and voice was complete; neither woman had ever heard its like from him before, and Arianeira paled, then flushed.

"Nay, call him rather by his true title: the next Cabiri Emperor! He who will make me his Regent here."

"His vassal, rather," said Aeron. "I think you will find the Prince of Alphor a far harsher master than I."

Arianeira's mouth tightened. "As to that, we must wait upon the time. Though you and those who follow you have but little left of that."

"If that is so, then your finding shall be all the sooner . . . But for me, Ari, I love you and pity you. I have ever been your friend and your sister before I have been your Queen, and no matter what befalls us both in the end, I shall ever be so." And Aeron turned away from Arianeira and headed back to the Keltic camp.

But Gwydion remained, and so he alone saw the look with which his sister gazed after Aeron. And as he watched he caught something of the conflict that was lacerating Arianeira's soul with claws of iron: the love against the jealousy, the loyalty against the perceived and imagined wrongs.

She felt the touch of his mind, and whirled around to face him. Tears were on her cheek.

"Why do you hesitate, Prince of Gwynedd?" she cried, and in the words was all the bitter despair she had kept hidden even from herself all these months and years. "Your sword is already drawn; strike! It would be a kindness, Gwion—"

The sound of the pet-name she had not used for him since their childhood staggered him like a blow to the face.

"Ari—your life is not mine to end. And even now your healing is not beyond you to accomplish." He came forward; she shrank a little, but lifted her head in the old proud defiance he remembered.

But he only took her hand and kissed it. "Gods with you, my sister." He looked down into her eyes, sea-gray into sky-blue, then turned to follow Aeron, who was by now a small dark figure far down the glen.

Arianeira looked after him with desperate eyes until he too was but a shape upon the moor, even the scarlet cloak he wore only a blurred patch against the autumn brightness. When she saw that the moor flamed with such patches, she knew that he was truly gone. She sank slowly down into the burned and withered bracken, and buried her face in her skirts.

Chapter Twenty-one

The second day of fighting was fiercer far than the first. By the time Aeron and Gwydion had come again to the Keltic camp, the armies had formed for the charge; there had been some skirmishing already, off on the Keltic left. But in the main the lines held firm, and Gwydion did not hold them long in leash.

By noon the battle had been lost and won several times over, no clear victor either way. Jaun Akhera ranged up and down along his hard-pressed line, shouting to his captains, rallying soldiers so weary they were dropping where they stood. And indeed his being there seemed to have as inspiring an effect upon his armies as Aeron's presence had upon her own, so that for a space of several hours the Imperial forces carried the field.

The field, but not the day, and not for long: for Gwydion threw Maravaun of Cashel and several thousand cavalry straight at the Imperial center. And Maravaun smashed the triple lines, wheeled left and right and came round again with the most of his riders still horsed, to take Hanno's infantry from the rear.

The sun was still two hours from setting when suddenly all along the front the Imperial ranks wavered, then made an abrupt and orderly withdrawal. A great yell went up from the Kelts, who in their battle rage would have harried the retreating enemy straight into the Imperial camp. But Gwydion sent swift word to the captains of the line not to follow, and the overeager Keltic warriors were soon collected and recalled.

Aeron, who had fought this day on foot, had made a strategic retreat of her own somewhat earlier, limping slightly from a bone-bruising blow struck at her by a Fomori pikeman. Her attacker had died for his pains under three Fian swords, but he had succeeded in putting Aeron, for the moment, out of the fight.

She had had the raxed muscles tended by Slaine, a talented healer, who had given orders that no word of the injury, slight as it was, should reach the army at large, and had also given orders that Aeron was to keep off the leg as much as possible for a day or two.

So it was that Aeron was in her tent, talking with Haruko, Ríoghnach and O'Reilly, when there was a sudden commotion outside in the faha, and then Sabia came flying in.

"They've taken Tindal," she gasped. "He was trying to escape in a singleship—Fergus's squadron caught him leaving the Kymric system, and Fergus sends him to you with his compliments."

If those present had hoped for a reaction from Aeron, they were disappointed. She made no outward sign either of pleasure or displeasure, but seated herself and spoke in a dry light voice that likewise held no clue to her feelings.

"Bring him in."

Tindal was escorted into the tent by Desmond and Grelun. The Terran was pale, and his customary expression of scorn was for once utterly absent. A streak of dried blood smudged his forehead, and his clothes were torn; evidently Fergus's kerns had not been over-gentle with him. As his eyes adjusted to the relative dimness within the royal tent, he saw Haruko standing behind Aeron's chair. He started to say something, but the look on his former captain's face caused him to think better of it, and he flushed and looked away.

"Doubtless you are sorry to be brought before me alive, Tindal," said Aeron crisply. "But no sorrier than I am for the necessity to bring you so, though I do not expect you to believe me. You were betrayed by Arianeira, of course."

He stared at her. "There was no 'of course' about it!"

" 'Ard-rían'," said Desmond in a very soft voice, and his hand moved almost imperceptibly on his sword-hilt.

"Ard-rían," amended Tindal mockingly. "Well, not at first, anyway—and without my help, she would never have gotten her message out to Jaun Akhera telling him to begin the attack."

"Perhaps not," said Aeron. "Any road, I had enough of that from her own mouth not twelve hours since . . . But it makes no odds. It is war; we here are all soldiers, and we know the rules that govern war."

"My diplomatic status—"

"—was forfeit by your own actions, as I have informed Captain Haruko. You will find no edge on that sword. Do you wish to pray to your gods, or make a last statement?"

"Only this—Ard-rían." Wrenching his arm from Grelun's grip, Tindal pulled a small square box of white metal from his sleeve, and with a sharp tug broke it in two, refitted it, and tossed it at Aeron.

With a cry Haruko dove to intercept it, catching it not six inches from Aeron's head, and flung it mightily out of the tent door into the faha where no one stood. There was a soundless concussion, a flash of blue light and a momentary wind.

Aeron for once looked fully as shaken as she felt. She had all through the brief interview not moved from her chair, but now she rose, eyes upon Tindal where Grelun and Desmond had brought him ungently to his knees. She was about to speak when Haruko, still breathing hard from his effort, detached the sword from his baldric, stepped forward, and, with a grim punctiliousness his samurai ancestors would have applauded, in one lightning motion beheaded Tindal where he knelt.

In the silence, Ríoghnach could be heard reassuring the speechless O'Reilly, who had been watching the proceedings with her from a corner of the tent.

"It is the law, truly. Any brehon will tell you."

But it was not so much Tindal's swift dispatch that had so stunned the Terran woman, nor even the fact that Haruko had been the one to effect it; but rather the apparent lack of emotion displayed by everyone save herself. O'Reilly put a hand to her mouth and stared at Tindal's crumpled body, headless upon the floor. Lawful retribution: It was a side of Keltia—and a face of Haruko, whom she had thought she had known well—that O'Reilly had never suspected, and it left her deeply shaken.

"But it is like that with adders," Desmond was saying. "Best to crush their heads as soon as they are caught." He looked up from the floor, which was awash in blood, to Aeron, whose gaze was still unfocused. "Forgive me, athiarna. He should not have come before you still bearing a weapon. I failed you."

Aeron came back into her eyes then, spoke with utter conviction.

"Not you, cousin. Never once you—nor you, Grelun." She gripped first Desmond's arm, then Grelun's, then turned to Haruko. "I must be more weary than I know, and less courteous than I thought . . . I have not thanked you, Theo, either for my life saved or my justice taken in hand." She kissed him formally on either cheek, then embraced him as friend to friend.

"I failed you also, Lady," muttered Haruko. "That was an ion-grenade, standard Navy issue. I should have known he'd have had something like that planned, or else you'd never have taken him alive."

"And *I* say, I have been failed by *no* one! Not you, not Grelun or Desmond, perhaps not even Arianeira . . . Let us speak of it no more."

When Gwydion returned to his tent it was full dark, and growing colder. Morwen was waiting for him, and while he ate a quick meal she told him of Tindal's capture and its horrifying sequels.

But he did not give way to anger as she had half-expected him to, merely inquired mildly enough as to Aeron's safety, and, when assured of that, commended Haruko's swift action; no more.

"You seem perhaps to make strangely little of this," she said, and her voice carried more of a rebuke than she had intended.

Gwydion sighed, and when he spoke at last his words came

low and weary and freighted with all the unconfessed emotion, all the unacknowledged sadness, all the pain and frustration and bafflement he had never before expressed.

"How? If I made more of it, both she and you would chide me for being overprotective. She is my prime and chiefest value, and I wish indeed to protect her, to shield her as best I can from whatever I can. But no more than that, and no more protection than is necessary; for to lift a burden from one whose dán requires that burden is no service but a grievous error . . . I know very well that she can take care of herself, Wenna, but she must also take care of Keltia, and I—I would spare her what little I can, or may."

Morwen felt tears sting her eyes. Never had she heard him speak so, whatever the provocation. Nor had any, save perhaps Aeron herself; the Prince of Dôn was not one easily to lay open his soul to even his closest friends.

But the events of the past fortnight had shattered a good many of his defenses, and Gwydion was suddenly glad of the chance to speak for once of the fears that harried his heart.

Morwen laid her arm across his shoulders, tentatively, as if she feared he would shake off her attempt at comfort, but after a moment he reached up to cover her hand with his.

"My dearest friend," she said, her face filled with pity and understanding, "do not torment yourself. She has declared openly to you now, and that means many things will change, and soon, as she grows accustomed to the idea. You of all people know how little she loves to depend on others for what she can do as well, or better, herself. But Aeron will ever do as she will do, indeed as she must do; nothing you or I or anyone else may wish can ever alter that."

He laughed shortly, and the old impassive mask fell once again over his face.

"I know that too, but it is good to hear you say so . . ." He rose, and her arm fell away, the moment over. "But stay a while. Morwen and Gwydion may have spoken, but the Taoiseach and the First Lord of War have much still to discuss."

Gwydion would have been surprised indeed to know just how much Aeron felt herself in need of his protection, and, more, how much in truth she longed for it. Yet ingrained pride, or Aoibhell obstinacy, or simple reluctance to admit a weakness—or what she perceived to be a weakness—kept her from going to him. She knew it well, and hated it heartily, that kernel of hardness in her soul that would not allow her to accept the protection she not only desperately needed but desperately wanted.

She was alone in her tent; the blood had been washed from the floor, but her nerves were still sorely rattled by the events of the afternoon.

Yet still would she not call him to her . . .

Was it Rhodri's death that had done this to her, she wondered bleakly; had made her so strong that she had grown less feeling? Unbidden, the picture that had haunted her memory for three years now formed before her eyes: the smoke-choked bridge of the crippled destroyer, the charred rubble left by Fomori laser torpedoes, the dusty light falling on a man's body stretched out at her feet, his eyes closed now, dead without her under far stars beyond the Bawn. Was that it, then?

Or was it rather that she still possessed the undimmed capacity to feel *too* deeply, and all this was simply terror of allowing another into her heart, for fear of losing him too? She brushed back her hair, stared blindly at the walls of the tent bulging with the wind. That was stupid, then; a willing, and loving, vulnerability was no weakness, but the gift of a very real strength. Perhaps she was not so strong after all?

Yet Gwydion had not come recently to her affections, but had been there always; she had chosen to make him king—had been sure enough and strong enough to forge that bond, for that title once bestowed could not be taken back again. Could she now not learn to rely a little more upon his strength and a little less upon her own?

She shivered a little, huddling down inside the plaid that wrapped her. These were questions that bore not at all upon her present straits. Fears or no, such speculation—and such emotion—would not help her to win the war, or even the next day's battle. It had not helped her earlier that day, not with Ari, not with Tindal. It scattered her purpose and destroyed her concentration, and it was a luxury a queen could ill afford in such a time; perhaps not in any time. No warrior could, not and still maintain a hope of real victory in the fight. And far too much depended on this fight, for her as for the rest of Keltia.

The stalemate of arms was broken on the fifth day of fighting, and it broke not to the advantage of the Kelts. Despite the heroic efforts of the Keltic starfleet, reinforcements had been brought up from Imperial and Fomori troopships and successfully landed at Rath na Ríogh. These fresh troops flung themselves into the battle, intent on turning the scales, and gradually the Keltic line began to curve in on itself like a bending swordblade.

"And the best blade in the world will break in the end, Ard-rían," said Struan Cameron, wiping blood from his eyes where a grafaun had struck him a glancing blow to the forehead.

"See to that cut, Struan," said Aeron. "But what do you suggest?" Still under orders from Slaine to rest her injured leg, she had taken no active part in the day's fighting, for the first time in five days, and now watched the conflict through field-glasses from the isolated, flat-topped hill called Orrest Law. A small knot of her commanders and personal guard stood with her under the Royal Standard.

"Fall back upon Ath-na-forair," said Gwydion. "Or, better, Tomnahara."

"To Ath-na-forair is a retreat of forty miles, and near twice that to Tomnahara. Can it be accomplished in time?"

Struan nodded. "With the help of the transports. If we begin at nightfall, all save for a rearguard can be in position at Ath-na-forair by dawn, or at Tomnahara by midday."

Aeron did not answer at once. Reluctant as she was to allow the conflict to spill farther down the Great Glen—and closer to Caerdroia and the risk of siege—every hour she had seen the necessity to do so grow plainer.

"Ath-na-forair, then," she said. "I would save retreat to Tomnahara as an option that may not be needed. Begin at once."

Gwydion looked relieved. "A wise decision, Ard-rían."

"A decision of necessity, King of Keltia." She marked

with hidden satisfaction the ill-concealed amazement that jolted all within earshot—for that was the first time she had addressed him so, in public or in private. Even Gwydion seemed a little taken aback, and said as much later, as he and Aeron watched the retreat begin.

"Was that well done, do you think?"

"To flaunt your future title in their faces?" She seemed amused. "They must learn, soon or late, to be easy with it—as must you."

But when Aeron emerged from the transport that had carried her, like any other common soldier, from Rath na Ríogh, she stopped short in surprise.

"This is not Ath-na-forair! This is—"

"Tomnahara," said Gwydion tranquilly. "We altered the plan somewhat, since the Fomori seemed to have gotten word of your destination, and we ourselves had word that they were preparing a surprise raid."

"But the army! Gwydion, I will not leave the army to—"

"Ath-na-forair is already under attack," he said, his face grim in the torchlight. "We did not even have the chance to garrison it before it was taken. We lost much strength, Ardrían, but we saved much also, and the most of the army is even now on its way here. They are doing what they can to protect the folk who live in the glen, as they come," he added.

"That at least is well . . . But another retreat—and the secret of my whereabouts will not remain a secret long. Bres will not have it so."

"He thinks you still at or near Ath-na-forair," he said, taking her arm and leading her inside the castle. "Please gods, he will continue to think so a while yet. But I have called together some whose opinions I know carry weight with you. There is a thing we must discuss."

In the gríanan of the castle perhaps a dozen people sat or stood in various degrees of uncertainty: Morwen, Slaine, Desmond, Sabia, among others, and off to one side, Haruko and O'Reilly. The Terrans had taken as active a part in the battle as any Kelt; O'Reilly, as Aeron's squire, close beside her, and Haruko attached, however informally, to Niall and Desmond.

Haruko had seen little of Aeron, therefore, in the past three days, save for the episode with Tindal, and now he had eyes only for her. *Had she been wounded?* he thought, appalled at the look of her . . .

"Sit, all you," said Aeron before they could begin to rise, and seated herself by the fire. "Gwydion it is who has summoned us, and I would hear straightway what he would say to us."

"Things go not so well on Tara as we could wish, and less well even than we thought." Gwydion's voice sounded a note of warning in their ears. "If we are forced from here, we must fall back upon Caerdroia and man a siege. And if that comes to be, I recommend certain measures be accomplished."

"Which are?" asked Sabia.

"The safe concealment of the Copper Crown, and various other of the royal insignia."

"That is well thought of," said Morwen at once. "But where in all Keltia would such things be safe? There has been war on all the major planets, and the struggle here is still—" She gestured, not completing the sentence.

"I have considered that too," said Gwydion. "The treasures would be safest at this time if they lie not in human hands."

"You would confide them to the care of the merrows?" asked Aeron, interested in spite of herself. "Or the seal-folk—the Sluagh-rón?" The merrows, Moruadha in the Gaeloch, were semi-aquatic humanoids who lived chiefly on the planet Kernow; the seal-folk, the silkies, were not humanoid at all, but an intelligent phocine race dwelling in the cold fresh seas of Caledon. The two races had been in Keltia since the beginning, and by now they had spread to most of the other worlds as well; they possessed all the civil rights of any subject of the Crown, and they were on excellent terms with each other and with human Kelts.

"It is not of them I thought, though they would be no bad guardians . . . Nay, I purpose to bring the Crown to the care of the Shining Ones."

If he had said he wanted to give it to the Coranians

themselves the surprise in the grianan could not have been more complete, and in the faces that now turned to Gwydion awe and fear were mixed in equal measure.

The Sidhe, the Shining Folk, the tall pale people, proud ladies and stern warriors all unearthly fair, whose hidden palaces shimmered on the high places where no mortal dared to step, the windy fells and bare uplands and the hollow mountain side—

How they had come to Keltia none living now knew, though it was said in the Bardic Colleges that St. Brendan had known. Some even claimed that it had been Brendan himself who begged his mother, she who was of high blood among them, to bring the old gods of Ireland with them in their flight, so that the Danaans might not go godless in their new home; and so did the Sidhe leave Ireland forever. Others held rather that the Shining Ones had been in Keltia from the first, and had called the Kelts to them across the starry gulfs of space. Most, though, were of the opinion that the Shining Folk, whatever their origin, were indeed gods; or the children of gods, for who knew how long it was given to a god to live? Even the gods were not immortal; only the high Powers were that, those who served the One and who spoke not to men save only through the lesser deities, who held more than enough divinity for most mortals to bear.

There were even tales that some of the old families had sprung from these divine progenitors: a goddess who had loved a warrior, or a lord of the Sidhe who had wedded a Keltic princess. Only the Ban-draoi and the Druids, if anyone, knew the truth of *those* tales. But no one who had seen Aeron Aoibhell call in her power, or Gwydion ap Arawn at full stretch as sorcerer, had any doubts whatever that there were yet children of Dôn and Dâna alive in the light of day.

"Is it lawful to call so upon the Shining Ones?" Morwen, the only non-sorcerer present who was brave enough to ask, looked as doubt-shaken as she felt. It was bred in the bones of every Kelt who ever had breathed: The People of Peace are not to be troubled in their hollow hills.

Even Aeron seemed to lack some of her usual assurance, and she had been as astonished as the others at Gwydion's suggestion, though this she did not allow them to see. But—

"Why not, then?" she asked, almost belligerently. "Keltia is their home as much as it is ours; let them shoulder their right share of the fight to keep it." She ignored the shocked silence at the near-blasphemy, pressed her point home. "Am I not then of their kin, as much a daughter of Dâna as any of them? They could not, surely, deny their help to a kinswoman."

But for all her confident speech, Aeron was none too sure of her welcome at the Court of the Sidhe. In living memory no known Kelt had ever gone to the Hollow Mountains and returned to tell of it, though there were songs and tales in plenty of those who had been taken to dwell among the Shining Ones, coming never again among mortal folk. But no one knew for sure.

"Granted that we need someone to go," said David Drummond. "But who?"

"I will go myself—"

"You will not, then," said Melangell. "Any road, Aeron, you are needed here."

"All of us are needed here, cousin. It is right that the Ard-rían be the one to bring the Copper Crown to the keeping of the People of Peace."

"I will take the Crown to the Hollow Mountains." The voice was Gwydion's. "I it was who had the thought, and I would take the risk of it too upon myself—if any risk there be. As Chief of the House of Dôn, I shall be welcome, and protected as few others are."

"There are other divine Houses," said Morwen.

"Aye—well, the Chief of the House of Dâna is Aeron, and she must remain here. The Chief of the House of Lír is slain; his heir goes missing, and we cannot tarry to find him. The Chief of the House of Brân is a child of eleven, and the Chief of the House of Mâth is a woman of nearly two hundred. The House of Fionn has stood chiefless for a hundred years. In the Dôniad is the only other power that will serve."

"There is Elved your brother," suggested Denzil. "He would go, surely."

"Surely he would; but this is an errand for a chief and a sorcerer, and Elved is neither . . . Nay, my friends, if any is to go it must be I myself who does so."

Aeron stared into the fire. "What will you ask of the

Shining Ones? Certain it is they cannot be bound by any mortal promises.''

"Can they not? Well, perhaps so. But I shall ask only what is needed: protection for the Crown, that they will hold it safe in their keeping. They care not overmuch for the things of our world, but in the Copper Crown is somewhat that will speak to them. They will know it, and honor it, and preserve it safe.''

"If we are to send the Crown to safety, Aeron,'' said Desmond, ''then perhaps other things should be sent as well.''

"What things?''

"The Scepter of Llyr, for one,'' said Morwen, ''and the Great Seal of Keltia.'' She saw the look on Aeron's face, spoke quickly. ''Aeron, it may have to be so. Only you can wield the Unicorn Seal, but the Great Seal may be used by any holder thereof. If it fell into the wrong hands much ill would follow.''

Turning over the Great Seal meant, effectively, turning over the governance of Keltia, and Aeron's face was dark with refusal.

"We shall consider this,'' she said, rising. ''Lords and ladies, we give you good night.''

Behind her she left troubled silence.

"What will she do?'' asked Haruko.

"It is ever a bad sign,'' said Melangell with a tiny shrug, ''when my cousin uses the royal 'we' . . .''

Tomnahara awoke well into the morning to the sounds of sudden battle. Aeron, dashing half-clad from the solar where she had spent the night alone in thought, met O'Reilly running toward her, arms full of battle harness.

"Chriesta tighearna!''—that was Aeron taking the name of the Christian god in vain—''What is happening here?''

"I don't know yet, Lady, but please get this on fast, just in case.'' O'Reilly pulled the lorica over Aeron's head and fastened the shoulder-clasps with flying fingers. ''Gwydion has rallied the guard—I think the castle is under attack.''

It was indeed. Grelun saw them as they ran out onto the battlements and spoke at once to Gwydion, who turned with a look of relief to see them safe.

"A surprise raid, Ard-rían," he said, pulling her aside into the lee of a tower. "Fomorian rig-amuis—paid berserkers—and Bres leads them himself."

"Does he indeed! But can the Fians not turn them back?"

"They hold them off," conceded Gwydion. "For the moment, at least. I blame myself for this. I should have been better prepared . . . Any road, I have summoned Struan's chariotry, but if they do not arrive in good time we are in very grave case."

"So. Then let us help with the holding-off." She drew her glaive and went to the edge of the battlements, and O'Reilly went with her.

Hours of bitter fighting later, Aeron paused atop the rubble of the castle's outer barbican. Great damage had been done by the Fomori mercenaries; but despite the heedless fury of the berserkers, the defending Kelts still held Tomnahara and the surrounding mains; and, heralded by a rising dustcloud, Struan's long-delayed chariots were even now at the mouth of the glen.

Then Aeron saw, for the first time that day, amid the blue uniforms of his bodyguard, Bres himself. There came over her on the instant blood-fury such as she had thought she had learned to forget, had schooled herself never to feel again. Her sight crimsoned, flooded from behind with blood, and the red mist narrowed her vision until Bres was all that she beheld.

He saw her in the same moment, and his reaction was even as hers. They began to move toward each other like comets in collision courses, impelled by the same volcanic and irresistible tide: two opposite poles of a magnet, or some new and dreadful double star, drawn together against all law and reason by the same force of hate.

Aeron was plunging headlong down over the burned and broken stone, and Bres was clambering up the long slope of the glacis with no less speed and eagerness, when a stocky figure in the brown uniform of the Fianna suddenly came between them, stepping with upraised lightsword directly into Bres's path. In her terrible single-mindedness Aeron did not at first recognize him; then the red mist lifted a little from her sight, and she saw with dawning horror that it was Haruko.

When the first alarms shattered the morning stillness, Haruko had raced with Desmond and Grelun to the outer bawn. In the last few days, he had fought as he had not thought he would—or could—ever fight again. Even Desmond had been impressed, and after the first day at Rath na Ríogh he had kept the Terran close by him at all times.

So Haruko had been with Desmond in the front lines all day long. From his position closer to the Fomori, he had seen Bres before Aeron had, and had actually been working his way toward the Fomorian king, intending to put an end personally to Aeron's nemesis, when Aeron had spied her enemy and launched herself toward him with murderous intent.

Which intent had been only too clear to Haruko—but he was way ahead of her. No matter what, she was not going to have to deal with this herself, there would be no more Fomorian blood on her hands. She had done so much for him, now he would do this small thing for her, sparing her this last task, and redeeming himself a little in his own eyes for that matter of Tindal, too . . .

Haruko flung himself down the glacis and did not stop until he stood directly in Bres's path. Behind him to his right, a confused, blurred impression of Aeron shouting to him in protest—but he ignored her. This was the karma the dragon ship had augured, and it could be neither altered nor forestalled.

Then Bres's face stood alone and clear in his sight, astonished and angry and fully aware of him. In the center of that crowded moment there was a gold flash as a laser-sword cut down, and Haruko's own weapon dropped from his hand.

As he fell forward into what seemed like unending slow-motion, Haruko saw, far and small above him now, Aeron's face like a bright silver moon-disk. Then a cloud seemed to come between to veil its brightness, and night came, and moonset.

Chapter Twenty-two

From atop the wall, Aeron saw Haruko go down beneath Bres's sword.

"Theo! *No!*" Her anguished cry was lost in the roar of the battle. No matter; if they could not, or would not, hear her, then by the gods they should see her, and feel the weight of her arm . . .

Before anyone could move to restrain her, she had flung aside her helm, vaulted the rampart and dropped down into the faha where Bres stood above Haruko. Her raxed leg gave way beneath her, as she had anticipated, and she came over and up again in a graceful roll, and as she came onto her feet she drew her sword.

She spared a glance for the ground: Bres standing quietly, watching her with some amusement; Haruko's fallen form a few yards away to her left. The faha cleared of all others as if by true magic; no one, neither Kelt nor Fomori, would be near when this fight was joined. It was not two swordsmen who faced each other here, but two kingdoms, two embodied hatreds.

She saluted Bres with grim formality. "Hazard your person, King of Fomor," she said. "This is the fíor-comlainn, the truth-of-combat. Or does treachery still sit more readily to your custom—and your courage?"

Bres smiled, refusing to be baited. "Go back to the castle, Aeron. Let one of your Fians fight for you. Though I shall but serve him as I did your tame Terran here."

"I call *you* to fight, Fomor—though I do not usually make war on primitives."

Rage flared in Bres's face. "Nor I on women and wounded," he snapped back. "Yet I can gladly make an exception, lady, if you will."

Aeron bit back a smile. "Accepted," she said, and brought up her swordpoint to engage his.

On the battlements above, Desmond surged forward, but hands caught and held him, and Aeron, catching the movement from the tail of her eye, waved him to stillness.

"Stand away! Keltia fights Fomor, I charge you thwart it not!"

Sabia laid a hand on Desmond's arm. "Be easy," she said. "Either will she defeat him, and end their quarrel once for all; or she will not, and we might as well all of us then roll up our bellies to Jaun Akhera."

Desmond shook his head angrily. "She is tired, she is injured, she is distracted for Theo. And not only that but she has brothers, sisters, cousins, fosterans, friends and a lord, every one of them a warrior—"

"This is something she must do herself," said Gwydion. He had raced up with the others when they saw what Aeron was about, and now stood, face impassive; but his hand was clenched white-knuckled upon his sword-hilt.

Morwen, very pale, looked up at him and away again. "Pray gods she can."

At first it appeared as if Aeron could indeed, and easily; she could not seem to put a stroke wrong. Her glaive seemed to move her arm, flashing green fire where it bit against Bres's gold-bladed weapon. He was taller by some few inches, heavier by far, and had the reach of her by nearly a span; but though he could break her guard with force he could not match her speed, and gradually she forced him back.

Bres had regretted his acceptance of the combat almost immediately. Too late he recalled Jaun Akhera's warning; his adversary was the quickest swordsman he had ever encountered, and she was fueled by fury besides. So swiftly did she strike that he felt nothing, neither touch nor pain, until many seconds later; but the blows he himself scored came down upon her like iron bars.

Yet triumph he must. Not his own people only but the Coranians and the Kelts alike watched this contest. Strange to think that none of it would be happening if, seventy years since, long before this one he now fought had even been born, he had not felt—whatever the right or wrong of it may have truly been—that Fionnbarr of Keltia had mortally insulted Bres of Fomor. And if he had not continued to nurse that grievance, and if he had not taken his long-delayed, long-anticipated revenge upon Fionnbarr only three years before this moment, then Fionnbarr's heir would not have felt impelled to wipe out Bellator as *her* revenge, and he himself would not then have felt the need to join Jaun Akhera's crusade in return for *that*—

Aeron seemed to have heard this train of thought. "You will catch your death of what-ifs, Bres . . ."

More than the words, the mocking tone enraged him, and he redoubled his attack, passing under her guard to draw his blade down her side from ribs to hip. Aeron parried almost contemptuously, but he had struck again before she could turn him back.

She had set up her strokes for a new line of attack when her leg betrayed her, giving way under her weight, giving Bres the opening for a death-blow as her guard fell away. Up on the ramparts, the Kelts froze. Aeron twisted violently to avoid the main weight of the downward-slicing blade, but her own sword was knocked from her hand. Regaining her balance, she pressed one hand to her side and backed slowly before Bres's now confident advance.

A dead galloglass lay a few yards away, and as Aeron moved cautiously backward over the paving-stones, she saw that he had worn a yellow cloak. *Close enough,* she thought, noting also that blood was beginning to well through the fingers held tight against her side. She ripped the cloak from the dead Kelt's shoulder-clasps and flung it up in front of her just as Bres's sword cut down. There was a dazzling gold flash, and a howl of pain and surprise from Bres, who was apparently either ignorant or forgetful of that particular trick, a favorite maneuver of desperate lightswordsmen. The gold laser had reflected from the gold color of the cloak, the color-frequencies cancelling each other out, and the lightsword had shorted and died in his hand—giving him a painful shock in the process.

An exultant shout went up from the watching Kelts, and Aeron took the instant to field the sword Desmond flung down to her. It was his own, with a blade of findruinna; Aeron was well used to conventional swords, but Bres, untrained to them, was not, and he was clumsy with the steel sword he grabbed up in haste from the ground.

"That should even it up," breathed O'Reilly, transfixed and horrified, her hands hugging her arms. "Oh, *please* . . ."

Except for the ferocity of it, what came next was not unlike any of the matches in which Aeron had been so often triumphant, or even her friendly lessons with Theo. In a flurry of cuts and lunges and parries overborne, it was over; one long moment caught out of time, even as it had been for Haruko, and at the end of the moment Bres was tumbling forward, eyes already glazed in death.

Aeron stood in the faha alone now. At her feet lay the wreckage that had been so lately Bres King of Fomor, and all around her rose a shout, part the triumph of the Kelts, part the fury of the Fomori. She could not bring to focus what had happened, her mind could not seem to make the knowledge real. She was aware, as from a great distance, of pain and stiffness and exhaustion greater than anything she had ever known, but all she knew for certain was that no sword came against her now, no longer the relentless clash of another weapon against her own. But she could not seem to understand how that should be . . .

She would have fallen right there but for some lingering memory that thousands of eyes hung on her every move; and that awareness, and the sword upon which she leaned so heavily, alone kept her on her feet. Yet there was something else dimly recalled, something so important, the very reason and soul of this fight . . .

"Theo," she whispered, and began to turn toward him, where he lay upon the paving-stones at the grassy verge of the faha.

Then suddenly Desmond was there beside her, and Gwydion, setting their arms carefully around her waist and beneath her arms, trying to avoid the terrible gashes, unclenching her fingers from their spasm-grip on the bloody hilt of her sword, leading her away, supporting her as they went back up to the castle, speaking steady encouragement to her though she could not comprehend a syllable they said, understanding only her need to walk from the field under her own strength, and not to fall where the world might see it.

Once within the concealing walls of Tomnahara, though, out of the sight of Kelt and Gall alike, she did collapse. Desmond caught her, lifting her effortlessly in his arms.

"Go," he urged Gwydion. "Slaine will care for her. Struan comes, and the fight still hangs in the balance."

The Prince of Gwynedd hesitated, then turned back to battle.

Aeron's retirement from the field meant as much to her enemies as her final victory over Bres meant to the Kelts. Yet now it seemed to all who saw her as if Bres would win in the end after all. She looked at point of death; all color had run away into the flaming hair, yet even that seemed somehow dulled. Her skin, always pale, had taken on a terrifying translucence, the veins showing clear blue at throat and arms and temples. Mercifully, she had fainted.

Morwen came running as Desmond, who had carried Aeron to the more spacious grianan rather than the little private solar, now placed his cousin gently on a low field-couch.

"Oh gods—where are the healers?"

"Slaine has been sent for, and Melangell, and Brychan and some of the Fianna healers also. Help me get her tunic off." Together they settled Aeron as best they could, then the door opened and Slaine hurried in.

"She must not sleep, not yet." She laid a hand on Aeron's brow. Morwen had removed the worst of the blood and grit and dust, and now the smooth skin felt cool. *Too cool,* Slaine thought, fear beginning to rise . . .

"Aeron, hear me. You must wake for a little, do you hear? Open your eyes."

For many minutes they tried to wake her, and all in vain, Slaine joined by Morwen and the Fian healer Brychan. Aeron heard them all perfectly well, in her white daze, and she was trying not to respond. So much easier to ignore them all, to slip quietly away out the other side, to sleep—

But then there came sudden hooks in her mind, much stronger, sharp and bright and insistent, that jerked and tugged and harried her reluctant spirit to return, and she sensed the aura of Melangell's personality. Well, she could certainly resist Melangell . . .

Then someone else strode into her fading awareness, someone who caught hold of her mind and dizzied her by the speed and strength with which he spun her back to the roaring world, someone she could neither ignore nor resist, someone she could not fight, and she knew it was Gwydion who so summoned her back.

On the rampart just outside the grianan, O'Reilly stood on the edge of the circle of light cast by the torches, trying not to cry. Since she had seen Haruko slain and Aeron cut down, she had been feeling incredibly lost and alone, and the whole past week had been full of fears. Oh, of course everyone was being as kind to her as they could possibly be, but their chief concern at the moment, and very rightly, was Aeron. And Morwen and Melangell, who could always be counted on for comfort, were desperately occupied at the moment trying to save Aeron's life—in terror, O'Reilly veered away from the thought that they might fail—and her only other real friends, Hathaway and Mikhailova, were long gone, far beyond the Curtain Wall by now, aboard the *Sword*. She felt an amazing pang of homesickness for that tiny ship. She was totally adrift, and very unimportant, and she was trying very hard not to cry.

Then an arm came around her shoulders, and she looked up, startled. It was Desmond, and his face was full of such compassion, such understanding, as he looked down at her, that she did cry. And once she had begun, she could not seem to stop—remembering Desmond's own dead father Elharn; remembering Tindal; remembering, oh God, remembering Theo . . .

He led her past the torches to a stone seat in the corner of the wall, and sat down with her, holding her against him until the sobs that tore up through her had quieted.

"All will be well, alanna," he said. "You shall see."

And the oddly comforting sound of the Gaeloch pet-name made O'Reilly think that, perhaps, indeed, it could.

Night had closed down again with rain, a needle-sharp icy mist driven along the glen by a bitter east wind. In the faha below Tomnahara, torches flared spitting in the cold gusts as a rider came up the slope at a gallop, his scarlet cloak whipping out behind him. At the castle doors, the Fians on guard snapped to the salute as Gwydion flung himself from his lathered horse and dashed into the keep, taking the stairs to the grianan three at a time.

Morwen turned at his entrance, with a cry half relief, half pain.

"I could not come before," he said, his voice roughened by the smoke and shouts of battle. "But the raid is crushed, Struan broke its back like a snapped stick . . . How is it with her?"

"We have done all we can. But she cannot, or will not, wake. Melangell says she hears us well enough when we call . . ." Morwen nodded toward the field-couch where Slaine, Melangell and Brychan kept vigil. They rose silently and withdrew as Gwydion crossed the chamber.

Aeron lay on the low bed, covered with furs and very still. Gwydion took in at one glance the blazing pallor, the breathing that barely stirred the furs, the torn and bloodied tunic folded neatly over a chair. *Yr Mawreth,* he thought in terror, and the word was both prayer and profanity . . . He knelt beside the couch and took her right hand in both of his.

"Aeron," he said, his voice deep and quiet and carrying a tremendous authority. He spoke no other word, and after a few moments she opened her eyes. They were emerald in the light, and languid with pain, but when she focused on his face, still wet with rain and streaked with the dust of battle, she smiled.

"I would just as soon not have come back," she said, managing a creditable version of her usual tart tone, and he laughed in spite of his fear.

"You do not get quit of us so easily, Ard-rian." He kissed her hands, scarcely less cold than his own. "Stay a while yet.'' He stood up again, flinging off his rain-soaked cloak and tunic, and turned to those who watched openmouthed from the doorway. ''Fetch me a piece of leather, a bullhide—they will have one in the tent of the Druid priests, or the Ban-draoi—strong enough to hold water, and big enough to hold Aeron.''

Slaine started violently. ''Gwydion, you cannot—''

''Slaine, I must. Now send for it!'' He bent again over Aeron.

Morwen touched Melangell's arm. ''I am no sorcerer. What does he plan to do?''

Gwydion spoke without turning. ''Since naught else can serve our need, I shall construct a crochan.''

''Never been done!'' gasped Morwen, for even she knew what that meant. ''Do you know how much power such a thing will require—it will kill you both! And you do not even know if you *can* do it!''

He had pulled off his boots now, and stood up clad only in shirt and trews.

''I know well enough that she dies without a doubt if I do not, and what shall we all be but dead without her. All you will help me. Fetch at once any high-degree sorcerers who may be near at hand—Druid, Ban-draoi, Dragon Kin, whatever. We shall need all the power we can raise.''

In a very few minutes all was ready. In the gríanan, Melangell had assembled perhaps a dozen people, trained magicians all, well-seasoned in their art. With no visible command given they arranged themselves in a loose circle and prepared themselves for the fearful effort to come.

Glad for something to do however desperate, the Fian guards rushed in carrying an enormous white bullhide, and some of them rolled huge keeves of water. They worked quickly and quietly; six guards held the edges of the stiff hide, and the others poured the water into it. Slaine and Morwen and Brychan themselves set hands to the bullhide, struggling to help control the enormous dead weight as the water began to fill its strange container.

''We are ready, Pendragon,'' said Melangell, touching

Gwydion's shoulder as he knelt beside Aeron. He nodded once, and the ring of sorcerers drew in around them.

But all eyes were on Gwydion. He stood apart from them within the circle as his power began to build around him, a clear white light like water over silver, a seashell glow; then he pulled back the furs that covered Aeron, gently stripped off the bloody shift and bandages, and lifted her in his arms. The strange glow spread to cover her also, and she stirred in protest.

"This will kill you all," she said, in a whisper so pain-torn that Morwen closed her eyes at the sound of it. "Gwydion, I absolutely forbid this—"

"Be still." The power in the command shook them all, and Aeron fell silent. He lowered her carefully into the water, and she gasped as the silvery cool liquid touched her wounds.

The surge of energy nearly knocked them all to their knees. "Gods," muttered one Fian, his eyes cast upward with the terrific effort, "don't let go of it now . . ."

Even Morwen, who was as she had said no sorcerer, could feel strength draining out of her and into Gwydion. And yet it was not her physical strength; for the more the water-filled bullhide sloshed and pulled at her fingers and threatened to break loose, the stronger her fingers seemed to grow, and the firmer their grip.

It was all so strange; she had always thought crochans to be the veriest legend, something out of the far myth-mantled past never to be met with in the real world. Yet Gwydion had created one, for Aeron . . . Morwen looked down in despairing anxiety. With the bandages gone, the terrible sword-cuts that ran down Aeron's left side from shoulder to knee were all too visible, dark red against the pale skin.

But something strange was happening, under the surface of the magic pool. The water seemed to have grown thick, viscous, like quicksilver, and cold vapors were rising like steam from its mirrored surface. The power came pouring in now; Morwen could feel it beating upon her like a strong wind against the walls of a tent, and what it must be like for the sorcerers, or for Gwydion, she could not begin to imagine. It grew in leaps, howled around her in sparkling spirals, until it was at the last almost unendurable, and she would have to shout or die . . .

"Hold!" Gwydion's command rang out. All sagged to their knees, or fell upon each other's shoulders, utterly spent, as suddenly the dead waterweight vanished, and the water also.

Morwen stared, astounded. Aeron lay wet and naked on the empty bullhide. She was unconscious, and there was no mark nor sign now of any wound upon her body.

There was a deep, awed silence as Gwydion, with the last rags of his own strength, gathered Aeron into his arms and placed her again on the field-couch, tucking the furs close around her.

From where she had collapsed upon the floor, Morwen looked up at him, half in fear of what he would answer, half in fear of him.

"Is it—it *is* all right?"

He nodded slowly. "The worst is past, any road. The wounds are healed, and now she must do for herself the rest of what is needed. She lay here long unaided—no fault of yours," he said swiftly. "You did all that you could, and you did well. But not even a pool can heal blood-loss and exhaustion, and now she must sleep as long as she may."

"She will so," said Slaine. "But now so must you, Pendragon. That is *my* order."

Gwydion smiled, but allowed himself to be led to an adjoining solar, where he threw himself down upon a wide bed and was instantly asleep.

The last of the leaves rattled like bones in the wind that swept, cold and damp and sleet-laden, out of the east, as O'Reilly came back to Tomnahara. Too distraught to remain in the castle, she had ridden out with Desmond and Sabia to the Fianna command post in the mouth of the glen, and then had come the glad news that Aeron had been healed by the sorcery of the Prince of Dôn.

"Magic has ever run deep in that line," said Sabia admiringly. "But Gwydion—Gwydion is a master . . . You are sent for, both of you, to Morwen and Slaine."

It was a long silent ride back, with much time for thought,

and those thoughts mostly dark ones. O'Reilly pulled her hood close and peered around her, grateful for Desmond's quiet presence riding alongside. He had taken a different route in the interest of speed, and the glen they now cantered through was unfamiliar to her. She could see little enough in the blackness, for the rainclouds masked the light of the Criosanna and the two moons had long since set, but the glen seemed far more savage than any she had yet traversed.

"What place is this?" she asked, more to hear a human voice than for any real interest in the answer.

"It is called Nandruidion," said Desmond, himself seeming glad of a chance to speak and chase some of the gloom. "Which means Valley of the Druids; the stream running through it is called the Velenryd. There have long been prophecies concerning this place . . . In ancient time it was the favorite retreat of the Archdruid Edeyrn, of whom you will doubtless have heard. He was a remarkable magician, and a very evil man."

O'Reilly had heard, and she wondered that Aeron would have chosen a place of such malignity near which to establish camp. Even in the light of day Nandruidion would be bleak indeed, its silence broken only by the sound of the Velenryd as it ran over stones beneath the dark stands of trees. And ever the wind swept through the frozen bracken.

Sleet slashed against the walls of Tomnahara, and a great gust of wind tore the casement open, blasting its way into the warmth of the grianan. The cold wet freshness of air touched Aeron's face, and she half-roused. Unbearable brightness, splinters of light, stabbed her eyes, and she retreated at once back into her dim dream-sanctuary.

All that wild night she drowsed half-waking in the great bed to which they had moved her, while the rain fell and the wind flared the torches and billowed the walls of the tents below the castle. Toward the cold silent hour known as Anrhod, the time of the turn of the Wheel, when stars pale and dark thickens and dying souls most easily shed the cumbrances of their bodies, Aeron opened her eyes, and this time they were lucid, free of pain, green and clear as the skies over Erinna.

''What of the battle?''

O'Reilly, whose very proud turn it was to watch beside her, shot upright in her chair.

''No concern of yours, Lady,'' she said earnestly, peering closely at Aeron's smiling face. ''Slaine and Morwen have given me very strict orders as to what to tell you if you woke, and your sister Ríoghnach—''

''Plague upon them.'' A shadow crossed her face. ''But Theo—''

O'Reilly kissed her hand with sudden fierce sympathy. ''You are not to fret about him, Aeron,'' she said through blinding tears. ''He died doing exactly what he wanted to be doing, he was so happy—and you avenged him. He lived long enough to see that, did you know? And he loved you so much—''

''And I him. He was my friend, and he was one of us—as you are.'' She touched O'Reilly's hand with real affection. ''We will speak more of this later. But tell them outside that I am awake, and send for Desmond and Niall. I would speak also with Morwen and Slaine.''

''Not Gwydion?''

Aeron breathed a laugh. ''Nay, let him rest. He has worked hard this night.''

''*Well?*'' A dozen voices pounced on O'Reilly when she emerged into the outer chamber.

She blushed, flustered. ''Aeron has awakened. She wants to see Morwen, Slaine, Desmond and Niall.''

''That may be what she wants,'' said Slaine grimly, even as she signalled a page to fetch Niall to them. ''But as her healer I say that what she wants and what she will get for the next few days, at least, are very different indeed. She will have to wait till morning to speak to her commanders. There is naught of the battle that cannot wait until then, and truly I care not if the war is lost for it, but she *shall* rest a few more hours yet; in fact, I will give her a draught to make sure of that.'' She vanished into the gríanan.

''I agree,'' said Morwen. She had been half-asleep in a camp chair, sitting wrapped in several cloaks and plaids, and now she struggled out of her swathings and got to her feet.

"It would scarcely profit us to win the war and lose the Queen."

"Yes, well, that's all very true," said O'Reilly, her shyness momentarily forgotten. "But once she starts feeling stronger, and knowing her a little I'd say that probably won't be too long, she'll want to be right back in the middle of things again. And how are you going to keep her out of it?"

But Aeron had no plans to fight again any time soon. She knew far better than Slaine, or even Gwydion, just how badly injured she had been. Never had she felt closer to death, never had she longed more desperately to sail out on that warm, strangely joyful tide and not turn again to the world no matter who summoned her. For the call from the other side had been strong too—she had felt Roderick's hand as real as Gwydion's had been, and she knew she had not been the one to make the choice between them.

There was little pain now, and even that little had been dealt with by that cup of athair-talam that Slaine had forced upon her; but against this incredible lassitude that now possessed her, this white whirling silence that roared like an ocean in her ears, there seemed no weapon save retreat and rest.

But her mind could not rest. It came back to her in waves, the fight with Bres, in little vivid pictures, soundless, disconnected, like some distorted nightmare tapestry. She turned her head on the pillows as the drug began to drag her down into sleep, as Slaine had intended, and she did not resist.

That had been a good fight, she thought, with something very like contentment. It was fitting that the long hatred should have ended so. Still, it had been a much nearer thing than anyone watching had known, or even suspected. Bres, though; *he* had known, and he had come very near to achieving her utter destruction, there in the faha. If he had succeeded, the war would perhaps be over by now. A strange thought—Ari—oh gods, and *Theo* . . . But it was not yet time for the luxury of grief. She felt someone's presence, forced her eyes open.

Ríoghnach leaned forward in the chair beside the bed, her face full of loving concern. "Sister?"

"Since my commanders seem to be forbidden to come to me, my commands must go to them. Give the order to fall back upon Caerdroia."

"Aeron, are you certain that is what—"

"Do it, Princess of the Name!" she snapped, and Ríoghnach hid a smile. "But tell them they must so manage it that the folk in the glens are protected as they go."

"At once, Ard-rían. Now will you not sleep again?"

Aeron nodded, black lashes already veiling her eyes. "And tell Gwydion, when he wakes—"

Ríoghnach waited, but there was no more; Aeron had fallen asleep again. The Princess sat a few moments longer, then pulled the furs up around her sister's shoulders and sent for Desmond.

O'Reilly quitted the castle and went out into the faha. The rainstorm had moved off down the Strath to the west, and the dawn sky was fresh and brilliant. Tomnahara was a thrum of activity, people with questions and worries and problems and fears, and all at once she could stand it no longer.

With a desperation near tears, she turned and scrambled straight up the steep gorse-covered hillside. Up behind the castle there was a little oak-wood that bordered on a clune, a tiny upland meadow, that would be very good to sit in for a while; to think, to remember, to try to regain her peace of mind.

Coming softly over the ground at the top of the hill, O'Reilly emerged from a narrow belt of trees and stopped short. Gwydion was standing in the little clune, quite alone. He was looking down toward the castle; the flying light fell upon his face, and he did not move. She stared at him as if she had never seen him before, and in spite of his art he seemed to be unaware of her presence.

And, unobserved, he suddenly appeared to her to be truly alien, as he had never seemed before, nor any other Kelt either. There was no one thing about him that could be said to give cause to this new strangeness: Still there was the same dark handsomeness, the same shaggy hair and beard, the same gray eyes. Yet something about him had changed, and as she watched him standing there, unmoving as the oaks around them, O'Reilly suddenly knew what it was. For the first time since she had known him, Gwydion's face bore the mark of tears.

She felt her heart go out to him in a violent sortie of pity and empathy, and in the same moment he became aware of her and turned. His expression did not alter, and the traces of tears seemed all the more terrible upon the iron set of his countenance. O'Reilly began to move, slowly at first, then quicker, until she was almost running, and his arms came up to catch her as she flung herself against him, sobbing for all her sorrow and his as well.

"Weep, then, alanna," he said quietly. "You see, I have done so myself, and so far the world has not ended for it."

She clutched at his cloak like a frightened child. "I was so afraid—first Theo, then . . . Did you see her, how she looked? She was so, so—"

Above her bent head, the ghost of a smile flickered over Gwydion's face. "So diminished. I know. We were all afraid."

"Even you?" she dared to ask after another moment, looking up at him and drawing away a little.

"Especially I. I had the most to lose, had I lost her . . ."

"And the most to save, and the most power to do it! They told me what you did for her."

"Power? That may be. I know only that I had the most need of her. If that need gave me power to save her, I am thankful. But I have done no more than you or Theo. Did you not give up everything to stay here with us, and did not Theo help when Aeron most needed that help? He died trying to keep her hands clean of Bres's blood. It was a hero's thought, but fated otherwise."

"He *died*! And I have done little."

"Twigs can turn floods, if they are in the right place when the first raindrop falls. That is not little." He saw that she had ceased to weep, and that all her awe of him had fled forever, and he smiled. "As for Theo, he shall be remembered for as long as Keltia endures . . . And if that is to be beyond this present moment, we must go back to the castle. Aeron is awake, I think, and she would speak with us."

Chapter Twenty-three

*I*n the gríanan, it was as he had said, and O'Reilly glanced up at him half-fearfully. How had he known? Up there on the hill . . . Then her rapidly returning awe was banished completely by the sight of Aeron.

She had badgered the healers into removing the restraint field and allowing her to sit up. She was paler even than usual, and purple smudges shadowed her eyes, but she smiled at them with all the old warmth.

"If you wish to know, First Lord of War," she said at once, "if the Ard-rían is fit to continue to order the battle, the answer is that she is not. Command therefore is yours absolute. Desmond will direct the retreat, and mac Avera will oversee the preparations for the siege of Caerdroia, since there appears to be one on the way. But they will both obey you in all times, as will the other commanders, and I have caused these orders to be known to the armies and the fleets."

He saluted her gravely. "As you command, Ard-rían."

"And, Gwydion—" They held each other's gaze, and the thought that flashed between them then was too quick and complex, too swift and subtle, for any other however skilled to catch. O'Reilly, watching them, was struck anew by the almost involuntary intimacy of their communication, and she dropped her eyes, feeling indecently like an eavesdropper.

Gwydion inclined his head briefly and was gone. Aeron gazed after him, then sighed and energetically kicked free of the furs that swaddled her.

328

"Enough! I need some air, walk with me."

O'Reilly helped her dress again in a fresh uniform, then hung a fur cloak over Aeron's shoulders and took her arm. They left the castle and turned from the faha, going slowly down a path along the walls to a small pine-wood. A little burn ran below them in a cutting through mossy banks, and its clear merry noise chattered up at them. Above their heads, the pines hissed and rustled in a wind which seemed to be gathering strength.

Aeron sat down somewhat more heavily than usual on a lichen-covered rock, putting back her hood and lifting her face to the wind.

"*Much* better," she said. "Slaine had that grianan far too hot—barely past Samhain—and I was getting a headache."

"Yes, well, Lady, but you mustn't stay out too long. It's cold all the same, and Slaine will feed me to the hounds if I let you catch a chill."

Aeron waved dismissing fingers. "As to that, you do but obey the Queen's orders . . . Sorcha, save for those few words last night, we have not spoken of Theo."

O'Reilly studied the lichen on the rock beneath her fingers, so as not to let Aeron see the sudden spurt of tears to her eyes.

"What shall I say?" she murmured at last. "He died very happy, and he died in our arms, Slaine's and mine, while Gwydion and Desmond were getting you back to the castle. There was nothing anyone could have done to help him. He said—" She inhaled raggedly against the sudden blank gale that shook her from head to foot, then went on resolutely, "He said to tell you goodbye, but that it was only goodbye for a while, and—and that if his karma had any justice in it at all, he was going to come back as a Kelt." She smiled, remembering, then looked up anxiously, for there had been no word in reply.

Aeron's green eyes were brilliant with the sparkle of unshed tears, but the smile she gave O'Reilly was one of love and pride. "And he will, then . . . Let us go to him."

She stood up, leaning on O'Reilly's arm, then turned her head sharply to the north and east, a look almost of hunger on her face.

"What is it?"

"Can you not feel the power on the wind? It rides down out of the Hollow Mountains—" She stared longingly into the eye of the wind, then turned back to her companion. "Let us go. I am growing tired, and I would see Theo, and there is a thing I must tell Gwydion."

In the Great Hall of Tomnahara, Haruko lay on a bier draped with the royal green, for he had died in the service of the Ard-rían, and his sword was naked in his hands, for he had fallen in battle.

Aeron gazed down upon the face of her friend. *He died so that I would not have to kill Bres*, she thought. He had died, and she had killed Bres anyway . . .

"Karma, Theo," she whispered, and kissed him gently on the brow. "Bydd i ti ddychwelyd . . ." She raised her voice. "Let it be set down that by royal fiant Captain Theo Haruko is declared a lord of the Court; he is to be barrowed in royal ground at Ni-Maen among the sovereigns of Keltia. I shall myself conduct the rites with Teilo; arrange it for sunset tomorrow . . . Sorcha ní Reille, come thou forward."

O'Reilly, who had been leaning against a pillar lost in memories, jerked upright in surprise, but obeyed at once.

"Kneel . . . I have been meaning to do this for some time now, but perhaps this is the moment most fitting, and in this company too. Cousin, your sword." This to Desmond, who instantly drew from its sheath at his side the blade that had slain Bres, and presented it hilt-first to Aeron.

O'Reilly, kneeling, heard incomprehensible words, felt something heavy strike her upon each shoulder, the sign of the circled cross traced on her forehead. Then Aeron raised her and kissed her on either cheek. O'Reilly stepped back a pace and looked at the Queen in total confusion.

"I hope that as a knight of Keltia you will wish to continue to be my squire," said Aeron, smiling. "But that, Lady Sorcha, is a decision I must leave now to you."

Lady Sorcha. O'Reilly's eyes sought Desmond's face, and he nodded. It was all true, then. She had actually been knighted, and Theo would be buried among kings and queens in royal ground . . . She found no words to say, but went briefly to one knee again and kissed Aeron's ring in pledge of knightly service.

"It is well, then." Aeron moved toward the door, and the others went with her. "Bid someone fetch the First Lord of War to my gríanan, and let Kynvael join us there, he that I sent to Caerdroia earlier this day, and Morwen also. Do the rest of you go where you please or where you are commanded. I must be private a while with those whom I have named."

Alone in the hall, O'Reilly went forward to the bier where Haruko lay. She touched with gentle affection the hand that lay upon the sword-hilt, not attempting to hold back either the loving smile or the streaming tears, Aeron's whispered words echoing and re-echoing in her heart. *Bydd i ti ddychwelyd*: "There shall be a returning for thee."

After a while she knelt beside the bier, letting her mind range back over the events of the past three tumultuous months. None of it seemed possible, or would have, even had she thought of it back then. Back when she had first laid eyes on the *Firedrake*; no, even before that, when she had first heard the scouts from the sloop addressing her in the Gaeloch—from that moment she had been won; she had ceased at that moment to be a Terran and had become, instead, forever, a Kelt. She had gone out exploring, and she had ended by discovering her own people; and she had lived among them ever since in a sort of glamourie, a magic glow as real and as potent and as transforming as any Druid's rann. Some of that glow had been dimmed forever, wiped out by war, by Tindal's execution, by Theo's death, by Aeron's ordeal; but O'Reilly had grown for its lessening, and her happiness if less idyllic was the more real for being the more aware.

Lady Sorcha. She hugged it to her like a lovely toy or a cherished pet, a few moments longer. Then she rose from her knees, kissed Haruko on the brow as Aeron had done, saluted him crisply in Terran fashion for the prescribed funeral count of three times the usual duration, and took up vigil position at the foot of the catafalque.

"In the early morning I ordered this done," Aeron was saying, "for I knew there should be little time for it later."

She beckoned, and Kynvael, a brown-uniformed Fian with the sword-and-crown badge of Aeron's personal guard on his sleeve, came forward. He was bearing a battered leather casket in his hands, as gingerly as if it had been a sack of eggs, and he set it down on the table before Aeron.

She put back the lid, and as one, all craned forward for a better view. Inside, upon faded purple velvet, lay the Copper Crown, gleaming redly in the light. To Gwydion's eye, it seemed to glow with more than reflected glory.

"Before you take up full command," said Aeron slowly, and her eyes never left his, "you shall take the Copper Crown to the Hollow Mountains, and you shall ask in my name and your own that the Shining Ones guard it until such time as I may come for it again."

"What of the Scepter of Llyr?" asked Morwen.

"The Dún of Aengus is not a jewelsmith's shop, nor yet a strongbox . . . nor is the Scepter as important as—as the other. Nay, the Scepter need not go with the Crown, but when we are again at Caerdroia it shall be hidden with the rest of the crown jewels in the place you know of."

"And the Great Seal?"

Aeron glanced down at the big emerald on her left hand. "That—shall remain on my finger a while yet. I have a thought as to that . . . But, Gwydion, I beg you be swift. I do not want the First Lord of War cut off in the north by the Imperial advance. If you take my ship *Retaliator*, you can be there and back at Caerdroia by sunrise, when with luck the rest of us shall be there as well." She looked at the crown. "I do not wish to do this thing," she said then.

"You have no choice, Ard-rían," said Kynvael at once.

"No more do I," she agreed with a bitter laugh. "For was it not laid upon me by Kynon of Ruabon? The first particular of his curse has already fulfilled itself: He cursed my crown from my head, and so it now is. Recall you the rest of his doom?"

"I remember it not," lied Morwen desperately.

"Do you not? I remember well. Next he cursed my lord from my bed, and last he bade the Shining Ones ride to war—a thing most unlikely of fulfillment—before I reign again as Queen in Caerdroia. I have only to wait."

"If that be so, Aeron," said Morwen, "then take comfort, for in the conceit of his malice he has promised that you *shall* reign again as Queen. In his folly and his mockery he named it as part of the curse, and so it will be as fated as the rest of it. Doubt it not."

Aeron made no reply, but with sudden decision closed the casket lid and fastened the heavy silver clasps. She picked it up and held it out to Gwydion.

"Gods with you, beloved," she said softly. "Greet the Shining Ones well from me."

He took the heavy casket from her hands. "They will guard it safe for you; none better."

"Aye, well, see that you guard yourself as closely; you are rather dearer to me than a piece of copper, however hallowed . . . And to that end there is another thing I would have you take with you—but to wear, not to leave." She had in her hands another scrap of the same worn purple velvet that had wrapped the crown. This piece, however, swathed something if less royal perhaps even more magical.

"The cathbarr of Nia the Golden," breathed Morwen.

Aeron had unwrapped the velvet to reveal a fillet of ancient silver knotwork set round with elvish crystals; an heirloom indeed, and one even she both loved and feared to wear. It had been a marriage-gift long since from the Sidhe themselves, given to Nia mother of Brendan, and passed down in Brendan's line for three thousand years.

"Older than all the crown jewels; older even than the Copper Crown itself, maybe." Aeron raised it in her hands, and Gwydion bent his dark head so that she might set the silver circlet upon his brow.

"It fits my lord!" Kynvael was startled into unsoldierly amazement.

"It fits any who wears it," said Aeron. "That is its nature, and its purpose . . . I would have you wear it—Prince of Gwynedd, King of Keltia—in token of the long kinship of the Houses of Dôn and Dâna with the folk of the dúns; and as protection also. There is great virtue in the cathbarr of Nia. Protection there is in your sword and your rank and your art, right enough, but I would take no chances. I would have you come back yet yourself, and no changeling from under the hill.''

For the first time since he had entered the gríanan, Gwydion smiled, and then grew as quickly grave again, and raised her hand to his lips.

"Look for me at Caerdroia."

Though the retreat to Caerdroia had begun almost as soon as Aeron's command was given to Ríoghnach the night before, the Keltic armies were slow to get on the move.

The invading forces, however, were moving toward the City more slowly still, for the terrain was unfamiliar, the glens hostile with folk who had remained to defend their places, and the baggage trains burdened with many wounded.

The Fomori had overrun Ath-na-forair as the Kelts retreated, and in their tents was no joy. Here it was that the news had been brought to Elathan of his sudden elevation to the kingship, and none had seen him since. He had received the news in silence, given orders that his father's body be brought back to the encampment, and then he had withdrawn to his own tent and his own thought. Even Talorcan had been denied access to his half-brother.

Elathan sat slumped in his chair, as he had for the past two hours and more. He knew very well that outside the tent the demands of his new position were mounting hourly, but he could not seem to summon the energy to rise and go out to deal with them.

His father was dead, and he was now King of Fomor. He had known always that this moment would come, but the long knowing did not make the present living of it any less difficult. What troubled him most, strangely and unexpectedly, was that his mother could not know. The Curtain Wall still blocked transmissions where it remained intact, and where it did not, the Keltic fleet had jammed all frequencies. No word of the war could reach the outside worlds.

So Basilea would not know she was a widow, and Camissa would not know that her betrothed was now her King— Elathan ran his hands over his face. Was this then how Aeron had felt, when she had become Queen Aeron? He made a sound that under any other circumstances would have been a laugh. Bres had made Aeron a queen, and now she had returned the favor, making Bres's son a king . . .

There was a commotion before his tent, then the tent flap was pulled back and Jaun Akhera entered. He was clad in dusty armor, and his black hair was disarrayed, but his smile was wide and joyful and for once utterly unfeigned. Elathan did not rise to greet him.

"Hail, King of Fomor!" Jaun Akhera dropped his cloak on a chair and sat down across the table from Elathan. "I heard the news last night, and came as soon as the army was well on the move. So Bres's great feud with Aeron is ended; though I hear he nearly ended Aeron too . . . I am sorry for your loss," he added, almost perfunctorily. "But I am sure you will understand me, Elathan, when I say that your accession argues nothing but good for our enterprise and our association—and our friendship."

Elathan looked at him darkly. "I understand you very well indeed," he said. "So that I know you will in your turn understand why I do what I do now." He raised his voice only a little. "Fetch my brother the Lord Talorcan and the war leaders Brudei and Salenn." The guard saluted and left.

Jaun Akhera frowned. "What is this?"

Elathan barely glanced at him. "I take my army home to Fomor," he said, "with the body of my father. I will fight no more with the House of Aoibhell."

Gwydion alighted from the sleek silver aircar—he had not flown Aeron's ship *Retaliator* after all; an anonymous aircar would attract less attention, and far fewer laser bolts, than the Keltic Queen's personal ship, which was, after all, well known by sight to the Fomori at least.

He looked up at the great gray mountain before him, the Hill of Fare, in whose depths was the Sidhe stronghold of Dún Aengus. It was one of the few known dwelling-places of the Shining Ones; as a rule they did not care to advertise to mortals the whereabouts of their dúns. But Dún Aengus was a place famed in legend as the chief seat of the Sidhe rulers, and it had seemed the best place for Gwydion's errand.

As he scanned the blank rocky face of the cliff, the ground began to rumble, the vibration faint at first, on the far edge of sensation, then quickly rising to a roar that shook the mountain. Gwydion felt himself trembling from head to foot. Then he mastered his fear, and straightened.

The vibration boomed and died away, and then with no sound at all the hillside opened, light pouring out to lap like a silver streamlet at Gwydion's boots. Music—a dancing-tune, harmonious and rhythmic, utterly enchanting—came from the depths of the hill, and he knew that the palace of the Sidhe stood open for him, that he was bidden enter. He set his foot on the broad smooth stair that now was where no stair had been a moment ago, and went in at the huge green doors.

He paused on the threshold of a great hall, dazzled by the light and music, aware of the gaze of many eyes and none of them human; but not so dazzled that he did not remember what it was he must now do . . . With some difficulty, for he was carrying the heavy casket containing the crown, he drew his sgian from his boot-top: the only iron upon him, the only weapon he had carried, its short, sharp blade gleaming in the torchlight. He raised it in his hand, then drove it deep into the doorpost.

A sigh seemed to go round the hall, then the music began, merrier even than before, and a young man clad all in red came forward.

"Hail, stranger!" he cried, his face both bright and curious, and he bowed to Gwydion.

Cumbered as he was with the casket, Gwydion bowed in return as best he might.

"Hail, lord," he said. "I am Gwydion ap Arawn, Chief of the House of Dôn, and a kinsman to your folk."

"So we know, and that which you bear upon your brow gives the proof to your words . . . Your errand also is known to us," he added. "But I am Allyn son of Midna; allow me of your grace to make you known to our lord." He gestured, and Gwydion followed him into the deeps of the dún.

"Before we begin our own retreat," began Morwen hesitantly, "Gwydion has charged me say this to you, Aeron: Will you consider flight for your own safety's sake?"

Aeron stared at her friend and minister, astonished and feeling somehow betrayed.

"Flight! The Prince of Dôn would have me flee the planet?"

"Not he alone, Aeron." Desmond, who had been sitting silent by the fire, looked up at his cousin. "I do not love to say it, but many of the Fianna, also, think it would go better for you if you fled."

"You forget yourself, Elharn's son!" snapped Aeron.

He was unperturbed. "Not for a moment, Ard-rían. We who love you have thought much upon this."

"And you who say you love me would counsel me to the action of a coward? What kind of queen is it would flee her planet and leave her folk to the tender mercies of the Imperium?" She looked away, added in a lower voice, "Or leave you whom she says *she* loves to face Jaun Akhera when he learns of your hand in my escape? Never. I shall go to ground in Armoy, or in the Kyles of Ra, help the Fianna and the Dragon Kin to assemble a resistance, if it comes to that."

"Are you mad?" Rohan burst out. He had arrived in the night from the *Firedrake*, and in spite of his battle-weariness had ridden straight to Tomnahara. "The Fomori may have seen the wisdom of the road home, but Jaun Akhera still has more than seventy legions left on Tara. Every one of them has been ordered to take the Queen of Kelts at any cost, and when they catch you they will kill you. I have no great wish to become Ard-rígh, my sister, so think of me if you will not think of yourself."

"Rohan speaks truth," said Morwen. "Jaun Akhera has set a price on your head of a million gold astari. No Kelt would touch a crossic of it, but I doubt if the Coranians will scruple so. Aeron, we have sent the Copper Crown to safety; if we take such care for the Crown, shall we take any less for the head that wears it?"

It was a powerful argument, and almost they thought they had reached her. But Aeron merely scowled and looked away.

"Morwen, you must go too," said Denzil Cameron into the charged little silence. Fergus, who had accompanied Rohan, looked up sharply in protest. "It must be so, mac Isla; she too is one of Jaun Akhera's chief quarries, and there is a price on her head also."

"Oh aye?" Morwen was all at once as indignant as Aeron had been. "And what of the rest of you? As Aeron has said,

Jaun Akhera will never overlook your aiding of our escape—if escape there is to be. Further, all those in this room, and many who are not, are just as much enginers of this war as Aeron and myself. Do you even dream the Coranian will leave you free—or alive—to reconstruct a striking force?''

A smile tugged at Aeron's mouth. ''Ah, now the boot is on the other leg, Lochcarron! And you seem to like the fit of it no more than I . . . Well, my friends, I shall consider what you have said, and give you an answer in good time.''

''When?'' pressed Denzil.

''*Ad kalendas Graecas*,'' said Aeron shortly, and turned the talk to other things.

'' 'At the Greek Kalends'?'' murmured O'Reilly to Rohan. ''When is *that*?''

''Never,'' said the Prince. ''The Greeks *had* no Kalends.''

Allyn son of Midna led Gwydion through the press of dancers in the crystal-roofed hall.

''This is a lesser and younger palace,'' he said. ''Those who enter the Hill of Knockmaa come not again among men. Nay, fear not that,'' he added with a laugh. ''Your iron in our door will keep that fate from you—though you might find it not so hard a doom as the one that now rides at your shoulder. Nor, very like, so high a one neither. But would you be less happy here with us?''

Gwydion, listening to the sounds of the revelry of the Sidhe, thought that he would surely die of the joy of it, and he could make no answer to his companion. For a bard and a musician, it was loveliness so complete as to be well-nigh unbearable, and he felt tears in his eyes as the music swirled about him. Somehow it sang to him of home, not Caerdroia nor yet Gwynedd, nor even Keltia itself, but *home*—

''So, tall lord?'' cried one who looked a queen among them. ''Will you not join our dance?''

It was all his bliss to join that dance, all that he had ever longed for, and he felt his entire being gather itself in a yearning sortie toward that bright circle. But the step died untaken even as he thought it, and he knew in that instant that he could not dance, not now. Someday, a dance for him; but not this dance, and so he smiled gently, ruefully, and raised his hand in denial.

"You must dance another measure, I think, before you dance with us," came the voice of Allyn from somewhere ahead of him. "But come."

Gwydion followed him into a chamber of such splendor that it could only be the throne-room of some king of the Shining Ones. And so it was, for a high seat was set at the far end, fair lords and fairer ladies thronging the steps around it. Their faces were turned to him in wonder, but he had eyes only for the one who sat in the throne beneath the golden canopy.

Stern of face he was, dark of hair and darker still of eye, and upon his brow was a circlet of silver twin to the one Gwydion bore, and had almost forgotten he did so, upon his own head.

As Allyn conducted him to the steps of the throne, Gwydion felt as Haruko had once said *he* had felt, entering the Hall of Heroes and seeing Aeron for the first time as Queen. But this lord of the Sidhe had a majesty no mortal monarch could hold, and when he came to the first of the steps to the throne Gwydion went to one knee before him.

The voice, deeper even than Gwydion's own, rolled out onto the air above his head.

"Welcome, Prince of the House of Dôn, to our halls. I am Gwyn son of Neith, and we are kin from afar. What would you of me?"

Gwydion lifted his head and looked the faerie King full in the face.

"In the name of Aeron Queen of Kelts, Empress of the West and Domina Bellorum, and in my name also," he said, in the bard-voice that carried easily without stress to all corners of the hall, "I have come to ask safekeeping for the Copper Crown of Keltia. There is war in the land, and a thing so precious should be surer kept than by our swords."

The dark eyes met his, and, mighty sorcerer though he was, Gwydion felt himself the veriest untaught child by comparison to the deeps that stood in the eyes of Gwyn.

"Aeron daughter of Dâna is known to us, and she is beloved of the Lady whom she serves . . . This is no hard asking, lord." Gwyn rose, towering above the courtiers who surrounded the throne. "Yet to come here alone were brave— not often do our mortal kindred come as guests to our halls. Or do you fear you shall wake in the morning to find the world a different place, your kin and your friends dead a thousand years?" He smiled then, and Gwydion rose from his knee. "No matter. It is in my mind, Prince of Dôn, that we shall know each other better in time to come . . . soon, as you count the days."

He came down the steps, and, bending, took the casket from Gwydion's hands.

"This we shall keep safe and sacred," he said gravely. "Tell your lady so. And this is our further word to her: Bid Aeron remember *Prydwen*, and seek the Treasures that were lost. When time is, the Copper Crown shall come to her again, and she have help unlooked-for in the last battle. As to thee, son of Dôn, the very trees shall be thy warriors. We shall meet again, thou and I, at the place called Nandruidion, and so that the moment be known, I give thee a token in pledge. The Queen of Kelts spoke true: This world is our home as much as it is yours, and we too shall fight to keep it safe."

Gwydion gasped. How could Gwyn, long leagues from Tomnahara, know the words spoken there days ago in private by Aeron? But he had no time to seek an answer; he felt his hand taken, something pressed into it, his fingers closed gently upon it. He saw nothing but the dark unknowable eyes of Gwyn, felt himself drawn into their incalculable depths, felt himself spinning, falling—a blur, a vibration—then the cold fresh wind of morning strong upon his face, and he alone upon the hillside in the winter dawn.

Alone, aye, but not empty-handed . . . Beside him on the ground lay the sgian he had thrust into the doorpost of the dún, as surety of his return to his own world, and upon his brow—he raised his fingers to touch it—the cathbarr of Nia still gleamed. But in his right hand . . .

He forced open fingers that had grown cramped and stiff in their unrelaxing grip. It was there, still in its proper form; it had not turned to dead leaves or dull pebbles, as the tales told all gifts of the Sidhe were wont to do, for no gift from the hand of Gwyn ever proved anything other than its true self.

Gwydion looked down at it with wonder: a small horn all of dull gold, wrought with great skill, coelbren letters carved upon its worn grip and a faded green silk baldric threaded through rings at mouthpiece and bell. He turned the horn one way and another, until the letters caught the light and blazed so that his eyes were dazzled. But for all his learning and lore, he could not read the writing on the horn.

He shivered suddenly, not entirely with the cold, then fastened the horn to his sword-belt and went down the hill toward his ship.

"I have to go too? *Me*?" O'Reilly was dismayed, and showed it.

Melangell touched her hand with real sympathy. "Jaun Akhera knows Terrans have been here, knows Aeron has offered Earth an alliance—and he has vowed vengeance on any Terran unlucky enough to be caught in Keltic space. Nay, do not worry," she said quickly, seeing the fear leap in O'Reilly's hazel eyes. "They are far, far from here by now—almost home, perhaps; but certainly safe. But now you too must leave Tara. Do you have any wishes?"

Where to go . . . "There was a Ban-draoi convent on Vannin that Aeron once told—told Theo about. If I could stay there?"

"Excellent," said Niall. "There's few places you'd be safer; the Sisters will see to that."

"Oh, it's not just being safe," explained O'Reilly candidly. "Though I can still hardly believe Jaun Akhera after *me* . . . But I need some time to think. So much has happened so fast, I feel I've left part of me behind, in the dust or in the *Sword*, maybe both. If peace can be found anywhere now, I need it very much."

"It is yours," promised Melangell. "You will find peace at Glassary; and safety, and anything else that you may need or we can give you. Go to Ffaleira within the next day or so, and she will give you letters and instruction. When it is time to leave, Desmond will get you out on a Fian sloop." Melangell marked how the Terran girl's face lighted at the mention of

Desmond, smiled to herself, and said nothing. *I wonder how Aeron will like having a Terran in the family*, she thought, and smiled again.

When Gwydion returned from the Hollow Mountains few indeed could look upon his face. Even his closest friends were shaken at the change in him, though no one could name what it was. He seemed taller, perhaps, or paler, or sterner, or more worn—

And fewer still could meet his eyes. Sea-gray they had always been, measuring and considering and ironic, with the far distance-look of the stars, or of one who spent much time gazing upon the stars. But now only Teilo, Ffaleira and Aeron herself could keep their gazes steady before his.

The strangeness was slow to pass from him, and he could speak of it only haltingly to Aeron, as they lay that night in the tapestried bed, together for the first time since the war began. But passion was far from their thoughts, and their hours were spent in quiet talk.

" 'Bid Aeron remember *Prydwen*,' " she repeated, musing, her cheek against his shoulder. " 'And the Treasures that were lost.' "

"Gwyn would say no thing that had no meaning; of that, at least, I am certain."

"Aye, but what meaning? *Prydwen* was Arthur's ship, the one he sailed out against the Coranians and Mordryth's traitors in the battle of the Roads of Camlann. It has always been thought he took *Prydwen*, and the Coranian flagship engaging her, into the Morimaruse, and neither came out again."

"And what of the Treasures, loremistress?" He was laughing.

"You, a Druid, to jest so! But why should a king of the Shining Folk speak of them to you?"

Gwydion put his free arm behind his head and lifted his gaze to the diamonded constellations of the bed-roof. Every child in Keltia knew of the Thirteen Treasures: spoils of Atland, saved from the great waves; or perhaps older still, brought to Earth from outside, when the Danaans first came there from their lost home. Who could say? Brendan and Nia had brought them to Keltia, all knew that; but there was no word as to what had befallen them later.

"I know not," said Gwydion at last. "And any road, he

bade *you* remember them, not me . . . But all his words were strange and full of presage. He told me that the trees should be my warriors, and what that might mean I cannot imagine."

"What means more to me is his pledge that the Shining Ones will indeed fight for Keltia, and the Crown will come back to me. I take no shame to admit to you that for a time I—" She broke off suddenly, twisted up on one elbow to stare down into his face. "The curse that Kynon spoke against me— He said that the Shining Ones would have to ride forth to war before I reign again as Queen in Caerdroia. And now has Gwyn promised that they shall." She lay down again beside him. "If that be so," she said, and now her voice was very small, "then two already of his dooms have come home upon me. And if two, then surely three."

"And that third?" he asked, though he remembered it well, for it had been set upon him as much as upon her.

"The stars' wandering between you and me . . . my lord from my bed." She tightened the arm that lay across his chest.

"That may be, or must be," he said, and kissed the top of her head. "But, Aeronwy, I am here now . . ."

Long after she had fallen asleep beside him, Gwydion lay wakeful, and the words of Kynon's curse and the words of Gwyn's promise interlaced like knotwork in his thought, until at last he too slept, and the chamber was still.

Chapter Twenty-four

"M'anam don sleibh!" swore Niall O Kerevan softly, his field-glasses tracking the enemy army across the blue distances of the plain below Caerdroia—Moycathra, it was called: Plain of the Battles.

"*My soul to the mountain*," translated Aeron absently. It struck her of a sudden what a very odd oath that was; she had heard it, had used it, all her life, yet never had consciously considered what it might mean. In view of the adventure Gwydion had had . . . Well, when all this was over, perhaps she would look into it. But her brother-in-law was right to be surprised and annoyed.

Without turning her head, she signaled Desmond, who had been standing near waiting upon her summons.

"Call the commanders to the War Room."

"At once, athiarna."

Aeron remained on the battlement, chin in hands, staring out at Jaun Akhera's legions. *Athiarna*, High One, the Fianna's form of respectful address to a superior officer. *Well*, she thought, *we shall see how high we still stand when this is done* . . .

Yet Arianeira's treachery had cut the ground from beneath them all. Not only her treason against Keltia, but the violence she had wrought against every tie of love and fosterage and friendship. Aeron was still more astounded than anything else, still in the mercy of shock that kept her from full realization of her pain. Perhaps the violation was still too new for her to feel the betrayal as she would come to feel it later. But there was surely one who felt it now to the fullest—

She looked sidelong to where Gwydion stood, giving his final orders to the captains of the wall in preparation for the siege to come. Clad in the unrelieved black of the Dragon uniform, his familiar scarlet cloak thrown back over his shoulders, he looked handsome as ever; but for the first time since the war had begun, his face showed his strain and his weariness.

He felt her attention on him, finished his briefing and came to stand beside her, and together they looked in silence at the marching cloud far across the plain.

"Sáinn an rían," she remarked after a while. " 'Check to the queen' —and by a pack of pawns."

"Check, maybe, but not mate; and not all pawns either. There is Jaun Akhera, who is for our purpose a king. Elathan too, though he has seen fit to withdraw from the board."

Aeron gave a short laugh. "King by my hand, as I am Queen by his father's; a fair trade, surely. But the Fomori were never noted for their skill at fidchell . . ." She glanced up at him. "I have summoned the commanders to the War Room to discuss measures to ensure the safety of the noncombatants within the City walls; will you come?"

"I am your war-leader. I have no choice but to come." He saw the shadow cross from him to her, and he took her arm. "Everyone's eyes are on you, Aeronwy; they look to you for their cue to action, and you cannot falter now." For a moment his mood lightened, and his face softened in a grin. "Do you know what they sing of you in the Imperial camp? 'Came I early, came I late, I met Red Aeron in the gate.' "

She laughed. "Sing they so? Well, I must be there to greet them, then, when they come to the gates of Caerdroia. Let us go, Pendragon, and discuss it."

Jaun Akhera pushed back his helmet and stared up at the walls of the city. In the low light of a somber winter afternoon, Caerdroia bulked vast as a couched dragon, and as ominous. *Girdle of Isis*! he swore to himself, *and I thought Escal-dun was well-fortified . . . but how can they defend seven miles of wall*?

He learned soon enough when the siege began the next

morning: The Kelts did not try. Having evacuated the outlying districts of all the civilian population, they then abandoned the defense of those areas, concentrating all their force
and all their folk behind the walls of the Old City that had its
center in Turusachan and its entrance at the Wolf Gate.

That day saw Moycathra prove its name from of old: Plain
of the Battles had it been called since the first days of Keltia;
through the time of Arthur and the Theocracy and the first
terrible wars against the Coranians; and now once more did it
earn its name anew. All day the armies of the Kelts fought off
the besiegers from the walls, and as the early winter dusk
closed down upon the Great Glen, each side retired exhausted
to its rest.

The weather had changed yet again. The air was now
uncharacteristically mild for the time of year, soft with sea-
mist and freighted with the half-muted sounds of siege, and it
slapped gently against Aeron's face as she stood on the turret
walk outside her tower, keeping a lonely vigil. And all the
inchoate sadness of the sea-wind entered her soul, so that she
faltered beneath the grief of it, and collapsed on the little
stone bench in the recess, and yet she could not bring herself
to weeping's release. Somehow it did not seem that sort of
sadness. She tried to fit images to it: her pity for O'Reilly,
her grief for Theo, her own ordeal at Tomnahara, what
Gwydion had done there to save her. The pressures of battle
and sovereignty had demanded that she set these things by
awhile in her mind and heart, and there had been until now no
chance to acknowledge them to herself, too much else with
which to contend to allow herself to mourn . . . But at the
thought of Gwydion, calm fell around her like a cloak. If, as
he had said, the people took their cue from her, then she took
hers from him.

Still, strength was not all the test. It was well within the
borders of possibility that this war could cost her her city, her
throne, her dearest ones, her lord, even her own life; but she
had acted as she had thought right and best, according to the
dictates of the moment, and she would do the same again in
the same straits. How else was a deed to be judged? There
was no changeless standard by which an act could be held
forever right or wrong, no bubble-sphere of time or place or

space in which inflexible judgment could be passed. The moment was all.

When Aeron got to the bubble-sphere, she stood up and shook herself free of the chill that had cramped her muscles and her soul. Kings have always died for their people, and that would be easy; but first they had to live for them, and that would be, again as always, something rather harder.

The siege of Caerdroia ground on into a third day, and a fifth, and a seventh. In the Imperial camp, the stresses were winding tight as a pirn. Hanno's orders came now with a harried snap to them that was utterly foreign to his usual smooth decisiveness; Sanchoniathon was beginning to move out more and more from the shadow of his brother, not entirely to his brother's satisfaction; and Arianeira became whiter and more withdrawn by the hour.

As for Jaun Akhera, he alone seemed to retain his usual mood, though his captains held out to him little hope for a victory of arms.

"The advantage always lies with the besieged," said Hanno. "You know that, my lord."

The Imperial high command was assembled in Jaun Akhera's tent to reconsider their strategy; since the departure of the Fomori, they had no cavalry arm at all and insufficient numbers to man an all-out assault on the city walls.

"Not only can they hold out indefinitely," added Garallaz, "with all the resources of the City on hand, and springs we cannot reach to foul, but once their fleets clear the other star systems, they can attack us here at their leisure. If Caerdroia is not in our hands within the week, we have failed, and we shall have little bargaining power when Rohan brings the fleet to bear on this planet. If we held the Queen as well as the City, our position would be even stronger."

Jaun Akhera looked at him with something like loathing. Garallaz was right, of course, but—

Sanchoniathon noted his brother's hesitation. "You are not still thinking that Aeron may yet accept that so interesting offer you made her at Rath na Ríogh? Not even to save her folk; she would sooner be burned alive in the Great Square

. . . Your obsession with her is a danger to everything we are trying to do here. Besides, what of the Princess Arianeira?''

The Prince of Alphor stared at his brother until Sanchoniathon looked away in confusion from the glowing golden eyes.

"Arianeira is a Kelt," said Jaun Akhera at last. "But Aeron is Keltia." He stood up, flexing shoulders stiff from many days of living in armor and sleeping in tents. "Summon the City to surrender at dawn. No, wait, I shall do it myself. If they agree, well and good; and they might, for they have their civilians to think of, and the destruction has been cruel. Also they have suffered heavier losses than have we, and they cannot call up reinforcements any more than we can.''

"I say she will not surrender the City," muttered Hanno.

"Most likely she will not," agreed Jaun Akhera. "But it is a chance I am going to try.''

Unnoticed by any of them, intent as they were on their talk, Arianeira had slipped from the pavilion, and pulling her cloak about her face she fled through the lines to a solitary place near a little clump of sea-pines. In the gathering dusk she stared up at the City she knew so well, and had loved so well, before she had persuaded herself she felt for it, and all it stood for, only hatred.

Oh Mother—the thought was a psychic moan, and she doubled over, folding up and falling to her knees as if she had taken a swordcut in the guts—*what have I done?* It could not be undone now, not now and never until the end of time; but somehow the hate and jealousy that had fueled her actions for the past few months had been swept suddenly aside. What stood now alone in their place was the memory of the love she had given and been given in return: Gwydion, Aeron, Morwen, all those others to whom her name was now become a hissing and an evil taste upon the tongue. Yet no matter what the rest of Keltia thought of her, there were two who loved her still. Even though they knew all her deeds, still did they love her, and had said so, back on that little hill near Rath na Ríogh. They had not changed their hearts since then; that she would stake her life on.

For that was indeed what she must stake, if anything was to be done to mend the havoc she had wrought. Her deed could not be undone, but it could still be atoned for; and by atoning she could yet buy some measure of final victory for those two she could now, at last, admit that she loved indeed—and some measure of final peace for herself. Yet the price would be a high one, and not hers alone to pay.

Dawn over the Wolf Gate. O'Reilly, on the ramparts to the west, rubbed her tired eyes and peered into the morning mists. It was much too quiet—something must be happening.

She turned to Niall, who stood nearby with some of his Dragons.

"What's going on?"

Niall jerked his chin down toward the Gate. "The Marbh-draoi would speak with the Ard-rían. Though what he thinks they have yet to say to each other, I do not know."

"Will Aeron speak to him?"

He nodded. "She goes now to the Gate."

O'Reilly waited to hear no more, but thanked him and fled down the long curving wall toward the Gate, arriving in time to see Aeron coming down from Turusachan. Reassured, she looked down over the battlements. Jaun Akhera and an armed escort sat their horses, waiting quietly under a white flag beneath the walls.

To O'Reilly, it was an outrage barely to be borne. There he sat on his horse, immaculate, elegant even, in a fur-trimmed white cloak, with his brother and his generals, and, most brazenly upon his left, the Princess Arianeira on a white stallion.

O'Reilly's gaze flew loyally to Aeron, who now stood on top of the Gate in plain view of all her Kelts and all her enemies, and her heart almost broke.

"She makes all too fine a target," muttered the Fian beside O'Reilly, and the Terran nodded grimly. Then Aeron raised her arm, and Jaun Akhera rode forward alone, and those both upon the walls and before them hushed to hear what those two would say.

Unlike their previous interview, this time both Aeron and Jaun Akhera knew that the balance of power had altered, and both knew also who it was now held that balance over the other.

He wasted no words this time on courtly civilities, and

spoke in Englic to be understood by the greatest number of his hearers.

"Aeron, yield up to me this City, this kingdom and yourself, and I swear to you I will spare your people."

"I have put them that choice already," she replied in the same tongue, her tone clear yet conversational. "And pledged them my word that whatsoever they asked of me, that even would I do."

"And?"

"And they choose to fight on. So long as they do choose so, I shall not lay down my sword to forsake the least, or the last, of my folk."

Jaun Akhera smothered a wave of irritation and reluctant respect. From all that he had heard, she had nearly been killed in that fight with Bres, and Isis alone knew how she had survived, yet here she was, as coolly intransigent as ever.

"If I take this city, Aeron," he said slowly and clearly, "I will take you with it, and I will nail your head above the Gate as I have promised."

On his left, Arianeira shifted in her saddle, and her horse pawed restively, perhaps catching her mood; but she neither spoke nor looked up.

Aeron shrugged. "I had rather have my head on a spike for this quarrel than my portrait in the Emperor's sitting-room."

Behind his brother, Sanchoniathon tried unsuccessfully to suppress a smile: Few people indeed had ever dared to so flout his elder brother, and no doubt Jaun Akhera was finding it almost intolerable.

Though he was unaware of his brother's assessment, Jaun Akhera would have agreed, and he stood in his stirrups to deliver his final words.

"So be it, then, Aeron! Did you not say it yourself—over your blood on the stones of Caerdroia?" He wheeled his horse savagely, cutting its mouth on the bit with the force of his jerk upon the reins, and spurred away, as, above, Aeron jumped down from the crenellation where she had stood. She looked deathly pale, as one who has trodden upon a viper or some other noisome thing, and hands caught her, but she shook them off.

"Let be," she said. "Where is Gwydion?"

"Here, Aeronwy." He came forward, his face unreadable to any save perhaps her alone.

"Order your battle, First Lord of War. Now comes the fíor-comlainn."

Long minutes' pause; then, outside, beyond the sudden quiet, the slow tide of the enemy advance began to beat again to Caerdroia's walls; in full flood, for this time Jaun Akhera held nothing back.

But those walls had been raised long ago, by Gradlon himself, he who had been Brendan's master-builder, and more than stone had gone into their making. Not easily do walls crumble that magic itself has mortared.

Behind the rising dust, the sun climbed to the top of its low arc and began to fall redly down, and still the battle raged. Like a tall tree in a windy wood, Gwydion stood watching the battle as Keltia fought for its life.

He turned presently to Struan, who stood by. "How much longer can the walls hold, Cameron?"

"I am a better judge of battle ahorse, Pendragon. The walls, I think, will hold forever; it is those who hold them will not endure so long."

"What do you counsel?"

"Cavalry does little good within walls; I say we ride out while yet we can."

"A sortie? We shall have to open all the gates, not just the Wolf Gate alone . . . But true it is they will not expect such a move."

Struan nodded. "And since they no longer have horse of their own to call upon for a counter, they will be hard put indeed to hold us off. But it is still a desperate tactic."

"What tactic might that be?" Aeron had come up behind them while they talked. Neither man had seen her since the moments after the dawn parley with Jaun Akhera; and in fact she had fought all day upon the walls. But now, even after the day's fighting, she looked her old self again, bright-faced in spite of the dust and blood that streaked her cheek. Morwen and Desmond were with her.

Gwydion explained, and she nodded.

"I agree," she said at once. "We must send them out, and

we must close the gates behind them. It is in my heart that the City will fall by this time tomorrow''—she impatiently waved off their protests—''and when that shall be, I want as many warriors as possible outside the walls. Trapped within, they can do nothing but be slaughtered; outside, they can flee off-planet to join the fleet, or regroup in the south or on the secured planets to form a resistance. And therefore the commanders will ride with them.''

Struan smiled. ''You learn quickly the ways of war, Ard-rían.''

''That's as may be—but we must take some thought now for ourselves. Desmond, you are to take O'Reilly at once to the convent of Glassary on Vannin. And do you not return to Tara—nay, argue not, this is not the whim of your cousin but the command of your Queen. When you have seen Sorcha safely there, Desmond, you will then join Rohan on the *Firedrake* and tell him all that has happened here.'' She turned to Morwen. ''What of the rest of the rígh-domhna?''

''All save Desmond and you are now safe away, either off-world or in sanctuary in the far south and east, or in the Kyles of Ra. Ríoghnach and Niall were the last to leave, she protesting bitterly, I might add; I think they have gone to Kieran on Caledon.''

''It is well, then.'' Aeron sighed, then took Morwen's hand and Gwydion's in her own. ''We shall stay, we three; that is fitting. Oh, my most beloved,'' she said, all her love for them plain in voice and face, ''whatever the dawn may bring or the day may take, yet it cannot alter this.''

The short winter dusk had long since given way to dark; the Imperial troops had withdrawn from the City walls, and again there was heated conference in Jaun Akhera's tent.

''You have little choice, lord!'' said Hanno passionately. ''If they succeed in rallying for a sortie, we are lost, as we no longer have Fomor's cavalry to offset their horse and chariotry. And if Rohan succeeds in breaking through with their fleet to reinforce them from space, we are doubly lost. You must take the City with them still trapped within.''

''And how do you propose we do so, Captain-General?'' snapped Jaun Akhera. ''Eight days, and still they hold us off.

Even the siege guns cannot blast through those walls; when we can use them, even—there is so much mist and fog and cloud about, the lasers are useless more than half the time.''

"I know a way would open the Wolf Gate in five minutes, and mists be damned.''

They turned as one, astonished, for the voice had been Arianeira's. She came forward now into the lamplight, smiling slightly.

Jaun Akhera ran a hand over his face, spoke with curtness. "What way is this, lady?''

"Magic. It is your last chance against Aeron. She would never use it against you; therefore must you use it against her.''

"Aeron's reasons for keeping her hand from magic are the same as mine,'' said Jaun Akhera doubtfully. "Or so Irin Magé, chief priest of my order, warned me before I left Alphor. Who first uses magic will fall in the end.''

"Superstition,'' said Arianeira. "Words and superstition—do they breed magicians on Alphor, or frightened children?'' She saw how her derision rocked them; now must she call upon every ounce of guile and trickery and power to sway that she possessed, or could summon up . . . "Did not I myself use sorcery to breach the Curtain Wall so that you might enter? If that law had been a true one, we should have been defeated utterly long ere now. And I suffered nothing for my use of power; indeed, the spell I made use of at Murias station was Aeron's own, the very one she wielded against Bellator. Or is it that you are not so strong a sorcerer as has been commonly held?''

She saw Jaun Akhera's golden eyes flicker, thought to herself behind deep shields, *Ah, that's touched you fair, Cabiri* . . . She continued suavely, "When your lord grandsir hears how you hesitated, will *he* praise your prudence in the use of your art? Or will he see only that you might have taken Caerdroia, and did not—because you feared to match spells with Aeron! Is your power so much less than hers—so much less than mine, even—that you dare not chance the hazard?''

The silence in the tent was absolute. Jaun Akhera stood motionless; Hanno stared at the scarred ivory tabletop; Garallaz and Sanchoniathon glanced at each other quickly and then away again; and Arianeira held her entire being to utter stillness lest some stray thought give the lie to that which she had said, and kill stillborn this last desperate strategy of hers to atone . . .

Then the tension broke, as Jaun Akhera raised his eyes to Arianeira's white face.

"What is magic," he said through his teeth, "but another weapon to my hand?"

Before the next day's sun was full risen, the Wolf Gate swung open for the first time in nine nights. Out beneath the vast stone arches, as was happening at the same moment at all the city gates, silently poured the Keltic cavalry, and most of the foot also; for Gwydion had emptied Caerdroia to make this final throw, and the walls were now nearly undefended.

Though in truth that mattered little, thought Aeron. If the sortie prevailed, the City would stand, and a defense would not be needed; and if the sortie failed and the City fell, a defense would not be needed still more . . .

As the Gate closed behind the last of the horse, Aeron stood alone in the wide stone-paved square behind the gate-pillars. Not entirely alone even so, for around her were the Fians Gwydion had set to guard her if the worst should indeed befall, but she paid no heed to them. Caerdroia, as she had said so long ago to Haruko, was not Keltia; and, no matter what Jaun Akhera might think, nor was the Ard-rían Keltia either . . .

She caught the trace of something, like a faint quick scent on the wind, and turned, frowning, to quest after it.

"What is it?" Gwydion had come down from the Gate parapet to join her, and noted her expression.

"I am not sure. Something strange—it has gone now."

"We carry the day out upon Moycathra; come and see for yourself." He took her arm to lead her up through the gate-house to the tower stairs, but she pulled away from him, and now her head came up like a hound's at a whistle no human can hear, and fear was in her face.

"Stand clear, all you, of the Gate!"

Gwydion dragged her to one side, throwing himself after,

for he too had now felt what she had earlier sensed: the beginnings of Jaun Akhera's magic.

"There is sorcery afoot—"

Over the battle's noise came a deep rumble that rose to a deafening roar. Above their heads, the findruinna of the Gate glowed briefly red, then blinding white, then burst apart in a shower of metal and stone. Aeron was flung backwards by the force of explosion and spell alike, for there had been time to prepare for neither. But her sword still hung at her side, and as the Imperial van began to pour like water through the breach, she struggled to her feet and reached to draw it from the sheath.

But the weapon jammed in the scabbard, and before she could tug it free she was surrounded by Coranians of Jaun Akhera's personal guard. Though by their lord's order they laid no hand upon her, a score of swords were levelled at her, and she took her own hand off her sword-hilt. In the empty space where the Gate had been she saw Gwydion fighting like a tiger with more Coranians. He had managed to cut down not a few of them already, but even as she watched he was overwhelmed by sheer numbers. Morwen she could not see at all.

Aeron returned her attention to the ruin of the Gate, as the guards opened an aisle among the dead and dying Fians, and Jaun Akhera strode between them into the City. He was on foot, and bareheaded, his sword sheathed at his side, and when he saw her, he halted.

Aeron said no word, but very deliberately touched her arm where a shard of flying metal had struck her near the shoulder. Her hand came away wet, and, still with that same formal air, her eyes holding Jaun Akhera's, she placed her palm to the stone of the gate-pillar, leaving a clear red print upon the granite.

Only then did she speak. "So I said."

"So, indeed, you said," he echoed, as shaken as he was triumphant. He looked past her then, to where his soldiers were ranging out to secure the strong points within Caerdroia, then back over his shoulder, where out on the plain the fight still raged.

"You have not won, Prince of Alphor," said Aeron, noting the direction of his glance. "True it is you have taken the City, but the most part of my forces are out there"—she pointed—"by the grace of the gods and the wisdom of my war-leaders. When they see the City is fallen, they will flee by my order, to save themselves and keep the fight alive. But that is only part of it . . . I said some days ago—though you were not there to hear me, and he who was is now slain—that whoever first resorted to magic in this quarrel would lose in the end. You who are a Cabiri doubtless received a similar warning, and though I know not who persuaded you to ignore it, I owe that one my thanks that you did so. For so have you ensured your own defeat; whatever may happen to me, Keltia shall be victorious in the end. I would endure much for that assurance."

Jaun Akhera had remained silent all through her speech, but his gold eyes had never left her green ones. Now he gestured, and his soldiers dragged Gwydion over to join them, and from another side of the square Morwen was escorted under guard. Jaun Akhera looked at each of them in turn.

"Escort these to the palace," he said to the captain of his guard. "See that they are kept close, and apart from each other. They may remain in their own chambers, if they wish, so long you first remove any weapons and other toys; and so long as I have your word, Aeron, that those rooms contain no hidden ways of escape?"

Aeron smiled, and laid her open hand over her heart to honor the oath. "Not my chambers, nor the Prince of Dôn's, nor the Duchess of Lochcarron's, contain any such. Hear me, gods."

Beside her, Gwydion seemed about to protest. She signalled him quickly in bardic finger language to desist—she dared not use even tight-focus telepathy with a Cabiri adept intent upon her—and he relaxed into the icy composure she knew masked fury. Behind Jaun Akhera, Arianeira had ridden up, still on her white stallion. She smiled as if she too knew, but Aeron did not even glance in her direction.

"Have we Your Highness's leave to go?" she snapped. "We are all of us very weary, and my arm pains me."

"Prisoners ask not; rather are they told," he replied evenly.

"But you may go indeed, and I shall send medics to attend each of you." As she turned away, with the guards closing in around her, "You do not make this easy, Aeron, for any of us."

"Ah well," she said. "Hard it is to get wool from a fish."

"What is it, Arianeira? Come in, and welcome."

Arianeira curtsied, the merest swirl of skirt, and entered the great state salon which Jaun Akhera had appropriated as his own personal quarters. It was the evening of the day after the fall of Caerdroia, and this was the first chance she had had for a completely private word with him.

After she had seated herself in a silk-upholstered chair and accepted a cup of wine, she smiled at him with all the old charm.

"Now that you have had time to consider at your leisure, lord, I would ask your intentions toward your royal prisoners. They are, after all, my near kin."

Jaun Akhera leaned back in his chair, his eyes as bright as the gold goblet in his hand.

"That is largely up to you, Highness," he said presently. "What would you?"

"I would be Regent in Keltia as you promised, lord, and that should I be a good deal easier if I knew that Aeron and Gwydion and Morwen yet lived."

"You who demanded their heads would now plead for their lives?" He was astonished, though secretly pleased. "I would be the last to deny their usefulness alive, and have been delaying their executions out of just such a hope, but they themselves have left me little choice. But if you think, Arianeira, that you can convince them otherwise, you have my full leave to try. Indeed, haven't you already spoken with your brother?"

She grimaced. "I have, and little good it did either of us . . . But I think I may have more success with the three of them together, if such is acceptable to you. Also I would have them brought to the Hall of Heroes, and speak to them there; the sight of the Throne of Scone might induce in Aeron a proper attitude of resignation."

Jaun Akhera laughed. "Somehow I doubt that," he said.

"But by all means do as you think best. You know her, and the others, far better than do I. You are not softening, are you?" he added.

"Not likely . . . Time was I would have liked to see their deaths, even my own brother's, but now perhaps I see things otherwise."

"I am glad of it," said Jaun Akhera honestly. "Those three are certainly of far greater value to me alive, and it would have gone hard to slay such worthy foes—though I should of course have honored my word to you . . . had you insisted."

"Would you indeed?" she murmured. "Well, I do not ask that now. Only let you send guards to conduct them to the Hall of Heroes. I shall await them there within the hour."

Aeron paced up and down her chamber, heedless of the guards at the door and outside upon the turret walk. She had not slept an hour since the fall of Caerdroia, and had barely ceased her pacing either. Now she knew how a mewed hawk must feel . . .

Still, she had managed to do all she could have done. The armies were dispersed as effectively as might be. The Terrans and the rest of the royal family were safely away. The Copper Crown was safe with the Sidhe, and the crown jewels had been hidden beyond anyone's power to discover, the scepter and other royal regalia with them. The records of state were inaccessible to anyone who lacked the Great Seal of Keltia, and she had in the last hour before the sortie attended to the Seal herself . . . It remained only for her to string herself to face whatever fate Jaun Akhera might decree—and of the many possibilities, death was by far the most preferable, since it alone held no terror of the unknown.

She did not look round as a small stir came at the door.

"Majesty?"

At that she did turn. Sanchoniathon, brother of Jaun Akhera, stood in the doorway.

He was smaller and slighter than his brother, much of a height and build with Aeron herself, with the dark beauty and amber eyes of all his family; and he so plainly hated having to be there, performing so distasteful a duty, that Aeron nearly laughed. But—

"My lord," she acknowledged gravely.

"You are to come to the Hall of Heroes, Majesty. The Prince of Dôn also, and Her Grace of Lochcarron."

"Whyfor? Has your brother something further to say to us?"

"I know nothing about that, madam." His expression as he looked at her was so openly admiring as to verge on the disrespectful; he had chided his brother for allowing himself to become infatuated with the Keltic queen, and never knew that he himself had done exactly the same. "I suggest you put on a warm cloak," he said, recollecting himself to the purpose for which he had been sent. "The weather has turned bitter cold in the past few hours."

"You and your brother are marvelous careful of my well-being: He sends medics to tend my battle scratches, you remind me to wear a cloak."

He said nothing, but watched her take a plain green cloak from a peg and buckle it at her throat.

"Well, my lord Sancho," she said with a smile, and he started at her use of the family nickname. "Shall we go, then?"

Chapter Twenty-five

*I*t was different from the last time Aeron had been in the Hall of Heroes, and not since the days of the Theocracy had any reigning monarch of the Six Nations been brought there as a prisoner under guard.

Sanchoniathon and his escort had not accompanied her beyond the doors of the Keep, but had there delivered her into the hands of a company of Jaun Akhera's personal troops. Morwen and Gwydion, similarly attended, were already there, and upon her arrival all three were escorted into the Hall.

As she paced the length of the vast chamber, Aeron found her thought flying unerringly back to the day the Terrans had come: the Hall filled with friends, she seated crowned upon the Throne of Scone, and coming toward her down the Hall's center aisle Haruko and O'Reilly and the rest . . .

With an effort almost physical Aeron wrenched her attention back to the present. Morwen glanced sideways at her, but Aeron would not look at her. Gwydion was a step or two behind them.

Aeron raised her eyes at last. Arianeira sat in the great carved stone seat, and as Aeron halted before the steps she found herself consumed by the flame of a white-hot heedless anger.

But it was Gwydion who moved forward, and the guards levelled their weapons at his chest.

"Why have you summoned us here, Ari?" he asked quietly. "Surely we have already said all there is to be said, the last time we spoke face to face."

"I craved the privilege of this meeting from my lord Jaun Akhera," his sister answered, "so that I may satisfy myself beyond all doubt that you three have had all possible chances to understand your position—and your peril."

"We understand well enough," said Morwen, after waiting a moment for Aeron to speak. "Have you anything new to say to us?"

"Only my best and strongest advice that you accept his terms. The alternative you know; and though Jaun Akhera is reluctant to take so final a step, be very sure he will do so if he must. Naturally, he knows of my deep concern for my kin, and so he willingly gave leave for me to try to reason with you one last time."

"You waste your time, his and ours, Ari," said Morwen, disgusted. "Your—*lord* has made his true position marvelous clear: Aeron dead and you upon the throne of a vassal Keltia. And so far has he succeeded." She nodded toward the throne. "Are you in truth so very eager to see the rest accomplished?"

Arianeira stared at Aeron, who returned her gaze untroubled.

"Clear the hall," said Arianeira then. "I will speak to Aeron Aoibhell in private."

"Highness," objected the Imperial captain, "we cannot leave you alone here with—"

"Can and shall!" snapped Arianeira, rising up out of the throne like an uncoiling piast, and he reddened. "They are your lord's prisoners, given into my hand. Also are they my own kin, my brother and my foster-sisters, and *I* say I shall speak to them privately."

"As you command, Highness."

"They will be my responsibility," said Arianeira, in a more conciliatory tone. "Go now." She waited until the guards had paced out of the Hall and closed the huge doors behind them. Then she dashed down the steps of the throne and flung herself at Aeron's feet.

"I invoke the mercy of the High Justice of the Ard-rían of Keltia, and ask royal pardon for my offenses against the Six Nations." She spoke the ancient formula of supplication with a depth of contrition in her voice that astonished her hearers.

Aeron stood motionless a moment, looking down in amazement at the bowed silver-gilt head. This was real and honest
repentance, she could ken it. But *why* . . . She extended her
hand to Arianeira in the ritual gesture of forgiveness. The
Princess kissed the unicorn signet, and Aeron raised her and
kissed her on both cheeks.

"You are forgiven, Ari," she said. "But I am confounded."

"Sometimes you can be denser than lachna, Aeron Aoibhell
. . . But Gwydion knows." She cast an unreadable look at
her brother. "I have made all arrangements. There are packs
and weapons hidden behind the throne. You are to escape
through the Nantosvelta, and, the gods being well disposed,
come through the Dales down to Keverango. There, at the old
spacebase, I have ordered your ship to be landed, Aeron.
There is a token Imperial garrison there, perhaps a hundred
troops; but with care you can easily avoid them. Your ship is
fully fitted and supplied for space, and you should be able to
get safely out-Wall with little difficulty. No Imperial craft is a
match for *Retaliator*."

Aeron had been watching Arianeira's face with a puzzled
frown. "I do not understand why you are doing this, Arianeira,
but nor did I truly understand why you betrayed us in the first
instance. Oh aye, I know what you said, but knowing is
hardly the same as understanding . . ."

Arianeira dismissed this impatiently. "But you will go?"

"Certainly I will not go! Gwydion, we have had this out
before. I will never leave the people, and three times never on
the word of a—" She bit back the word before she spoke it.

"You forgave me, Ard-rían," said Arianeira. "Did you
not say yourself that you are still my sister and my friend?
Well, perhaps I have come, however late, to believe that . . .
Still and all, Aeron, if you must know, I do this not so much
for you as for myself; not so much for myself as for my
brothers and my House; and not so much for them as for
Gwydion alone."

"Ari, Ari, whomsoever you may do it for, it will be
suicide all the same! When Jaun Akhera learns you have
betrayed him in his turn—"

"He is meant to find out." Arianeira busied herself with
the heavy tapestries that backed the throne. "This is not the

first time I have betrayed him, though he knows it not: I it was who swayed him to break the Gate with magic—and you know what that must mean in the end. And it is not suicide, but execution . . . Aeron, I beg you, go!''

She had wrestled the hangings aside to reveal a granite slab, its highly polished black surface broken only by a small shield inlaid at eye level: the device of the winged unicorn, set flush with the facing of the stone.

"Gwydion, you knew of this?" asked Aeron, her voice dangerously soft.

"I did, Aeronwy; Ari spoke of it to me yesterday in private . . . You will go, Queen of Kelts, and your Taoiseach with you."

The silence sang like a plucked harpstring. Then Aeron laughed.

"Very well, then, Prince of Dôn. I will go if you will also. All it needs is another pack."

But Gwydion shook his head. "That is not the bargain, Ard-rían. I remain so that you have a realm to return to. And any road, as you yourself said, all this has been fated by Kynon's doom laid upon you—and spoken of by Gwyn."

Aeron shrugged. "Fates have been altered before now, and the counsels of faerie kings set aside. Join me in flight, or I stay."

"If you stay, Aeron, you will die," Gwydion answered, with a certain weary patience, for they had been over this ground a good many times before.

"And you? You are the designated king-consort of Keltia, or have you already forgotten? Are you so sure of your own life under an Imperial occupation?"

"I am of more use to the Coranian alive than slain; he knows that, and knows I know it too. And I am of more use to you and to the kingdom if I stay. You and Morwen serve us all best by fleeing."

Aeron remained unmoved. For many minutes Arianeira pleaded with her, Morwen could not shake her, and at last even Gwydion appeared to capitulate.

"We waste precious time here . . . Very well then, I go too. Another pack can be as swiftly obtained. But let us await it in the tunnel entrance, so that we are in less chance of discovery." He exchanged with his sister a look that even Aeron could not interpret. Arianeira gave a small nod, and looked again at Aeron.

"You must open the gate to the Nantosvelta, Ard-rían," she said. "That is in your power alone. The guards will soon begin to grow suspicious."

Aeron stepped slowly up to the granite slab, raising her hand to set her ring to the inlaid seal. True it was that only the reigning monarch, he or she who bore the Unicorn Seal, could open this hidden gate. It led to the Nantosvelta, an underground tunnel running beneath the mountains of the Loom and emerging in one of the high hidden valleys of the Dales to the south. Partly it was the long-abandoned bed of an ancient river, and partly it was shaped by the lasers of the builders of Caerdroia; and it had been used ever since the days of the Fáinne for just such desperate moments as this.

The seal on the signet and the seal on the stone met, and the huge granite block slid silently aside, revealing half-open gates of findruinna, three feet thick, and beyond them a tunnel sloping down into darkness.

At the back of the throne lay the packs provided by Arianeira. Morwen hefted one experimentally, testing the weight of it, as Aeron, stepping into the tunnel entrance, turned to make a final farewell to Arianeira.

For the first time in their meeting, Arianeira smiled, the old sunny smile without malice or bitterness that all of them remembered.

"Gods with you, Queen of Kelts."

"Ari—"

"Now, Gwion!" his sister shouted, and whirling upon Morwen pushed her into the tunnel. Gwydion tossed Aeron's pack to follow, then pinned her arms beneath her cloak and kissed her swift and hard upon the mouth.

Aeron grasped his intent immediately. "Gwydion, I will not go without you—"

"Aeronwy, you must." He held her close a moment with a final fierceness, then flung her from him so violently that, entangled in her cloak, she overbalanced and fell. But, as he intended, she fell beyond the automatic sensors that operated the findruinna gates, and those gates rang shut between them even as she was scrambling to her feet.

"*Gwydion!*"

Her cry was cut off as the stone wall too slid back into place. In the reverberant quiet left in the Hall of Heroes, Gwydion leaned his forehead against the throne's carved back, his shoulders bowed in grief and relief. Arianeira leaned against him, her head bent to his, then both of them looked up as the great copper doors crashed open at the far end of the hall.

Jaun Akhera's guard poured through, and among them, not first, was the Prince of Alphor himself. He strode down the hall and stopped at the steps to the throne.

"Where is Aeron, Gwydion?" he demanded. "And Morwen Douglas?"

"They are gone, lord."

"Gone! Dead?"

"No, gone, and long gone too," said Gwydion, lying serenely. "They are well away off-planet, far beyond the reach and speed of such ships as you still command."

"Who arranged this escape? You? I promise you, Gwydion—"

"Nay, I will claim that promise for my own, Emperor's Heir." The voice was Arianeira's. She had been standing in the shadows to one side of the throne, and now she came slowly forward. Her face was white and set, but triumphant contempt danced in her eyes.

Jaun Akhera's face grew black with anger as realization of how she had tricked him struck home.

"You! You damnable both-sides traitor—"

"My mistake, that I have tried to right as best I could. They are both safely fled where neither you nor your spies shall find them." She smiled down at him. "That is my reparation to Keltia and to Keltia's Queen; and in return I have forgiveness."

"Forgiveness, is it? I shall give you a forgiveness shall requite all sins forever—" Jaun Akhera started forward, hand to sword-hilt, but her expression stayed him.

"Coranian fool!" she hissed. "And do you think me a like fool, to boast to you of such and not to have made—

arrangements? Look you—'' She held out the hand that had been hidden in the folds of her cloak. In it was the writhing form of the little red-eyed white snake that is called marbh-fionn, white death, on the Keltic worlds, to which it is not native; the most venomous known in all the settled galaxy, that bites and dies with its victim.

With her other hand Arianeira pulled down the high round neck of her gúna, revealing the small puncture mark over the heart-vein, startlingly red against the pale skin. Gwydion made as if to speak, then caught back his words unsaid.

"I have but little time left," she said, looking not at Jaun Akhera but at her brother. "Yet time enough to know that there has been here not defeat but victory. And that victory, Jaun Akhera, is not yours."

"Victory!" jeered her former ally. "Caerdroia fallen, the Keltic army scattered, your own death but moments away, and Aeron Aoibhell fled off-planet like a runaway serf? You claim this as victory?" Yet for all his mocking tone, his eyes showed fear and uncertainty.

"Victory indeed," she repeated calmly. "But not yours, and not yet. You shall see." Her body swayed as the poison began to riot in her blood. Gwydion leaped forward to catch her in his arms, and lowered her gently to the steps. The small white snake lay upon the floor, already dead.

"Gwynfyd, the Circle of Perfection," murmured Arianeira, looking past Gwydion now, past him, past Jaun Akhera, to something neither man could see. "Ah! The Light—Gwydion, my dearest brother—you do not know how—" Then the incredulous look of joy froze upon her face, as her body sagged in his arms and her head fell back against his chest.

Gwydion kissed his sister gently upon the brow, and when he raised his face again to Jaun Akhera, only love and pride and triumph marked his features.

Jaun Akhera looked long at him in silence, then down at Arianeira.

"She was a true Kelt after all," he said. "Come when you will, Prince of Gwynedd." Turning on his heel, he left the Hall of Heroes, and the guard followed after, to wait outside the door, leaving Gwydion alone awhile with his sister.

*   *   *

On the other side of the throne, Aeron flung herself weeping against the gate, hammered on the cold metal with her fists and clawed at it with her fingernails. Beneath her grief and frustration and fury, she knew well that that barrier would not yield to siege lasers, much less to fingernails, and it could not be opened from this side. Nor from the other side either, now . . .

Morwen pulled roughly at her arm. "Come away, Aeron. There is no time for this. Put these on." She held out the fur-lined white leather leggings and hooded doublet worn in the deep cold, spoke as to a grieving child. "There, so—now your boots—snowcloak—"

Moving like a sleepwalker, Aeron put on the heavy garments, then stood there, her face remote and gray. Morwen, having finished her own preparations, looked closely at her friend and then fetched her a sharp slap to the face. Aeron rocked beneath the blow, then seemed to come back from the far place into which shock had thrust her.

"I am here," she said, catching Morwen's wrist. "Let it be, and let us go. Ari and Gwydion have bought us time at a high price indeed, and we wrong them to waste it."

Up in Aeron's tower rooms, which he had taken over as much for his own solace as to prevent their desecration by Jaun Akhera, Gwydion stood looking out at the invisible sea. It was late, and he was exhausted, yet he could not sleep, and most especially he could not sleep in the curtained bed, but had asked instead for a field-couch to be brought. It stood over against the north wall of the chamber, uncreased and unused.

He knew very well that he could not go on sleepless many more hours; knew also that for Arianeira, death had come as a triumph, more of a blessing even than usual. She was happy now, she would be seeing all things clear, and all her pain and fear and hurt would be taken away. He had wept for her, some lost time in the night. But his tears had been for the child-sister he remembered: Since the day of their conception they had never been truly apart. She was part of him, and she would not now die in the world until he did, and he had no more fears for her at all.

Aeron . . . Well, Aeron was another tale, and one far from sung. It was a great comfort that Morwen was with her, for Morwen had a good deal of good sense, and she would not allow Aeron to run over-wild. But all the same, they were gone into the unknown, into a perilous uncertainty surpassed only by the far more certain peril they would have faced had they remained in Keltia. He had no doubts whatsoever that Jaun Akhera would have wasted any more time in setting Aeron's head above the Wolf Gate, and Morwen too had been sentenced to the block. Of his own danger he did not trouble to think. It was well that none knew where they had fled, though Gwydion had a few ideas of his own as to that. And he was glad of his ignorance; for had he known, he would have feared above all things that he might somehow reveal it to Jaun Akhera. Kelts were not the only skilled telepaths in the universe. . . .

Well, ignorance would preserve him from that at least, if not from other worry. They might very well have gone to Earth, or to one of the Protectorate worlds, even. There were any number of safe places to which they might have gone . . .

Gwydion ran his hand over his face, putting resolutely aside the thought that they might decide not to leave the planet after all—Aeron was extremely persuasive when she chose to be—or, worse, had already been captured. And even if they did succeed in escaping, space right now was laced with terrors, the Imperial fleets crossing and recrossing the star-roads; remnants only, thanks to Rohan—and Elharn—but still strong. But they would be in *Retaliator*, he countered. Elharn had designed that ship's armaments, Rhain and the Fianna scientists had overseen her construction, and Aeron had contributed several useful ideas of her own. The result had been a beautiful, deadly, elegant ship that looked as if it had been cut with a laser from a black diamond. It was the ship that had carried Aeron to Bellator—and back.

For once, remembering Bellator gave Gwydion some comfort.

Beneath the roots of Mount Eagle, Aeron and Morwen walked steadily and silently on in the darkness. The glow of illuminant crystals swept over their faces at widely spaced intervals, activated by their passing, then, once the human electrofields were out of range, again extinguished.

The Nantosvelta was bitterly cold, and it was well that they had clad themselves warmly; well too that their boots were sturdy, for the rock floor was uneven and difficult to walk on. After some hours, Morwen, who was in the lead, reached back to touch Aeron's arm.

"Look ahead."

They were coming to the mouth of the Nantosvelta; thin blue light that came from no crystal was seeping down to them. The tunnel sloped sharply upward, skewed round to antisunwise, and ended abruptly in a dripstone screen. The waterfall that masked the entrance was not Keltia's highest: That pride belonged to Lightwater, which fell from Mount Keltia such a downward flight that all its water turned to ionized mist and recombined again before it touched the earth. But Waterharp, so called for its peculiarly musical sound, was big enough, taking as it did all the runoff from the clouds that came in off the Western Sea, to spill their water on the slopes that barred their way in the air.

It did not sing this day. The cold that had fastened its fangs on all the High Dales had turned the entire waterfall to milky marble, a great smooth swelling frozen curve that burst from the rockface like a plume of ice.

They emerged from behind the ice-curtain and skirted the small pool into which the frozen stream vanished. It had begun to snow heavily, the unearthly snowlight that lay on the land dazzling to eyes so long accustomed to the dark.

"Snow," said Morwen, dismayed.

"Our friend the snow," Aeron corrected her. "And see how strong the wind is; our footprints will be cold and covered before our boots are fairly out of them."

They repacked their gear—thoughts of Arianeira, who had furnished it, uppermost in their minds, though neither spoke of her—then masked their faces with the lower part of the furred hoods and went out into the storm, and the driving blizzard blotted their tracks from sight.

* * *

"I have summoned you here, Prince of Gwynedd, to discuss with you some few points bearing on the nature of your position here."

"Your position also, lord," said Gwydion, undisturbed by Jaun Akhera's threatening overtone. "In certain ways it may be even more precarious a one than my own."

The two princes were in Aeron's marble-walled office, which Jaun Akhera had commandeered for his own use along with the rest of the State Apartments. Gwydion was grateful for the choice of location: The big luxurious room had never been a favorite of Aeron's, and did not carry so vivid an imprint of her to cause him pain as another chamber might have done.

Jaun Akhera scowled. "Yes, well, let us leave that for the moment. You had every chance to escape, yet you deliberately remained in the City and allowed yourself to be taken with Aeron and Morwen. Again, you could have escaped when they did—doubtless your late sister urged you to do so; yet again you stayed. You have a certain value as a hostage, as I need not point out, and I want to know why you chose to remain."

Gwydion laughed. "I would think that to be obvious even to you: so that the Ard-rían of Keltia has a kingdom to come back to."

"If you think to organize a resistance, Gwydion, be warned I will not tolerate it."

"It organizes itself," said Gwydion, still smiling. "How many members of the royal family did you capture? How many officers of the Fianna? How many Kin to the Dragon are still free?" Jaun Akhera was silent. "You see? You cannot hope to stop it; whether I lift a finger or no, it is moving even as we speak. Yours is an army of occupation: You hold, but you have not conquered. Ours is an army of—let us call it suspension. We have been checked, but not destroyed, and certainly not defeated."

"Your Curtain Wall has not been repaired."

He nodded. "And very likely will not be, not even when the last of you is gone from within the Bawn. Long past time those barriers were let fall. Aeron herself said that the Curtain Wall keeps out more than just invaders; it keeps out ideas.

But I am more interested in your position, lord. It is true that you hold Caerdroia hostage, indeed the entire Throneworld. But it is equally true that the planet is blockaded. Our forces must regroup in secret on other of our worlds, but your forces cannot be relieved, or at least not without very great cost. You occupy Caerdroia; it is just as accurate to say that you are besieged in it.''

Jaun Akhera sat back in the big chair behind the desk, studying the man who faced him with such apparent equanimity.

"Have you no fear for yourself, then? I might find it useful to make an object lesson of the fate of the Prince of Dôn—the obstructive Prince of Dôn.''

"I think not.'' Gwydion seemed unconcerned. "If you kill me, you lose a bargaining counter of some importance. More than that, you would lose somewhat of a chance to lure Aeron back. I think you will want to keep me here a while yet.''

Jaun Akhera regarded him with exasperation, some amusement and a good deal of grudging admiration.

"Perhaps, Prince Gwydion, you and I may come to be, if not friends, at least, possibly, less bitter enemies.''

For the first time in their interview, Gwydion turned the full depth of his gray gaze upon the Imperial heir. In his eyes now was not only the druid-power but the bale-look of one whom Gwyn had touched, and in his voice was all the cold of the stars.

"Sooner will geese grow fur.''

Chapter Twenty-six

Aeron trudged up the snowy slope, halting at the crest to try to catch her breath—a difficult feat in the bitter air. The cold was now intense; so white and so still it seared the bone, it burned in silence until one moved, and then it filled laboring lungs with pain like crystal knives.

She looked back to view their progress. They had made a good job of it in the deep snow; another few hours and none would be able to say which way the fugitives had taken. Behind her, the short winter day was falling down to darkness. The sky was clear for the moment of stormclouds, and a huge deep blue shadow hung over much of the dale. From the west came a glow as the sunset layered itself in banks of color, where the cold wind down from the hills had piled great masses of cloud in the lift, gold-barred purple, clear green, frosty red shading upward through rose-light into blue.

"Where are we?" she asked presently.

"Wolfdale," said Morwen. She pulled a water-flask from her pack and passed it first to Aeron. "At least until we cross the Ill Step. After that, Black Sail will shield us until we pass over the Stile and drop down into Upper Darkdale."

Aeron drank sparingly and returned the flask. "And then?"

"And then to Keverango, in the end; a long and weary way. I could wish the secret port had been made more convenient to those who would stand in need of it! We must hope that the others will keep Jaun Akhera's attention away from the south a while yet."

372

"We must hope so indeed."

Morwen glanced at her friend's face and spoke to what she had really said. "It is not cowardice to flee, Aeron. You should know that by now."

"I thought I did," she said with a bitter laugh. "Come then, Taoiseach, we must find some sort of shelter before dark."

They lay out that night in a small cave Morwen found, at the back of a wild corrie only the winter foxes knew. Even with their furred garments, and the warmth of the hand-crystals from their glaives, the cold was unforgivable. The mountain creaked with it; the frozen tarns rang like slow chimes as the ice shifted, groaning musically.

In the morning, snow lay deeper than ever all round, having fallen again in the night, and the clouds were swagged dark gray above their heads, big-bellied with the promise of more snow to come. The whole valley seemed lit from beneath, and the voice of the little burn rang loud in its ice-cut bed. A wind got up during the forenoon, sweeping down the desolate fells and troubling the deep unfrozen waters of Deer Tarn, that lay on their left as they walked, cold ruffles of foam lying on its black surface like lace on velvet.

This was wild country, and few folk lived here. The valleys closed in toward the northeast, rising in great tumbled slopes of quartzite scree to the huge barren uplands of the central massif of the Loom. From that high purple hub, the Dales radiated out like the spokes of a wheel. Standing across the path Aeron and Morwen now took out of Wolfdale, the giant whaleback of Black Sail loomed like a breaking wave, its sides, usually slate-colored, cloaked now with white.

Looking back, Aeron saw through the lowering clouds the shapes of Traprain Scar, Malisons and the Bellstones, at this distance seeming to be hewn from topaz crystal, rapidly vanishing behind the advancing veils of snow. Then some wind aloft caught the veils aside for a moment, and she saw stand out briefly, far behind them now, the tremendous three-horned bulk of Mount Eagle, Eryri, its mighty back turned toward them across the miles of air.

Only for a moment; then the snow shut down again, the

path bent southward; and Aeron could no longer see the mountain upon whose knees her city lay.

They had been several hours going down into Darkdale when Aeron, coming down the fellside, lost control of her speed, and plunged through the ice-crust into a crevasse concealed by the drifted snow. The rift swallowed her left leg to the thigh, but she managed by main force and good reflexes to keep her other leg out of the cleft. Morwen floundered through the snow to her side.

"Aeron, are you all right?"

"I think not." Together they managed to extract her leg from the twisting fissure; once freed, Aeron fell sideways on the snowbank and Morwen eased off the thigh-high cross-gartered snowboot.

"Well," she said after a long anxious silence, "it is certainly not broken, Aeron. Can you walk on it?"

"Let us find out." She tugged the boot back on, stood up and took a few firm steps. "Not well, and not for long. It is the same leg was hurt at Rath na Ríogh."

"No matter," said Morwen, trying to conceal her dismay. "I remember from the maps there are farmsteadings not much farther down the dale. There we can get help." *If we dare*, she thought privately; but this fear she kept to herself.

They went on some while into the morning across Upper Darkdale. For the most part they plodded through the snowy wastes in silence, saving their strength and concentration, but after a while Aeron began to talk.

"Do you ever think of Rhodri, Wenna?" she asked with no preamble.

Morwen, if she had been less cold, would have been chilled to the heart by the strangely casual tone in which her friend had couched the question. Aeron never, never spoke of her dead lord; even to Morwen, Roderick's own sister, Aeron had not once spoken his name since his death. His brother Tarsuinn now bore Roderick's title of Prince of Scots, and it seemed that, to Aeron, none of it had ever been. Though Morwen could understand such a reaction, she herself had, once the first violence of her grief was past, desperately longed to speak of her dead brother to the others who had loved him. But she had been unexpectedly shut out: Aeron was locked away with her own grief and her new sovereignty and the guilt of having killed a planet for revenge; and Gwydion, the only other who shared the full measure of their loss, had likewise withdrawn into himself, going into a Druid monastery for silent retreat. And so Morwen had been forced to turn elsewhere for comfort. She had turned to Fergus, had married him six weeks later, in a whirlwind but undoubted lovematch. Still—

"Often, Aeron," she said at last. "Why do you ask?"

Aeron waved a hand. "No reason, truly. I was but thinking how matters might have fallen out had he been here . . ."

Alarm flared in Morwen's blue eyes at the offhand conversational mode. Was this uncharacteristic nonchalance, and unprecedented topic, the herald of the snow-sickness? Aeron had nearly died at Tomnahara, had been injured anew at the siege of the City, had lived under crippling stress for weeks. The delirium caused by high altitudes and low temperatures and snow-glare would strike her first, maybe, sooner than Morwen, who if in no better emotional state was at least something sounder.

"Look! A steading!" Morwen pointed down into the dale, all reluctance to approach strangers vanished in the face of this new peril. "Aeron, look—you can see the warm air rising from the hearths."

"I go no farther," said Aeron, in a voice as cold as the air around them, and sat upon a rock, closing her ears to Morwen's entreaties and seeming to drift off into some other reality.

Snow-sickness for sure . . . "Well, rest here then, and I will go for help," said Morwen doubtfully. "I'll not be long. Aeron? You *will* stay?" Receiving no answer, she backed away uncertainly, then hurried down the snowy fellside toward the valley bottom.

Coming round a projecting corner of rock, Morwen ran full-tilt into a tall man cloaked and hooded in sheepskin. She stared at him blankly, then he reached out to catch her arms as she swayed on her feet.

"Lassie, are you snow-mazed? How came you here? None has come up the dale past Tintock these ten days gone."

Morwen found her voice. "We—came over the Loom from the City."

"Ah, you flee the fighting, then. Is it that you need refuge? You look to want food and warmth and shelter, certainly, and for those you are welcome to our house."

"I thank you indeed, sir, but the—my sister is still up on the fell, she is too weary to walk any farther."

"Well then, we must fetch her down."

When they reached Aeron, she had fallen into a sort of dreamy doze, and she took no note of their presence. The man lifted her into his arms with no more effort than if she had been an exhausted lamb.

"This one is ill of the snow-sickness," he observed. "And that is not all."

Morwen scrambled alongside him as he strode easily through the drifts. "She fell and hurt her leg. I think it is only strained, but I am no healer or sensitive to tell for certain, and she has raxed that same leg before."

"Well, no great matter. Muscles can be eased, and snow-sickness is a thing that swiftly passes. My wife will care for her."

In a very short time they reached the ancient farmstead called Tintock—the House in the Mist. It was a graceful old manor, built of the gray-brown stone of the fells and set within a ring of tall pines. Within, all was snug and warm, with a delicious smell of cooking. Morwen received only a confused impression of greeting by the ban-a-tigh, who spoke her name as Ithell, before Aeron was whisked away into the culist, the traditional best chamber directly behind the enormous free-standing fireplace on the ground floor.

In the warmth of the house Aeron sensed the nearness of others and seemed to come out of her daze. She was half-lying on a soft, wide wall-bed in a room illuminated only by the firelight. Someone had stripped off her snow-sodden outer garments, wrapped her in a soft swanskin plaid to keep the chill away, and was now examining her leg with gentle pressure. She struggled to sit up.

"Nay, lass," came a quick thick country voice. "Lie still

now. You've raxed your leg sore, but it will mend quicker if you rest quiet. You are safe here, and your friend with you.''

"I put you all in peril," muttered Aeron. "I will go."

"You will not, then! We know all about it, and you will stay here until you are better fit to travel." An old woman's face came into the light; strong of bone and brow, with expressive dark eyes. "I am Ithell, and it was my man Brioc who helped you from the snow."

"Mistress Ithell, you do not understand—"

"We understand very well. You are Aeron the Queen, we knew you as soon as we saw you. The Marbh-draoi has his armies searching for you all over Tara, you and young Morwen. Both of you will be safe hid here for as long as you need."

Aeron felt tears burn behind her eyes. "I cannot thank you as is fit, mistress, for your kindness. But we shall go in the morning all the same."

"Well, I do not argue with my Ard-rían, but we'll leave that till morning, to see how your leg is then. And no need of thanks; are there not still sacred laws that rule such? As well you know, lassie—Lady, rather—no Kelt would turn away any who stood at the door in need, not if the stranger had the blood of his host's father upon his blade. That is the reality of our law, lass, and they do not change in time of testing."

"That indeed I know," said Aeron. "But perhaps I knew it less well than I thought . . ."

When Ithell had gone, vowing to prepare her guests a meal truly fit for queens, Aeron sat back thankfully, feet to the fire, and listened to the snow seething again on the windows. No trackers would be moving through these storms, even with a clear trail to follow; and the traces of passage she and Morwen had left would have been obliterated within minutes.

And that too was a strange thing, she thought with drowsy wonder. The storms that had saved them had come out of the Hollow Mountains, whence no storm came but that it was called—or sent. And no weather-worker, she knew, had summoned these. Maybe Rohan had been right. Maybe the Shining Ones did fight alongside.

In the morning Aeron's leg was much improved, and all trace of the snow-sickness gone; and, over the respectful objections of the folk of Tintock, she and Morwen resolved to continue their flight. Though no guest in Keltia need ever offer payment for hospitality—indeed, even to hint that a guest should feel obligation was an offense of criminal stature—it was nonetheless considered a serious lapse not to offer some token for courtesies rendered and received, and Aeron wished to do so now. Coin would be an unforgivable insult, even though the Ard-rían herself should give it, and in any case they would need all their store of gold to sustain them off-planet. All the same—

Aeron unhooked the smallsword from her belt and held it out to Ithell. It was not an heirloom of her House, but Aeron had carried it for years: a weapon of great age and beauty, with heavy silver fittings and blue stones inlaid in patterns, hilted with a single large sapphire.

"Take this and my thanks for the kindness you and your man have shown us. If ever you need a thing, bring it to my brother Rohan, or to Gwydion Prince of Dôn, and tell them how you came by it; they will know it, and will redeem it for a hundred times its value."

Ithell stared down at the glittering weapon, stammered, "Lady, I cannot accept it! This is too valuable by far! We did only what was right, lassie, and it was joy to do it. To leave you weaponless in your flight—"

Still Aeron held it out to her, smiling. "Take it, my friend. I shall not need it if I win through to *Retaliator*, and I shall need it still less if I kneel upon Jaun Akhera's scaffold."

Far away on Vannin, in the cloister of Glassary, O'Reilly took Desmond's hand.

"You won't forget I'm here?"

His dark eyes lighted as he looked down at her. "No fear of that. I go now to lead my squadron back to Erinna, and then I must go to Rohan as I have been bidden. But I shall see that you receive all news, and I will return as soon as I can. You will do very well here; the Reverend Abbess is foster-kin to Melangell's mother's family, and she will look after you." He kissed her fingers, surprising them both, and was gone in a swirl of brown cloak.

"Gods with you," said O'Reilly softly, and it was the first

time she had used the formal Keltic farewell, though he did not hear.

There was a rustle beside her, and she turned to see a tall woman standing a yard away, robed in the soft gray of a Ban-draoi nun. Her face was strong of feature and serene of mood, her eyes clear and of the same gray as her robes.

"I am Indec," she said, taking O'Reilly's hands between both of hers. "Abbess of this house. Prince Desmond has told me of you, Sorcha. You are welcome to us indeed; you will be safe here, and happy, and we will do what we can to make your time with us serve you best."

"How shall I call you?" murmured O'Reilly, suddenly shy, though at the same time feeling greatly comforted.

Indec laughed, and put her arm around the Terran girl's shoulders, drawing her into the cool dim cloister.

"Well, as makes you feel easiest: Indec, or Abbess; the Sisters call me Mother, but you, of course, need not do so."

"On the contrary," said O'Reilly slowly. "I think I should like to, very much."

The folk of Tintock had furnished them supplies enough to last a fortnight if necessary, and horses to ease the long road that still remained to Keverango, and it was these sturdy, rough-coated mountain ponies that Aeron and Morwen now rode down out of the Dales and, next morning, across the grassy expanse of the ten-mile-wide Pass of the Arrows, Bwlch-y-Saethau.

Both knew well that this was the most dangerous part of their long flight, for the Fianna had had certain information that a strong force of Imperials and Fomori had been dispatched that way to cut off just such an escape. And to cross the Bwlch in daylight was deliberately to court capture, but—

"There is no choice," said Morwen shortly. "We cannot afford to lose still another day. Who can tell what may be happening by now in the City? And the pursuit may be hotter than we know."

"Or there may be none."

"As you say, though I think that unlikely—Please, Aeron, let us ride on. We can speculate to your heart's content once we are safe up there." She pointed south to the high peaks of the Dragon's Spine, stretching away before them in the clear air.

They rode the first five miles through upland desolation; but then, because of the way the land lay in the Pass's southern reaches, they were forced to take to the only road, a narrow track winding through steep folds of the foothills.

Morwen was in a fret of apprehension. "We must go faster," she urged. "If we are caught here we are surely finished."

No sooner had she spoken than they heard voices ahead, echoing in the narrow combe, and an eddy in the wind carried to them the smell of cookfires.

"A camp," whispered Aeron, unnecessarily, and her companion nodded.

"Nowhere to hide or flee and time too short for magic. So we must do the other thing—" Morwen reached across and tugged off Aeron's hood, flung back her own as the camp came into view around a bend in the road. "They look to be Coranians by their uniforms, and perhaps less quick to recognize us than Fomori might be. Better it is that we ride past without guile, as if we were concealing naught. They may be more like to allow us to pass, so. Please gods," she added doubtfully.

Aeron raised her brows, then ran a hand under her collar and lifted out the unmistakable hair to cascade down the back of her cloak. If she was to be taken by her enemies, far rather it be so, without mask or concealment, not skulking in disguise like some runaway fudir . . .

As they came level with the camp, which was set back a length or two from the road, no one seemed to mark them, and Aeron dared to begin to hope that just perhaps they would be able to—

"Halt! You there!" A guard had risen from where he sat beside the road, and they saw that although he carried his blastgun loosely cradled in the crook of his arm, still it was aimed at them. Morwen reined in her horse; Aeron's, imitating, stopped of its own accord.

The soldier was big, and undoubtedly a Coranian.

"Well now," he said. "And just who might you two be?"

Morwen replied unhesitatingly, "I am Morwen Duchess of Lochcarron and this lady is Aeron the Queen."

The soldier roared with laughter. "Forgive a poor alien soldier for not having known you at once," he gasped. "I beg your royal indulgence—But may a common warrior ask Your Exalted Graces where you might be bound?"

"To our winter palace on the southern coast, where it is a good deal merrier than it is now back at Caerdroia." Morwen smiled winningly down at him. Now if only Aeron would match her mood . . .

But the soldier's attention had already shifted. "And you, flamehair? Or should I say Your Majesty. You too are for this southern palace?"

Aeron nodded, eyes wide and guileless. "Indeed so, sir."

"Truly," interposed Morwen, "my sister and I are merely returning to our home, a small farmstead in the foothills to the south." She pointed vaguely, not daring to chance meeting Aeron's eyes. "It is perhaps two days' ride from here. When the battle was on, we thought to be safer north of the Bwlch—the Pass—but now all that is over and things are settled, and we are going home."

The Coranian did not appear disposed to question this.

"Pity," he commented. "Could you not be persuaded at least to stop and share a cup of hot wine with us? We're not used to such fierce weather, and it's been boring here—such pleasant company would be welcome."

Morwen shook her head with a fine show of regret. "Another time, perhaps, good sir."

"Well, pass then, and go safely. And good luck to Your Highnesses on returning to your kingdom."

He laughed heartily again, but he stood back to let them by. Though their backs crawled, they rode on at a sedate trot until they had rounded a turn in the road and passed out of the combe.

"My thanks for that wish," muttered Aeron savagely, and spurred her horse to a gallop.

But the evil genius that rules chance meetings was surely upon them that day, for in the last valley before the safety of the true hills began they ran straight into a Fomori patrol.

By the grace of the gods they were at least slightly better prepared for this encounter, for during the forenoon they had come across the hastily abandoned camp of another Imperial troop. Five minutes' plundering had yielded them the cloaks and cowled tabards of two Imperial lieutenants, which they now wore over their own gear.

Morwen, riding ahead, gave the leader of the Fomori company a crisp salute. Women were not so usual in the Imperial or Fomori forces as in the Keltic armies, where they made half the numbers, but they were numerous enough so that Aeron and Morwen should arouse no suspicions; or, at least, so they hoped.

But this time the officer studied their faces with sharp attention, and, as his gaze rested longest upon her, Aeron felt ice begin to touch the back of her neck. The telltale hair was hidden under the uniform hood, but she was suddenly certain that he knew her.

He turned back to his men, spoke briefly in his own tongue. Aeron, who spoke the Fomorian Lakhaz as well as the Imperial Hastaic, understood him to be ordering his troop on ahead; and they cantered past incuriously, hardly sparing a glance for the two supposed Imperials. Then he looked straight at Aeron.

"Good faring to Your Majesty."

"You are much mistaken, sir," said Aeron evenly.

The captain laughed. "What, do I not know the Queen's grace well enough?" he asked. "I attended Elathan of Fomor in Jaun Akhera's embassy on the plain near Rath na Ríogh."

Deep silence. Aeron knew that Morwen, slightly behind her and to one side now, was fully prepared to obliterate the officer by whatever means was quickest and quietest; and, if necessary, the two of them along with him. She lifted her face now without thought of concealment, and she and the Fomori captain looked long into each other's eyes.

Then he smiled. "Go your ways, Aeron," he said, "for all of me. You proved yourself a noble enemy upon the plain of Moycathra, and I would prove to you—and to your illustrious First Minister—that Kelts are not the only folk capable of honor on the field of battle, or off it either."

Morwen stared incredulously, but Aeron's face did not change.

"Courtesy to the enemy has long been the tradition of the Fianna," she said. "But I had never thought to find it among the Fomori. How are you called, my lord?"

He drew himself up proudly in the saddle. "Captain Borvos, attached to the Royal Guard of His Grace the Prince—of His Majesty King Elathan. We are the last of our forces left on this world, and we ride now to our ship to make our own way home. We were on patrol in the region at the orders of Jaun Akhera himself, to block Pass of the Arrows lest any Keltic royalty attempt to flee this way, looking to escape off-planet."

Aeron laughed. "I am not surprised at his foresight. But you will, truly, allow us to go free and unpursued?"

"I have said so, Majesty. My men will not speak of the two Imperial officers we met on the road to the Dragon's Spine. Nay, I shall order it so, for you *are* on a secret errand, are you not?" His face was vivid with amusement.

"I would have chosen to meet you in happier time, Borvos of Fomor," said Aeron. She held out her hand to him, and he kissed it; then withdrawing it again she touched heel to her horse's flank. Morwen, still too astounded for speech, saluted him as he rode by. Before they had passed from sight, Borvos had turned his own horse's head again to the north, and ridden on to rejoin his troop.

Chapter Twenty-seven

Whether it was the drunken good wishing of the trooper, or the noble courtesy of Borvos, by some agency they were spared further encounters with anyone, either Kelt or invader, and by hard riding and snatching food and drink in the saddle they managed to gain the safety of the Dragon's Spine by sunset that day—the fourth since their flight began.

The cold held, though here, south of the Loom, little snow lay at present upon the ground. At the top of a saddle pass, a ballach, leading from the shoulder of one huge nameless purple mountain to another, Morwen pulled up her horse and swung about in the saddle to look behind her.

Swift concern crossed her face as she saw Aeron still far below her on the switchbacked trail. *I should not have pushed the pace so hard*, she thought with a pang of guilt, *she is so very weary* . . . She began to ride down again, but Aeron looking up waved her to stay where she was.

The long trek up the mountain had not troubled the tough hill ponies, but Aeron, who was still far weaker from the demands of the past few days than she had permitted anyone to see, was trembling with fatigue by the time she came up with Morwen in the mouth of the ballach.

"We will camp here," said Morwen quickly, and for once Aeron did not demur.

There was a little sheltered hollow just beyond the bend in the pass, and after they had tended their beasts they set up a small quartz-hearth and prepared a hot meal. After, Aeron leaned back against the grassy bank and stared up at the arching Criosanna. She had spoken no word for all that time.

"Why do you think he let us go?" burst out Morwen, unable to contain her curiosity any longer.

On the other side of the hearth, Aeron brought her hands out of her cloak and warmed them at the glowing crystal hearth.

"Well, for what he said, surely . . . that he wished us to know all honor was not dead among the folk of Fomor. Why else?"

"Oh, naught else, but I had heard—" Morwen broke off, and, amazingly, blushed. To cover her confusion, she began with great show of absorption to brew a flask of shakla.

"What had you heard?"

"Campfire tales, gossip, naught to pay heed to."

"Lochcarron—"

"There was some talk," said Morwen with immense reluctance, "that Elathan of Fomor did not share his father's antipathy toward you. That in fact he thought of you—rather otherwise."

There was a long silence, broken only by Aeron's pouring herself some of the freshly brewed shakla.

"I had heard that too," said Aeron then. "What a goleor of alien admirers—first Jaun Akhera, then Elathan." Her voice had taken on a sardonic bite. "Pity it is I am already pledged to Gwydion; otherwise I had had my choice of out-Wall thrones. So—you think that the admirable Captain Borvos allowed two royal fugitives, each with an enormous price on her head, to escape simply because it was gossiped that his new King might harbor feelings of affection toward one of them, and that one the sworn enemy of his people?"

"Well . . . I thought it not totally impossible."

"Put it out of your mind," said Aeron sharply, swinging her legs around and sitting up all in one fluid movement. "I had it from a captured Fomori lord that the first thing Elathan did upon learning that I had slain his father was to swear to avenge himself still further upon me—and mine."

"It makes little differ in the end, Aeron, so that he *did* let us escape. And we will not be able to make good that escape unless we move more quickly tomorrow. I know you are desperately tired, but it is still at least another day's ride to Keverango.''

"Let us see the maps.''

They spread out the maps, and by the light of the quartz-hearth bent over them in silent study. Arianeira had marked out a safe way for them, but not the shortest. Presently Aeron pointed to a finger of land along the coast.

"If we took that path across the headland, we could cut off hours. See how it bends round—''

"And runs close by that townland,'' said Morwen. "Great risk of being seen, and once seen, surely recognized. From all reports neither Imperial nor Fomori troops got so far south in any province. It would be only our own folk that we would encounter, and they would know us.''

"And since what time, Taoiseach of Keltia, do we fear our own folk? Did we fear to ask help at the door of Tintock?''

"Aeron, be reasonable. We have no way of knowing if we keep the loyalty of the people. As for Tintock, that was a calculated risk, and, aye, I did indeed fear to ask, and if you had not been ill of the snow-sickness I would not have asked at all . . . Besides, did not Arianeira send us this way? She herself admitted that Keverango was garrisoned by Imperials—how if it is but a trap? That when we finally come to Keverango we walk straight into the arms of Jaun Akhera?''

"Ah. We don't know, do we . . . And I for one choose to believe Ari. So, we shall go by the coast road.''

Morwen gave up. "As Your Majesty wishes.''

"Yes—my majesty.'' Grinning, Aeron pulled her cloak around her and huddled herself down beside Morwen to sleep.

Gwydion was stretched out on the bed, gazing up at the constellations, when the guards at the doors of the room snapped to flustered attention.

Jaun Akhera entered unattended, and an air of extreme irritation—tempered by curiosity, for these were Aeron's private rooms, and he had not seen them before—came with him. Gwydion made no move to rise.

"Where is the Great Seal, Gwydion?'' demanded Jaun Akhera with no prelude. "Aeron's finger was bare of it at the breaking of the Gate, and we have found no trace of it in the days since. If you know where she has concealed it, it would go best for you if you were to tell me."

"Nay, I can do better still. I shall show you." Gwydion rose lazily and headed toward the door that led out onto the turret walk, all under the dumbfounded stare of the Prince of Alphor. After a moment's nonplussed pause, Jaun Akhera nodded to the guards to let him by, and himself followed his hostage onto the battlements.

They had not far to go. Gwydion vanished up the curving stair that led to Aeron's chamber of magic, Jaun Akhera close behind him, and halted at the heavy bronze doors.

"The Seal is within," said Gwydion, and lifted the latch.

Jaun Akhera looked at him with sharp suspicion. Gwydion's manner was far too blandly casual, and mockery was plain in the gray eyes.

"As simple as that?"

Gwydion laughed. "You shall judge. Look."

He pushed the doors open, and Jaun Akhera peered past him into the round room beyond. The light from the lantern windows lay in thin jewel-colored strips across the slate floor, and there in the middle of the room, on the low bench between the four torches, the huge emerald of the Great Seal of Keltia caught the light and blazed like a green beacon.

Jaun Akhera stared hungrily at the prismed sparks spilling from the heart of the stone, then drew a deep breath and made as if to step forward into the chamber. But Gwydion's arm was flung suddenly in front of him, barring the way, and on the Prince of Dôn's face was a look of honest warning.

"Even you, Jaun Akhera, I should not wish to step through that door. Think you Aeron left the Seal all unguarded?"

Jaun Akhera favored him with a long measuring stare, then snapped his fingers. A soldier of his guard was up the stair in seconds.

"Lord?"

"Fetch me out that ring," said Jaun Akhera, and he never took his gaze from Gwydion's face. But Gwydion was silent, though his eyes were clouded now, dark as iron, and as hard.

Without a moment's hesitation, the soldier stepped beneath the carved lintel. At once he went rigid, as if frozen, or suddenly caught in amber, immobilized, and on his face a look of stricken terror. He did not have to endure it long: There was a blue flash, and the two men watching closed their eyes. When they looked again, the doorway was empty. Jaun Akhera stared in disbelief, then turned slowly to Gwydion.

The Prince of Dôn's face reflected a sort of implacable compassion, not for Jaun Akhera, and not a trace of remorse.

"Aeron guards her possessions well," he said. "She did not wish to take the Great Seal away with her, yet she feared to leave it with anyone she held dear. So she brought it here before the City fell, and it has lain here ever since, and will lie so until her return."

"That soldier—"

"—might well have been you. He was the victim of an advanced form of restraint field—combined with certain ranns. Be assured he felt no pain . . . but his death is on your head nonetheless."

"But—*how?*"

For answer Gwydion stepped through the doorway himself, and Jaun Akhera gasped in involuntary horror. But the field did not catch upon him, the light did not blast him. He went over to the bench, picked up the ring and tossed it in the air. It flashed green fire as it tumbled over and over in its descent; then he caught it again in his fist and set it down gently once more, and came back through the door to Jaun Akhera's side.

"As you see," said Gwydion. "Did I not tell you you might wish to keep me unharmed a while yet? Not very like that I should ever give over the Seal into your hands, but without me you have no way in all the hells of coming at it, and I think you will not throw away even a chance of that. Aeron keyed that door to three people besides herself, and I am the only one of those three that you have, or are likely to have, to hand. Anyone else attempting to pass into the chamber will meet the same fate as that poor bodach of a guard. And if you think to try reaching the Seal without entering the room, I assure you the consequences will be more unpleasant still. Even to you, Prince of Alphor: Your magic cannot break Aeron's in her own place of magic, and mine will not serve your purposes."

Jaun Akhera dragged his eyes away from the green gleam

of the emerald. Without that Seal, he had no access to any of
Keltia's documents or databanks or military records or treasuries or any other thing of import. But, just as plainly,
without Gwydion he had not even the smallest possibility of
access . . .

"Will it not?" he asked quietly. "At least, Prince of
Gwynedd, not yet."

He went back down the stairs, and Gwydion went with
him.

After a bare four hours' rest, Morwen's time sense roused
her, and she shook Aeron awake in turn. They saddled the
horses and were riding down the mountain's far side by
midnight.

As dawn broke they came to the coast. The rising sun flung
a cold gold glory across the waters, and like a flat blue shield
in the southeast the isle of Imaal rose up out of the morning
mists.

Here the mountains of the Dragon's Spine fell away sheer
into the waters of a vast, almost circular bay. Across the
south-facing curve of the cliff where they stood, a tiny track
clung, almost invisible among the tumbled scree and tough
stonevine.

Aeron pointed across the bay. "That is the way we must
go. Once by that headland, we can come down upon Keverango
from the north, and still remain unseen as we do so."

"Aye, but we can take the horses no further. The path is
too steep for them to cross, and any road I'd not abandon
them at Keverango to be ill-treated by Imperials. They will
find their way home well enough."

To that Aeron agreed at once. They dismounted, removing
the sheepskin saddles from the beasts that had served them so
well on the long hard flight. They made much of the animals,
with many affectionate pats and words of praise, and were
just removing the headstalls when Aeron suddenly froze. A
few seconds later, the horses shied violently, snorting with
terror and prancing nervously sideways. The sea beneath
them seemed to hush, and no birds sang. Morwen turned,
puzzled, to her friend.

"Aeron?"

Before the word was full-spoken she heard the answer: a long slow roar that sounded as if it came from the very depths of the earth. Which in truth it did: The mountain reeled beneath them. All around bounced small boulders and loose scree, shaken from the slopes by the earthquake that now billowed under the fugitives' feet. The horses screamed in fear, and, ripping free of the headstalls, bolted away back through the pass. At the first tremor, Aeron flung herself face down upon the breast of the mountain, pulling Morwen with her, and they lay unmoving until the first shock had passed.

"Is that it?" whispered Morwen in the huge shaking silence. "Is it over?"

"Not yet. Come quickly, we must cross the path before it falls away, or worse."

They grabbed what gear they could carry and half-ran, half-slipped along the track that led vertiginously out over the roiled waters of the bay. Another quake came, stronger; this time, trapped on the narrow path, they were helpless, and could only close their eyes against the likelihood that the mountain would pitch them from their precarious foothold into the sea.

At last that quake too ceased, and Aeron moved out cautiously along the talus-choked track. Her face showed that she expected worse to come, and Morwen plucked at her cloak.

"What is it?"

For answer Aeron pointed out to sea, and Morwen understood. Something had happened to the horizon, for she could no longer see it. A giant fold of the sea seemed to have been pinched upward, a smooth blue swelling that suddenly burst into white plumage on top. All the water in the bay beneath them trembled and fell away, sucked out by the approaching monster.

"The earthquake has troubled the ocean bed, and now the water will come, and quickly too."

It came almost quicker than she could speak of it. Again they flattened themselves against the rock face, thanking the gods that the part of the path where they chanced to be trapped was above the reach of the coming wave.

But only barely higher: One after another, glass-green and

colossal, the tremendous wave and its successors swept roaring by, only a few yards away.

"We cannot cross," said Morwen. She pointed; the path ahead wound upward to safety, but first it angled sharply out and down, disappearing regularly in the foaming skirtedge of the tidal waves as each moved majestically past.

"We must cross." Aeron flinched as another wave surged through the bay to crash in thunder on the far shore.

"Is there nothing you can do, Aeron?" begged Morwen. "Neither of us can endure very much more of this . . ." Her voice shook as she spoke and her face was wet with the spray that came hissing off the waves.

Aeron did not reply straightaway to her friend's plea. She possessed, by both art and nature, a strange inborn affinity with the forces that shaped the lands and moved in the waters, a more than animal instinct that had enabled her to sense the coming quake even before the horses. But that same sensitivity worked to her detriment once the event was at hand, and now she was deathly sick with her own reaction to the earth's torment. She barely heard Morwen's voice imploring her to action. But, far from subsiding, the waves were only growing huger; perhaps, out to sea, the earth tremors had not ceased. And her nerves were as ragged as Morwen's, not with the earth-sickness alone, but with a race-memory preserved thirteen thousand years from the drowning of doomed Atland; the inherited terror of the great waves that had taken all but a few of her people . . .

But Morwen was right. They could ill bear more of this, and they must pass.

Aeron unclenched her fingers where they had dug into the face of the cliff, and stepped out onto the path. It was streaming with cold salt water, and out to sea another set of waves was forming. She lifted her arms in front of her and spoke a short rann.

Morwen watched in real awe as the water fell away; the waves seemed to hang back, and the path to safety lay clear and temporarily dry before them.

"Hurry, Wenna," gasped Aeron. "The rann will not keep the water back for long."

Morwen needed no second telling. But Aeron was nearly

spent— She caught her under the arms and dragged her along the cliff-path, to where a tunnel had been cut through an outcrop of stone to the other, inland side.

They were barely in time. Angry, perhaps, at having been balked, the wave now approaching was twice the size of the biggest that had yet struck. It would cover the path completely as it passed. In a panic Morwen pushed Aeron ahead of her into the tunnel mouth, leaped in after her, and by main force threw both of them as far down the passage as she could.

They felt rather than saw the wave pass, for its might shook the mountain to the roots, and its passing tore the air from the tunnel for a moment. A moment only, then it was gone; the vacuum broke, and the air rushed back as a torrent of cold seawater and broken stone surged into the tunnel. It reached to their knees, and the force of it knocked them off their feet. For a moment they floundered splashing in it; then it drained away, and Morwen scrambled unsteadily to her feet.

"Aeron!"

"Over here." Aeron pushed herself upright against the wall of the tunnel, and gave her friend a tired smile. "I hope the horses got away."

"They'll come safe home, Aeron. You will see."

"Please gods, I shall."

After a brief rest and a quick meal, they used hand-crystals to dry out their packs and clothing, and then started on the last leg of their long flight. Toward noon they lay hidden on the slopes of the mountain that towered over Keverango on the north.

"We should stay here until it is full dark," said Morwen. "And you need some rest. Go to sleep, and I will watch a while."

Aeron was too tired to argue; Morwen made her as comfortable as she could, then settled down herself to her vigil. Clouds began to roll in from the south; at least they would help to make the night as dark as possible, though they would also, very like, make the hours till then damp and chill . . .

As the skies darkened to evening, Aeron woke, much refreshed, to a hand on her shoulder.

"Is it time? You should have roused me earlier, you are as weary as I."

"Not quite—but look below." Down in the cleft of the glen, lights were coming on in the buildings of the spacebase. They gathered up all their gear, to leave no trace that they had been there, and began to move carefully down the mountain.

Three hours later they lay concealed among boulders and high ferns on the edge of the base. Keverango was small as such ports went, tucked away among shielding mountains and open on one side to the sea. Built in the reign of Aeron's great-grandfather to the fifth Brendan XXVIII, it had been maintained ever since as a center of clandestine operations. But its chief purpose, now as then, was to serve as a possible escape hatch in the face of such calamity as had now befallen Brendan's descendant.

But neither Aeron nor Morwen thought much on this, as they lay hidden in the scrub. Presently Morwen nudged her friend, and jerked her chin silently toward the base.

As Arianeira had said, Keverango was indeed garrisoned by Imperial troops, though, again as Ari had said, not many, and not heavily armed. At the moment, all the personnel in sight appeared to be going into the main hall, no doubt for the nightmeal. Only four guards could be seen, all of them at some distance from Aeron's ship *Retaliator*, which stood alone in an apparently disused area of the main field.

"That at least is well," said Aeron. "And the ship looks spaceworthy enough—but how are we to reach it? It must be half a lai away, and there is no cover."

Morwen studied the bracken in front of her nose. "I thought perhaps you could—do something again?"

Oh gods, not more magic . . . "If I had the time and strength for such a spell as that which we need here, I had done it long since, Wenna," she said gently. "And we'd not have had to fret ourselves with that trooper or with Borvos . . . The rann for quieting the water is a cantrip by comparison to a rann of control."

Aeron rested her chin on the boulder she leaned against. There was one thing she might try: the fith-fath, the shapeshifting spell. It was not especially difficult, but something tricky of sustaining, and exhausting in the end if it had to be long maintained. Still, it would be for but a few minutes and a short distance, and she would have to cast the illusion only for those few guards—not so taxing as if the entire garrison should be watching. And she could rest after . . .

"Aye, then," she said. "Gather our things, and be ready to run when I say." She raised her fingertips to her temples and closed her eyes. Strength suddenly flooded into her from some unknown source; she swayed with the unexpected force of it, and Morwen watched her closely. "Now."

Even as they ran, Morwen looked down at herself, then over at her friend.

"We are unchanged, Aeron."

"Only to our own eyes. It is less strainful so. But to any who see us, we appear as wolves."

Wolves . . . "Was that your best choice?"

"It was my easiest. Now be silent. It is not a true fith-fath, but glamourie only, and I have not changed our voices."

As it turned out, only one guard saw them pass; and he saw not two fleet gray forms, but three, the third a huge brindled male, twice as big as the others . . .

They ducked around the side of the ship away from the rest of the base, panting a little from the long run. Moving forward along the line of the hull, Aeron set her bare palm to a silver plate waist-high in the seamless black metal. Doors slid aside where no doors had been before, and they tumbled through into the ship.

Once within, Morwen helped Aeron to a blastcouch, then ran forward to the cockpit. Lying in white exhaustion upon the couch, her strength all but gone, Aeron felt from what seemed a million miles away the motion of *Retaliator* rising beneath her; then that was replaced by the motionless illusion that was true flight, as Morwen threw in all power to get them out of the planet's pull. They flashed beneath the Criosanna and were away.

Epilogue

And now all the threads that the gods had spun were strung upon the frame of the loom, all their color and gleam and complexity planned into the pattern, the weaving begun in true earnest . . .

On the mist-mantled planet of Vannin, O'Reilly walked in the cloisters of Glassary, looking out across the shining sea-loch toward blue hills. Around her, the gray-clad Sisters of the Ban-draoi moved and worked and prayed, with no more noise or fuss than one of their planet's mists.

There was more than a touch of envy in the look O'Reilly bent upon them. Though utterly elsewhere, they seemed so—*here*, so all of a piece, while she herself was sadly scattered. Part of her was here, and part on its way to Earth with those who sailed the *Sword*, and part at Caerdroia with Gwydion and the ghost of Haruko, and part—a rather larger part than she was at present prepared to admit—was with Desmond on his way to the *Firedrake*. But the largest part, the central part, the part most to the forefront of both her conscious and unconscious minds, was with Aeron. And O'Reilly didn't even know where that might be . . .

And at Caerdroia, Jaun Akhera looked out at the winter rain that had been falling steadily upon the City since midday. *Was the weather here never any better than this*, he wondered, vexed. He had never been so damp and so cold in his

395

life, he was chilled to the bone. Why couldn't the Kelts have built their capital somewhere warm and dry and sunny? But no, that was undoubtedly not perverse enough for them.

He had been in an evil temper all day, ever since Gwydion had shown him where the Great Seal of Keltia had been hidden. Hidden! He laughed bitterly. He could see it, plain as salt, any time he wanted . . . and he could come no closer to it than if it had been on the other side of the universe.

Still, all was not black. He held the City, and all within it, and most particularly Gwydion Prince of Dôn; and while he did so no Kelt would lift a hand against him.

Not even Aeron, presumably. But what *about* Aeron? His soldiers had scoured the lands in all directions around Caerdroia, and found no trace of her. He shrugged impatiently: If she had died in the escape attempt, and Morwen Douglas with her, so much the better. If not, no doubt but that he would know of it in very good time; she would raise a stour that would be heard from one end of the galaxy to the other.

His thought veered to his grandfather. He must get a message out to him, somehow, as soon as he could; a carefully worded message, of course, since as yet he had not succeeded in all that he had so rashly promised.

For a moment, the thought of Alphor overwhelmed him with longing: Escal-dun, his home, and Tinao—the way she had been when last he had seen her, all smooth honey skin glowing through white silk, her hair tumbled about her.

Jaun Akhera pressed interlaced fingers to the back of his neck, banishing the tension that knotted the muscles of his shoulders. They were waiting on him for the nightmeal, Sancho and Hanno and the others, and finally he headed reluctantly toward the small banqueting hall he had taken over for his own use.

But a small corner of his mind remained on Alphor—and on his grandfather. The Cabiri Emperor had his own ways of gathering information, even when—especially when—the information was not over-eager for itself to be gathered . . .

And on the Imperial planet of Alphor, in his garden city of Escal-dun, the Cabiri Emperor lay upon his golden longchair, feeding the carp that lived in the lilied pool. Strephon's eyes were half-closed, and at first any who watched would have said that he slept.

But then suddenly his hand would move, a flick quick as a fish's tail, and the golden carp would rise goggling to the surface, their fat glistening bodies crowding each other aside in their haste to mouth the bits of soft bread.

And sometimes his hand would flick, and there would be no bread at all falling from his fingers, but the fish would contend for the nonexistent morsels just the same.

For you never know, thought Strephon lazily, and his eyes gleamed like opals under the hooded parchment lids. *It might be there, and then again it might not. You have to try regardless, because fish or princeling, you just never know . . .*

And again at Escal-dun, in another part of the sprawling white palace, deep behind the aurichalcum walls, where pierced grillwork windows cast lacy shadows upon mosaic floors, Tinao wrapped herself in a big-sleeved robe of stiff yellow silk and sat down before the computer. Her gold-tipped fingers thrummed expertly over the touchboard, and presently data began to flow across the viewscreens, beneath the hologram portrait of a red-haired, green-eyed queen . . .

And on Fomor, in the royal city of Tory, the crown of his ancestors was set upon Elathan's head. He looked out over the heads of the cheering crowds in the huge square before the palace, then smiled as Camissa, first of all his subjects, came forward to do reverence to her newly crowned King and future husband. Her eyes cast demurely down, her dark head bowed beneath a diamond coronet, she gave him a deep, billowing curtsy, then took her place upon a gold chair set slightly below and to the left of his jewel-encrusted throne, for they were not yet wedded, and she could not yet share honors as his queen.

And Elathan's mother came forward, the Dowager Queen Basilea, her face full of loving maternal pride, her curtsy straight-backed and regal. And his sister the Princess Rauni, tall, coltish, honey-haired, who winked at him as she rose from her obeisance.

And Talorcan came forward, splendidly attired in crimson velvet slashed with gold, and knelt before his half-brother, placing his hands between Elathan's own in the age-old ritual of fealty. He took the oath in a clear carrying voice, and the face he turned up to his monarch's kiss of peace was correct and cold. Only the eyes were alive, and in time to come Elathan would have cause to remember the expression those eyes had held; although he had not believed it at the time, and so swiftly was it gone that he could not say it had truly been there.

But it had been there. In Talorcan's eyes, as in his heart, was nothing but purest hatred . . .

And on the bridge of the *Firedrake*, Rohan stood leaning against the curve of the viewport, his hands hugging his arms and his gaze turned out upon the stars. Desmond stood behind him; the new High Admiral, Caradoc Llassar, had tactfully withdrawn, leaving the cousins alone to speak with each other.

"Then they are gone," said Rohan. "No one knows where?"

Desmond shook his head. "It was better so, Gwydion said; in case one of us should be captured, and the Coranian should decide to try to coax the information from our minds."

"Ah gods, Gwydion . . . Of us all, he has put his hand deepest into the lion's mouth—" For an anguished instant Rohan's despair broke through his control; then the mask, so like his sister's, shut down again over it.

"Truly, Rohan, Gwydion knows very well what he does," offered Desmond, himself feeling as helpless as his cousin. "He it is will be master of Caerdroia in the end, and Aeron with him. You shall see. I have no fears for him."

"You were ever a poor liar, Elharn's son," said Rohan, and the face he turned to Desmond was haunted and haggard. "Nay, cousin," he said in a low voice, turning again to his contemplation of the stars, "I have naught *but* fears—for any of us . . ."

And alone again in the round room overlooking the sea, Gwydion paced restlessly around the chamber, trying to restore his shattered peace. He had not permitted servitors in since the night of Aeron's flight, and the guards who kept constant watch on him went in too much fear of him, and of the room's absent owner, to dare meddle with anything. Untidy evidences of Aeron's recent occupation were therefore everywhere: a blue leather boot lying under the chair where she had kicked it; a book face-down on the window seat as she had left it; a gold and ruby torc tilting out of a carved casket on the table beside the bed.

Gwydion found the clutter comforting, as if any time now Aeron would be back in the room, to read the book or pull on the boots or fit the torc around her neck. He tipped the necklace inside the casket and closed the lid, catching as he touched the rubies a brief clear picture of the last time Aeron had worn the torc. It was night, and she was laughing up at him . . .

He smiled at the memory, then laughed in good earnest at another memory: Jaun Akhera's frustration of earlier that day. She had been so clever, his Aeronwy. No one, not even he, had noticed that the Great Seal was no longer on her hand, not until that moment at the Gate when Jaun Akhera had looked for it and it was not there to be found. No, folk had seen what she had wished them to see, and she had left Keltia in his hands—that was the message of the Seal.

Reaching inside his tunic, Gwydion closed his hand over the Dragon medallion that hung on a leather cord against his chest; Aeron's it was, as she wore his. The little silver disks were telepathically keyed each to their owners, and they were not lightly exchanged, for they could be used to speak or to summon, even to compel. But though Gwydion now sent all his considerable strength out to its conscious limits, he could not reach her anywhere, and he knew that she must be truly gone from Keltia.

There were, of course, other possibilities . . . If she were dead, though, he would know it. No matter the distance, he would feel her going. But no Gwynedd gwrach had been heard on the wind, the royal banshee had not keened, and the Faol-mór, the great wolf that was the fetch of the Aoibhells, had not appeared on Mount Eagle to howl the lament. Gwydion would not need such telling, even so, to know—and if she had been captured, the Imperials would have trumpeted the news to the stars. Nay, she was still alive, still free. But far from him now, very far.

The stars' wandering between us . . . Suddenly desolate, he caught up the old brown gúna from a chair and buried his face in it. Immediately she was there: Her faint sea-rose fragrance still clung to the cloth, and caught in the hood's silver clasp were a few long strands of golden-red hair.

"Oh gods, Aeron," he said aloud, and the wolfhounds looked up sharply at the sound of the familiar name. "What else was I to do? You could not stay, and I could not go with you . . ."

The rain that drenched Caerdroia that night fell, small and fine and softly wetting, on the circle of Ni-Maen, up in its little valley between the peaks of Eagle, the huge blue-gray trilithons gleaming wet and black in the rainy dark.

And the rain fell on the packed earth of a barrow so new it had not yet even been turfed over, a dolmen at its foot, the carving upon the stone knife-bright and sharp from the hand of the graver. Within, Theo Haruko, FSN, slept as peacefully as the royal dead who lay in their own beds beside him.

And the rain fell into the dry bracken more than fifty long leagues to the east, where cairns marked the ashes of the honored fallen below the walls of Rath na Ríogh, where neither cairn nor honor graced the grave of Hugh Tindal, unmarked and already forgotten, buried begrudgingly, with less ceremony than a dead beast.

And the rain fell over the leaves of the little wood up behind Turusachan, dripping soundlessly onto the pine-needle carpet of the forest floor that lay, thick and green and velvety, over the grave of Arianeira, a princess of Gwynedd . . .

And in the enormous vault of space, where no rain had fallen since the Beginning nor would even after the End, Aeron stirred upon her couch. She heard through a sleepy dimness Morwen speaking over the transcom in Thari, the secret Fianna battle-language, but her mind refused to decode the words. She started to sit up, but encountered a rigid invisible barrier, and a wave of panic hit her.

"Wenna—"

Morwen was beside her at once. "I am sorry, Aeron. I thought you slept."

"I cannot move—"

"Oh, that is but a restraint field, to keep you still awhile." She switched off the field, and Aeron struggled gratefully up onto one elbow. They had changed into flightsuits upon coming aboard, and the suits were not the most comfortable of sleeping garments.

"I heard you speaking just now?"

"A coded message to the *Firedrake*, to let Rohan know we are safe away. I used bardic codes; the Imperials will never be able to break it. Also I have altered our trajectory several times, so we cannot be traced; nor answered, for that matter." She paused. "I have been checking the ship's stores. There is gold enough to last us for many months, and food, and both Imperial and Fomori dress. Ari provided well for us."

But Aeron let it pass. "Where are we now?"

"Just heading past Droma."

"Droma!" That was several orbits outward from Tara. "How long did I sleep?"

"No time at all. You forget how fast this ship is, even in space-normal."

"Can you handle her?" asked Aeron presently, a bit jealous.

"Easily. Except that—Aeron, I could not go into hyperspace, because I do not know where we are going."

"Not hard." She pushed herself up on the pillows, tucking her feet beneath her in her usual posture, and smiled at her friend's bewilderment. "Well, though I say it as never thought to, we are going for help. We are going to find Arthur."

For a moment Morwen watched her expectantly, waiting for more, or for clarification. Then—

"Arthur! Arthur the *King*? But he has been dead these fifteen hundred years!"

"Well, so we must assume . . . But if he himself is dead, Morwen, his ship *Prydwen* may not be. And he took things with him on that last sailing may save Keltia for us now—if only we can find them."

Morwen frowned, obscurely troubled. She had heard, of course, as no Kelt had not, of *Prydwen* and the lost Treasures: magical things, sacred things, things that ought not to be used for vengeful purposes . . .

"Do you know, then, where the ship may lie?"

"Let us say I have a good idea of where to begin to seek it."

"You do? You do," amended Morwen thoughtfully, studying her Queen's smiling face. "What will you do with the Treasures, if we find them?" Her voice came slow and doubtful, and Aeron answered the reason for the doubt.

"It is not like Bellator, Wenna, not this time . . . I will use them to save Keltia. I will use them to win back my crown." Aeron's smile had turned wintry. "I will use them to make myself Empress."

"But in Council you said you had no wish to be Empress!"

"And no more do I now. But even more than I wish not to be Empress, do I wish Jaun Akhera not to be Emperor. And if I must seize some form of Imperial sovereignty—even his—to stop him, be very sure I will."

Morwen fiddled with her betrothal ring, as she did when upset, and did not look up. "And after that?"

"After that—I do not yet know. But I will know . . ."

They spoke no more for a little while, as *Retaliator* raced through the fringes of the Throneworld system and headed out into empty space, on its way toward the Curtain Wall and the world beyond that was not Keltia.

"How did you learn where we must search for *Prydwen*?" asked Morwen at last.

"I was told, and we are sent."

"Who sends us?"

"The Shining Ones."

"Who told you?"

"Gwyn ap Neith."

"What shall we use for maps?"

"Taliesin ap Gwyddno, greatest of bards, shall be our guide. In his histories of Arthur—there is a poem—but I shall show you all presently. We must sail in strange places, Wenna, if I am right in my reading. To, and through, the Morimaruse; to the planet Fomor, very like—"

"Fomor!"

"And even to Kholco," continued Aeron. In spite of her cares, her face sparkled with anticipation. "Where only the Salamandri, the Firefolk, do live; the oceans boil there, it is said, and the lands sail upon seas of liquid stone. And before we are done, we may well come to Earth herself . . . Oh, Wenna, to see Earth! Where we came from, and where Brendan was born, and Theo—''

She fell abruptly silent, and Morwen, sensing her wish, left her to her thoughts and went back to the cockpit.

Alone again in the little cabin, Aeron thrust her hand inside her flightsuit to touch the silver medallion that lay on its silk cord between her breasts. It was too far a stretch even for her, she could not reach him—but she could conjure him, not the austere prince nor the deft politician nor the consummate warrior, but the real Gwydion that she loved . . .

"Oh, beloved," she said aloud, "And so I will take my own other hand, to touch this life once more . . ."

So now across the hollow dark three ships did move; they went with purpose and celerity, and they went each alone.

Not so swift nor so elegant as *Retaliator*, nor yet so deadly, the *Sword* continued on her way to Earth. In their coldsleep bunks, Straloch and Fionnuala, Morgan and Emrys, all slept in the same bright dream-filled peace as Mikhailova and Hathaway, and around them the *Sword* sailed herself home without fuss . . .

And far across the long lazy arc of the galactic spiral arm, another ship, bigger and faster and altogether more impressive, was preparing to leave its home system. Upon its hull it bore galactic ensigns of embassy, and it carried a hundred people, all of them very much awake. The Earth ambassador's vessel, for such it was, had departed the Terran starharbor some four local days ago, and now it was sweeping past the dark ringed giants that graced Sol system's outer orbits. Soon it would swing its bows to Keltia, and go into the hyperdrive that would bring it there in a thousand hours . . .

And in *Retaliator*, Aeron had taken the helm. They were nearing the Curtain Wall now, the familiar blue werelight of the energy barrier showing clear on *Retaliator*'s screens. It shimmered and flared around the ship for an instant, and then they were through.

Aeron put her ship's nose to the distant Morimaruse, then stared at the screen that showed Keltia receding rapidly astern.

" 'Sé do bheatha," said Aeron to Keltia as it fell away behind her. Then she lifted her eyes to the viewports ahead and sent *Retaliator* into hyperdrive.

The stars became a blazing lattice of smudged light, set with milky jewels at the interstices, and the heavens rolled tremendously into new patterns around them: the same constellations seen by Brendan, and by Arthur. And now Aeron too had taken them for guide, bound as she was to seek help from the past—and from the unknown.

(Here ends *The Copper Crown*, a book of THE KELTIAD. The sequel is called *The Throne of Scone*.)

Appendices

History of the Tuatha De Danaan and the Keltoi

The Tuatha De Danaan, the People of the Goddess Dâna, arrived on Earth, as refugees from a distant star system whose sun had gone nova. They established great city-realms at Atlantis, Lemuria, Nazca, Machu Picchu, and other centers of energy. It was an age of high technology and pure magic: lasers, powered flight in space and in atmosphere, telepathy, telekinesis and the like. There was some minimal contact with the primitive Terran native inhabitants, who, awed, regarded the lordly Danaans as gods from the stars.

After many centuries of peace and growth, social and spiritual deterioration set in: faction fights, perversion of high magical techniques, civil war. The Danaan loyalists withdrew to the strongholds of Atlantis, or Atland as they called it, there to fight their last desperate battle with those of their own people who had turned to dark ways. Atlantis was finally destroyed, in a fierce and terrible battle fought partially from space, and which resulted in a huge earthquake and subsequent geologic upheaval that sank the entire island-continent. (The battle and sinking of Atlantis were preserved in folk-myth around the world; obviously the effect on the Earth primitives was considerable.)

The evil Atlanteans, the Telchines, headed off back into space: their descendants would later be heard of as the Coranians. The Danaan survivors made their way as best they could over the terrible seas to the nearest land—Ireland—and to the other Keltic sea-countries on the edge of the European land mass. There had long been Atlantean outposts in these lands, and they made a likely refuge.

But the refugees had yet another battle to fight: with the Fir Bolg and the Fomori, the native tribes currently in occupation of Ireland. Atlantean technology carried the day, however, and the Danaans settled down to rebuild their all-but-lost civilization.

After a long Golden Age, the Danaan peace was shattered by invasion: the Milesians, Kelts from the European mainland. War exploded; the new race was clever, brave, persuasive and quarrelsome. The Danaans, at first victorious in defense, were at last defeated by the strategies of the brilliant Druid Amergin. They conceded possession of Ireland to the sons of Miledh, and obtained sureties of peace.

The peace and amity between Danaans and Milesians lasted many hundreds of years; there was much intermarriage, informational exchange, joint explorative and military expeditions against raiding Fomori and Fir Bolg. Then a period of Milesian distrust turned to outright persecution, and the Danaans began to withdraw to live strictly isolated, although even then there continued to be marriages and friendships and associations. With the coming of Patrick to Ireland, bringing Christianity, the persecutions resumed with redoubled intensity, as Patrick and his monks called upon all to denounce the Danaans as witches and evil sorcerers.

Brendan, a nobleman of the House of Erevan son of Miledh, was also half-Danaan by birth—and more than half one in spirit. His mother was Nia, a Danaan princess, and he had been taught by her in the old ways. He rebelled against the persecutions, the narrow-mindedness and prejudice and condemnation of all the high old knowledge, and he resolved to relearn all the ancient lore, to build ships and take the Danaans back out to the stars, to find a new world where they could live as they pleased. All who felt as Brendan did might go, and did: Druids, priestesses of the Mother, worshippers of the Old Gods and followers of the Old Ways, all now so ruthlessly put down by the Christians.

After much study, instruction, construction and a few short trial runs, Brendan was ready at last, and the Great Emigration began. Following the directions of Barinthus, an old man who was probably the last space voyager left on Earth, Brendan and his followers left the planet. After a two-year search, they discovered a habitable star system a thousand light-years from Terra. He named it New Keltia; eventually Keltia, as it came to be known, would command seven planetary systems and a very sizable sphere of influence.

The emigrations continued in secret over a period of some eight hundred years, with Kelts from every Keltic nation participating in the adventure, and not human Kelts alone; the races known as the merrows and the silkies also joined the migrations.

After the first great voyage, or immram, Brendan himself remained in the new worlds, organizing a government, ordering the continuing immigrations, setting up all the machinery needed to run the society he had dreamed of founding: a society of total equality of gender, age, nationality and religion. He personally established the Order of Druids in New Keltia; his mother, Nia, who left Earth with him, founded the Ban-draoi, an order of priestess-sorceresses.

Brendan, who would come to be venerated by succeeding generations as St. Brendan the Astrogator, became the first monarch of Keltia, and his line continues to rule there even now.

By about Terran year 1200, the Keltic population had increased so dramatically (from both a rising birth rate and continued waves of immigration from Earth) that further planetary colonization was needed. The Six Nations were founded, based on the six Keltic nations of Earth: Ireland, Scotland, Wales, Man, Cornwall and Brittany, called in Keltia Erinna, Scota, Kymry, Vannin, Kernow and Brytaned. A ruling council of six viceroys, one from each system, was set up, called the Fáinne—"The Ring." The monarchy continued, though the Fáinne had the ultimate sovereign power at this time.

This was the Golden Age of Keltia. The mass emigrations ended at around Terran year 1350, and the dream of Brendan seemed achieved. There was complete equality, as he had intended; a strong central government and representative local governments; the beginnings of a peerage democracy; great advances in magic, science and art.

It could not last, of course. By Terran year 1700, increasingly vocal separatist movements sprang up in each nation, and, a hundred years later, the Archdruid of the time, Edeyrn, saw in the unrest the chance to further his own power, and the power of the Druid Order. A fiercely ambitious and unquestionably brilliant man, Edeyrn succeeded in engineering the discrediting and ultimate dissolution of the Fáinne, in forcing the monarchy into hiding, and in installing those Druids loyal to him as magical dictators on all levels. Civil war broke out all over Keltia, and the realm was polarized by the conflict.

This was the Druid Theocracy and Interregnum, which was to endure for nearly two hundred unhappy years. Edeyrn and his Druids were joined by many politically ambitious and discontented noble houses, who saw in the upheaval a chance for their own advancement.

There was of course a fierce and equally powerful resistance, as many Druids remained loyal to the truths of their order, and joined forces with the Ban-draoi, the magical order of priestesses, the Fianna, the Bardic Association and some of the oldest and noblest Keltic families.

This resistance was called the Counterinsurgency, and it opposed Edeyrn and his Druids with strength, resource and cleverness for two centuries. Consistently outwitting the aims of the Theocracy, the loyalists managed to preserve the fabric of true Keltic society. Through the efforts of the Bardic Association, they also succeeded in salvaging most of the important lore, science, art and records of the centuries of Keltia's settlement, and the records from Earth before that.

The terrors of the Theocracy raged on for two hundred years, with the balance continually shifting between Theocracy and Counterinsurgency. The general population was sorely torn, but most did in fact support the loyalists, in their hearts if not in their outward actions. Then full-scale alien invasion, by the races called by the Kelts Fomori and Fir Bolg after their old Earth enemies, hit Keltia, causing enormous destruction and loss of life. But even in the face of this appalling new threat, Edeyrn continued to dominate, and some even said he was responsible for the invasions. Though he himself was by now ancient beyond all right expectation, his adopted heir Owain served as his sword-arm, and Owain was as twisted as ever Edeyrn was.

Though their most immediately pressing need was to repel the Fomori and Fir Bolg invaders, the Kelts had first to break free of the grip of the Theocracy; and in the midst of that chaos, a mighty figure began to emerge.

Arthur of Arvon, a minor lordling of a hitherto minor noble house of the Kymry, rallied boldly the forces of the Counterinsurgency. Arthur proved to be an inspired leader, and, more importantly, a military genius, and he quickly smashed Owain's Druids in the Battle of Moytura. The Theocracy, its military power broken, caved in, and Arthur was named Rex Bellorum, War-Chief, by the hastily reconstituted Fáinne and the newly restored monarch Uthyr. Arthur then led the Keltic forces out against the invaders; the aliens were not prepared for such a concerted counterattack, and Arthur succeeded in utterly crushing the invasion.

But King Uthyr had died in battle. Arthur married the royal heir, Gweniver, and with her assumed the sovereignty of Keltia by acclamation. The wars behind him, at least for the present, Arthur turned his genius to political and social reform, establishing elective bodies of legislators, the Royal Senate and Assembly, restoring the House of Peers, formulating a new judicial system on the remains of the old brehon laws, and laying the groundwork for a standing battle force. He commanded a purge of the Druid Order, setting his closest advisor and old teacher, Merlynn Llwyd, to undertake the task, and he gave new power and prestige to the loyal orders of the Ban-draoi, the Fianna and Bardic Association.

* * *

Arthur and Gweniver reigned brilliantly and successfully for nearly fifty years, and had two children, Arawn and Arwenna. Then, in Terran year 2047, he was betrayed by his own nephew, Mordryth, and the infamous Owain's heir, Malgan. Their treachery let in the invading Coranians, descendants of the Telchines, who had evolved into a race of sorcerous marauders whose savagery made the Fomori and Fir Bolg look like sheep. This was Arthur's first chance to test his reforms, and he was well aware that it might be his last also. He dealt with Mordryth and Malgan, then led a space armada against the Coranians, with devastating success. Tragically, he disappeared in the climactic battle, sending his flagship *Prydwen* against the Coranian flagship and taking both vessels and all aboard them into hyperspace forever. His last message to his people was that he would come again, when he was needed.

In the absence of proof positive of Arthur's death, he is still King of Kelts, and all succeeding monarchs have held their sovereignty by his courtesy and have made their laws in his name . . . for who knows when Arthur the King might not return?

The monarchy, after Arthur's disappearance, became a Regency, the only one in Keltic history. Arthur's sister Morgan, his wife Gweniver, and his mother Ygrawn ruled jointly, until such time as Prince Arawn should be old enough to take the crown.

All three women were strong characters, skilled in magic, but Arthur's sister Morgan, called Morgan Magistra, was the greatest magician Keltia would ever see.

After taking counsel with the the Ban-draoi, Merlynn's newly rehabilitated Druids, the Fianna and the Bardic Association, and with her own co-Regents, Morgan undertook the immense achievement of the raising of the Curtain Wall. There was no other feat like it, even back to the days of the High Atlanteans.

The Curtain Wall is a gigantic force-field, electromagnetic in nature and maintained by psionic energies; it completely surrounds and conceals Keltic space, hiding suns, planets, satellites, energy waves, everything. Once outside its perimeters, it is as if Keltia does not exist. Space is not physically blocked off, and radio waves and the like are bent round the Wall, but any ship attempting to cross the region is shunted into certain corridors of electromagnetic flux that feed into the Morimaruse, the Dead Sea of space, and now no one goes that way, ever.

So the Keltic worlds and their peoples became a half-legend of the galaxy, a star-myth to be told to children or to anthropologists. But behind the Curtain Wall, the Regency carried on Arthur's work, and when in time Arawn became King, he proved almost as gifted as his parents. The dynasty he founded was followed in peaceful succession by the closely related royal house of Gwynedd, and that by the royal house of Douglas.

For fifteen hundred years Keltia prospered in her isolation—not a total isolation even then, for still there were out-Wall trading planets and military actions, and ambassadors were still received.

In the Terran year 2693, the Crown passed to the House of Aoibhell. Direct descendants of Brendan himself, the Aoibhells have held the monarchy in a grip of findruinna for eight hundred years, according to the law of Keltia that the Copper Crown descends to the eldest child of the sovereign, whether man or woman.

In the Earth year 3512, a Terran ship, a long-distance stellar probe, approaches the Curtain Wall and is hailed by a Keltic scout ship. Aeron Aoibhell, the seventeenth member of her House to occupy the throne, has been Ard-rían, High Queen of Keltia, for just under three years.

After three millennia, the Earth has caught up with the Kelts at last.

Glossary

(Words are Keltic unless otherwise noted.)

aircar: small personal transport used on Keltic worlds

alanna: "child," "little one"; Erinnach endearment

amadaun: "fool"

An Claideamh Soluis: "The Sword of Light"; a Keltic constellation

an-da-shalla: "The Second Sight"; Keltic talent of precognition

An Lasca: "The Whip"; the ionized northwest wind at Caerdroia

anwyl: "sweetheart"; Kymric endearment

Annwn: (pron. *Annoon*) the Keltic religion's equivalent of the Underworld, ruled over by Arawn, Lord of the Dead

aonach: an assembly, gathering or fair

ap: Kymric, "son of"

Ard-eis: the royal High Council of Keltia

Ard-rían, Ard-rígh: "High Queen," "High King"; title of the Keltic sovereign

astar, pl. **astari:** gold currency unit of the Imperium

athair-talam: "father-of-the-ground"; a magic herb used by healers of the Fianna, with narcotic/analgesic properties

athiarna: "High One"; Fianna form of address to a superior officer

aurichalcum: (Hastaic) a type of metal-stone mined on the Imperial planet of Alphor and used extensively in building there

ballach: a saddle pass leading from one mountain to another

ban-a-tigh: woman householder

Ban-draoi: lit., "woman-druid"; the Keltic order of priestess-sorceresses in the service of the Mother Goddess

bards: Keltic order of poets, chaunters and loremasters

Bawn of Keltia: the space enclosed within the Curtain Wall (*bawn*: the area enclosed by the outer barbican defenses of a fortress)

Beltain: festival of the beginning of summer, celebrated on 1 May

bodach: term of opprobrium or commiseration, depending on circumstances

brehons: Keltic lawgivers and judges

brugh: a fortified manor house, usually belonging to one of the gentry or nobility; in cities, a town-palace of great elegance and size

bruidean: inn or waystation, maintained by local authorities, where any traveller, of whatever rank or wealth, is entitled to claim free hospitality

Cabiri: (Hastaic) Coranian magical order of adepts, similar to the Druids or the Ban-draoi

camur: feral scavenger canine; usually runs in packs

cantrip: very small, simple spell or minor magic

cariad: "heart," "beloved"; Kymric endearment

cath, pl. **catha:** military unit of 5,000 warriors

cathbarr: fillet or coronet; usually a band of precious metal ornamented with jewels

ceili: (pron. *kay-lee*) a dancing-party or ball; any sort of revelry

Chriesta tighearna!: lit., "Lord Christ!"; name of the Christian god, used as an expletive

cithóg: "port," as on board ship (cf. *deosil*)

clarsa: Keltic musical instrument similar to Terran harpsichord

clochan: dome- or yurt-like structure used by the Fianna in the field

coelbren: magical alphabet used by Druids

coire ainsec: "the undry cauldron of guestship"; the obligation, in law, to provide hospitality to any who claim it

Coranians: ruling race of the Imperium, hereditary enemies of the Kelts; they are the descendants of the Telchines, as the Kelts are the descendants of the Danaans

coroin: unit of Keltic money (large silver coin)

corp-dira: fine exacted, according to the brehon law, for honor-price violations

Crann Tarith: "Fiery Branch"; the token of war across Keltia. Originally a flaming branch or cross; now, by extension, the alarm or call to war broadcast on all planets

creagh-rígh: "royal reiving"; in very ancient times, the traditional raid led by a newly crowned monarch to consolidate his rule

Cremave: the clearing-stone of the royal line of St. Brendan

Criosanna: "The Woven Belts"; the rings that circle the planet Tara

crochan: magical healing-pool that can cure almost any injury, provided the spinal column has not been severed and the brain and bone marrow remain undamaged

crossic: unit of Keltic money (small gold coin)

culist: "back-room"; traditional best chamber in Keltic farmhouses

cursal: very fast light warship of the Keltic starfleet

Curtain Wall: the artificial energy barrier that encircles and conceals Keltia

Cwn Annwn: (pron. *Coon Annoon*) in Keltic religion, the Hounds of Hell; the red-eared, white-coated dogs that belong to Arawn Lord of the Dead, that hunt down guilty souls

daer-fudir: "outlaw"; a legal term, used in banishment of a malefactor

dán: "doom"; fated karma

deosil: on board ship, the starboard side (cf. *cithóg*)

Dragon Kinship: magical-military order of Keltic adepts

Druids: magical order of Keltic sorcerer-priests

dúchas: lordship or holding; usually carries a title with it

duergar: in Kernish folklore, an evil elemental or place-spirit

dún: a stronghold of the Sidhe, the Shining Ones (also *liss* or *rath*)

enech-clann: brehon law system of honor-price violations

Englic: unofficial galactic Common Tongue

éraic: "blood-price"; payment exacted for a murder by the kin of the victim

faha: courtyard or enclosed space in a castle complex or an encampment

Fáinne: "The Ring"; the six system viceroys of Keltia

fetch: the visible form taken by the spirit-guardian of a Keltic family

Fianna: Keltic officer class; order of military supremacy

fiant: royal mandate which cannot be altered by parliamentary action and from which there is no appeal

fidchell: chess-style game

fidil: four-stringed instrument played with a bow

findruinna: superhard, silvery metal used in swords, armor and the like

fíor-comlainn: "truth-of-combat"; legally binding trial by personal combat

fith-fath: spell of shapeshifting or glamourie; magical illusion

Fomori: ancient enemies of the Kelts; sing., Fomor

Fragarach: "The Answerer"; moon-size laser-cannon emplacement that defends the throneworld system of Tara

fraughans: dark-red berries, similar to raspberries, often found growing wild in Keltia

fudir: "criminal", "outcast"; term of opprobrium

galláin: "foreigners"—sing., Gall; generic term for all non-Kelts

galloglass: Keltic foot-soldier

gauran: plow-beast similar to ox or bullock

glaistig: on the planet Scota, a legendary demon or hag-creature

glaive: (from Erinnach, *claideamh*) lightsword; laser weapon used throughout Keltia

goleor: "in great numbers, an overabundance"; Englic *galore* is derived from it

grafaun: double-bladed war axe

grianan: "sun-place"; solar, private chamber

gúna: generic name for various styles of long robe or gown

gwrach: on Gwynedd, a spirit that sings mournfully to lament the death of one of the ruling family

hai atton: "heigh to us"; the horn-cry that rallies an army

Hastaic: the language of the Imperium

Hu mawr: Hu the Mighty; father of the gods in the Kymric pantheon

immram: "voyage"; the great migrations from Earth to Keltia
iron-death: curse inflicted upon anyone who refuses to take oath upon the Cremave (q.v.)
(I)'s é do bheatha: lit., "life to you"; traditional Keltic salutation

jurisconsult: brehon engaged in law-court cases

keeve: breaker or barrel
kenning: telepathic mood-sensing technique originally developed and used almost exclusively by Ban-draoi and Druid adepts
kern: Keltic starfleet crewman

lachna: heavy, superdense metallic ore with anti-magnetic properties
lai: unit of distance measurement, equal to approximately one-half mile
Lakhaz: the language of the Fomori
leys: lines of electromagnetic flux found in the Morimaruse (q.v.)

maenor: hereditary dwelling place, usually a family seat
"M'anam don sleibh!": lit., "My soul to the mountain!"; Keltic oath
marana: "meditation"; thought-trance of Keltic sorcerers
Marbh-draoi: "Death-druid"; Jaun Akhera's epithet among Kelts
marbh-fionn: "white death"; Keltic name for the virulently poisonous, non-native snake known elsewhere as the annic
marca-sluagh: cavalry squadron; usually refers to the bodyguard of a Keltic sovereign or high-ranking commander in battle
marchra: "cavalcade"; small horsed company of a military or recreational nature
master-otter: a magical beast used by sorcerers

merrows: (An Moruadha) the sea people of Kernow

mether: a four-cornered drinking vessel, usually of wood or pottery

Morimaruse: vast electromagnetic void; the Dead Sea of space

moscra: animal of the equine family, similar to Terran zebra

nathair: generic term for any of various poisonous snakes of the adder type

némed: "sacred"; one whose person is sacrosanct by law; usually a royal personage or a bard, according to tradition

nemeton: ceremonial stone circle or henge

ní, nighean: "daughter of"

ollave: a master-bard; by extension, anyone with supreme command of an art

palug: a graceful, red-furred, lynx-like feline, native to the island-continent of Môn on the planet Gwynedd

piast: a large amphibious water-beast found in deepwater lakes on the planets Erinna and Scota; the species was known to Terrans as the Loch Ness Monster

Plumed Dancer: the star Rigel

púca: mischievous, sometimes malevolent, spirit of darkness

quaich: a low, wide, double-handled drinking-vessel; can be made of metal, pottery or leather

rann: a chanted verse stanza used in magic; a spell of any sort

rechtair: steward of royal or noble households; title of planetary governors; title of Chancellor of Exchequer on High Council

rig-amuis: Fomori mercenary berserkers

rígh-domhna: members of the royal family, as reckoned from a common ancestor, who may (theoretically, at least) be elected to the Sovereignty

riverhawk: very fierce, large sturgeon-like fish native to the Great River on Alphor

ros-catha: battle-cry

saining: rite of Keltic baptism

saining-pool: another name for crochan (q.v.)

Salamandri: the Salamander-race, Firefolk; inhabitants of the volcano planet Kholco

Samhain: (pron. *Sah-win*) festival of the beginning of winter, celebrated on 31 October

sgian: small black-handled knife universally worn in Keltia, usually in boot-top

shakla: chocolate-tasting beverage brewed with water from the berries of the brown ash; drunk throughout Keltia as a caffeine-based stimulant

Sidhe: (pron. *Shee*) the Shining Ones; a race of possibly divine or immortal beings

silkies: (Sluagh-rón) the seal-folk of the Out Isles

Six Nations: the six star systems of Keltia (excluding the Throneworld system of Tara); in order of their founding, they are Erinna, Kymry, Scota, Kernow, Vannin and Brytaned (or Arvor)

sluagh: a hosting, as of an army

Solas Sidhe: "The Faery Fire"; a natural phenomenon similar to the will-o'-the-wisp, usually seen in the spring and fall; also, a magical wall of fire, created by sorcerers as a means of attack or defense

Spearhead: the polestar of Tara

Stonerows: the lower circles of Caerdroia

sun-gun: moon-sized laser cannon used to defend planets or systems

sunmice: tiny, brightly colored schoolfish native to the Great River on Alphor

taghairm: "echo"; magical trance technique used by Druids and Ban-draoi

Tanist, Tanista: designated heir of line to the Keltic throne

Taoiseach: the Prime Minister of Keltia

telyn: Kymric lap-harp

torc: massive neck ornament worn by Kelts of rank; a heavy, open-ended circle usually of gold or silver

usqueba: "water of life"; whiskey, generally unblended

Warrior: the star Sirius

Yamazai: "Amazon"; warrior-woman race of a matriarchal system, whose homeworld is the planet Aojun

Yr Mawreth: "The Highest"; Kymric name for Kelu or Artzan Janco, the One God who is above all other gods

Keltic Orders and Societies

The Dragon Kinship

The Dragon Kinship is a magical and military order of adepts, under the authority of the Pendragon of Lirias. Members are the most accomplished adepts of all Keltia, elected strictly on the basis of ability. All professions and ranks are equally eligible.

All those of the Kinship are equal under the Pendragon; no formalities are observed, no titles are used, no precedence of rank is followed. The only other office is Summoner; chosen by the Pendragon, this officer is what the name implies—the person responsible for calling the Kinship together on the Pendragon's order.

The Pendragon is chosen by his or her predecessor to serve for a term of seven years; this choice must be confirmed by a simple-majority public vote and may be renewed only by a unanimous secret vote of the entire membership (not surprisingly, such a renewal has never taken place). At the moment, Gwydion Prince of Dôn is Pendragon; he was preceded by a farmer from the Morbihan, a poetess from Vannin, a weaver from the Out Isles and a bard from Cashel.

To call someone "Kin to the Dragon" is the highest tribute possible. Most members are public about it, some prefer to keep it a secret, but all possess a certain unmistakable and indefinable air of apartness and assurance. It is a severely demanding society: More than any other power, save only the Crown itself, the Dragon Kinship is responsible for the well-being, the welfare and the quality of life and spirit of Keltia, on all levels. As a magical order, the Kinship takes precedence over all other factions; much of its membership, in fact, comprises members of other orders such as the Druids, Ban-draoi or the Bardic Association. It is truly a cross-section of Keltic society, for it reaches from royalty to farmers to artists to techs to soldiers to artisans to householders. There are no age limits either upper or lower, and no entry requirement save the possession of psionic Gift.

That Gift must include all psionic talents, and feature supreme proficiency in at least one: healing of body or mind; seership; broad-band telepathy, either receptor or sender; magical warfare, attack, defense or strategic; energy control; psychokinetics; retrocognition or precognition; shapeshifting; transmutation; pure magic; or any other magical discipline or talent. Members are recruited through observation and direct approach by a current Dragon. There are generally no more than ten thousand members at any one time, though in time of war or other great emergency the membership may be increased, if acceptable candidates are available.

The Dragon Kinship have their own brugh in Turusachan and rich lands on Brytaned and Dyved; their main training establishment, Caer Coronach, is in a remote part of Caledon. A Dragon is by tradition named the sovereign's Magical Champion, as a Fian is always named Military Champion.

The Druid Order

The Druid Order is, with the Ban-draoi, the oldest order in Keltia, founded by St. Brendan himself in the direct tradition of the Terran Druids. The Order is limited to men only, who may present themselves for membership beginning at thirteen years of age. As with the other orders, preliminary training is begun as soon as a child begins to show promise of talent, sometimes even as early as three or four years old.

The Druids are an immensely powerful body; they concern themselves with sorcery and politics, not necessarily always in that ranking. There are three degrees of Druidry: Novice, Ovate, Master. Head of the Order is the Archdruid, who is chosen by his predecessor upon his deathbed, and who then rules until his own death. The Archdruid sits in the House of Peers as Lord of Carnac, and is a member of the High Council which advises the monarch.

The training is long and intensive: all forms of magic, lore, herbalism, alphabets, correspondences, alchemy, psionics, chants, music, healing, seership, trance mediumship, and other occult disciplines. A fully qualified Druid is a master of magic, and very few can manage to withstand him when he puts forth his power.

There have been a few doubtful passages in the history of the Order, most notably the appalling two-hundred-year period known to infamy as the Druid Theocracy and Interregnum.

At a time of unusual political polarity and turmoil, the Archdruid, a brilliant and devious man called Edeyrn, saw in the divisiveness a chance to seize power for his Order—which is to say, for himself. A series of battles and massacres called the Druids' Wars followed, effectively demolishing all semblance of civil order in Keltia, and Edeyrn installed himself as magical overlord. He was supported in this by his fellow renegades and quite a few equally opportunistic noble houses. He was opposed by the remnants of the Fáinne, the Bandraoi, the Bardic Association, the Fianna, most of the noble houses and many of his own Druids who had remained loyal to the teachings of their Order. This opposition was the Counterinsurgency, and they were very, very strong.

This horrific state of affairs existed for nearly two centuries, with the balance of power continually shifting from one side to the other, until the invasion of Keltia by Fomori and Fir Bolg space fleets resulted in enormous destruction and panic. The Theocracy, now led by the ancient Edeyrn's heir Owain, tried to make a deal with the invaders but failed, opening the way only for full-scale war.

Arthur of Arvon, himself a Druid, rallied the Counterinsurgency in one great desperate throw and defeated Owain's forces at the Battle of Moytura. With the help of his chief teacher and advisor Merlynn Llwyd, who assumed the Archdruidship, Arthur went on to pull Keltia together and become King of Kelts, as has been told elsewhere. But throughout his long and glorious reign, Druid precepts remained Arthur's guide to action.

The Druids, under Merlynn Llwyd, began a period of severe purge and purification, and eventually were restored to their former high standards.

The current Archdruid is Teilo ap Bearach; the ranks of Master-druids include Gwydion Prince of Dôn, Aeron's uncles Deian and Estyn, and her cousins Alasdair and Dion.

The Druid Order has a brugh of its own in Turusachan, and its chief college is at Dinas Affaraon on Gwynedd.

The Ban-draoi

Equal in rank and antiquity with the Druid Order, the Ban-draoi are the evolvement of the incomparably ancient Goddess-priestesses of the most deep-rooted Keltic tradition. The Order was founded in Keltia by St. Brendan's mother, Nia daughter of Brigit, who many said was of divine parentage herself, and who became the ancestress of the House of Dâna in Keltia.

Divine or not, Nia of the Tuatha De Danaan was brilliant, beautiful, foresighted, and incredibly gifted in magic, and the Order she established had power, respect and influence right from the start.

Open only to women, the Order of the Ban-draoi (the name is Erinnach for, literally, "woman-druid") has as its chief purpose the worship of the Lady, the Mother Goddess; but they are sorceresses as well as priestesses, and their magic matches that of the Druids spell for spell. All women, whether initiates or not, participate to some degree in the ways of the Ban-draoi, as do all men in the ways of the Druids, since both systems are at their deepest hearts paths of worship. But the mysteries of the Ban-draoi are the Mysteries of the Mother, the things of most awe in all the Keltic worlds. Priestess or not, every Keltic woman shares in this awe, and every Keltic man respects it.

The Ban-draoi were never so politically oriented as the Druids, but when the Theocracy began, they became the chief focus of the Counterinsurgency and gave the resistance movement much of its force. Later, Arthur's mother Ygrawn and sister Morgan, and his wife Gweniver, were all three high priestesses of the Order, and gave him invaluable aid in his task of defeating both Druids and aliens. After Arthur's departure, it was Morgan who raised the tremendous energy barrier of the Curtain Wall, thus protecting Keltia from the outside worlds for fifteen centuries.

Obliged by circumstances to assume a critical political role, the Ban-draoi adapted, and have retained a position of political preeminence down to the present day. Aeron Aoibhell holds the rank of Domina, or a High Priestess of the Order, as does her sister Ríoghnach.

The training of a Ban-draoi (the word is both singular and plural) is as intensive as that of a Druid, and includes the same body of magical knowledge. Due to the heritage of Nia, however, it also emphasizes many branches of arcane lore known only to the priestesses. It is not so hierarchical as the Druid Order; an aspirant to the Ban-draoi is initiated as a priestess once her training is judged complete. If she wishes, and if her teachers agree, she may then seek the rank of high priestess, which carries with it the deepest knowledge of all and the title Domina.

The Chief Priestess is elected for life by a conclave of all the high priestesses; she bears the title Magistra, sits on the monarch's High Council, and sits in the House of Peers as Lady of Elphame. The office is currently held by Ffaleira nighean Enfail.

The Ban-draoi have a brugh of their own within the walls of Turusachan, and their chief training school is at Scartanore on Erinna.

The Fianna

The Fianna is a purely military organization, comprising the most skilled and talented warriors of Keltia. To become a Fian, a candidate must pass a series of incredibly rigorous tests of his or her warrior skills: a test of knowledge, in which he or she must demonstrate mastery of a specified body of lore; a test of soul, in which the candidate must face psionic examination by a qualified inquisitioner, who may be Druid, Ban-draoi or Dragon; and finally a formal combat with a chosen Fian of the First Rank.

So rigorous are these tests, in fact, that it seems astounding that anyone at all ever becomes a Fian; but many do indeed succeed, and rightly are respected. Membership is open to all ranks, ages and professions; candidates must be at least eighteen years of age, for physical reasons, though training may often begin at age six or seven if a child shows talent.

Skills a Fian must learn include all forms of combat and martial arts: sword-mastery, both classic and lightsword techniques; fencing; archery; wrestling; four forms of unarmed combat approximating to Terran judo, karate, kung-fu and foot-fighting; boxing; riding; marksmanship with all forms of weapons; tracking; running; spear-throwing; and the piloting of all types of vehicles from starship to snow-yacht.

The test of knowledge requires extensive study in the fields of history, both Keltic and Terran; literature; brehon law; the arts; heraldry and genealogy; politics; and science, both pure and applied. Fians are expected to be able to speak all seven Keltic tongues, Latin, and as many alien tongues as possible (the minimum is three, and Hastaic, the Imperial tongue, is mandatory). In addition, Fians are taught the secret Keltic battle-language, Shelta Thari.

The test of soul could well be called an ordeal. It involves deep-trance, telepathy, and astral travel, and no candidate, whether pass or fail, will ever speak about it afterward.

The final formal combat is determined on an individual basis by the Captain-General of the Fianna; choice of weapon and combat form will vary, but there is always one armed and one unarmed duel for each candidate. The Captain-General also selects the First-Rank Fian who will oppose the prospective member. No allowance is made for sex or physical size: Women, for instance, are expected to know how to defeat a male warrior who vastly outmeasures them in height, weight and strength.

The Fianna have their own training establishment, Caer Artos in Arvon, and their quarters in Turusachan, the Commandery, are directly across from the royal palace. Military champions for trial-by-combat are always selected from the ranks of the Fianna; the Royal Champion is always a First-Rank Fian, and the monarch's personal bodyguard is made up of Fians.

The current Captain-General of the Fianna is Dónal mac Avera.

The Bardic Association

The Bardic Association has a long and honorable history. From its founding in Keltic year 347 by Plenyth ap Alun, the society of bards has held without stain to its high principles and rigorous requirements, and bards of all degrees have traditionally been granted hospitality, honor and semi-royal precedence throughout Keltia.

Although bards receive a good deal of magical training in the course of their studies it is not emphasized; the primary training of bards is words. Any and all literary disciplines: poetry, sung or spoken; satire; history; sagas; ballads; myths and legends; drama; genealogy; precedent—all belong to the bardic tradition. Unlike magical schooling, the bardic discipline may begin at any age; there are records of peers in old age handing over their titles to their heirs and going to the bardic Colleges to end their lives in study.

Bardic aspirants spend five years as apprentices; five years as journeymen; five years as institutional bards. Having completed the fifteen-year training program (which does not preclude other study; Gwydion of Dôn, for instance, is both Druid and master-bard), they are then permitted to take the examination for the rank of ollave, or master-bard, if they so wish. If they are successful in this bid, they may then represent themselves as master-bards of the schools and seek the very highest employment. Not all bards choose to seek the status of ollave, however; and many do not remain even to become institutional bards. Any bard who has successfully passed the examination at the end of the journeyman term may serve as a teacher of children, and many choose to leave at this level to work in such capacity.

Bards of all degrees, whether journeyman, institutional bard or ollave, are much in demand throughout Keltia; they are employed by royal or noble families, or by merely wealthy families, as poet of the house and artist in residence, encouraged to recite the old lore and to compose creatively on their own. Exceptional bards of high degree are often entrusted with delicate diplomatic or social missions, including—not to put too fine a point on it—spying; though this last is done only in cases of the gravest national importance, for if too many bards did it, all bards would be suspect. The Ard-rían Aeron makes great use of bards, and gives them greater honor than they have had from the monarchs of Keltia for some years.

Bards have by law and custom several odd privileges: A bard may demand the nightmeal from anyone, in exchange for a song or a poem; the royal ollave (or ríogh-bardain) has the right to a seat at the high table in Mi-Cuarta not more than seven places from the monarch's right hand; an ollave is permitted by law to wear six colors in his cloak (only the reigning monarch may wear more—seven, if desired).

The Chief of Bards is chosen by a vote of senior masters; he serves until death or retirement, and sits on the monarch's High Council. Chief of Bards at present is Idris ap Caswyn.

The Bardic Association has a brugh of its own, Seren Beirdd—"Star of the Bards"—within the walls of Turusachan, and the Bardic Colleges are located on Powys.

Partial Chronology

3400	Fionnbarr born at Caerdroia
3405	Bres born at Tory
3434	Emer born at Coldharbor
3438	Haruko born at Old Kyoto
3442	Quarrel of Bres and Fionnbarr
3455	Fionnbarr and Emer marry
3467	Jaun Akhera born at Escal-dun
	Roderick born at Kinloch Arnoch
3470	Gwydion and Arianeira born at Caer Dathyl
3472	Desmond and Slaine born at Drumhallow
3473	Elathan born at Tory
3475	Aeron born at Caerdroia
	Morwen born at Kinloch Arnoch
3476	Rohan born at Caerdroia
3477	Ríoghnach born at Caerdroia
3479	Fionnbarr's reign begins (death of Lasairían)
3480	O'Reilly born at Sandiangeles
3482	Kieran and Declan born at Caerdroia
	Melangell born at Bryn Alarch
3489	Fionnuala born at Caerdroia
3509	Aeron's reign begins (deaths of Fionnbarr, Emer and Roderick)
3512	Arrival of Earth ship *Sword* in Keltic space

Dates given here are in Earth Reckoning (A.D.); to find the date A.B. (*Anno Brendani*) or A.C.C. (*Anno Celtiae Conditae*), subtract 453 and 455, respectively.

The comparative ages can be misleading, as Terran lifespans average 100–110 years, while those of Kelts, Coranians and Fomori run to 160–200. Therefore, the "younger generation" of protagonists (Aeron, Elathan, Jaun Akhera, et al.) are very young indeed, while Bres and Haruko are well into middle age.

Note on Age

The average Keltic lifespan is 160–175 years, and many individuals reach, even surpass, the two-century mark in full possession of their faculties both physical and mental. Physical development occurs at the same rate as in shorter-lived races, with full physical maturity coming between the ages of 18 and 21.

There is no single legal majority age. At 18, all Kelts, both male and female, are liable for military service; the mandatory term is three years. They may also vote in local elections and assume minor titles.

At 21, citizens may marry with consent (though marriage at this age is almost unheard-of—thus the scandal of Emer ní Kerrigan's elopement with Prince Fionnbarr as he then was; most marriages occur at around ages 30–35), vote in planetary elections, and hold minor public office.

At 27, Kelts may marry without consent, vote in major (system and national) elections, hold major public office, and succeed to major titles.

And no one under the age of 33 may hold the Copper Crown unregented.

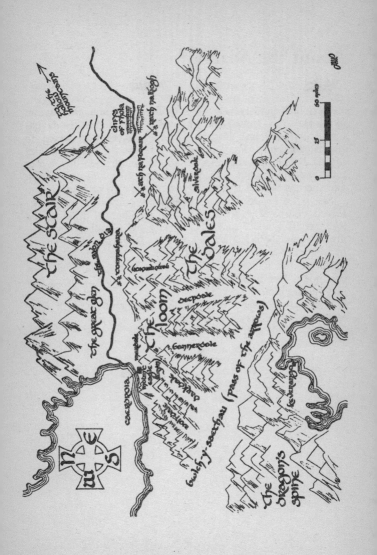

About the Author

Patricia Kennealy was born in Brooklyn and grew up in North Babylon, New York. She was educated at St. Bonaventure University and Harpur College, taking her degree in English literature. For three years she was the editor-in-chief of JAZZ & POP magazine, a national publication devoted to rock and progressive music in the late 60's and early 70's, and she has written extensively in the field of rock criticism.

She is an award-winning advertising copywriter; a former record company executive; and a member of Mensa, the Richard III Society and The Society for Creative Anachronism (where she is known as Lassarina Douglas of Strathearn). In 1970 she exchanged vows with the late Jim Morrison, leader of the rock group The Doors, in a private religious ceremony. Her leisure pursuits including riding, fencing and playing the violin.

She lives in New York City and Stephentown, N.Y. Her ambition is to christen a warship.

WORLDS OF WONDER

☐ **BARROW by John Deakins.** In a town hidden on the planes of Elsewhen, where mortals are either reborn or driven mad, no one wants to be a pawn of the Gods. (450043—$3.95)

☐ **WIZARD WAR CHRONICLES: LORDS OF THE SWORD by Hugh Cook.** Drake Douay fled from his insane master, a maker of swords. But in a world torn by endless wars, a land riven in half by a wizard powered trench of fire, an inexperienced youth would be hard-pressed to stay alive. (450655—$3.99)

☐ **THE HISTORICAL ILLUMINATUS CHRONICLES, Vol. I: THE EARTH WILL SHAKE by Robert Anton Wilson.** The Illuminati were members of an international conspiracy—and their secret war against the dark would transform the future of the world! "The ultimate conspiracy . . . the biggest sci-fi cult novel to come along since *Dune*."—The Village Voice (450868—$4.95)

☐ **THE HISTORICAL ILLUMINATUS CHRONICLES, Vol. 2: THE WIDOW'S SON by Robert Anton Wilson.** In 1772, Sigismundo Celline, a young exiled Neapolitan aristocrat, is caught up in the intrigues of England's and France's most dangerous forces, and he is about to find out that his own survival and the future of the world revolve around one question: What is the true identity of the widow's son? (450779—$4.99)

Prices slightly higher in Canada.

Buy them at your local bookstore or use this convenient coupon for ordering.

NEW AMERICAN LIBRARY
P.O. Box 999, Bergenfield, New Jersey 07621

Please send me the books I have checked above.
I am enclosing $＿＿＿＿＿＿ (please add $2.00 to cover postage and handling).
Send check or money order (no cash or C.O.D.'s) or charge by Mastercard or
VISA (with a $15.00 minimum). Prices and numbers are subject to change without
notice.

Card #＿＿＿＿＿＿＿＿＿＿＿＿＿＿ Exp. Date ＿＿＿＿＿＿＿＿
Signature＿＿＿＿＿＿＿＿＿＿＿＿＿＿＿＿＿＿＿＿＿＿＿＿＿
Name＿＿＿＿＿＿＿＿＿＿＿＿＿＿＿＿＿＿＿＿＿＿＿＿＿＿＿
Address＿＿＿＿＿＿＿＿＿＿＿＿＿＿＿＿＿＿＿＿＿＿＿＿＿＿
City ＿＿＿＿＿＿＿＿＿＿ State ＿＿＿＿＿ Zip Code ＿＿＿＿＿

For faster service when ordering by credit card call **1-800-253-6476**

Allow a minimum of 4-6 weeks for delivery. This offer is subject to change without notice.

If you and/or a friend would like to receive the *ROC Advance*, a bimonthly newsletter featuring all the newest and hottest ROC books and authors, on a complimentary basis, please fill out this form and return it to:

ROC Books/Penguin USA
375 Hudson Street
New York, NY 10014

Your Address

Name _____

Street _____ Apt. # _____

City _____ State _____ Zip _____

Friend's Address

Name _____

Street _____ Apt. # _____

City _____ State _____ Zip _____